"I WAS LOOKING FOR YOU AT CHURCH TODAY,"
WENDY SAID TO HER SISTER OVER THE TELEPHONE.

Kim had known this conversation would take place
eventually. "Really."

"What happened? When we left Soul Sistas Friday
night you said you were coming . . . Are you all right?
You act like something is wrong . . . You sound sort of
stank."

"Never mind how I'm feeling. What about you? How
are you feeling, Sister Sunday?"

"Good," Wendy said cautiously. She was unsure why
Kim called her the same name that they had created for
their grandmother. Kim was always joking about how
fake Frances acted around other church members and
suggested the nickname Sister Sunday—implying that
the only time Frances appeared to be saved was on
Sunday morning.

"You know you never did tell me what the doctor
said about the baby."

"Uhhh . . . yeah—I'm straight." Wendy had been
meaning to make up a story to tell Kim, but she forgot.

———

"Need a little good news in your novels? Look no further."

—*Essence*

# Soul
# Matters

## Yolonda Tonette Sanders

Walk Worthy Press

West Bloomfield, Michigan

**WARNER BOOKS**

NEW YORK    BOSTON

This book is a work of fiction. Names, characters, places, and incidents are the product of the author's imagination or are used fictitiously. Any resemblance to actual events, locales, or persons, living or dead, is coincidental.

Biblical quotes throughout this book come from the King James Version.

Copyright © 2005 by Yolonda T. Sanders
All rights reserved.

Published by Warner Books with Walk Worthy Press™

Warner Books

Time Warner Book Group
1271 Avenue of the Americas, New York, NY 10020

Walk Worthy Press
33290 West Fourteen Mile Road, #482, West Bloomfield, MI 48322

Visit our Web sites at www.twbookmark.com and www.walkworthypress.net.

Printed in the United States of America

First Edition: September 2005
10  9  8  7  6  5  4

Library of Congress Cataloging-in-Publication Data

Sanders, Yolonda Tonette.
    Soul matters / Yolonda Tonette Sanders.—1st ed.
        p. cm.
    Summary: "A young Christian woman struggles with mistrust, disorder, and tension after an act of infidelity threatens her family and friendships."—Provided by the publisher.
    ISBN 0-446-69441-X
    1. Christian women—Fiction.  2. Young women—Fiction.  I. Title.
PS3619.A529S67   2005
813'.6—dc22
                                                                2004030853

Book design and text composition by L&G McRee

Cover design by Tracy McCutchion

*This book is dedicated to my husband, children, and mother for their unwavering love and support.*

# Acknowledgments

First and foremost, I want to give all glory and honor to God. Thank You for the continual favor, grace, and mercy that You have shown me. Without You, writing this book would have been impossible. Thank You for using an imperfect being like me to do works according to Your perfect plan.

Before I acknowledge individuals for their specific contributions, let me say that there are countless others whose thoughts, prayers, and well-wishes were with me throughout this process. Many of you continuously expressed your excitement about what God is doing in my life. For fear of inadvertently omitting any one of you, I will not list your names. However, please know that I truly appreciate your support and encouragement.

To my husband and best friend, David—I praise God for the blessing of you. You have been extremely supportive of me. Thank you doesn't seem like enough for the sacrifices you've made. I love you!

To my children, Tre and Tia—you both inspire me to

be better and to do better. It's a joy being your mother. I love you both very much!

To my parents, Eddie Brown and Wilene Brown—I love you guys. Thank you for all that you deposit into my life and the lives of my children. Ma—you are such a strong woman, and I greatly admire you. Your prayers have gotten me through many hard times.

To my pastor, Bishop Timothy J. Clarke, and First Lady, Clytemnestra Clarke—I love you both. Thank you for your dynamic leadership at First Church. Bishop Clarke, it is a direct result of your teaching and preaching that causes me to be where I am today. You have planted the Word of God in my life on a continual basis, thus contributing to my spiritual growth. Thank you for being a blessing to me.

A very special thank you goes to Kim Hahn, Danella Hicks, Carla Laskey, and Janice Sanders. I cannot thank you all enough for helping me every step of the way. I appreciate your honesty by telling me when there were glitches in the storyline, giving me new ideas to explore, reading (and sometimes rereading) every chapter of the book, and most importantly, your belief in me. You all invested a lot of time in *Soul Matters* way *before* I'd been offered a contract. The fact that you were willing to work so hard without any tangible proof that I would be signed with a publisher shows the degree to which you believed in me. Thank you not only for your support but your hard work as well. Both have been invaluable.

To John Anderson, Peggy Brown, Kem Dicken, Toni DiSalvo, Calvin Harris, Lynn Henry, Sharon Lindsey, Kelly McCoy, Nevy Payton, Jennifer Schwind, Pat Shade, and Sue Tobin—each one of you helped me along this journey by giving me feedback on sample chapters and/or the synopsis, thus playing an important role in my producing the finished product. Thank you so much for your help!

I also want to thank both sides of my family members, and my husband's family, for all of your love and support throughout the years. I love you guys! To my cousins, Mark and Tonya—thank you for being my "big brother" and "big sister." No matter what happens in life, remember that God is able to turn things around!

To my sister/friend, Robin Thornton—I love you doesn't even sum up how I feel. You are truly an inspiration. Your gift of faith has increased my level of faith. You believed in God's ability to use me even before I began to believe it myself. Thank you for the many times you've gotten me back on track using the Word of God. We have such a wonderful divine connection. You are a blessing to me.

To my publisher, Denise Stinson—I truly believe that my signing with Walk Worthy Press was a divine arrangement. Getting a publishing contract in and of itself is a blessing, but then to have a publisher who aims to please and honor God is an abundant blessing. I greatly appreciate the times of prayer and words of encouragement you've spoken to me. Thank you for being a vessel and giving me the opportunity to share with others what God is doing through me.

To my editor, Frances Jalet-Miller; my copy editor, Karen Thompson; and my production editor, Tareth Mitch—thank you all for your hard work in getting *Soul Matters* ready for publication. I thank God for your thoroughness, professionalism, and kindness. There are numerous others at Walk Worthy Press and Warner Books who have assisted with the publication process. I do not know your names, but I do want to thank you for all of your help as well.

To my graduate school advisor, Ruth Peterson—the lessons I learned from you while writing my thesis carried over into writing this novel. Thank you for being meticulous and always demanding my very best effort. The training I received from you was crucial to my being able to write this book.

To Michael Everhart, owner of Baby Love Studio (Columbus, OH)—thank you for the photographs. It was truly a pleasure working with you. I pray the blessings of God upon your business.

To everyone who reads this book, THANK YOU! It is my sincere desire that God's Word comes through and that you are blessed.

Love,

*Yolonda*

www.yolonda.net

# Soul
## Matters

# Chapter One
## The Perfect Package

IT WAS TEN MINUTES TO THREE, and Wendy was eager to get out of work on time. "Start cleaning up now," she said to her first-grade class. They had crayons, markers, and books all over the place. "Be sure to put everything back where it belongs. After you're finished, line up at the door and wait there until the bell rings."

Much to Wendy's surprise, her instructions were followed with little resistance. A few students mumbled about not being able to finish what they were doing, but even they cooperated without her having to say anything else. Maybe they could sense that something was different about her. Toward the end of each day the children usually had exploratory time and were allowed to choose among various activities such as reading, coloring, playing educational games, or anything else Wendy deemed appropriate. She normally walked around the classroom and interacted with several students during that time. However, this entire week she had sat at her desk like a watchdog, responding only when needed.

*"Just a few more days . . ."* Wendy murmured to herself. Next Wednesday the school would be closed for Christmas break, and as much as she hated to admit it, she was looking forward to having some time off. Although she was only seven weeks pregnant, she was beginning to feel the effects this pregnancy was having on her body. She used to have the vitality of a three-year-old, but lately she felt like she would lose in a race against Methuselah. She was convinced that the term *morning sickness* was deceptive. If the feelings of nausea, vomiting, heartburn, and headaches were confined only to a few hours of the day, it would make the first trimester of her pregnancy much more bearable. Instead, she was liable to experience *morning* sickness at any given moment of the day.

While the children were cleaning up, Wendy was on the edge of her seat as she waited for the bell to ring. *Thank God it's Friday.* She didn't think she would be able to make it another day. She was going straight home after work. She would not leave the house until it was time to go to church Sunday morning. After service, Wendy would then go over to her parents' house to celebrate her father's birthday. Wendy hoped to feel better by next Friday, when she and her husband, Kevin, were scheduled to go to Philadelphia and visit his family for the holidays. The Ohio native would rather spend her Christmas vacation recuperating from her ailments in the comfort of her own home, but there was no way she could back out of the trip now. Her mother-in-law was ecstatic about the pregnancy and could not wait until they got to Philly so she could show Wendy some of the things she had already bought for the baby.

"Keep your hands to yourselves," Wendy said to two young boys who were shoving each other.

"He started it!" David stated, pointing to Jeffrey.

"Nuh-uh, he did!" Jeffrey pointed back at him.

"It doesn't matter who started it—both of you knock it off," Wendy replied sternly. Secretly she knew that David probably was at fault, but she didn't feel like investigating the issue. David was bigger than the other first-graders in both height and weight. Jeffrey was one of those children who looked like he had been born premature and his small size made him an easy target for David. Even though David was sometimes a bully, Wendy had taken a great liking to him; probably because he reminded her of herself.

Wendy had never been a bully, but she had been heavy and tall as a child. She used to feel awkward standing next to other children in her class. It irritated her when adults would ask how old she was and then say, "You look like you should be older than that." It wasn't until the summer before her freshman year of high school that she began to thin out. All of her adult years, Wendy managed to remain a size eight, but she had to work hard at it, contrary to her younger sister, Kim, who naturally wore a six.

When the bell rang, it was music to her ears. "Okay, let's go." Wendy jumped up and escorted her class to the pickup area. Once they were there, another staff member would stay with them until their bus or a parent came to get them. When they reached their destination, Wendy said good-bye to her students and headed back to her classroom.

"Attention, all teachers and staff: Mrs. Phillips, please come to the office. Wendy Phillips to the front office, please," she heard Donna Burchett, the office secretary, announce over the PA system.

*For what? Maybe I should go ahead and leave. No one would be able to say for sure that I was in the building during the announcement.* Wendy was only a few doors away from her classroom, so all she had to do was grab her stuff and head home. However, she reluctantly turned around and walked toward the office at a medium pace. Her shoulder-length hair often bounced as she walked. Today it was pulled back in a ponytail. Wendy actually hated ponytails and only wore her hair in that style when she worked out. But ever since she had been experiencing morning sickness she devoted less time to her appearance. She even had her glasses on, and Wendy normally wouldn't be caught dead in a pair of glasses.

"Wendy Phillips, please come to the office," Ms. Burchett repeated.

*Coming!* she wanted to yell. *I hope it is something simple like a signature needed on some paperwork I filed.* She dreaded the possibility that a parent would be waiting to speak with her about his or her child's behavior.

"Hi, you paged me?" Wendy inquired as she burst through the door into the administrative office.

"Yes, dear. You had a telephone call," Ms. Burchett replied, exposing the gap between teeth stained from years of smoking.

"A telephone call? From who?" Wendy asked, scrunching her eyebrows. *No one ever calls me at work.* Her friends and family knew that she taught and was unavailable during the day. "It must be from a parent. I'll take the message, but I'm not calling anyone back until Monday."

"No, honey. It wasn't from a parent. Someone called from a Dr. Korva's office."

"Oh," she said nervously, trying hard to keep her composure and not panic.

"I wrote down the number." Ms. Burchett handed Wendy a piece of paper and pointed to the phone on her desk. "You can call from here if you'd like." She carefully studied Wendy's response.

"That's okay. I'll wait and call later since I'm getting ready to leave anyhow."

"The lady didn't tell me why she was calling, but it sounded important."

Wendy could tell that Ms. Burchett was fishing for information. Odds were she had already tried to gather as much as she could from the person who called. Wendy hadn't told anyone at the school about her pregnancy yet, and now was not the time to make that announcement. "Thanks so much, Ms. Burchett, but I'm sort of in a hurry so I'll just call back from my cell phone on my way home."

"Okay. I just hope everything is fine," she said with her narrow, bluish green eyes peering from the top of her glasses. "Are you sick, honey?"

"No ma'am," Wendy said honestly. Her mind was so boggled with getting to a phone to return Dr. Korva's call that the feelings of morning sickness had been temporarily suppressed.

"Then why would someone from a doctor's office call you?"

As much as Wendy wanted to tell Ms. Burchett to mind her own business, she couldn't. The woman was at least in her late fifties or early sixties and Wendy couldn't strike up the nerve to tell her off. *If only I was a little more like Kim,* she thought. Her sister would not have wasted any time getting Ms. Burchett out of her business. Wendy and Kim did have similar characteristics, with their dark brown hair, brown eyes, and dimples. However, Wendy's complexion was just a little lighter than Kim's, and she was also a few inches taller than her younger sibling. Both ladies favored their mother, but it was Kim who had been blessed not only with the high metabolism but also with the ability to speak her mind audaciously. Although Wendy generally liked Ms. Burchett, this interrogation was testing her patience. "I'm not sure, but I better run so I can find out, huh? You have a good weekend, Ms. Burchett," she said, backing toward the door.

"Okay, you too—and I'll talk to you on Monday."

*Not if I can avoid it you won't!* Wendy walked out of the office and raced back to her classroom. She was so disturbed by the call that she rushed by several of her co-workers without speaking. *Why did Dr. Korva call me at work?* Wendy was desperate to find out.

When Wendy returned to her classroom, she grabbed the cell phone out of her purse only to discover that there was a message waiting. That was nothing unusual because her phone stayed on vibrate during the day. A lot of times Kim called her from the hair salon where she worked and left messages when she was between clients.

"Hi, Wendy, this is Susan, Dr. Korva's nurse. She would like you to come into the office today, if possible, to discuss your test results. She's leaving around four this afternoon. If you can't make it before she leaves, then you definitely need to come sometime early next week. Please call the office and let the receptionist know what'll work best for you. The number here is 555-3794. We hope to see you soon."

Wendy's heart sank. *Dr. Korva told me that they take blood and vaginal swabs to run tests on all expectant mothers. The only reason they would call was if something came back abnormal.*

She looked at her watch. The time was now three-fifteen. It would be a stretch to make it from the southeast side of Columbus to the northern suburb where her gynecologist's office was located. Such a trip would take forty minutes this time of day, at the very least. Still, she tried to call the doctor's office anyway, hoping that, with any luck, they would squeeze her in.

Shaking and short of breath, Wendy wiped her sweaty palms on her clothing and dialed the number. "Hi, this is Wendy Phillips," she said, trying to hold back tears. "I'm returning a call to Dr. Korva. Will she be able to see me today? I can be there in about a half hour?" She altered her traveling time, expecting to increase her chance of being seen.

"Oh," she said solemnly when the receptionist stated that Dr. Korva was running behind schedule. Wendy couldn't be seen until Monday morning. "Well, can you tell her I'm on the line? Maybe she can just tell me the results over the phone." She crossed her fingers, praying that she would be transferred to the doctor. No such luck. Dr. Korva preferred to talk in person. "Okay, I'll be there at nine on Monday," she said, confirming the time of her appointment, and hung up the phone in despair.

*How am I going to make it until then?* She dreaded going back to the office and arranging for a substitute through Ms. Burchett. *Forget it. I'll just call in,* she opted. Sure, not submitting a request for a substitute beforehand was inconsiderate and very unprofessional, but she didn't care at this point. Her main concern was finding some way to make it through the weekend without losing her mind.

Wendy got her stuff and headed for the car. She tried to talk herself into remaining calm, but it wasn't working. She felt light-headed. *What if my baby is retarded? What if it's deformed or has some kind of genetic defect?* she tormented herself. She was afraid of what the doctor would say. She knew it was bad news. Her fear turned into anger toward Kevin. *I told him his smoking could cause damage to the child, but he didn't believe me.* If Kevin just smoked cigarettes, she could probably deal with it a little better, but he sometimes smoked marijuana, and Wendy couldn't stand that.

Whenever she complained about his recreational activities, Kevin got upset. He would tell her that he was not doing anything she hadn't been aware of before they got married. True, Wendy had known about his smoking when they were dating, but it was different then. She was attracted to his street-but-sweet personality. She had never dated anyone so successful yet a little rough around the edges. Plus, he was very pleasing to the eye. He reminded her of a Denzel Washington wrapped up in a Barry White voice. He was the perfect package: sexy, successful, and single.

Kevin's accomplishments intrigued her most of all. He worked hard for everything he owned and had built his real estate business from the ground up. He was very successful and made well over six figures a year. He didn't have parents who could afford to pay for his education. He'd paid for it himself. He hadn't grown up in the suburbs of some major city, but had lived in various ghettos of Philadelphia. His father left home when Kevin was only three, and his mother raised him, his older brother, and his sister with money she received from the federal government. He hadn't let his life's circumstances prevent him from making something of himself, and Wendy respected that.

Foolishly, she had convinced herself that Kevin would change the things she didn't like about him once they married, but he hadn't. Now, nearly six months into the marriage, the honeymoon was well over and reality had settled in. *If something is wrong with the baby, I know it'll be all his fault,* Wendy told herself.

# Chapter Two
## No Ordinary Sunday

IT WAS COLD AND WINDY OUTSIDE, but the atmosphere inside the two-story home owned by Michael and Marlene Tibbs for the last twenty years was very warm and cozy. The house was just the right size for a couple with two adult children, two grandchildren, and more on the way. They had three bedrooms with a full bath upstairs and a half-bath downstairs in the partially finished basement. In the summer, Marlene enjoyed sitting outside on the deck that Michael had built and watching the kids play or having barbecues with her family. When they first bought the house, it had been painted green outside and every room inside was a different color. After much debate about the exterior, the couple finally settled on a soft, baby-blue paint job, and the inside rooms were all painted the same neutral color.

The living room was Marlene's favorite place in the house. Its decorations constituted a miniature African museum. Marlene had always harbored a great love for

Africa. During her childhood, her best friend had been from Morocco, and Marlene learned a great deal about African culture from her. As a thirtieth-wedding-anniversary present to their parents, Wendy and Kim had bought them a two-week vacation package to Kenya. After that trip, Marlene had embarked on giving her living room an African decor.

Although Marlene took pride in how well she had decorated the living room, the kitchen was where she often did her best work. In honor of her husband's fifty-fifth birthday, she had made all of his favorite dishes. Marlene had spent the afternoon cooking corn on the cob, macaroni and cheese, homemade mashed potatoes and gravy, dinner rolls, and fried chicken. She also made a pot of green beans; not because they were Michael's favorite, but because she just couldn't stand having a formal dinner without any green vegetables.

"We can eat now," Marlene announced, walking out of the kitchen and carrying the last entrée. Seeing her family gathered around the dining room table reminded Marlene of when Kim and Wendy were children and how all of them would eat dinner together every night. Now the girls had their own lives. Newlyweds, Wendy and Kevin were expecting their first child, and Kim's two small children, Tori and Tyler, along with her boyfriend, Terrance, kept her busy. Unfortunately, the Tibbs family didn't get together very often for formal dinners unless it was a holiday or some other special occasion.

"Baby, everything smells really good," Michael said.

The rest of the family agreed.

"Thanks," Marlene said, and took her seat. After their girls moved out of the house, Michael and Marlene had enjoyed being empty nesters for a while. The telephone didn't ring as much, the TV wasn't on all night, and the radio stayed at a volume that was enjoyable. Now they had Marlene's mother, Frances, living with them. She was in her early seventies and brought a whole new set of issues for the couple to deal with, such as waking up to the smell of BenGay, uncontrollable flatulence, or finding teeth soaking in one of their *good* cups.

Everyone bowed their heads and closed their eyes as Michael said grace. "Father, I want to thank You for this meal that has been prepared for us. Please use this food to strengthen and nourish our bodies. In the name of Jesus, I pray, amen." He kept his prayer short and simple. Church had let out a little later than normal that day and Marlene still had to go to the grocery store afterwards. It was almost six o'clock, and Michael hadn't had anything to eat since breakfast. Being nearly six foot tall and one hundred and ninety-seven pounds, he normally didn't go too long without food.

"Pastah know he brought forth some good word today." Michael looked up as Frances began speaking, only to see remnants of macaroni and cheese between her chubby cheeks. He wished that his mother-in-law would learn to swallow her food before striking up a conversation.

"Mm-hmm, he sho' did," Marlene said, seconding her mother's statement. "Kim, the choir sang that one song you used to like when you were a little girl. What's the name of it, Wendy?"

" 'Safe in His Arms,' " Wendy announced quietly. She

wasn't in a talkative mood. The entire weekend she'd been stressing about what the doctor would tell her tomorrow.

"Yeah, that's right," Marlene confirmed. "Sister Rogers sang lead and tore that song up! That woman can really sing."

"What did Pastor Jones preach about?" Kim asked.

The question caught Frances so off guard that her semi-pleasant expression turned into a scowl and she became very defensive. "Well, you can't expect me to remember ev'rything he say word for word. I just know it was some good word. Maybe if you show up ev'ry now and then you would know for yourself what he was preachin' about and you wouldn't have to rely on secondhand information." This time it was the green beans that everyone, except for Michael, got the displeasure of seeing. He knew to keep his eyes on his plate.

"Mama, please don't speak to Kim that way. She asked a reasonable question." Marlene sighed. She knew that Frances's comments had lit a fire, and she desperately wanted to put it out.

"I know what that chile was doin'. She was tryin' to question my Christianity." Frances imitated Kim: " 'What did Pastah Jones preach about?' Like she really care about what he said. If she did, she would have been there. Ain't that what the Word say? Forsake not the assemblin' of ourselves together. You ought to take them children to church yourself instead of sending them with your mama ev'ry Sunday."

The more Frances spoke, the higher Kim's blood pressure rose. Her almond-colored skin wrinkled as she frowned. Her temples began pulsating and everyone could tell she was angry. Kim had completely lost her appetite as her eyes glared at her grandmother. Terrance reached over to pat Kim on the back as if to say *Calm down, sweetie*, but it was too late. By the time he touched her, Kim had already made up her mind that she wasn't going to sit there and let that woman attack her without striking back.

"First of all," Kim began, "I wasn't trying to question your Christianity. And even if I was, why would you be upset *if* it's as secure as you claim it to be?" Frances had indeed started the fire; Kim was just adding fuel. Her emphasis on the word *if* cut Frances as sharply as a knife. "You were saying how good he was like you were about to start speaking in tongues and now you can't tell me what he spoke about. Okay, maybe I do need to go to church, but it looks like you need to stay awake when you go. You apparently got just as much out of the service as I did: *nothing!*"

The heat in the Tibbs household rose ten degrees and no one had even touched the thermostat. A very uncomfortable silence filled the air. Michael continued eating as though nothing had taken place. The silence was interrupted only whenever his fork hit the plate. Although he thought Kim was being very disrespectful, he believed it was about time someone told Frances about herself.

Everyone knew that what Kim said was true. Frances was known to fall asleep during church and wake up every now and then just to join the rest of the congregation in saying "Amen." Even so, no one ever had the audacity to

call her on it until now. There had been tension between
Frances and Kim ever since Kim had gotten pregnant with
Tori. Frances gave her such a hard time about it that Kim's
tolerance for her grandmother's verbal abuse had gotten
very low. Today everyone got a glimpse of just how tired
of Frances Kim was.

"Pastor spoke on three reasons why we have pain in our
lives and why God allows us to go through some things,"
Wendy interjected. She knew that things could get a lot
worse if she didn't speak up, and she didn't feel like wit-
nessing a family feud.

"It was a really good sermon, Kim," Marlene replied.
She was glad Wendy had broken the code of silence.

"I got that part . . . that it was a really 'good sermon' "—
Kim was still very irritated—"but what did he say?" She
glanced at her grandmother, who was clearly upset that
someone was going to fill her in on that morning's events.
Frances sat with her eyes closed as she folded her plump
arms across her chest. At this point, Kim no longer cared
what the service was about. The whole ordeal with her
grandmother had made her uninterested. Nevertheless,
she would listen anyhow because she knew how much it
would bother Frances.

"Basically, he gave three reasons why God allows pain
in our lives. The first one is that it teaches us how to
handle blessings humbly," Marlene stated.

"He said that God hates pride. There will always be
something in our lives that keeps us humble," Kevin
jumped in.

"Like what?" Terrance asked.

Kevin shrugged his shoulders. "It could be anything. Most likely something you've done in the past, like skeletons that you don't want falling out of the closet."

"Oh, I see . . ." Terrance paused to reflect on the point. He hadn't grown up in church like Kim had. He went with Kim occasionally when they were teenagers, but when she stopped going, so did he. He enjoyed listening to her family talk about Pastor Jones's sermons, however. It seemed like Pastor Jones didn't talk at his congregation as though he was three steps closer to heaven than they would ever be. Rather, he appeared to be very down-to-earth and spoke in such a way that they understood what he said and could apply his messages to their lives.

"Secondly, our pain teaches us how to submit to God's will," Marlene revealed. "One of the ways we learn to submit to God is through our failures, because sometimes our failures are back doors to blessings."

"What was the third reason he mentioned?" Kim asked her mother as her interest in the sermon was sparked.

"That our pain or even our problems teach us to rely on God."

Kevin looked at Terrance. "It was real cool, man. You and Kim should come with us one Sunday."

Kim wanted to laugh when Kevin added his two cents to the conversation. He only went to church every blue moon, yet he said they should come with *them* as though he was there faithfully every Sunday.

"Maybe one day we will; I'm sure Kim and I have done some stuff worthy of repentance," Terrance responded to Kevin's invitation.

"I think that's the case with all of us. Ain't that right, honey?" Marlene nudged her husband.

"Yeah, um-hmm," Michael said. He hadn't planned on joining the conversation. While everyone else had stopped eating or slowed down to start talking, he was getting ready to work on his second round of food.

"As Pastor Jones always says, 'It doesn't matter if you've committed many sins or a few. Either way, it's a debt we couldn't pay and we're all covered under the same blood,'" Marlene affirmed.

Everyone except Frances nodded in agreement. "I don't see why y'all waste your time tellin' her what Pastah preached on," Frances blurted out, interrupting Kim's state of tranquility. "It ain't like she gonna take the Word and live by it. Um-hmm . . . we sho' nuf is covered under the same blood all right, but the Bible also say that if one should sin willingly after they have received the truth then there is *no* other sacrifice for that person's sins. Oh Glory Hallelujah," Frances said, and lifted her hands in the air as though she just felt *The Spirit*. "I hate to be the one to tell y'all this, but that chile is goin' to hell!"

The nerve Frances had previously struck in Kim was reignited. "You know what? You might as well reserve your seat right next to mine 'cuz I won't be burnin' by myself," Kim snapped.

"Uh . . ." Frances gasped.

"Kimberly Michele Tibbs, apologize to your grandmother right this minute! I will not allow you to disrespect her like that," Marlene said sternly, although she knew that her mother was out of line. Still, she had raised her kids to be respectful toward their elders. No matter what Frances said, Kim had no right to respond to her the way she did.

"Mama, I get tired of her getting on my back all of the time," Kim said defensively.

"She is right, you know. You *do* need to go to church every now and again."

"Oh boy, here we go with the 'you need to go to church' speech!" Kim abruptly left the table and marched into the kitchen. Terrance followed behind her.

If Michael hadn't grabbed Marlene by the arm, she would've been on her way into the kitchen to knock some *do right* into that child of hers.

"Baby, just let her go," he said calmly.

"The girl's gotta a lil' attitude, I see. There's always a bad apple in every bunch. I know the devil when I see him and that girl is full of him," Frances sneered.

"Mama, please stop—"

"Well she is. Y'all wanna get mad at me and I'm just speakin' the truth. John 8:32 says, 'And ye shall know the truth, and the truth shall make you free.' Y'all don't wanna be set free. I know the devil when I see him. I got the gift of discernment," Frances said smugly.

"Mama, just drop it, please. We are *supposed* to be celebrating Michael's birthday today. Have you forgotten that?"

Frances mumbled, imitating Marlene. " 'Mama, just drop it, please.' I can't help it that your chile is evil. It's a good thing that she don't go to church—as much wrong as she's done, she wouldn't feel comfortable there nohow!" She tried to take a bite of her corn, but the lump left in her throat from Kim's outburst made it hard for her to swallow.

Michael always tried to stay out of it when the ladies argued, but it really got under his skin hearing his mother-in-law verbally assault his baby girl. Sure, he didn't like the fact that Kim had given birth to her children out of wedlock and was living with her boyfriend. However, none of that changed the fact that she was his daughter and he loved her. "Ladies, please! Mama Gibson, out of respect for my house, my daughter, and me, I am going to insist that you be more cordial to Kim. No matter what you think about her, she is *still* our daughter *and* your granddaughter."

"Well ex-*cuse* me! I thought that I lived here too, but thank you for reminding me about whose house this is."

Marlene put her head in her hands. She would jump in between her mother and her daughter, but when it was her husband and her mother she tried to stay out of it. Michael was a man of few words. When he did say something, it was a clear indication that he'd had enough.

Tyler was so busy playing with his food that he was unaware of what had been going on. He drowned out the adults and entertained himself by mixing all of his side items together. His resemblance to his father was eerie. Take away the mustache, the muscles, and about three feet, and left standing would be a four-year-old replica of Terrance. It was as if Kim didn't have anything to do with Tyler's genetic makeup at all.

Unlike her brother, six-year-old Tori was very attentive

to the debate going on around her. She didn't like hearing her great-grandmother say negative things about her mother. She would have liked to say something in Kim's defense, but she knew she'd better stay in a child's place. Getting in "grown folks' business" would guarantee chastisement by her mother, grandmother, and possibly Aunt Wendy. Her small brown eyes lit up when her paw-paw spoke. A tiny grin appeared on her face, exposing her missing front teeth and showing off the dimples she had inherited from her mother.

Before Michael had a chance to say anything else, Marlene jumped in, changing the subject in an attempt to ease some of the tension. "Wendy, why are you so quiet, honey? Are you feeling okay?"

"Yeah, I'm fine. I'm just tired, that's all."

"Try and get more rest. You really need to take care of yourself now that you're carrying a little one inside of you," Marlene encouraged. "Are you taking your prenatal vitamins?"

"Yeeeeees."

"You're just abnormally quiet today. Are you sure you're all right?"

"I think Wendy is a little nervous about the pregnancy," Kevin spoke up.

"I . . . I just don't know if I am ready to be a mother," Wendy confessed.

"That's nonsense. I know you love kids. You're a teacher, for God's sake—how could you not?" Marlene reasoned.

Wendy tried to explain, "Yeah, I do love kids, but—"

"Just be thankful that you can have children. Some folks can't, you know."

Wendy had her reasons for not being excited about the baby, but she would never be able to convince her mother of that. Instead, she just nodded in agreement. Everyone else was happier about the pregnancy than Wendy. It was ironic, especially since her motive behind getting married was to start a family.

Under different circumstances she would be delighted. However, Kevin was not being the husband she desired him to be right now. Even his money couldn't change that. She didn't understand how someone who was just a couple hundred thousand dollars shy of becoming a self-made millionaire could spend his weekends hanging out in clubs, drinking and getting high with his no-good friends. She could strangle him on Sunday mornings when he preferred to sleep in rather than go to church. Every weekend they had the same argument ending with the same results: Wendy went to church mad and came home even madder when he was still in bed. He hadn't gone out last night, which was probably the only reason he'd gotten up for church this morning.

Kevin was the most successful man Wendy had ever dated, and the only one who had respected her decision not to have sex until she married. Many of her other relationships hadn't lasted long for that very reason. Last year Wendy had met Kevin at a Christmas fund-raising event hosted by a nonprofit organization, only weeks after ending another relationship. Kevin's company was a big contributor and Wendy was a volunteer. They hit it off and six months later they were married. At first, Wendy thought Kevin was the one. Now she wasn't so sure she would be spending the rest of her life with him. Everything happened for a reason, a season, or a lifetime. Depending on how severe the baby's defects were, Kevin's involvement in her life might only be for a season. Her visit with the obstetrician would clarify things. She hadn't told Kevin about the appointment and didn't intend to until it was over.

"Are you still going to take some time off from teaching after the baby is born?" Michael asked his daughter.

"Yes. I'll put in my resignation for next year in a few weeks."

"I told her to go ahead and resign now, but she doesn't want to," Kevin admitted. He made more than enough to support both of them. In fact, Wendy had had the option of being a stay-at-home wife prior to finding out about her pregnancy, but she wanted to continue teaching. She loved working with kids. Plus, she was afraid of becoming a bored housewife who did nothing all day except watch soap operas and talk shows. She planned to take some time off after the baby was born, though. She didn't know how long; maybe a year or two, or maybe indefinitely, since taking care of the baby would be a full-time job. In any event, she wasn't willing to abandon her students in the middle of the school year.

"Resigning now may not be a bad idea," Marlene agreed with Kevin. Kim and Terrance walked out of the kitchen just as Marlene finished speaking. Terrance took the kids upstairs to wash their hands. Kim sat down at the table.

"What's not a bad idea?" Kim was curious.

"For your sister to go ahead and resign from teaching now. Every time I see her she complains about being tired," Marlene answered.

"I *want* to finish out this school year," Wendy said persistently. "And anyhow, I didn't complain. You asked me what was wrong so I told you."

"Okay. We're only concerned about you and the baby," her mother reassured her.

Frances looked at Kim and began doing her own rendition of Aretha Franklin's "Respect." "M-A-R-R-I-E-D find out what it means to be, M-A-R-R-I-E-D before you have ba-a-bies."

Kim wanted desperately to slap the woman. However, she chose to ignore her like everyone else. "We're getting ready to go," she announced to her family.

"No, you can't. Your dad still has to open his presents and cut the cake. You *can't* leave before he does that," Marlene protested.

"She can go if she wants to," Michael said. "I won't be offended. It's not like this is my first birthday, and hopefully it won't be my last."

"But still, you know Tyler and Tori will want some cake," Marlene pressed her case.

"We'll stay, but you can wrap up our cake and we'll take it home." Kim gave in, knowing that this was a special day for Michael.

When Terrance and the kids came back into the dining room, Marlene went into the kitchen and brought out the birthday cake. They all gathered around the table and sang "Happy Birthday" to Michael as he blew out his candles. Tori and Tyler then sat on his lap and helped him open his presents. Because it was getting late, Wendy and Kevin requested to take their cake home also.

Kim gave a round of hugs and kisses to her sister, brother-in-law, and mother while conveniently neglecting Frances. Kim walked over to her father and gently rubbed his bald head. "Daddy, I'm sorry for messing up your birthday," she whispered in his ear and kissed him on the cheek. He smiled and winked at her, indicating that he wasn't the least bit upset.

Marlene walked her family to the door and watched them get into their cars. She smiled as the thought of becoming a grandmother for the third time excited her. So much had happened that day with church getting out late, Michael's birthday, and Kim arguing with her mother. Marlene closed the door, leaned her head back, and said to herself, *Today has been anything but an ordinary Sunday!*

## Chapter Three

# What's the Worst That Can Happen?

"WHAT?" Wendy could not believe what she heard. She sat in the chair, staring at Dr. Korva while her mouth dropped to the floor.

"You tested positive for a sexually transmitted disease," Dr. Korva restated. "You have chlamydia, which is why I needed to see you again so quickly. I want to begin treating you in order to minimize any effects this could have on the baby."

Having the gynecologist repeat herself only confirmed that Wendy had heard her right the first time. Dr. Korva, who appeared to be of Asian descent, spoke with a slight accent. She pronounced chlamydia as "chlæmydia," using the long *a* sound, which made the word stand out even more. "B-b-but how?" Wendy stammered and slumped over, putting her face in her hands.

"I understand that you're upset, but instead of focusing on how you contracted the disease, we need to concern ourselves with getting you treatment right now. Okay?"

*Oh shut up! I know how I got the disease!* Wendy wanted

to say as feelings of rage boiled inside her. She knew that Dr. Korva was just doing her job, but she was ready to explode on anyone who rubbed her the wrong way. Tears formed in her eyes, but pride kept them from falling. Crying would only add to her embarrassment. She almost would have preferred it if Dr. Korva had confirmed her suspicions that something was wrong with the baby. At least then she wouldn't feel so dirty. "But . . . I never had any symptoms," Wendy contested.

"I'm sure you did. However, they were probably so mild that you didn't recognize them. It's common for people who contract chlamydia not to notice or feel anything different."

"Is my baby going to be all right?" Wendy asked, still fighting back the tears.

"Chances are"—she handed Wendy a tissue—"your baby will be just fine. We found out early enough to treat you before any significant damage occurred."

"What do you mean by *significant*? What's the worst that can happen to my baby?" Wendy accepted the tissue from Dr. Korva and blotted her eyes to prevent a down-pour. This whole conversation seemed so unrealistic that Wendy could swear she had entered *The Twilight Zone*. She had never engaged in premarital sex, and Kevin was the only one she'd been with during their marriage. Yet she felt as dirty as a cheerleader who'd slept with half the guys on the football team.

"If left untreated, the bacteria could spread to your baby's eyes during childbirth and possibly cause blind-ness," Dr. Korva explained. "However, there's no point in discussing this because you're only in your seventh week of pregnancy. There will be no danger to your child by the time you deliver," Dr. Korva assured.

Wendy let out a sigh of relief.

"I'm writing you a prescription for ofloxacin."

"Oxa what?" Wendy blurted.

"O-flox-a-cin," Dr. Korva pronounced. "It's an antibiotic. You'll take one 300-milligram tablet every twelve hours for one week." She handed Wendy the prescription. "Once you have taken all of the medication, I need you to make an appointment to come back into the office so we can run more tests to make sure that no traces of the disease still exist."

"What are the side effects?"

"Some people experience such things like nausea, insomnia, headaches, dizziness, vomiting, or diarrhea. But don't let that scare you. In those instances, there is usually an allergy to the drug. You'll be able to tell right away if you are allergic."

Wendy nodded to indicate that she understood. She wasn't alarmed by the side effects at all. It sounded like what she was going through on a daily basis with the morning sickness.

"If you have any bleeding, call the office immediately and *please* drink lots of water."

"Okay." Wendy spoke softly.

"Before you have sexual intercourse again, your partner needs to be treated or—"

"You mean my husband," Wendy interrupted, indicating that she did not like the term *partner*. It implied engagement in reckless sexual activity.

"Yes, excuse me—your husband," Dr. Korva said apologetically, sensing the tension. "Anyhow, he needs to be treated before the two of you have intercourse again or you will become re-infected."

Wendy nodded her head in agreement, but she could care less whether or not Kevin got treatment. He would definitely hear about her visit today, but that wouldn't be all she'd have to say. *There is no way he is going to touch me again after this.*

"Well, if you don't have any questions for me, you're free to go. Just make sure you stop at the front desk and make a follow-up appointment."

"Actually, I have one request, if you don't mind."

"Yes?"

"If you need to reach me during the day, just call my cell phone or even leave a message on my home phone, but please *do not* call me at work. I'm uncomfortable receiving personal calls there," Wendy admitted. This morning she had called the school and said that she couldn't come in because of a family emergency. It was the best thing she could think of; the message she'd received on Friday *was* urgent, and the baby *was* part of her family, so *technically* she hadn't told a lie.

"Sure, no problem," Dr. Korva said. "I apologize for any inconvenience I may have caused you."

"It's okay."

"Well, have a good week and try not to stress yourself out over this. Your baby will be fine." She gently rubbed Wendy's back to reassure her.

"Thanks."

After Dr. Korva left the room, Wendy was temporarily paralyzed from the numbness she felt. She sat for a few minutes before going to her car. Once she was outside, it was a while before she could actually drive off the parking lot. She was finally able to process everything that had taken place. She thought about her life and how it was not going the way she had planned. *All I ever wanted was to get married and have children. I have both, and neither is satisfying.* "God, what did I do to deserve this?" she asked out loud, looking toward heaven.

Wendy was angry with herself, Kevin, and God. *How could I not know that Kevin had been cheating on me? How could he even do such a thing? Who is the other woman?* Wendy pondered these questions.

She should've known something was going on. Married men don't stay out in clubs with their single friends till the wee hours of the morning doing nothing. Birds of feather flock together! Kevin's friends were no good and apparently neither was he.

*How can God observe my faithfulness to Him and not bless me with a good and faithful husband? What ever happened to never leaving or forsaking me?* she thought. Her whole life she had aimed to please God, and this was how He repaid her. "Why, God? Why did you allow this to happen to me?" Wendy cried out of frustration as she beat her fist against the steering wheel.

# Chapter Four

# A Christmas to Remember

IT WAS ABOUT FOUR O'CLOCK IN THE AFTERNOON. Tori and Tyler were downstairs in the den playing with all of their new toys while their parents, grandparents, and great-grandmother lounged in mini-Africa watching Christmas specials on TV. Everyone was trying to recover from the feast Marlene had prepared earlier. The remainders of ham, turkey, dressing, collard greens, potato salad, macaroni salad, and chitterlings lay on the dining room table. For dessert, Marlene had made sweet potato pie, strawberry cheesecake, and banana pudding. Everyone desired to eat more, but their bodies wouldn't tolerate another bite without exploding.

"Looks like it turned out to be a white Christmas after all," Marlene said joyfully to her family while gazing out the window. She loved watching the snow fall, concealing everything it touched.

"The snow is pretty and all, but I can do without the cold weather," said Kim. She was seated directly in front of the fireplace and still had a blanket wrapped around her. Kim had lived in Columbus all twenty-four years of her life, yet she had never gotten used to the cold winters. Each year she complained as though she had never experienced this weather before.

"Girl, you just need a lil' meat on your bones," Frances joked. "You don't have enough fat on your body. You see all this meat on me"—she grabbed a chunk of her stomach—"it may not keep your man around, but it'll sho' keep you warm."

Everyone laughed, including Michael, although he felt sick after watching Frances's actions. He prayed that Marlene wouldn't adopt her mother's appearance as they grew older. Frances truly did have a lot of internal *insulation*. She, Marlene, and Kim were all just a few inches over five feet, but they varied greatly in size. One of Frances's dresses could wrap around Kim three times and still be too big. Marlene was somewhere in between the two.

Kim liked seeing her grandmother act silly and laugh instead of being so cantankerous. By now both of them had gotten over the spat they'd had on Michael's birthday. "Mama, have you heard from Wendy?" Kim wanted to know.

"She called on Saturday and said that they made it to Philadelphia okay."

"How long are they stayin'?" Frances inquired.

"Until after the New Year."

"It's different celebrating Christmas without Wendy," Michael confessed. Christmas was one of Wendy's favorite holidays, and he missed the excitement and joy she brought with her.

"Honestly, I'm glad they went this year, so the baby can

spend its first Christmas with us," Marlene said. She missed Wendy too, but she would have a fit if Wendy took her newest grandbaby out of state next year.

"I agree," Kim admitted. The baby would be her first niece or nephew. "Was Wendy feeling any better?"

"She didn't say, but she sounded all right."

"That's good, 'cuz I was worried about her getting ill on the plane with all of the problems she was having with morning sickness. I wouldn't have wanted to fly when I was pregnant."

"Girl, you're thinkin' of a coach experience; Wendy flew first class." Frances laughed. "I'm sure she was just fine."

"I think morning sickness is just a conspiracy by women to get men to feel sorry for y'all and be at your beck and call," Terrance playfully instigated.

"Whatever," Kim replied. "You got your nerve; it's not easy having another human being growing inside you."

"I don't know . . . Terrance might be on to something," Michael joined in.

"Oh be quiet," Marlene said to her husband. "God trusted women to bear children because men are big crybabies."

"What?" both Michael and Terrance said in unison.

"Y'all are. At least I know Michael is." Marlene imitated her husband: " 'Baby, can you rub my back. . . . Baby, I got a headache. . . .' All I hear is baby, baby, baby . . ."

"I don't sound like that," Michael defended himself.

"Yes you do, Daddy. I've heard you."

"Um-hmm, I heard you before too," Frances chimed in.

"Kim, stay out of grown folks' business," Michael teased

his daughter. "I'll address your comment when I think of a good response," he said, looking at his mother-in-law.

"There ain't one. You know we tellin' the truth," Frances stated.

"Kim, tell your father that he can't tell you to stay out of grown folks' business anymore 'cuz you're grown also," Marlene mentioned.

"Yeah, Daddy, that's right, I am grown," Kim said wittily, and smiled at her father. "Now, as I was saying, you do sound like that. As a matter of fact, you were whining about your stomach hurting after we ate." Kim intentionally deepened her voice in order to mock her father. "Oh baby . . . that food was good but it sho' messed me up. I think I ate too much or somethin' 'cuz my belly's startin' to ache."

Everyone laughed.

"I simply mentioned having a little stomachache, but I didn't whine," Michael stated, rubbing the tire that had grown around his waist over the years.

"Terrance, I don't know why you're laughin' at my daddy—you're just as bad, if not worse."

"Why you gotta put me in it?" Terrance said for lack of anything better.

"You're the one who started it."

Terrance was stuck. He had opened up the door to the battle of the sexes. Marlene, Kim, and Frances continued teaming up against Michael and him, who denied being adult babies. The women's coalition fell apart when the telephone rang and Marlene got up to answer it.

"Hello?"

"Hey, we were just talking about you," she said. From

the high pitch of Marlene's voice, everyone suspected she was talking to Wendy, and they focused in on her conversation. "How are y'all doing?" Marlene's face lit up as she spoke.

"Is that Wendy?" Kim asked for verification.

Marlene nodded.

"Oh, okay . . . well, tell Kevin that I said hi and Merry Christmas." Marlene paused for Wendy's response. "Okay, love you too, sweetie."

She hung up the phone.

"Why didn't you let anyone else talk to her?" Michael was irritated.

"She said she and Kevin were on their way out the door and she didn't have time to talk to everyone, but she wanted to call and wish us all a Merry Christmas."

"But still, she could have at least said hi or called at a time when she would be able to talk." Kim spoke sourly.

"Well, she said she'll call back later. Right now they are on their way to visit some of Kevin's relatives." If it weren't for the fact that Marlene was the one who'd answered the phone, she also would have been upset if she hadn't gotten a chance to speak with Wendy.

"That still don't sound right." Frances frowned.

"Mama, please don't get started with one of your conspiracy theories. Maybe Kevin was rushing her. Maybe she didn't want to be rude and stay on the phone—who knows? Anyhow, she sends everyone her love and said she will drop our presents off when she returns."

Kim agreed with Frances, but she wouldn't dare say so out loud. Wendy had been making such a big deal around Thanksgiving about how she was going to miss spending Christmas with everyone this year. It was strange that she would call on her first Christmas away and speak only with one person.

"The next time she calls I want to talk to her," Michael said firmly. He was more upset than anyone else because he hadn't gotten to speak with her the last time she'd called, either.

"Okay, I'll tell her next time that you want to talk to her."

"Mommy!" Tyler came yelling from downstairs.

"What's wrong with you?"

"Tori said that I'm ugly."

Everyone wanted to laugh, but poor Tyler had huge crocodile tears in his eyes, and it was clear his feelings were very hurt.

"Are you ugly?" Kim asked.

"No, but she said I was."

"If you know that you're not ugly then it doesn't matter what anyone else says, right?"

Tyler nodded in agreement.

"Look at my baby's hair, Mommy?" Tori walked in the room to see what Tyler had told Kim.

"Oooh, that's pretty," Kim beamed.

"Thank you," she said, stroking the doll's hair after getting reassurance from her mother.

"I told Mommy that you said I was ugly." Tyler scowled at his sister.

"So what?" Tori snapped.

"Hey guys, don't start. Not today—it's Christmas," Kim scolded.

"But he said my baby's hair was ugly!" Tori pouted.

Tori had diligently worked on that doll's hair, combing and recombing it to make it look good, but Tyler was right. The doll's hair was hideous. Kim couldn't admit that to her daughter, though, without crushing the six-year-old's self-esteem.

"If y'all can't say anything nice to one another then just don't speak at all. Maybe y'all need to take a nap. Is that the problem?"

"No ma'am," they both said.

"Well chill out or I am gonna make both of you put away your toys and go upstairs and lie down."

Neither child said a word. They both looked at their mother and then at each other. "Sorry for calling you ugly," Tori mumbled to her brother.

"Okay," Tyler said and ran back down the stairs without apologizing. Tori followed behind him just as the doorbell rang.

"Terrance, that's probably your parents," Michael stated.

"What?" Kim said in surprise.

"Uh . . ." Terrance uttered. He'd known this moment was coming, but he hadn't prepared a response.

"I invited Evelyn and Doug over to spend the evening with us," Marlene quickly responded.

"Why the evening? That doesn't make sense. Why didn't you invite them to eat Christmas dinner with us?" Kim asked.

"They couldn't make it for dinner so I asked if they could come over this evening."

"I thought we were going over their house." Kim addressed Terrance.

"We were going over to their house until your mother invited them over here."

"So when was someone gonna fill me in?"

"I'm sorry. I thought you knew." Terrance was aware that she didn't know, but he couldn't think of anything else to say at the moment.

*Liar!* Kim said to herself and rolled her eyes at Terrance.

"Actually, it's my fault, honey. I asked Terrance to invite them over and I should have told you."

"Mm-hmm." Kim didn't believe Marlene either. It was nothing against his parents. In fact, she loved them. As much as she stressed open communication with Terrance, he knew that she didn't like to be caught off guard. "If you knew they were coming, why did you have me leave their presents in the car?"

The doorbell rang again.

"I'll get it," Terrance responded before Marlene could get up. If he didn't move, Kim would continue questioning him until he answered her.

"Well, they didn't tell me nothin' either," Frances said after Terrance went to get the door. She was telling the truth, but there was a good reason for that. The family had learned a long time ago that Frances could not keep secrets. The surest way to guarantee that someone would find something out was to tell her.

"Well, everyone knows now, so that's all that matters, right?" Michael winked at Kim.

"But some of us didn't find out until the last minute," Kim rebutted.

"Merry Christmas," Evelyn and Doug Carter called out as they walked into the living room.

"Merry Christmas," Kim replied. "This is quite a surprise."

"We forgot to tell Kim that you guys were coming over.

She is a little upset with us because she thought they were going over to your house later," Marlene told Terrance's mom and dad.

"Oh, honey, I'm sorry." Evelyn said to Kim. "I assumed you knew we were invited. I guess I should have said something when I talked to you the other day."

"That's okay. It's no big deal. I was just shocked, that's all." After seeing Terrance's parents, Kim didn't know why she had been upset in the first place. They were like her second parents. Before she and Terrance started going together, they'd always said Kim was the daughter they never had.

Evelyn was beautiful, and Kim hoped she could keep her figure when she got older like Terrance's mom had. Evelyn and Doug made a very attractive couple, although they seemed like complete opposites. Doug was casually dressed in a pair of jeans and a T-shirt, while Evelyn entered the room wearing slacks and a metallic silver shirt. She claimed to be forty-eight but looked at least ten years younger. Her skin was flawless, and she didn't have one strand of gray hair. Even Doug would look younger if it wasn't for his receding hairline.

"And how are you?" Kim asked Doug as she hugged him.

He smiled. "Fine, sweetie."

"Hi, Grammy. Hi, Grandpa," the kids yelled as they ran up the stairs.

Both Evelyn and Doug bent down and gave them big hugs. Even though Terrance wasn't Tori's biological father, he and his parents treated her as though she carried their blood. They had all been a part of her life since the day she was born.

"Where are Wendy and Kevin?" Evelyn asked after greeting her grandchildren.

"They went to Philadelphia to spend Christmas with Kevin's mother," Marlene answered.

"Oh. Well, we brought some presents for them. Will it be okay to leave them here?"

"Sure. They won't be back until after the first of the year, but I'll be sure they get them."

Evelyn handed the presents to Marlene, who set them underneath the now empty Christmas tree.

Terrance went to the car to get the presents he and Kim had bought for his parents. Tori and Tyler eagerly opened more gifts. The children couldn't have had a better Christmas. Both sets of grandparents had spoiled them completely rotten. Earlier that day, Kim's parents gave them brand-new thirteen-inch televisions to go in each of their rooms. From Evelyn and Doug, Tyler now received a PlayStation 2 with several games, while Tori got a collection of dolls, purses, toy jewelry, and makeup.

The children spent the rest of the evening playing with their new toys while the adults continued chitchatting in the living room. Frances, Terrance, and Michael all dozed off after getting leftovers. Later, Marlene asked Kim if she would start the dishes while she and Evelyn straightened up the mess in the living room. Doug helped the kids gather all of their toys.

Kim was standing at the sink doing dishes and thinking about what a good time she'd had today with everyone, including her grandmother. She thought about Wendy and was a little hurt that she didn't get to talk with her, but she would see her in a week or so. Kim and Wendy had always spent the holidays together. Even though they were five years apart, they had grown to be very close. Wendy had spent a lot of time taking care of Kim when they were younger. She would help Marlene do her hair, get her ready for school, and even help Kim with her homework. Wendy was always very protective of her little sister. Kim was confident that Wendy would be an excellent mother.

The phone rang.

"Will someone get the phone?" Kim yelled. "My hands are wet."

The phone continued to ring.

"I guess I'll get it," she said sarcastically. She was tired, ready to go home, and she was trying to finish the dishes as quickly as possible.

Kim wiped her hands on the dish towel and answered the phone before it clicked over to the voice mail. "Hello?" she said, a little frustrated.

"Uh . . . hi, Kim. This is Kevin." He sounded nervous.

"Hey. What are you doing?" Kim hadn't expected him to be on the other end. She'd figured it would be one of Marlene's friends from church.

"Nothing much. Just sitting around my mom's house."

"I thought Wendy said that y'all were going somewhere."

"Huh?"

"I was sort of mad that she didn't talk to me, but she said that y'all were on the way out the door."

"Wendy called you and said that we were leaving?"

"Yeah. She didn't talk to me; she talked to Mama."

"Kim . . ." Kevin hesitated. "I was calling to speak to Wendy."

"What do you mean?"

"She didn't come to Philadelphia with me. I called the house. When she didn't answer I assumed that she was over there."

"Hold up—Wendy isn't with you?"

"No, she's not."

"Then why did she call here and say that she was?"

"I'm really not sure. . . . I . . . I had no idea. . . ."

"Why didn't she go?"

"I . . . Look, maybe you need to talk to her. I'm sorry, I shouldn't have called. I've said too much already. Listen, if you talk to her, just tell her that I was thinking about her. I'm sorry, Kim." Kevin hung up the phone, leaving Kim outraged.

She dialed star-six-nine to get the number he had called from, but the recording stated that the call came from a non-published number. "Dang!" she grumbled. She was confused by the conversation and mad that he had hung up on her before she had a chance to figure out what was going on. She had started to dial Wendy's home number when Michael called her from the living room.

"Yes," Kim said, trying not to let the frustration show in her voice.

"Can you come here, please?"

"Okay." She hung up the phone and swore that she would find out what was happening with her sister somehow.

"Who was on the phone?" Marlene wanted to know.

"Huh?"

"Just a few minutes ago . . . who was on the phone?"

"Oh, it was the wrong number," Kim lied. She didn't want anyone to know that Kevin had called. There was no need to have her parents panic, especially since she didn't know all of the facts. "What did you need, Daddy?" Kim asked.

"Terrance wanted you."

"I have a Christmas card I want to give to you," Terrance announced.

Kim now noticed that someone had turned off the TV, dimmed the lights, and lit a few candles on the mantel. Her children were also sitting quietly on the couch, and everyone else was staring at her. "Okay, why does it have to be a public forum when you give me a card?" she asked, giving Terrance a strange look.

"Just open it up," Terrance replied impatiently.

Kim sighed but obediently opened the card while Terrance bent down to tie his shoe. Inside was a handwritten note that read: *Christmas is not over. Look down at me.*

She looked down and saw Terrance on his knee holding a one-carat diamond ring; her heart began racing.

"Kimberly Michele Tibbs"—his voice cracked—"will you marry me?"

She wanted to scream from the top of her lungs "Yes!" but could barely speak.

"Well?" Terrance summoned her reply.

"Of course!" She managed to squeeze out those words through her tears. Everyone started clapping and yelling.

"Y'all were in on this, weren't you?" Kim said, sobbing, to both sets of parents. She then pointed to Evelyn and Doug. "That's why no one told me that y'all were coming over."

Everyone laughed as an admission of their part in the surprised proposal. Kim wasn't exactly sure if the kids understood what the proposal meant, but she would talk to them about it later. She glanced at Frances, who mumbled congratulations and quoted some scripture about it being better for them to marry than to burn. Kim could tell she was slightly offended because no one had let her in on the surprise. *Oh well*, she thought. Tonight was one of the most memorable nights of her life. Even with all of the excitement about the proposal, Kim couldn't keep from wondering about the phone call she'd received from Kevin. *If Wendy's not in Philly, why isn't she here?*

## Chapter Five

# More Than Just
## a Little White Lie

I'M COMING!" Wendy shouted to the annoying person banging on her front door. It had been less than two weeks from the time she'd confronted Kevin about her visit with Dr. Korva. Kevin had left that day, and she hadn't said much to him since then. For now, he was temporarily staying at one of the apartment buildings he owned. Before he went to Philadelphia he'd left Wendy a message saying that he would like to talk to her when he got back. *You can stay in Philly until you die, for all I care,* Wendy thought as she reflected on Kevin's voice-mail message. She was in no hurry to hear what he had to say. Chances were he'd use this time in Philly to think of some crafty way to explain how she contracted chlamydia, but nothing he said would change the fact that he had cheated on her.

"I said I'm coming," Wendy repeated as the knocking became more aggressive. This would be the fifth time Kevin had sent roses to her since the night he left. Wendy hadn't even taken the time to place them in water or read the attached cards. Rather, she'd trashed them, just like she intended to do with the roses she expected to receive now. She tried using the intercom to tell the delivery person just to leave them at the door, but something must have been wrong with the system because no one responded.

She was so frustrated by the time she got to the door that she swung it open without even looking through the peephole. "You don't have to knock so—" Wendy's plan was to give the man or woman a snide remark for beating the door down. However, she was taken by surprise when Kim stood in place of the supposed delivery person. "Kim? What are you doing here?"

Kim was fuming after the long drive from her east side town home to her sister's exclusive New Albany residence. It would have been more convenient to come last night since her parents lived closer to Wendy than she did, but doing so was impossible. The fact that she was out under two conditions she loathed, early morning and cold weather, did nothing to appease her anger. Her red Mitsubishi Eclipse had came close to nicking several cars as she skidded along the snow-covered highway. "Back from Philly so soon?" she asked sarcastically with one hand on her hip while the other was apparently used as a weapon against the door.

"I . . . um . . . I . . ." Wendy searched for words, but nothing came to mind.

"Next time you decide to play hooky, you ought to tell your husband not to call over to Mama's house looking for you," Kim snapped with eyes piercing Wendy.

*Dang!* Wendy had been so determined not to answer any of Kevin's calls yesterday that she had ignored both her cell phone and the home phone each time they rang. The possibility of him calling anywhere else never crossed her mind. She sighed and reluctantly asked, "Are you coming in?" She really didn't feel like talking, but it was evident that her sister wasn't leaving until she did.

Kim folded her arms and walked into the foyer, looking at Wendy and waiting for an explanation.

Normally, Wendy would have had a fit if someone dragged snow-covered boots across her oak floor. However, she knew that she wasn't in a position to remind Kim to take off her shoes.

"Are we just gonna stand here or are you gonna tell me what's going on?"

"Can we *please* go sit down? I'd prefer not to stand here while you interrogate me." *Why did you answer the door? Why, why, why . . .* she questioned herself while walking down the foyer. Kim followed silently behind her.

When the two ladies entered the living room, Wendy was glad to see that Kim had taken off her boots before stepping on the light beige carpet. The living room usually had such a warm feeling, being decorated in hunter green and white. The cathedral ceiling helped create a classy look. It was evident that Wendy had put a lot of thought, time, and money into furnishing the room. She even had a custom-made ceiling fan with a white base and see-through hunter green blades. What Kim liked most was the hidden TV that sat directly above the fireplace. At first glance, it was just a wall. However, with the touch of a button, what appeared to be a wall opened up and a thirty-two-inch flat-screen television emerged.

"Where are the kids?" Wendy inquired, trying to break the ice as she sat on the couch and Kim stood over her.

"They're with Mama."

"Does she know you came over here?"

"No, I didn't tell her. I didn't even tell Terrance. After he left for work, I called Mama and asked her to keep Tori and Tyler so I could go help out at the salon for a few hours."

Wendy was relieved. "Thank you for not telling her."

"Thank me, for what? I said I *didn't* tell her, but it doesn't mean that I won't."

"Look, Kim. I know you're upset, but I really need you to calm down if you want to talk. There's a lot going on and I really don't need to deal with you and your feisty attitude."

Kim gave Wendy a blank stare. "What do you expect? Maybe I wouldn't be upset had I not just caught you in a bold-faced lie."

"I know. . . . I'm sorry. . . . Just hear me out, will you?"

"I'm listening."

"What exactly did Kevin say when he called you?" Wendy asked curiously. She wanted to know how much Kim knew about her situation. If Kevin hadn't gone into details then neither would she.

"That's just it. He didn't say anything. I asked him what was going on and he said I needed to talk to you, then he hung up on me. So tell me, what's going on?" Kim demanded.

"Well Kevin and I . . ." Wendy hesitated for a moment. "We . . . we split up."

"Really? When?"

"A little over a week ago. In fact, it was the day after Daddy's birthday."

Kim sat down next to Wendy. Her expression of anger twisted into concern. "What happened?"

"I found out that he cheated on me. That's why I didn't go to Philadelphia." It angered Wendy to say that out loud.

"Oh my God." Kim covered her hands with her mouth. "How did you find out?"

"It's a long story and I really don't feel like going into any details right now," Wendy said, desperately wanting to avoid telling her about the appointment with the gynecologist.

"Okay," Kim stated, respecting her sister's privacy. She hated it when people tried to force her into talking about something she wasn't ready to discuss. She was not going to put Wendy in that position. "Why didn't you come over to Mama's house and spend Christmas with us?"

"You know how big a deal Kevin was making about us going to Philly. If I had showed up over there, everyone would have been asking questions and I guess I'm not ready for everyone to know yet. Plus, you know how Gramma is. I wasn't in the mood to put up with her."

"But what about me? Why didn't you tell me?" Kim sounded hurt. "I wouldn't have told them anything."

"Yeah, I know. I was going to tell you, I promise. But what good would it have done for me to tell you before Christmas?"

"What do you mean by that?"

"I would have ruined your Christmas. You would have been over there worried about me. It's not like you could have come and spent any time over here. Everyone would have been suspicious."

"But still, I would have found some way to work it out."

"How, Kim? Then that would have interfered with the proposal Terrance had planned."

"How did you know about that?"

"Everyone knew except for you—oh, and Gramma. How did she react?"

"She was a little bitter," Kim recalled with a slight grin, "but she'll get over it."

"I was with him when he bought the ring."

"You what? See, he didn't tell me that. I'm thinkin' the brotha picked it out on his own."

"He did. I went along to steer him in the right direction." For the first time since her sister had been there, Wendy put on a smile. "You like it, don't you?"

"Of course I do. Thank you so much." Kim gave her sister a hug. The only thing that would have made her proposal more special was if Wendy had been there. Kim still hadn't expressed how excited she really was about the whole thing. Last night she had been stressing over Kevin's phone call. Now she was even more concerned in light of what Wendy had just told her. It was sort of hard for Kim to be happy about her engagement after hearing about her sister's marital problems. "I'm sorry for the way that I came over here. I had no idea what was going on with you, and I was worried."

"I know. I'm sorry too. I'm very sorry for not being there to see your face when Terrance gave you the ring. I just didn't think I would be able to handle the pressure of everyone questioning me."

"So what's gonna happen now? Are you guys getting a divorce?"

"I'm sure we will eventually," Wendy replied solemnly.

"What are y'all gonna do with the house?"

"I'm not sure. We haven't even discussed it. I guess we'll figure that out later. I just want to move on with my life, and the only way I can do that is by not being with him. If that means giving up the house, so be it." Wendy hated the thought of leaving her luxurious five-thousand-square-foot home. She and Kevin had bought it a few weeks before they were married, for $2.6 million. It was her dream home, but if she had to give it up in order to get rid of him, then she would.

"That jerk!" Kim said angrily. "I can't believe he would do something like this to you, especially with the baby on the way."

"Well, the baby won't be an issue anymore after—" Wendy stopped mid-sentence. *Dang it!* She had not meant to share her thoughts out loud.

"After what? What were you gonna say?"

Wendy wished she hadn't opened her big mouth. Sure, she would have to tell Kim eventually, but she hadn't planned on doing it that day. "After . . . the . . . miscarriage," she answered slowly.

Kim's eyes got big. "You had a miscarriage?"

"No . . . not yet. My doctor said that I'm in jeopardy of having one, though."

"Why? What's wrong?"

"You saw how sick I was. I've also been having a lot of cramping and bleeding."

"Oh, I am so sorry." Kim hugged Wendy again. She knew how badly her sister wanted children, and she felt like crying. She wouldn't have held back the tears if she didn't think Wendy would start crying also. "Are you okay?"

"Yeah, I have no choice but to be," Wendy said, looking at the floor.

"You're not going back to work after the New Year, are you?"

"Yes."

"*Why?* You need to try and take care of yourself and the baby."

"There's nothing I can do about the baby. It's out of my hands."

Kim felt horrible about being so abrasive earlier. She would like to wring Kevin's neck for everything he'd done to her sister. "How long are you pretending to be in Philly?"

"Kevin and I aren't supposed to come back until after the New Year, so I guess until then."

"What are you doing on New Year's Eve?"

"Nothing. I'll just sit around the house like I did yesterday. I really can't go to church 'cuz Mama and Daddy will be there."

"Well, I'll be over that night. Maybe we can go downtown to First Night Columbus," Kim suggested, referring to the annual community New Year's Eve celebration.

"I don't know, Kim. I'm trying to keep a low profile, seeing how I'm really supposed to be out of town and all. Besides, what about Terrance and the kids? You can't bring Tori or Tyler with you."

"I'll think of something. I'm gonna tell Terrance the truth, but I promise I won't tell Mama."

"Let me think about it." Wendy didn't like dragging Kim into her lie.

"No. There's nothing to think about. You're spending New Year's Eve with me and that's final."

"Yes ma'am."

"You may at least want to call Kevin so he doesn't call Mama's house again. You're lucky I answered the phone."

"Yeah, I will." The thought of talking to Kevin irritated her, but it was something that definitely had to be done if Wendy was going to keep up her charade.

"Well, I have to run. I told Mama that I wouldn't be gone too long. She already thought it was crazy that I was getting up early to work, especially since I told her that I'm off the rest of the week. I wouldn't want her to call the shop."

"That would be a disaster."

"Call me if you need anything."

"Okay."

"I mean it," Kim said. "You don't have to go through this alone. That's what sisters are for."

"Thank you."

Kim hugged her sister a third time. "I love you."

"I love you too."

As Kim walked toward the front door, she was glad she had made the trip over to Wendy's house. Wendy's openness about her situation confirmed to Kim the closeness of their relationship. Besides Terrance, Wendy was her best friend.

Wendy, on the other hand, was engulfed by feelings of guilt. What she had told Kim about the miscarriage was much more than just a little white lie.

# Chapter Six

# A Choice in the Matter

"How can I help you?" the receptionist asked.
"I have an appointment," Wendy shyly stated.

"May I have your name, please?"

"Wendy Phillips."

She leaned closer to verify what was said. "Did you say Cindy Phillips?"

"No, Wendy Phillips," Wendy repeated louder this time.

"Oh, I'm sorry." She looked at her schedule. "I show that we sent your registration form and state-mandated literature to you by mail, correct?"

"Yes."

"Did you bring the registration form with you?"

"Um-hmm." Wendy glanced over her paperwork to double-check that all necessary information had been filled out: name, birth date, address, telephone number, and medical history. There was no way she would give out her work number. If she got a call at work from here, Ms. Burchett would make it her business to hunt Wendy down for information. "Here you go."

"Thank you." The receptionist also looked over the paperwork. "You need to sign this form giving your consent to be treated today." She handed Wendy a different document, pointing to the dotted line where her signature was needed.

Wendy scribbled her signature on the paper and gave it back to the lady.

"Now I just need your payment. We only take cash or credit."

Money was the least of Wendy's concerns right now. She handed the lady cash that she'd withdrawn earlier that morning from the bank.

"Okay, you're all set. Just have a seat and a nurse will call you back shortly."

Wendy searched for an empty seat. The waiting room was more crowded than she'd expected it to be. The lighting was dull, which gave the place a depressing aura. She was shocked to see how many young women were there. Some appeared to be terrified and others were calm, like they'd done this before. Wendy was especially glad not to see any familiar faces. She'd driven nearly an hour from Columbus to ensure anonymity. Wendy found a seat next to a frightened young lady who looked like she'd turned eighteen just days ago. She searched for words to comfort her but couldn't think of anything to say. They were in the same position, and she was scared herself.

Tears welled up in her eyes as she saw one woman come from the back crying. She closed them to prevent having to look at the face of anyone else. Wendy nervously rocked back and forth in the chair as frightening thoughts raced through her head. *People bomb places like this. What if I'm here and it blows up? This is not where I want to die.*

Spiritually, Wendy knew that what she was planning to do was wrong, but she continued justifying her actions. *It'll make separating from Kevin much easier.*

Wendy had called him the other day after Kim left. He said that he loved her and apologized again for what happened. He asked if she would see him when he got back. Although she wasn't thrilled about seeing him, she knew that she couldn't avoid doing so forever. There were a few things that needed to be taken care of, so she agreed to meet with him next Friday. Lying to Kevin wouldn't bother her after all he'd put her through, but it would be hard lying to everyone else in her family. She felt bad enough about telling Kim. *Maybe I'll tell Mama and have her tell Daddy and Gramma.*

"Wendy Phillips . . ."

Wendy was so consumed with her thoughts that she hadn't even noticed when the girl next to her had been called. Her legs trembled as she got up and walked toward the nurse.

"How are you today?" the nurse asked Wendy.

"I'm fine, thank you," she lied. "My sister's name is Kim also, but she spells her name with an *i* instead of with a *y*," Wendy mentioned after noticing the nurse's name tag. It was all she could think to say during such an awkward moment.

"Yeah, I guess it is uncommon to spell it with a *y*," Nurse Kym acknowledged. "Will you step on the scale so I can get your weight, please?"

Wendy did as she was told. The name was the only thing Nurse Kym had in common with her sister. They did not resemble each other at all. Kym had extremely pale skin that was in desperate need of a tan. She looked like she was probably in her late thirties or early forties and needed a touch-up to her blond hair because the brown roots were starting to show.

Wendy looked at the scale and was astonished by the amount of weight she had gained. In the last couple of months, she had put on fifteen pounds. There was no telling how big she would be if she carried this pregnancy to term.

"I'm going to have to take a urine test to verify your pregnancy before we go any further," Kym announced.

Wendy really didn't think it was necessary. She wouldn't be here if she wasn't pregnant. Nevertheless, she took the cup from Kym, went in the rest room to do her business, and returned a few moments later.

"Thank you." Kym took the urine sample from Wendy. "You can wait in Room Three. Please get undressed and put the gown on that's on the table. I'll be in there shortly to draw your blood and do an ultrasound. After that, you'll have to watch a short video before we actually do the procedure."

Wendy obediently walked to her assigned room and waited. She thought about her relationship with Kevin and wished she had taken more time to get to know him before they got married. She had been in her late twenties and had felt like time was passing her by. All of her friends had been either married or engaged. Wendy had felt like she was always a bridesmaid, and she'd desperately wanted to be a bride. Even those who weren't married had children like her best friend, Gwen, and her sister.

Kym walked into the room. "You are most definitely pregnant." She spoke matter-of-factly.

"Yeah, I kind of figured that," Wendy replied for lack of anything better.

"A lot of women don't understand why we take urine tests. We have to by law. It's sort of stupid since women come here because they're pregnant, but rules are rules and we must follow them." She put on gloves and pulled a needle out of her pocket. "Now I need to draw some blood to determine what blood type you are."

"What does my blood type have to do with anything?"

"We need to test the iron levels in your blood and check to see if your blood type is positive or negative."

Wendy still didn't understand why it would be important. Kym picked up on her confusion. "I don't mean to scare you, but if something were to happen while you were here, say you began hemorrhaging or something, we need as much information as possible to be able to help you."

Kym's answer only made Wendy more terrified.

After taking blood, Wendy lay down so Kym could perform the ultrasound. She accidentally caught a glimpse of the monitor as the cold ball rolled against her abdomen. She recalled the pictures of a previous ultrasound she had received from Dr. Korva. Kevin had been so happy. He swore that he could see the baby's face, while the only thing Wendy could see was a fuzzy black-and-white image of something that definitely didn't look like a baby.

Kevin had already picked out possible names for the baby. If it was a girl, he wanted to name her Maya Nicole after his sister who'd died several years ago. That didn't bother Wendy, especially since her middle name was Nicole also. It would have been like naming the baby after herself. If it was a boy, he wanted to name him KJ, short for Kevin Jamal Phillips Jr. Wendy wasn't too eager about having a junior, but she would have been willing to let Kevin have his namesake. *If only he hadn't cheated on me . . .*

"According to this, you're about nine weeks pregnant," Kym announced.

"Can you tell when the due date is?"

Kym looked at Wendy strangely. "Are you sure you want to know that?"

"Yes." Dr. Korva had already told her, but for some reason, Wendy wanted to hear it again.

"Okay . . . let's see here . . . approximately August second."

"Thanks," Wendy said softly. She would intentionally make plans for that day so she wouldn't spend it thinking about what could have been.

After the ultrasound, Kym stepped out of the room so Wendy could watch the required video that explained the procedure and the finality of having it done. Wendy felt ashamed about watching it. Until recently, she never thought this would be something she would do. She tried to divert her attention by thinking about her class and the activities she would do with them when school resumed. *Maybe I'll ask Principal Schoff for permission to have lunch in the classroom one day instead of going to the cafeteria. Maybe we could go for a nature walk during recess. Maybe—*

The door opened and Kym walked in with the doctor. "Hi, Wendy. I'm Dr. Bullock," he stated and stuck out his hand to greet her.

She wanted to jump off of the table and run out when this tall, thin, dark-haired man entered the room. There were certain things she felt uncomfortable discussing with a male physician. At a crucial moment like this, Wendy felt that a woman would be more sympathetic to her situation. "Hello," she finally said, and shook his hand.

"Do you have any questions about the procedure?"

Wendy shook her head no.

"Okay then. I'm going to give you an anesthetic. It'll take a few minutes to kick in, but I promise that you won't feel a thing afterwards."

As Wendy sat silently, her mind went into overdrive. *What if he makes a mistake and I'll never be able to have kids again? What if I'm allergic to the medicine?* She bit her lip trying to contain her thoughts, but they overpowered her and ran wild.

*Children are a heritage of the Lord. . . . Thou shalt not kill. . . . Have we not one Father? Has not one God created us?*

"Okay, Wendy, I need you to lie back," Dr. Bullock instructed. "You'll feel a little poke at first and then you won't feel anything else for a couple of hours."

The very moment he was about to inject her with the medicine, Wendy cried out "Wait!"

Dr. Bullock dropped his medical equipment and Kym grabbed her. "Is everything okay?" she asked.

"No, I—I'm not ready yet," Wendy bawled.

"Look, if you're not one-hundred-percent sure that this is what you want to do, then take some time and think about it," Dr. Bullock suggested. "You're only nine weeks, so you have plenty of time to decide. Our office does abortions up to twenty-four weeks. This doesn't have to be done today."

Wendy sat silent.

"Kym and I are going to step out of the room so you can

get dressed. She'll come back in and discuss your options with you from here. If you decide to go through with the surgery, I'll see you another time. If not, best of luck with your future."

"Thank you," Wendy mumbled and put her clothes back on when they left the room.

"Are you okay?" Kym asked when she returned.

"Yes," she murmured, though her dried, tear-stained cheeks told a different story.

"Please take these business cards. One is the number to our twenty-four-hour counseling center. They can help you make the right decision. The other number is to a support group. If you do decide to proceed, they'll help you deal with the aftermath of having an abortion."

Wendy took the cards and placed the information in the zippered pocket on the inside of her purse. "Do you think I'll be able to come back later today?"

"I don't know how full the schedule is. You'll have to check at the front desk on your way out. Remember, you have plenty of time to decide. This doesn't *have* to be done today," Kym stressed.

"I know. . . . It's just that it would be easier if it were. I hate to have driven all of this way for nothing."

"I can't tell you what to do, but it doesn't look to me like you're ready. I think you should take time and really weigh all of your options because once it's done, there's no turning back," Kym warned before leaving the room.

*I just need a little more time, that's all*, Wendy thought to herself. On her way out of the clinic, she stopped at the front desk to see if there was any possibility she could come in later that day.

"It looks like you're in luck," the receptionist said. "We

just had someone call in and cancel. We can get you back in at one-thirty. Will that work?"

Wendy looked at the time. It was ten after eleven. "That's fine." She wasn't familiar with the small town, and she didn't want to sit in the waiting room for over two hours until it was time for her appointment. "Is there someplace quiet that I can go around here to pass time?" she asked.

"Down the street there's a library and a small diner. They are in walking distance if you wanted to leave your car parked."

"Which way?"

"When you go out the door, make a left and walk about a block and a half. You can't miss either of them."

"Okay, thanks," Wendy said and left with the intention of returning soon. She just needed some extra time to get her thoughts together before going through with this.

Wendy had been in the office for so long that she had forgotten how cold it was outside. The air was very crisp. Walking down the steps to the sidewalk, she looked back one more time at the sign on the building. It read: PREGNANCY ALTERNATIVE: WHERE WOMEN HAVE A CHOICE IN THE MATTER. Wendy turned around and told herself she was doing the right thing. *As far as my family and Kevin are concerned, I will have a miscarriage. What they don't know won't hurt them. This whole thing will be over and I can divorce Kevin without any reminders of our time together.*

Initially, she headed toward her fully loaded silver BMW 5 Series sedan, which Kevin had gotten her as a wedding present. Once inside the car, Wendy changed her mind about driving despite the fact that it was cold. She figured it would be more of a hassle driving down the street and finding parking than it would be just walking and leaving the car there. She got out of the car, reactivated the alarm, and proceeded in the stated direction.

She walked very briskly, and it didn't take her long at all to reach the diner. She ordered a cup of hot cocoa and sat in the corner at a small table, trying to silence the voices in her head that had prevented her from going through with the abortion the first time. *It is the only way!* she argued with herself. She'd pretty much made up her mind. At one-thirty, she was going to terminate this pregnancy and close this chapter of her life for good.

In order to pass time and to keep the voices of reason from changing her mind, Wendy got a newspaper from the newsstand and began doing the crossword puzzle in the back of it. The puzzle was more difficult than she'd anticipated, or maybe she couldn't concentrate as well as she would've liked. In any event, she succeeded in passing time until twelve-forty-five. She wanted to solve the last few problems before heading back to the clinic. *Seventeen Down: The art of fine handwriting.*

"Wendy?"

She jumped at the mention of her name and spilled the now cold cup of cocoa all over the crossword puzzle. "Um . . . hi." Her smile was forced.

"Here, let me help you with that," the man said as he got napkins together and assisted in cleaning the spill. "I'm sorry. I didn't mean to startle you. I just finished having lunch with a friend of mine who pastors a church here. I wasn't sure if it was you or not. What brings you out to this neck of the woods?" Pastor Jones asked.

Wendy was at a loss for words.

"Are you okay?" He picked up on her nervousness, as her hands were shaking.

Tears began to creep from her eyes.

"Do you want to talk about whatever it is that's bothering you?"

She really didn't want to talk. However, her head mechanically nodded yes against her will.

"Come with me. We'll go next door, where we can talk privately." Pastor Jones took her hand and led the way.

# Chapter Seven
## A Back-Door Blessing

"EXCUSE ME, MA'AM, do you have a meeting room available?" Pastor Jones asked the librarian.

"Yes, it's a small one, though. How many people do you need it for?" she responded.

"It's just the two of us." Pastor Jones pointed at Wendy, who sat down at an empty table while he was at the desk.

"In that case, all I need you to do is fill out the top part of this paper and sign here at the bottom," the librarian stated, and waited for Pastor Jones's signature.

"It's all yours. Be sure to return the key when you're finished."

"Yes, I will. Thank you so much, ma'am," Wendy overheard Pastor Jones say. He looked very intimidating with his six-two, two-hundred-and-thirty-pound frame. His voice was very deep and heavy. It reminded her of Kevin's voice except she didn't get the same sensual feeling hearing Pastor Jones speak as she used to with Kevin. Pastor Jones's looks were very contradictory with his character. Underneath his dark complexion and large stature he was nothing more than a big bundle of love. He motioned to Wendy and she followed him into the conference room.

"Wendy, what's going on, darling?" Pastor Jones asked once they were both seated.

"I'm not really sure where to start," Wendy admitted.

"Why don't you begin by telling me what's on your mind?"

"I'm sorry. I'm just stressed. I didn't expect to run into anyone I knew here, especially you."

"Stressed about what? I thought things were going good with you. Marlene tells me that you're expecting."

Her eyes filled with tears. "I came here to have an abortion," she confessed, staring at the floor. She couldn't bring herself to look him in the face.

"Did you already have it?" he asked somberly.

Wendy nodded her head no.

Pastor Jones exhaled loudly. "I don't understand. Why would you feel like you have to do something like that? Is your husband—I'm sorry I can't remember his name . . ."

"Kevin."

"Yes, thank you. He's happy about the baby, isn't he?"

"Yes."

"Well, what's the problem? Is there something wrong with the baby?"

"No sir."

"Wendy . . ." Pastor Jones looked confused. "Is the baby Kevin's?"

"Yes! Yes . . ." Wendy looked up for the first time. She definitely didn't want her pastor to believe that she was having a baby by another man.

Although Pastor Jones was happy to hear Wendy confirm that the baby was indeed Kevin's, her answer only added to his uncertainty about the situation. "Why do you want to terminate your pregnancy?"

Wendy looked back down at the floor.

"Wendy?"

"Yes," she answered.

"I can't help you unless you tell me what's going on."

"I . . . I'm just not ready to have a baby right now," she murmured.

"Why not? What's wrong?"

By now a continuous flow of tears raced down her cheeks. "Kevin"—she paused to catch her breath—"he cheated on me."

"What?" Pastor Jones didn't know Kevin very well, but he hadn't expected to hear that Kevin had been unfaithful. "Are you certain about this?"

"Yes."

"How do you know?"

Wendy told Pastor Jones about her visit to the gynecologist the day she found out about having chlamydia. She had never intended to tell anyone that story. However, now that Wendy had started talking, she didn't seem to be able to stop. She told Pastor Jones about how Kevin partied on the weekends, drank alcohol, and got high with his friends. She admitted her insecurity whenever he went out. "It looks like I had every reason to be insecure after what happened," she stated. "I just want him out of my life for good, and having an abortion would ensure that."

Pastor Jones listened to Wendy patiently and managed to understand everything she said through her tears. "Let me ask you a few questions." He paused for a moment as though he was trying to figure out what to ask first. The news about Kevin was shocking. But then again, Wendy had chosen not to take any of the premarital classes required by the church and had married elsewhere. "Did Kevin get high and stay out late before you two were married?"

*Uh-oh.* Wendy knew where this was going. "Yes."

"If you didn't agree with his behavior then, why did you marry him?"

"I don't know . . . because I thought . . ."

"You thought he would change?"

"Yeah, I guess," Wendy confessed. "I don't know, I was tired of being alone. Kevin was interested in me and he was available."

"Um-hmm." Pastor Jones nodded his head as though she had confirmed what he already thought in the first place. Wendy felt like she had to keep explaining herself. "I mean—I thought he was a nice person. . . . I didn't think that our marriage would come to this."

"Did you want children?"

"Yes, but then I felt that Kevin needed to mature before we could start our family."

"So in other words, you're willing to abort this baby because Kevin is not the ideal father you would like to have for your child?"

That statement sounded harsh coming out of Pastor Jones's mouth, but it was true. Wendy had always been a perfectionist. The main reason she wanted to get rid of this baby was because things weren't perfect between her and Kevin. She didn't want to be a divorced mother. She didn't want the burden of having to explain to her child why they had split up. Wendy had almost gotten the nerve to make eye contact with Pastor Jones until he made that last statement.

"Listen, I'm going to tell you a little story," he began. "There was a woman who served God faithfully for sixty years. One night she prayed and asked Him if He would do one simple thing for her the next day. She wanted Him to come by her house. God answered her and said that He would. The next day, she received three visitors: a homeless man, a little boy, and an unmarried, pregnant woman. Each one of them needed a place to rest for a couple of hours while they were on their journey. She turned them all way. She said that on any other day she would have helped them out, but today she was expecting a very important visitor. God was coming by and she didn't want anyone else to intrude on the time she would be spending with Him. She waited patiently the entire day for God to show up. By nighttime, the woman was extremely upset because she felt that God did not keep His word to her. That night when she prayed, she was furious. She reminded Him that she had served Him *faithfully* for sixty years and all she asked was for Him to do this one thing and He didn't do it. All she wanted was for God to come by her house. God replied by telling her that He had come by that day. He showed up three times, and each time she turned Him away."

*What does it have to do with me?* Wendy thought.

As though he could read her mind, Pastor Jones answered her question. "The point of the story is that sometimes we expect God to come one way and He comes another. You wanted to start a family and He has given you the opportunity to do so. Don't let your circumstances dictate how you will respond to God's blessing. Children *are* a blessing. Despite everything that is going on around you, He still trusted you enough to raise His child. You were looking for Him to bless you with a child, but *only* when it was convenient for you. You wanted the perfect husband and the perfect situation. Now you're pregnant without all of that. You see, sometimes God comes through the back door and not the front. Either way, He still brings your blessing."

Wendy put her head in her hands and continued crying. She had been so focused on how Kevin had hurt her that she hadn't even considered this child to be a blessing, but more of a curse.

"God has a purpose for every life he creates. That child is not an accident. You don't know what God has in store for your baby. Take my life, for example. My mother had me out of wedlock by a married man. I'm not ashamed to tell you that my siblings and I don't have the same father."

*Really!* Wendy thought while her face was still buried in her hands.

Pastor Jones continued speaking. "I was conceived in sin, but look how God has used my life to teach others about Him. Just like God had plans for me, He has a plan for your child as well. If He didn't, He would have never planted that life inside of you. Think of what God says to Jeremiah in chapter one, verse five. He says 'Before I formed thee in the belly I knew thee; and before thou came forth out of the womb I sanctified thee, and I ordained thee a prophet unto the nations.' Sweetheart, God doesn't make mistakes. You never know what He has planned for that child. Don't interrupt His plans and invoke your own. Wendy?"

"Yes sir." She gave a tearful, muffled response.

"Look at me, please." She lifted her face just high enough that her eyes were exposed, and she looked directly at Pastor Jones. "Honey, you're never going to be perfect. We all fall short of God's glory. No matter what, know that God loves you and He is willing to forgive you, but you're also going to have to forgive yourself."

Wendy completely removed her hands as she meditated on Pastor Jones's words.

"Have you and Kevin discussed the future of your marriage?"

"No sir."

"What does he have to say about the affair?"

"I'm not sure. I really haven't talked to him about it."

"I suggest that you pray about your marriage and not make any hasty decisions. Pray for God's wisdom and direction. He's able to restore even the most strained marriages. You first have to be willing to yield your all to Him. I know that Kevin has hurt you, but there is absolutely no hurt that Jesus cannot heal. If you really don't want to give up on your marriage, then don't. It's not wise to make a permanent decision based on temporary hurt feelings. Turn Kevin and your entire relationship over to God. What you think is a mess God can turn into a blessing."

Pastor Jones grabbed Wendy's hands and held them. "Before we go, I would like to have a word of prayer with you," he said.

Wendy nodded in agreement and Pastor Jones began what she thought was a rather lengthy prayer, but it was exactly what she needed right now. "Thank you, Pastor," Wendy said when he had finished. She was deeply appreciative to him for taking the time out of his day to address her needs.

"You're welcome, sweetheart. Please remember to seek God for answers in every area of your life—including your marriage."

"Okay," Wendy agreed, although she already had her mind made up. *Maybe there is hope for my baby and me after all*, she thought. As for Kevin, he was still out of the picture as far as she was concerned. God apparently wanted her to have this child, at least. To make sure she would, He had sent a little divine intervention her way.

## Chapter Eight

# The Pot and the Kettle

Y OU HAVE TWO UNHEARD MESSAGES," the recording on
Wendy's voice mail announced.

"First message, sent today at 2:29 P.M.: 'Hey, Wendy, I
was calling to see how your visit was with Mama and how
you're feeling. Give me a call when you get a chance. My
last appointment is at three-thirty today. Once I finish, I
plan to be home all evening. I hope everything goes well
with Kevin tonight. And *please* try not to get upset, no
matter what he says. Your health and pregnancy are more
important. He's definitely not worth losing the baby over,
so try to stay calm. Okay? Call me if you need anything.
I'll give you a call tomorrow if I don't hear from you
tonight. All right then. I'll talk to you later. Love ya!' "

As Wendy listened to her sister's message, she made a
mental note to get Terrance's parents' telephone number
so she could call and thank Evelyn for the Christmas presents that were left at Marlene's house. Wendy also
couldn't help but be consumed with guilt since Kim still
thought that she was in jeopardy of having a miscarriage.

Only a few days into the New Year and instead of feeling better about herself, Wendy felt worse. *I gotta find some way to get out of this*, she thought, referring to the lie she'd told. She and Kim had gone out for New Year's Eve after all. The entire night, Kim had kept a close eye on Wendy. She'd even rented a wheelchair so Wendy wouldn't have to be on her feet. As if lying to Kim wasn't enough, she'd dug herself deeper into the pit of dishonesty with the rest of her family today.

Wendy had spent the entire afternoon visiting with her parents and grandmother. She also got to see Tori and Tyler, who were at her parents' house, for the first time since supposedly leaving for Philadelphia. Wendy would have enjoyed being with them much more if she hadn't pretended that she'd had such a wonderful time on her trip with Kevin. She even put her wedding ring back on so that she wouldn't arouse suspicion. She snatched it off her finger the minute she pulled out of her parents' driveway.

The visit with her family was strange. Marlene and Michael didn't seem like themselves. Although they were glad to see Wendy, they weren't overly ecstatic like she'd thought they would be. Rather, they seemed somewhat nonchalant while she jabbered. They didn't ask her a single question about her trip. Wendy got the mild impression that they didn't care, but she knew that wasn't true. Maybe Frances had gotten on their nerves, which was not unlikely. They had made a lot of adjustments since she'd moved in. Still, there was something different about them, and Wendy couldn't quite put her finger on what it was. Then again, the awkwardness she felt could have been guilt resulting from the lies she'd told about her visit to Philadelphia.

"Next message," the voice mail continued, "sent today at 3:43 P.M.: 'Wendy, this is Kevin. . . . I tried contacting you when I got back in town on Wednesday, but I never heard back from you. I hope we are still on for tonight. I should be there no later than six-thirty. Call me if anything changes. I look forward to seeing you soon. Oh— and Wendy, I love you.' "

*Yeah, whatever!* She was totally untouched by Kevin's last statement. *Love doesn't give chlamydia!*

It was about 4:30 P.M. and she had some time before Kevin would arrive. She'd decided to relax by taking a bath. She had a hard day mentally and needed to clear her mind in order to regain focus before he came.

It would be the first time she and Kevin would see each other since he left the house. At this time last week, she had been planning on having an abortion. Thanks to Pastor Jones, she no longer considered abortion an option.

As Wendy lay in her spa bathtub, she closed her eyes and listened to the soothing sound of ocean waves playing through the in-wall speakers. The porcelain tub was black and came with a heat-maintenance feature that sustained the temperature of the water so it didn't get cold. The entire bathroom was decorated in cranberry and black to match the furnishings in the master bedroom. Wendy laid her head back as the bubbles smothered her body up to her neck. She tried to organize the things she wanted to discuss with Kevin. *We definitely have to talk about the house.* Originally, Wendy had been willing to give up the house, but that was when she was planning to terminate her pregnancy. *Now I have a little bargaining power,* she thought. She had been packed and ready to walk out on Kevin the day of their big blowout. However, he refused to allow the mother of *his child* to be without a home. He'd done the chivalrous thing and left himself. The disparity was that Kevin *thought* the separation was temporary while Wendy *knew* it was permanent. *If only I can get him to pay enough child support and alimony,* she told herself. That would be the only way she could afford the house without him living there.

Wendy dozed off while in the tub and was awakened by Kevin's voice whispering in her ear: "Wake up, Sleeping Beauty." She was so startled that she splashed water all over his Armani suit. "Please get out until I'm finished!" she demanded.

"Sor-ry," Kevin said, backing away from the tub. He grabbed a towel to wipe his face and suit. "I'll be in the living room." He threw the towel on his side of the bathroom and walked out.

*Great!* The night was off to a bad start already. She hadn't meant to react that way; Kevin had frightened her. *He shouldn't have come in here like that anyway, considering our situation. He could have knocked on the bathroom door and that would have been fine.*

Wendy quickly dried herself off and slipped on a pair of navy sweats and a T-shirt. She put her hair up in a clip and then walked to the living room, where Kevin was waiting. "Look, I didn't mean to yell at you, but you should have knocked on the door," she confessed in a cold but apologetic way.

"I would have if the door had been closed."

"Oh." Wendy had been so frustrated by Kevin's entrance that she'd completely forgotten about leaving the door open. Still, she didn't like him coming in there.

There was an awkward silence while Kevin sat on the

couch and Wendy stood looking at him with her arms folded. "Well, what did you want to talk to me about?" she inquired.

"Sit down." Kevin patted the empty space next to him. "I have something to tell you."

There was something about sitting on the couch with him that made Wendy feel uncomfortable. "Can we go in the kitchen? I don't want to talk in here."

"Fine." He got up and walked toward the kitchen.

As she stepped onto her ceramic-tiled kitchen floor, Wendy realized that she should have moved the conversation into the dining room instead. There was a small round kitchen table located next to the bay window. The window overlooked the gazebo in the backyard, where the newlyweds had once spent many nice summer evenings enjoying each other's company. The kitchen table had been used numerous times for candlelight dinners. It was a romantic spot, not the tone Wendy wanted to set for the evening.

Kevin noticed Wendy's hesitation to sit down. "Just have a seat. Is all of this really necessary?"

"Is all of what necessary?" She slumped into the chair.

"Us. The way we're acting. What's up with all the formality?"

"Yes, Kevin. Considering our circumstances, I think it is necessary."

He sighed. "I know you're still upset with me, but will you give me a second to explain?"

"Explain what? How can you possibly explain what happened?"

"I know that I didn't have an answer for you the last

time we talked, but I do now. I promise if you'll just hear me out, it'll all make sense."

"Honestly, I don't feel like getting into any heavy discussions about your infidelity. I think we just need to figure out where our relationship goes from here. Most importantly, what do we do until the baby comes?"

"Dang it, Wendy!" Kevin said angrily, and banged his fist on the table. "Why do you have to be so stubborn? You won't return my phone calls. You won't give me a chance to explain. Will you just listen for one single minute? All I'm trying to do is get my wife back."

"Please don't go there," Wendy said, trying not to get upset. *He's got some nerve getting mad at me when he's the one who destroyed our marriage!*

"Why not? I listened to you say how much you hated me, how I destroyed your life, and how much of a dog I am. It's okay for me to hear all of that, right? But you can't listen to anything that I have to say."

Wendy began to let her irritation show. "There is absolutely *nothing* you can say that will erase what you have done. You say that you love me, but if you really loved me, you wouldn't have betrayed me."

"That's just it! I haven't done any—"

"Whatever!" Wendy interrupted him by raising her voice. "You haven't done anything. Yeah, right! Then how did I end up with an STD? I may have been a virgin when we first met, but I'm not stupid. I didn't catch it from a public toilet. Why do you keep lying? Just fess up."

"There you go again, believing only what Wendy wants to believe. I came over here hoping that you would listen to me and we would work things out. As always, Wendy has to have it her way." Kevin pulled an envelope from inside his suit jacket and threw it on the table. "Maybe if you won't listen to me, you'll at least read this."

"What is it?" She picked up the envelope.

"It's everything that I wanted to say tonight. Funny thing is, I wrote it because I had a feeling that you were gonna act like this. So instead of wasting any more of your *precious* time, I'm leaving. Read it and call me later." Kevin got up from the table.

"Wait. You can't leave yet."

"Why?"

"We still have some things to discuss."

"Like what?"

"*Like* what we are going to do until the baby comes."

"If you would just hear me out or at least read the letter, I think that would solve everything."

"I'm sorry, but nothing you say or I read will change my mind. Our relationship is over."

"Fine, Wendy. Then what else do you want from me?"

"Please sit back down."

Kevin reluctantly sat back in his chair. He had his elbows on the table, and he put his head in his palms. He felt hopeless. He wished he had listened more closely to how she felt about him staying out late. Maybe then she would be more likely to believe him.

"How should we handle things until the baby comes?" Wendy asked softly.

"You tell me. You're the one calling all the shots." He removed his hands from his face.

"Seriously, we need to make some kind of arrangements. We have the house—"

"Oh, so that's what this is about—the house." Kevin smirked.

"No . . . not really."

"Now who's lying?" he said sarcastically. "Miss Holy Ghost herself can't even tell the truth. Yet she calls me a liar. If that ain't the pot calling the kettle black."

Wendy glared at him.

"It's true, isn't it?" he continued. "Did you not make up a story about going to Philadelphia? I'm anxious to hear how you explained that one, 'cuz Kim was mad when I spoke with her."

"Forget you, Kevin."

"Oh, I'm sorry. That must be a sore topic."

"You can go ahead and leave. Forget I ever said anything," Wendy declared. *How dare he throw Philadelphia in my face.*

"Let me just make this easy so you don't continue lying. I know you want to stay in the house. That's fine with me. Like I told you before, I wouldn't send you and my baby out on the street."

"Kevin—" Wendy wanted to say something, but he held his hand up to stop her.

"Let me finish. You don't have to worry about paying the mortgage; I'll take care of that and the rest of the bills. I honestly believe that once you read that letter we will be able to work things out. If I'm wrong and you still think our marriage is over, then I'll accept your decision and we can work out the details at a later date. Promise me that even if you don't take me back you'll wait until after the baby gets here before making any permanent arrangements."

"Okay," Wendy agreed.

"Well, I'm leaving right now while things have quieted down." He got up from the chair, walked over to Wendy, and kissed her forehead. "No matter what you think, I love you."

Before Wendy could respond, Kevin walked out of the kitchen and she heard the front door close. She sat at the table and cried. *God, why does it have to be like this?* She recalled Pastor Jones's suggestion that she not give up on her marriage and opened the letter Kevin had given her.

*Dear Wendy,*

*If you're reading this letter then it must be the last chance I have of making things right with you. I'm sorry for everything that happened. I swear to you that I didn't cheat on you.*

That was all she read. Wendy crumpled up the letter and threw it across the kitchen. She intended to read it. However, the fact that he still denied being unfaithful infuriated her. *How can he continue lying like this?* Part of her wanted to know why he had cheated. She had searched her mind for the answers over and over. *Did I not show him enough attention?* She would never be able to find out his motive for going astray if he didn't admit to doing it.

Wendy got up from the table and picked the letter up off the floor. She tried to fold it back neatly. *I just can't deal with this right now*, she thought to herself and headed toward the study. She placed the letter inside her desk, where she kept other *junk* she didn't plan on getting to right away.

She was now exhausted. Wendy went into the bedroom to change into her nightclothes and go to bed. In a couple of days school would resume, and she was determined not to take all of this baggage into the classroom with her. She wasn't ready for anyone at work to know that she and Kevin had split up, especially Ms. Burchett. She knew someone would notice that her wedding ring was missing. *I'll just tell them that my fingers have swollen,* she decided before turning out the light. When school resumed, she would announce her pregnancy. Her co-workers were bound to find out eventually.

"Father God . . . uhh . . . Dear Heavenly Father . . . I—um—bless . . ." Wendy was on her knees trying to say her prayers, but she struggled with the words. She sighed. Her mind was so consumed with the events of the day that nothing would come out right. Frustrated, she abandoned the idea of praying, lay down, and cried herself to sleep.

## Chapter Nine
## The Grapevine

OKAY, WENDY, YOU CAN DO THIS. She paced back and forth on her kitchen floor with the phone in her hand. For the third time, she was going to attempt to dial her parents' house. She nervously began pushing the buttons. 5-5-5-7-0-9—before completing the call she hung up, just as she had done two times previously.

*Wait! Figure out exactly what you're going to say first,* Wendy silently told herself as her pulse increased with each passing minute. Earlier she had received a phone call from Kim indicating that her lie about being in Philadelphia over the holidays had hit the fan and was on its way down to smack her dead in the face.

She had been home from school for only about an hour before the phone had rung. Wendy recalled answering it.

"Wendy, you need to call Mama and tell her that you didn't go to Philly *now!*" Kim whispered.

"What? Why?" Kim's insistence caught Wendy totally off guard.

"Gramma knows. I swear I didn't tell her, and neither did Terrance."

"Okay, so what makes you think that she knows something?" Wendy asked nervously.

"I stopped by Mama's house to drop her cake pans off. Remember, she donated a few pound cakes for the bake sale at Tori's school to raise money for that little girl in her class that was severely burned in a house fire?"

"Yeah, and . . ."

"Her mother didn't have health insurance so some parents were trying to raise money to help out with her medical bills."

"I know, Kim. You told me all of that. What happened with Gramma? And speak up—I can barely hear you," Wendy said impatiently. Although she was saddened by what had happened to that child, she was more interested in what Kim had to tell her about Frances.

"Hold on and let me go in the bedroom. I'm trying not to talk loud so the kids can't hear me."

Kim's transition from one room to another took only a second, but it seemed like an eternity to Wendy.

"Can you hear me now?" Kim asked much louder this time.

"Yes. Finish what you were saying, please."

"I'm trying. Well, I got off of work early because my last appointment canceled on me so I called Terrance and told him that he didn't have to pick up the kids. I went by Mama's house to return her pans and she wasn't there. Gramma said that she'd left to run some errands."

"Um-hmm."

"Anyhow, do you know who Sister Binford is?"

"I'm trying to think—is she a lady around Gramma's age, like in her early seventies or so?"

"Probably. I don't know how old she is."

"If I am thinking of the right person, she wears this reddish brown wig that never seems to be on straight."

"Yeah, that's her."

"She's one of Gramma's gossiping buddies at church. Why do you ask about her?"

"How well do you know her?"

"Well enough. She's only been a member of our church for a little over a year. I think she moved here from Illinois with her daughter. I try to say hi and bye to her and leave it at that. She's too nosy and keeps up too much junk. Why?"

"She was at the house when I got there."

"Are you serious?"

"Yeah. I saw her sittin' there, but I didn't know who she was. I said hi and went in the kitchen to put back Mama's pans. On the way out, that lady asked me if I was at the First Night Columbus New Year's Eve celebration. She said that she thought she had seen you there that night, but figured she was mistaken when Gramma told her you were in Philadelphia. After seeing me, she said that she was absolutely certain that you were there and I was with you. She even mentioned that you were being pushed around in a wheelchair."

"Oh no! What did you say?"

"Nothing! I didn't know what to say. I just stood there."

"Oh my God!"

"I was glad that I left the kids in the car 'cuz I was

totally blindsided. I get on them all the time about telling the truth, so they didn't need to hear that."

"What did Gramma say after that?"

"That old witch sat there the whole time with a smug look on her face. She said that she wondered how you could be in two places at one time. I didn't want to argue with her so I just said 'Whatever' and walked out. But you know she's gonna say something to Mama. I suggest that you call her before Gramma gets ahold of her."

"Great!" Wendy murmured as her phone call with Kim came to a close. Before she hung up, Kim had reminded her that either way Marlene would be mad, but she wouldn't be as upset if she heard it from Wendy rather than Frances. Wendy agreed, and now she was trying to figure out what to say to her mother.

It had been nearly three weeks since she and Kevin had had their discussion. They'd talked a few times since then, but nothing in depth. He'd asked her what she thought about his letter. Truth was, she hadn't read it. What was the point? He started off the letter with the lie about not having cheated on her. How could she believe anything else he wrote? Not wanting to rehash the whole situation with Kevin, she told him that she'd read it and it didn't change how she felt about their marriage. Kevin was clearly disappointed. However, he apologized for everything and said that he wouldn't pressure her any longer.

Since the night Kevin was over, Wendy had intended to tell Michael and Marlene that they had split up, but each day it became harder to confess. Even when she did get around to telling them about the separation, she definitely hadn't planned on mentioning that she had never gone to Philadelphia.

*Just call. You might as well get it over with*, Wendy convinced herself. She sat down; the nails of her left hand drummed on the table while she held the phone in her right hand. She was so light-headed and nauseous that she felt like she could throw up at any moment. Except this time it wasn't morning sickness that caused her illness, but fear. Now that she was beginning her second trimester, she didn't get sick like she used to.

Once again, she started pushing the number buttons. 5-5-5-7-0-9—3. *There!* She did it. She nervously listened as the phone rang. She heard the first ring and held her breath. She heard the second ring and could swear that the baby turned a flip in her stomach. When the phone rang for the third time, Wendy let out a deep breath. *No answer yet.*

"Hello?" Marlene answered the phone as though she had picked it up just in the nick of time.

Wendy was quiet for a moment.

"Hello?" Marlene repeated more assertively.

"Hi, Mama," Wendy said quietly. It was a wonder that Marlene didn't mistake her for a prank caller since she was breathing so heavily into the phone. She had stopped tapping her nails on the table and they found their way between her teeth.

"Hello, Wendy. I was wondering how long it would be before I heard from you."

"Uh . . ."

"I suppose you're calling because of what Sister Binford said to your grandma, right?"

"You know already?"

"Yes, I know all about you and Kim going downtown for New Year's Eve," Marlene said plainly.

"But . . . I don't understand." Wendy was confused. She had expected to go deaf from all the yelling she anticipated her mother would do. Marlene's calmness was eerie.

"I just found out you were downtown, but hearing that you were actually in town wasn't news to me. I found that out a while ago."

"How?"

"From Pastor Jones."

Wendy's heart sank. "What did he say?"

"He looked for you after Watch Night Service. He asked your daddy and me if you had come. Of course we told him that you were in Philadelphia with Kevin for the holidays. Imagine our surprise when he mentioned running into you days earlier," Marlene said sarcastically.

There was an uncomfortable moment of silence as Wendy wasn't sure what to say. She prayed that Pastor Jones hadn't mentioned to them where he had seen her. He hadn't known that she was supposed to be out of town. Even if Wendy had told him, she would not have expected him to lie for her. "Mama?"

"What?" Marlene snapped.

"I'm sorry," Wendy said as tears welled up in her eyes.

"Oh really? Exactly what are you sorry for?" Marlene's anger was starting to show. "Are you sorry that your dad and I sat with Pastor Jones for an hour after service was over because we were so stunned by what he said that we were trying to make sense of the whole thing? Not only did you inconvenience us, but you inconvenienced his family, because they stayed there with us. Are you sorry for all of that? Or are you sorry that you got caught in a lie? Which one is it, Wendy? Do you know how embarrassing it was for us?"

Wendy sat silently as tears rolled down her cheeks. She could hear the hurt in her mother's voice.

"Do you know how it felt to discover that you had lied to us—your own family?" Marlene continued. "You betrayed us by allowing us to believe that you were out of the state." Her voice got louder. "Not only that, but you prance over here after New Year's and instead of coming clean, you sat here and put on this show about the *wonderful* trip you had. The whole time I watched you lie through your teeth and wanted to slap the truth out of you. I couldn't help but ask, what happened to the child I raised 'cuz surely this can't be her?"

"Why didn't you or Daddy say something?"

"Why should we even have to? You're a grown woman. You know better."

Now Wendy understood why her visit at her parents' house had seemed so uneasy. Apparently Marlene and Michael didn't tell Frances what they found out. From the way Kim sounded on the phone, Frances probably thought she was going to be the one to drop the bomb. Wendy wondered just how stupid she must have looked to her parents talking about her trip when, the entire time, they knew she hadn't gone anywhere.

"Don't think that I didn't have a mind to come over there and strangle you after talking with Pastor Jones that night. You oughtta be thankful that he encouraged us not to say anything. He said that you are going through some things right now and that Michael and I needed to sit back and let God deal with you. Why is it that Pastor Jones knows more about you than we do? We didn't have a clue that anything was going on with you."

"Mama, Kevin and I split up," Wendy blurted out, hoping that sympathy would be on her side.

"Oh good Lord, Wendy. What happened?"

"He cheated on me, Mama," Wendy cried.

"Well for heaven's sake, why would you pretend to go on a trip with him?"

"I didn't want to ruin the holiday for everyone else because of what I was going through."

"Well, I'm sorry to hear about you and Kevin, but don't you ever alienate your family because of him or any other man. Families lean on each other during hard times; they don't lie to each other."

"I know."

"And another thing, when I see Miss Kim, I got some stuff to say to her too for not telling us that you were in town. I didn't know that Kim knew anything until this evening."

"Mama, please don't be mad at Kim. She didn't know from the beginning. She sort of found out by accident. She took me out so I wouldn't be by myself. I made her promise not to tell, so *please* don't get upset with her. She was just looking out for me."

"Yeah, I guess. She still should have told us. So I take it she knows about you and Kevin too, then, huh?"

"Yes."

"Um-hmm, I figured she did. So what makes you think that Kevin cheated on you? Did you catch him with another woman?"

"Sort of . . ." Wendy hesitated.

"I'll be darned. I never would have thought he would do such a thing."

"Me neither."

"Well, whatever happens between y'all, your daddy and I will support you."

"Thank you. I know."

"If you knew, then why have you been lying to us for so long?"

Can we get off of this topic now? Wendy wanted to ask but didn't dare. She knew that Marlene's feelings were hurt. Marlene often stated how proud she was of the communication she had with her daughters. Wendy was certain that her mother felt betrayed. "Mama, I *am* sorry."

"What hurts most is that you didn't trust your daddy and me. We had to find out through the *grapevine*."

"Is Daddy there now?"

"No, he went to pick up your grandmother's prescriptions from the pharmacy. Do you want him to call you when he comes back? I'm sure he would like to speak with you now that everything is out in the open."

"Yes, please. I think I need to talk to him."

"Well, I'll tell him. We're both disappointed in you, honey. Michael especially because he was so worried about you when you were gone. Rather, when you were *supposed* to be gone. He really wanted you here for Christmas."

Wendy's conversation with her mother didn't last much longer. Marlene got off the phone so she could prepare dinner. It wasn't too long after she'd hung up with Marlene that Michael called. Like her mother, he was saddened by the way Wendy had handled the situation, but he didn't go off. Marlene had informed him about the separation before he called. He said that he wasn't going to pry, but he did have one question for Wendy: Did Kevin lay his hands on her? Luckily for Kevin's sake, Wendy was able to say no. Lord have mercy on any man who would dare hit one of his daughters. It would be best for that fellow if he left Columbus and never came back. If Michael Tibbs got hold of him, he might forget that he'd been saved, sanctified, and filled with the Holy Ghost.

## Chapter Ten

# The Young and Restless

M OMMY," Tori whispered in Kim's ear, trying to wake her while tapping her on the shoulder. "Mommy."

Kim managed to pry her eyes open and saw the silhouette of Tori's nightgown as the streetlight shone through the blinds. "What?" she moaned, still half asleep.

"I'm scared," the six-year-old confessed. She had been awakened by the wind beating against her bedroom window.

Without mumbling a word, Kim scooted closer toward Terrance to make room for her daughter. Every now and then one of the children would come to sleep with them in the middle of the night because they couldn't sleep well for one reason or another. Kim used to get up out of bed, go to their rooms, and comfort them back to sleep. That process would last up to an hour, if not longer, and Kim would be exhausted by the time daylight hit. It was much simpler to placate their fears by allowing them to sleep with her, especially when she had been awakened from a deep sleep.

Tori hopped into the bed and lay on her stomach. A minute later, she changed positions onto her side. Unable to get comfortable, she then tumbled onto her back.

"Be still," Kim demanded. Each time Tori moved, she accidentally jolted her mother with a foot, knee, or elbow, making Kim's attempt to doze off impossible.

Tori looked up at the ceiling. Although her fears were suppressed by being in the same room as her parents, she found it difficult to go back to sleep. "Mommy?" Her tiny voice rose over the stillness in the night.

"What?" Kim croaked as if she was in pain.

"Can I turn the TV on?"

Kim heard Tori's question but couldn't formulate her words to give an answer right away. Tori's soft voice echoed loudly through her mother's head. Kim desperately wanted the peacefulness she had felt prior to Tori walking into the room.

"Mommy, can I turn the TV on?" Tori repeated with a louder whisper this time.

"No. Go to sleep."

"But I can't."

"Uhhhh," Kim moaned. "I don't care if you go back to sleep or not, just be quiet and be still." *Why do they always come on my side of the bed?* she wondered and once again covered her pupils with her eyelids.

It was only a few minutes before Kim was disturbed yet again by the sound of Tori's voice whispering in her ear. "Mommy."

Kim felt like putting a muzzle on Tori. She would pay money for that child to go back to sleep. *"What?"* Kim answered in a loud voice, hoping Terrance would wake up and deal with Miss Young and Restless. Contrary to her wishes, Terrance kept snoring and didn't budge.

"Are you going to church with me and Tyler today?" Tori's head scarf had come off sometime during the night and she lay there twirling her ponytails with her fingers.

"No. You're going with your grandmother. You know that." Kim threw the covers over her head, wishing that she could block out the sound of Tori's voice. *Just go to sleep!* she whined inwardly.

"When I get older, are you going to take my kids to church?"

"You can take them yourself. Honey, Mommy really doesn't feel like talking right now." Kim tried to stay calm. "I don't think you realize what time it is, but it's *very* early."

Tori looked at her mother's digital clock. "It's fifty-three-zero," she said proudly.

"Five-thirty," Kim corrected her. "It's way too early for this. If you are not going back to sleep, then you need to go in your own room."

"But why won't you take my kids to church?" Tori asked as if she hadn't heard the latter part of her mother's statement.

"I just told you why—now leave me *alone!*"

"Last week we learned a new scripture."

"Great. Go back to your room."

"It's Proverbs 22:6. Do you know what it says?"

"I really don't care right now."

"It says to train up children in the way they should go and when they are older, they will not stray from it."

"Good. Now go to sleep." Kim was ready to carry Tori into her room but was too tired to do so.

"Our church teacher said that it means a lot of stuff. Like parents should take their children to church themselves if they want them to go when they get older. I told her that you and Daddy don't come to church with us and she said that I should ask you to come. Will you come, Mommy?"

Kim was so exhausted she would have agreed to cut off her right leg if Tori asked her to. "Fine, I'll go with you sometime, but just leave me alone and *go to sleep*."

"Will you go today?"

"*Yes!* Did you learn the scripture about obeying your parents?"

"Yes ma'am. Our church teacher said that God wants all the little children to listen to their mommies and daddies."

"Well, I'm telling you to go to sleep, so do it."

"Okay." Tori shut her eyes tightly and then opened them back up suddenly. "Mommy."

By this time, all of the interacting with Tori had completely woken Kim up. She glanced enviously at Terrance, who lay beside her undisturbed by the conversations and commotion that had taken place. "What?" Kim wanted to cry.

"I have to use it."

"What are you telling me for? Just go!"

Tori jumped out of bed and went into her parents' bathroom. She left the door open so the light shone in Kim's face, and every noise the toilet made while flushing magnified Kim's inability to go back to sleep.

After Tori came out of the bathroom she settled down, and it wasn't long before she was knocked out. Now it was Kim who tossed and turned, longing for time to freeze until she regained every second of sleep that was lost. By the time it was a quarter to seven, Kim figured she might as well get up since her alarm clock was scheduled to go off at seven. Hitting snooze at this point would do nothing but irritate her.

"Train up a child in the way he should go: and when he is old, he will not depart from it." Kim had never thought more about Proverbs 22:6 than she had the last hour. A couple of months ago she had tried explaining to the children what it meant now that she and Terrance were engaged. It was difficult because she found herself telling them not to do things the way she did.

She remembered Tyler asking why "Aunt Wendy" didn't have kids before she got married. "People are really supposed to wait until they get married to have children," Kim had explained.

"Why did you have us, then?" he further questioned. The only explanation Kim could give was that they were very special gifts to her. Although she wasn't married, God blessed her with two of the most precious children in the world. At the time, Kim had been satisfied with the answer. Now she was wondering about the kind of example she had set for her children.

Kim got out of bed and took a shower. The warm water felt good as it ran down her body. "Train up a child in the way he should go: and when he is old, he will not depart from it." Kim prided herself on getting her own apartment, not living off of the welfare system, and raising her children herself instead of leaving them for her parents to raise, as many young girls did. *But is all of that enough?*

*Starting today, I will be a better role model,* she pledged. Her pledge had nothing to do with church. In fact, she was hoping that Tori would forget coercing her into agreeing to go that morning. *That scripture can mean a lot of things. I don't have to go to church in order to train them up right. I'll stop cursing around them, I'll spend more time with them, and I'll be more careful about the type of music I listen to in their presence.*

*All of this will be good. I may go to church every now and then, but I'm not regular church-attendance material.* With the exception of her parents, her sister, and a few other people, she was completely turned off by the behavior she saw "Christians" exhibiting. Most of the time how they acted on Sunday was in direct contrast with how they were Monday through Saturday. *I'm better off the way I am,* Kim thought, referring to the fact that she was herself every day of the week.

After Kim got out of the shower, she was surprised that her little Sleeping Beauty was no longer lying on her side of the bed. She slipped on her bathrobe and walked down the hall to Tori's room. To her amazement, she found Tori getting dressed for church already. Kim always laid her clothes out the night before. Tori had even taken the initiative and woken Tyler. He was in the bathroom washing up.

"Good morning," Kim said, and kissed her daughter on the forehead. "You know you kept me up this morning."

"I'm sorry. I had a bad dream and couldn't sleep."

"Do you remember what your dream was about?"

"No, not really. I just remember that it scared me."

"You do know that there's nothing to be scared of, right?"

"Yes ma'am."

"I'm going to finish getting dressed and then go and fix

y'all something to eat." Kim turned to walk out of Tori's room.

"Mommy."

"Yes?"

"Are you still going to church today?"

*Dang!* "Sure, I said I would, didn't I?" If Tori hadn't remembered her mother's promise, Kim wouldn't have brought it up. Maybe she would be more eager to go on a Sunday other than this one. Today was the first Sunday in February. As far as Kim could remember, first Sundays were always the longest church services.

"Will Daddy come too?"

"I don't know, honey. He's still sleeping, but I'll ask him," Kim replied and proceeded to walk back down the hall.

*What am I going to wear?* Kim thought. She didn't have a huge selection of church clothes. Increasing her church attire had never been a priority on her shopping list. There were a few things she could wear, but nothing fancy like most people often wore on Sundays. She was about to go back to Tori's room and say that she didn't have anything to wear for church but changed her mind. *But Jesus said to come as you are . . .* she could hear her daughter respond. Kim wasn't sure if Tori knew that scripture or not, but she didn't want to take any chances.

Kim went through the process of taking her clothes out of the closet, laying them on the bed, holding each outfit up to her while looking in the mirror, only to put it back in the closet again. She had been doing this for about twenty minutes before Terrance finally woke up from noisy hangers squealing across the rack.

Kim always found a way to wake him up earlier than he would like on the weekends. If she wasn't hitting snooze on her alarm a half dozen times, she was yelling at the kids or doing something else distracting. It was as if she didn't realize that he would enjoy sleeping in occasionally. He got up at 3:00 A.M. Monday through Friday to get to the television station where he worked by 4:30 A.M. In college, Terrance had majored in communications with a minor in electronics. His senior year he landed an internship at the CBS affiliate station WBNS in Columbus. He started working on the production team. As luck would have it, a permanent position came open and he was asked if he wanted the job. Although they couldn't officially hire him until after graduation, they kept him on as an intern even when his internship was up. Now Terrance was in charge of running the TelePrompTer for the morning news crew and then he switched to lighting and sound production. He didn't make nearly as much money as Kevin did. However, he got a pretty decent salary that would steadily increase as the years went by and he gained additional experience.

"Do you have to be so loud?" an irritated Terrance asked Kim. He enjoyed his job, but getting up early morning after morning took its toll sometimes. The weekends were the only days he had to rest.

"Sorry. I'm trying to find something to wear to church."

"You're what?" Terrance heard her, but it was one of those things she needed to repeat in order for him to believe what she said.

"I'm going to church with the kids."

"What are they having today?" Terrance sat up in the

bed, afraid that he'd missed the announcement of a program. Kim never went to church unless it was a special occasion.

"Nothing. Tori asked me to go and I said yeah," Kim said, while taking more items out of the closet. "She wants you to go, also."

"Really?" Terrance laid his head back down on the pillow. "Aw, man."

"What?"

"I really don't feel like going."

"Then don't."

Terrance didn't plan on doing anything today but relaxing. However, he was amazed by Kim's willingness to go and he decided to follow her example so Tori wouldn't be disappointed.

Kim finally settled on wearing a long blue-jean skirt with a black turtleneck and her black leather boots. She figured that she would be somewhat underdressed but didn't care. If she was going to be there all afternoon, she was going to be comfortable.

She had planned to cook breakfast that morning, but with the curve ball that had been thrown and the amount of time she took getting dressed, there was no time left even to boil water. She and Terrance decided that they would pick up something on the way to church and everyone could eat in the car.

"I can't wait until we get to church," Tori stated while her father was driving. "Gramma is going to be glad to see us."

"Oh, I gotta call your grandmother so she doesn't come to pick y'all up. I'm glad you said something about her."

Kim grabbed the cell phone out of her purse, praying that Marlene hadn't left the house yet.

"Mama," Kim said with relief when Marlene answered the phone.

"Yes?"

"You don't have to pick up Tori and Tyler. We're taking them to church today."

"Okay. Are you coming over afterwards to pick them up or do you want me to drop them off?"

"No, Mama. We're coming to church, meaning that we are actually staying for the service, so they can just come back home with us."

"You're staying at the church for the entire service?" Marlene asked uncertainly.

"Yes."

"Praise the Lord!" she shouted. "What made you decide to join us today?"

"Tori wanted us to come."

"Both you and Terrance are coming, right?"

"Yes, Mother."

"Glory to God. Michael, guess what? Kim and Terrance are coming to church today."

"Good," Kim overheard her father say.

"Ain't that wonderful?"

"Yeah," Michael said unemotionally. His personality was more laid-back than his wife's.

"Oh, girl, you don't know how glad I am to hear that. God sho' is good. I've been praying for y'all for a while. The effectual fervent prayer of the righteous availeth much!" Marlene paraphrased the second part of James 5:16.

Kim feared that her mother was getting melodramatic. "Relax, Mama. We're just coming to church. Nobody said we were going to join. Don't go gettin' all excited about nothin'."

"Well, it's a start and I'm praising God anyhow. So I'll see you there."

"Okay." Kim ended the call. She silently rode in the car, repeating the scripture that Tori had recited to her: "Train up a child in the way he should go: and when he is old, he will not depart from it."

# Chapter Eleven
## Soul Sistas

Y OU FEELIN' ALL RIGHT, KIM?" Gwendolyn, the owner of the hair salon where Kim worked, questioned.

"Yeah. Why you ask that?"

"Girl, you seem like you've been out of it all day," Gwendolyn said as she swept hair off the floor from around her workstation. Many of the other hairstylists were either with clients, waiting for clients, or also cleaning up their stations. Kim was sanitizing her combs and making sure that her area was stocked with the supplies she would need the next day.

"I'm just tired, that's all."

"You sure that's it?"

"Yeah, Gwen. I'm fine," Kim protested.

"Okay, if you say so. You know I'm here if you need me."

"Yeah, I know. Thanks." Kim didn't want to say anything to Gwen, but she was contemplating whether or not to go to church with Wendy tonight. For the last two months, Kim had consistently gotten up on Sundays and gone to church with her children. Terrance had gone a couple of times, but he wasn't as committed as she had been.

Each week when Pastor Jones invited people to join the church, Marlene always looked at her and smiled, but Kim never stepped forward. She didn't intend to continue going so diligently. Right now she was anxious to hear the rest of the series that Pastor Jones was preaching entitled "Living the Christian Life." She had no intentions of claiming Christianity. It was just fascinating for her to see how many "Christians" lived in direct contrast to what he preached about. Now that spring had rolled around, it was not so much of a sacrifice for her to get up and out of the house in the mornings as it had been in the winter. However, when the series ended, Kim believed that her consistent church attendance would also.

If she went with Wendy tonight, it would be the first non-Sunday event she had attended since she was a teenager. Wendy had invited Kim to the Soul Sistas meeting, which met on the first Friday of each month. It was a women's ministry that aimed to address the spiritual, mental, emotional, and even physical needs of women. From what Wendy said, it was an awesome ministry. They often invited guest speakers and planned special trips for the women. Kim didn't know if she was ready to participate in something like that, especially since she was not interested in becoming a member of the church.

"Do you need me to do anything before I leave?" Kim asked Gwendolyn after she finished getting her station in order.

"Naw, you go ahead and get out of here. You look like you need the rest," Gwen responded as she looked in the mirror and fluffed her hair with her hands. She had owned and operated her shop for the last seven years and had been quite successful. The name of the salon, GWEN'S, pointed to the confidence she had in herself as a hair-stylist and as a person. Gwendolyn was a very thick woman, but one of the most secure people that Kim had ever known.

Gwen refused to allow her excess weight to keep her from feeling or looking good. She had all the curves that guys liked. Hers were just a little fuller. She was blessed with naturally arched eyebrows and dark brown skin that never seemed to break out. Gwen was beautiful and she knew it. Anyone who didn't know her personally might think that she was conceited because she walked with so much assurance. However, Gwen was not conceited; she liked to use the term *convinced*.

She was convinced in her ability to succeed. At sixteen Gwen had had her first child, who was now about to turn fourteen. She lived with her elderly grandmother, who raised her after her parents were killed in a car accident. For a while Gwen worked at department stores and fast-food restaurants after high school because she couldn't afford to go to college. However, when her grandmother died she left Gwen a lump sum of money that Gwen swore she would put to good use. By the time she was twenty-three, she had gotten her cosmetology license and opened up her own shop, which had grown to be one of the most successful hair salons in all of Columbus.

Gwen was also convinced that even though she had a little extra packaging, she could get the finest brothers if she wanted. A few of her ex-boyfriends turned the heads of the skinnier girls in the shop. Gwen knew her limitations, and she dressed sexy, not sleazy. Guys were attracted to her outgoing personality, fun nature, and warm smile. Contrary to what anyone may have thought, she had always been the dumper and not the dumpee. When Gwendolyn Marie Simmons stepped onto the scene, even a man with a woman who measured 36-24-36 at his side would take a second look. Gwen demanded respect and attention, and she definitely got both.

"Thank you for calling Gwen's. How can I help you?" Kim overheard Gwen answer the phone as she walked toward the backroom to get her purse and jacket.

Once there, she carelessly grabbed her purse off the hook and the strap snapped, flinging all of her stuff on the floor. "Shoot!" she said. Normally, she would have used another word, but ever since that first Sunday when she went to church with the children, she'd been trying to improve her vocabulary. She had slipped and used profanity on occasion, but now, unlike before, the curse words sounded awkward coming out of her mouth.

"Gwen said to tell you that your sister is on the phone," one of Kim's co-workers announced when she came into the backroom to throw dirty towels in the washer.

"Okay, thanks." There was a phone located back there that Kim could easily have answered, but she wanted to gather all of the belongings first. Besides, she knew Gwen and Wendy wouldn't mind talking to each other for a few minutes. Wendy and Gwen had gone to grade school, junior high, and high school together. They had been best friends for years. It was Gwen who had encouraged Kim to get a cosmetology degree and work at the shop.

Tori had been born a few weeks after Kim graduated

from high school. Kim had had no idea what she would do with her life. All of her plans had gone down the drain when her former boyfriend virtually abandoned her. She and her ex-boyfriend, Darius, had been going together since their sophomore year. At the beginning of their senior year of high school, his dad's job transferred to Atlanta and his family moved just when Kim found out she was pregnant. At that time, the plan was for Kim to move down there after the baby was born. She and Darius intended to marry—or so she had thought.

Kim began looking into colleges in Atlanta where she could major in accounting. Darius's mother had volunteered to keep the baby while Kim and Darius earned their degrees. His mother planned to work only part time because her husband's new salary increased so that she didn't need a full-time job. However, once Darius moved, the time between his phone calls became longer and longer. One day Kim received a letter from him stating that he wanted to postpone their wedding plans. He felt a little overwhelmed about becoming a father and husband before he had a chance to really experience life. Kim was devastated and never wrote back. To this day, Darius still did not know if the baby had been a boy or a girl.

With a baby, no job, and a grandmother who swore that she was about to make a mess of her life and soak up the welfare system, Kim jumped at the opportunity when Gwen offered her a job at the shop. But she had to get her license. To help pay for school, Gwen allowed her to work as an apprentice and even donated supplies to her so that Kim didn't have many out-of-pocket expenses. Kim never thought she would enjoy doing hair, but it wasn't bad. Sometimes she wished that she were able to get her accounting degree, but she would forever be grateful to Gwen for looking out for her. Gwen took a great risk considering that her shop was only a little over a year old at the time and she still needed to build her clientele.

Unlike Gwen, Kim had a "replacement" father for her child. Throughout the whole ordeal with Darius, Terrance had been right by her side. He and Kim had been friends since they were twelve, and he was asked to be Tori's godfather way before Darius broke up with Kim. Even though he went to school full time, Terrance would baby-sit between classes and worked part time on the weekends to help Kim financially. It was obvious that he had a huge crush on her. Everyone knew they would eventually hook up despite their protests of being "just friends."

Kim finally picked up all of her scattered belongings and answered the phone. "Hello?" Her frustration about her purse breaking showed in the tone of her voice.

"Ugh, what's wrong with you?" Wendy asked.

"Girl, she's been acting funny all day. She wouldn't tell me what's wrong—maybe she'll tell you," Gwen stated.

The last thing Kim wanted to hear right now was her older sister and her surrogate big sister analyzing her. "I'm *fine*. All of my stuff just dropped out of my purse."

"Oh, that's what took you so long. Well I'm gonna hang up and let y'all talk. My client just walked through the door. I'll talk to you later, Wendy."

"All right." Gwen hung up the phone. "Kim?"

"Yeah, I'm still here."

"Are you going with me tonight?"

"I was, but now I gotta go to the store and get a new purse. My strap just broke."

"Don't even try that. I've seen your closet. You have plenty of purses at home."

"Yeah, I know, but those are the ones that I like to carry with special outfits." Kim was dressed in a pair of slacks with a cotton short-sleeved shirt. "This is my everyday purse and I wasn't planning on dressing up tonight 'cuz you told me that I didn't have to." Her outfit was still clean because she had worn a cape while doing hair.

"If you need a purse *that* bad, you can use the black one I carried this past winter 'cuz I just bought a new Gucci purse the other day."

"But I still want to buy my own purse."

"You can, but you don't have to do it tonight. You're just trying to get out of going to church."

"Fine, I'll come. What time do you want me to meet you there?"

"Let's see, it's almost five now. It starts at seven, so meet me in the lobby about ten 'til."

"Okay."

Kim hung up with her sister, said good-bye to everyone in the shop, and headed out the door. She planned to stop at home for a few minutes before going to the church.

## Chapter Twelve

## *Sister Sunday*

I WAS LOOKING FOR YOU AT CHURCH TODAY," Wendy said to her sister over the telephone.

Kim sat flipping through the channels on the twenty-seven-inch television screen in her living room. She had known this conversation would take place eventually. As much as she tried to prepare herself, she was unable to rise above the feelings of hurt and disappointment she now had toward her sister. "Really."

"I was surprised when Mama told me that you weren't there," Wendy said without noticing Kim's dry response. "What happened? When we left Soul Sistas Friday night, you said you were coming. Remember, we talked about going out to eat after service today, just the two of us?"

"Yeah. Well, I changed my mind," Kim said nonchalantly.

"Well, thanks for calling and telling me," Wendy said sarcastically. She was disappointed that Kim hadn't followed through with their plans. She had been looking forward to spending that time with her. "Maybe we can go next week."

"We'll see."

"Thanks for returning my purse. I told you Friday that there was no need for you to rush out and buy a new one. You really could have kept this one if you wanted to. Why'd you give it to Mama to give to me? It's not like I needed it."

"Um-hmm." Kim had had every intention of going to church that morning and out to eat with Wendy until yesterday evening. After work, she'd gone shopping for a new purse and also bought clothes that she anticipated wearing specifically to church. Terrance even made plans to take the kids over to his parents' house and have dinner with them. He asked her to come with them once Kim told him that she was canceling her plans today, but she declined. She wasn't in a socializing mood and wanted to stay home by herself. She was uncertain as to what to think about Wendy in light of what she had discovered last night as she took her belongings out of Wendy's purse and transferred them into the new one she had bought.

"Are you all right?" Wendy asked.

"Yeah, I'm fine."

"You act like something is wrong. I don't mean to offend you, but you sound sort of stank."

"Maybe I'm just tired of people continually betraying my trust."

"*Maybe* you need to address that issue with *those* people and not take it out on your sister," Wendy responded. "Do you want to talk about whatever is bothering you?"

"Never mind how I'm feeling. What about you? How are you feeling, Sister Sunday?"

"Good," Wendy said cautiously. She was unsure why Kim called her the same name they had created for their grandmother. Kim was always joking about how fake Frances acted around other church members. Although she believed that she had everyone fooled, very few people thought of Frances as anything other than a busybody and tolerated her only for Marlene's sake. Marlene had been a faithful member of Mount Calvary Missionary Church ever since she was saved as a young adult. However, Frances hadn't started going to that particular church until she moved in with Marlene and Michael. Prior to living with them, she had attended another church, where she made more enemies than she did friends. Kim suggested the nickname Sister Sunday, implying that the only time Frances appeared to be saved was on Sunday morning.

"You know, you never did tell me what the doctor said about the baby," Kim said.

"Yes I did. I told you that my gynecologist said that she could tell me the sex of the baby now since I'm in my fifth month, but I don't want to know. I want to be surprised."

"That's not what I'm talking about. So now she thinks that you will carry the baby to term, right? Before she was afraid that you would miscarry."

"Uhh . . . yeah—I'm straight." Wendy had been meaning to make up a story to tell Kim, but she forgot. She and Kim had been spending so much time together that correcting the lie she told had slipped her mind. "Girl, I'm way past that. That was in the beginning when I was feeling sick and all. The baby is fine now."

"Liar!" Kim said and slammed the phone down. She was even madder now than she was before Wendy called.

The remote control left her hand and soared across the room. She had just given Wendy a chance to tell the truth. Instead, Wendy chose to continue lying to her, and it infuriated Kim.

The phone rang again. Kim knew it was Wendy calling back. "What!" she answered hatefully.

"What in the world has gotten into you? You just hung up on me for no reason at all!" Wendy was confused. The last time she was with Kim they had had fun together. She couldn't recall saying or doing anything that night to upset her.

"I'm starting to wonder if it was really Kevin who had the affair," Kim lashed out. She really didn't think for one minute that Wendy had been unfaithful; she was just being cruel.

"What's that supposed to mean? How could you even say something like that?"

Kim detected the hurt in Wendy's voice, but she didn't care. "Silly me to think that although you were lying to Mama and Daddy, you would at least tell me the truth. After all, I thought that we were more than sisters, I *thought* you were my best friend."

"Kim, what are you talking about? I didn't cheat on Kevin! He cheated on me!"

"You know what? I don't even care anymore. I have too many problems of my own to concern myself with yours. I thought you didn't believe in abortions anyhow."

"I don't. Where did that come from?"

"Then tell me why there was a card from Pregnancy Alternative in your purse. You told me that you were at risk for losing the baby when the entire time you were planning to have an abortion."

When Kim mentioned Pregnancy Alternative, Wendy felt like all of her dirty laundry had been exposed. She had completely forgotten about placing the business cards from the abortion clinic in the inside pocket of her purse. She had never used that pocket before or after that day. Once Pastor Jones had gone back with her to cancel her appointment, she didn't think twice about the clinic. "Kim . . . wait . . . you don't understand."

"And I don't want to. It's not the fact that you considered having an abortion that bothers me. It's the fact that you have continuously lied to me. You have taken advantage of my love and trust. Do you know how many nights I couldn't sleep because I was concerned about you?"

"Kim—"

"Had you told me that you'd lost the baby, I would have blamed Kevin for stressing you out. You've betrayed me, Wendy. The fact that you didn't tell me the truth proves to me that you don't trust me."

"No, that's not true—"

"Did you think I would judge you or something? I don't see why you would have. I have lied for you, I have looked out for you, and I have even broken plans with my fiancé to be with you. I have never lied to you about anything. You have taken advantage of my feelings for the very last time."

"Kim, please listen—"

"Forget it. If you really loved me, you wouldn't have betrayed me. I don't care what happens to your baby or marriage from here on out." Kim hung up once again. She was too angry to admit that she really did care about the baby and Wendy. She had been eager to become an auntie and spoil the child rotten. Everything she said to Wendy stemmed from the hurt she felt from being misled.

—◠

Wendy sat stunned on her living room couch. She was embarrassed and angry with herself. Most of all, she was hurt by the things Kim had said to her. She thought about calling her back, but feared the rejection that was inevitable. She knew that Kim had every right to be upset with her. *Why didn't you just tell her the truth about everything when she came over after Christmas?* Wendy recalled trying to avoid discussing the details about her relationship with Kevin the day Kim confronted her about not being in Philadelphia.

As tears stormed down her face, she thought about Kim's words. "If you really loved me, you wouldn't have betrayed me." Ironically, that was the same thing she had said to Kevin.

# Chapter Thirteen

## Nuttin' Like an Otis

IT WAS ABOUT TWELVE-THIRTY IN THE AFTERNOON. Kim and Marlene were sitting in Marlene's living room watching television, talking, and looking through bridal catalogs. Kim didn't have to work and had decided to spend the day with her mother. They didn't have plans to do anything special. In fact, Kim would have loved a nice quiet afternoon to herself since Terrance was working, Tyler was in preschool, and Tori was in elementary school. But, from the sound of her mother's voice yesterday evening, Kim suspected that she was in desperate need of company. Marlene had been at home with Frances the entire week by herself because Michael had gone to visit his brother in Florida who had been diagnosed with prostate cancer. His brother's prognosis was good since the doctors detected the cancer in the early stages, but Michael just wanted to spend some quality time with him because the two didn't get to see each other much. Marlene would have gone with him, except someone needed to be home with Frances.

Dealing with Frances was enough to drive anyone crazy. Marlene enjoyed the level of sanity Kim brought to the place. Sometimes Marlene wondered if it had been a good idea to retire from nursing after twenty-two years and move Frances in to care for her full time. Frances suffered from high blood pressure and diabetes. She used to live at the senior center. There, Michael and Marlene had paid for a nurse to check on her each day and make sure she took her medicine. They'd made the decision to move Frances in with them so Marlene could care for her when Frances complained about being mistreated.

Although Michael didn't quite believe Frances, he was sympathetic to his wife's concern. The decision affected him also because he had always been a self-employed repairman and spent most of his time at home when he wasn't out on jobs. Now that Frances was living with them, Michael found other ways to keep busy. He started volunteering at the local Boys and Girls Club. In addition to the duties that he and Marlene had serving on the deaconate board at the church, he was the repairman there and at some other properties the church owned. The church elected to pay him a salary instead of paying him per repair. As a result, the income that was lost when Marlene quit working was replaced.

Frances would always be herself. That is, opinionated, stubborn, illogical, and judgmental. However, she got a little more outrageous when Michael wasn't around. If Marlene said something to her, she would respond by saying "I'm the mother. Remember, I bore you—it wasn't the other way around." However, she couldn't say that to Michael. Marlene tolerated Frances more than Michael did. When Frances had gotten on his last nerve she knew because he didn't keep quiet about it—unlike Marlene, who usually ignored her or went into another room.

"I think this dress is pretty," Marlene said while flipping through a bridal catalog that Kim had brought over.

Kim looked at the picture of a wedding dress with a satin top and a chiffon skirt that flared out at the end. It was nice for someone who liked the Cinderella-ball-gown look, but it wasn't what she had in mind for herself. "It's really not my style," she said with a twisted look on her face.

Marlene shook her head. "And what style is that?" She should have known better than to think she could find a wedding dress that her daughter would like. She and Kim had different ideas when it came to fashion. Marlene had never been able to buy her any type of clothing without having to return it or hang it in the closet until she donated the item to charity.

Kim shrugged her shoulders. "Anything that doesn't look like that," she kidded.

Marlene playfully folded up the magazine and hit Kim on the head. "I can tell already that you're going to be difficult."

"No I'm not. I just want something nice and elegant, but not big at the bottom."

"Since you're thinking about dresses, it must mean that you and Terrance have finally set a wedding date," Marlene nudged gently. She hadn't heard Kim say much of anything about planning the wedding.

"No, not officially. We've talked about sometime next summer."

"Why next summer? Why didn't y'all want to do it this summer?"

"I don't know. Not enough time to plan, I guess. Plus, I *was* gonna ask Wendy to be my matron of honor. I figured it would be better for her to wait until after the baby is born. Now it's too late to plan anything for this summer."

"So does that mean you're not going to ask Wendy to be in your wedding now?"

"No, I may ask Gwen."

Marlene closed her eyes then laid her head back on the couch. Kim had a feeling she knew what her mother was about to say. "I really think that you should still consider having Wendy as your matron of honor. Although Gwen may be *like* a sister to you, Wendy *is* your sister. I love Gwen like a daughter, but at special moments in your life such as your wedding, you should never put friends before family. I think it would really hurt Wendy's feelings if you asked Gwen to stand up for you and not her."

"Mama, you promised not to get in the middle."

Marlene opened her eyes. "I'm not." At least she was *trying* not to. When Wendy called her and told her what had happened with Kim, Marlene said that she would let the girls work it out by themselves. She had never had to go through this with them before. Her daughters had always gotten along great. At first, Marlene thought the girls got along well because Wendy was five years older than Kim. However, several of her co-workers had children who weren't close in age and, according to them, their children still fought. Wendy and Kim never did any of that, so this sibling rivalry was all new to her. It had been over two weeks since their argument. Marlene felt it was definitely time for them to make amends. The rift between them had gone on long enough. "You never did call her last week and wish her a happy birthday, did you?"

"No, I forgot."

"C'mon, Kim, how could you forget your sister's thirtieth birthday? Your dad even said he talked to you that day and reminded you to call."

"I know, but I started doing something and lost track of time." Kim defended her actions. She didn't feel like discussing Wendy any longer. She started gathering her belongings. Her intention was to leave before Marlene could continue lecturing her. "Can I have that?" she asked, referring to the catalog that rested on Marlene's lap.

"Oh, you gonna run out of here now that I brought up your sister, huh?" She gave Kim the bridal catalog.

"No. It's almost time for me to go anyhow. I'm picking up the kids today." Kim was telling the truth. On her days off she picked up the kids. She still had some time to spare before she needed to be at their locations, but if Marlene was going to start preaching to her, it was time to go.

"Um-hmm," Marlene replied. She knew all too well what her daughter was up to. "Are you going to church Sunday? You haven't been for the past couple of weeks. Why is that?"

"I don't know. I just haven't felt like it." Honestly, Kim had been enjoying the church services. After the Soul Sistas meeting she went to with Wendy, she had even considered walking up front during the altar call for salvation. Now she was having second thoughts about whether she would be able to live up to Christian standards, especially since Wendy couldn't.

Kim had always thought Wendy was perfect. It was Wendy who went to college and graduated summa cum laude. It was Wendy who remained a virgin despite the peer pressure from her friends. It was Wendy who got saved at a young age and remained faithful to her commitment. In Kim's eyes, Wendy had never made a bad decision. She had even hit the jackpot by marrying Kevin. It was love Wendy was looking for, not money, but she got both. Kim had never been jealous of Wendy. Rather, she admired her and looked up to her. After constructing this image of her sister in her mind, Kim was surprised by what she had found in Wendy's purse. If Wendy, who had basically been a good girl all of her life, had trouble doing things the Lord's way, how could she?

"I hope you don't let what's going on with Wendy prevent you from coming to church," Marlene stated as though she knew how Kim's mind worked. "It really surprised me that you didn't come on Easter with Terrance and the kids."

"I told you I wasn't feeling well that day."

"I know that Wendy's actions were not appropriate. However, I want you to remember that we all have to see God for ourselves. We're not accountable for what others do; we're accountable for what we do. You can't let what Wendy did prevent you from seeking a relationship with God."

*Yeah, yeah, yeah,* Kim thought. She glanced around the area to make sure she had all of her stuff.

"You need to get over this issue with Wendy and move on," Marlene said bluntly.

"Easy for you to say. You're not the one she lied to for several months."

"Wendy has hurt us all. She may not have lied to me about the baby, but remember she did lie to me about her trip to Philadelphia. And so did you, I might add."

"Yeah, but that was different."

"How was it different? You don't think that hurt me?"

"Yeah, but still—"

"There's no buts. You're just being stubborn."

Kim sighed. *So what if I'm being stubborn.* She was so focused on her own hurt feelings that she didn't even stop to think how her actions were hurting her sister or even her parents, who had to witness their children at odds with one another.

"Do you even know the circumstances that prompted Wendy to do the things she did?"

"She said that Kevin cheated on her and that's why she didn't go to Philly."

"Oh, so you do believe that Kevin cheated on her and not the other way around."

"Yeah, why do you ask that?"

"Wendy said you implied that she had the affair."

Kim shook her head. "I know she didn't cheat on Kevin, Mama. I was just mad at the time."

"Well, you need to call and tell her that."

"If Wendy wants to talk to me, she knows how to get in touch with me," Kim replied.

"Do you know how ridiculous that sounds? Why would she want to call you after you spoke to her the way you did?"

Kim wished she had stayed home and enjoyed this time she would have had to herself. The day had gone well until now. "Mama, I'm not in the mood for this lecture. I gotta go anyhow." With her catalogs gathered under her arm, she took her keys out of her purse and stood up.

"Nobody's lecturing you, smarty pants. I'm just saying that there's more to her story than you know."

"Like what?"

Frances was supposed to be upstairs taking a nap, but no one ever knew when those ears of hers would be tuned in to what was happening. Frances knew that something was going on with Wendy and Kevin and was upset because no one would give her the details. If Frances ever got wind of what had really happened, she would tell Sister Binford and the two of them would be sure to have it around town before sundown. "She went to the doctor and found out that she had chlamydia," Marlene whispered.

Kim's eyes widened. "Are you serious?" She sat back down.

"Shh!" Marlene put her finger over her mouth and pointed upstairs to remind Kim that they were not alone. "Yes. That's why she didn't go to Philadelphia and that's why she was considering having an abortion."

"Wow!" Kim's jaw fell to the floor.

"Now, I don't agree with how she handled things in the least bit. I know she hurt you by lying. She hurt all of us. But we don't know how we would have acted under those circumstances. If she ever needed us, she needs us now."

"I really had no idea." Kim was dumbfounded.

"I know you didn't. That's why you need to make things right with her."

Before Kim could speak, she and Marlene heard footsteps coming down the stairs, indicating that Frances was up. Marlene hurriedly grabbed a catalog from Kim and opened it to make it look like that was all she and Kim had been discussing.

Frances strolled in the living room wearing the blue house robe she normally wore when she didn't expect company or plan to go anywhere. It had seen its fair share of washings so its color was no longer a vibrant sky blue, and it had several rips and tears. Marlene had bought Frances several robes throughout the years. However, they all hung in her closet, many untouched and with the tags still on. Frances continued to wear the blue house robe as though the others didn't exist.

"Hello." Kim spoke to be polite.

"What are y'all down here doin'?"

"Nothing. Kim's getting ready to leave soon. We were looking at bridal catalogs."

"Umph." Frances looked at Kim without replying to Kim's initial greeting. "I hope she don't plan on wearin' white. You know that color is for virgins."

Under normal circumstances and if Marlene hadn't been present, Kim would have liked to tell her grandmother where to go and give her a map to get there. However, her mind focused on what Marlene had just told her about Wendy. Kim felt awful for being as mean as she had been.

"Mama, that was unnecessary," Marlene said. Frances ignored her and went into the kitchen. "Please don't pay her any attention."

"Don't worry, I'm not," Kim responded. "I don't see how you kept your sanity growing up in the household with her."

Marlene laughed. She often wondered the same thing. "Believe it or not, she wasn't always like that."

"Yeah, right."

"I'm serious. It wasn't until after my daddy died that she began to change."

Kim listened intently. Marlene rarely mentioned the death of her father. He had passed away when Marlene was young.

"Sometimes I wonder how things would have turned out had he not killed himself." Marlene spoke solemnly. For some reason her father had suffered from depression for about six months and had begun drinking heavily. One night, Frances had come home and found him lying on their bedroom floor. He had shot himself in the head. "I think Mama became angry and bitter after that. It was a struggle for us. Mama even sent me to Tennessee to live with my grandmother."

"How did you end up back here?" Kim asked, wondering. She never knew Marlene had been sent away after her father's death.

"My grandmother died a few years later. My Aunt Edna lived there also, but she had three children of her own she was struggling to raise. Mama didn't have a choice. She had to come and get me." Marlene was quiet for a moment, as though she were reliving that period in time. "I don't think Mama has ever gotten over all of that."

"That still doesn't give her the right to treat other people like crap."

"I know it doesn't, baby. Just pray for your grandmother. Lord knows I do. I pray that God will truly touch her soul before she dies."

Kim looked at her watch. "It's *really* time for me to go now."

"Okay, honey. Thanks for coming by. I've enjoyed your company today."

"Me too. Tell Daddy that I said hi when he calls."

"Okay, I will." Marlene hesitated for a moment. "Please think about what I said to you about your sister. She needs you."

"I will," Kim said, and walked out the door. She rushed to her car and called Evelyn, Terrance's mother. Kim asked if she could drop the kids off for a few hours after she picked them up from school. She had something she wanted to take care of before going home.

～

Wendy stood at the departure area waiting for the last few students to leave. All teachers were required to take turns every six weeks to wait for buses and parents to come. This happened to be her week in the rotation. Wendy made sure to stand up straight, afraid that if she leaned over the slightest bit, she would fall due to the disproportionate size of her stomach compared to the rest of her body. She was more than halfway through her pregnancy and she hoped that the second half would not be as stressful as the first half.

In about a month and a half, school would be out for the summer and Wendy would be done teaching for a while. It was a break that she was looking forward to. Before their separation, Kevin had agreed that she could stay home as long as she wanted to, but she didn't know if that agreement still stood. Hopefully he'd pay her enough support so that she could afford to stay home for at least a year. She had already turned in her resignation, so Kevin better come through for her. All of this was his fault, anyhow.

When the last student was gone, Wendy strolled down the hall to her classroom. She figured that the parking lot would still be crowded with buses and cars, so getting out quickly at this point would be impossible.

*Thirty, Pregnant, and Alone* was the title Wendy had come up with on her thirtieth birthday. That night she had cried and couldn't help but wonder what could have been if Kevin hadn't cheated on her. Although she was starting to miss him terribly, she was too stubborn to admit that to herself or anyone else.

Wendy walked into her classroom and straightened her desk. It was pretty unorganized with papers here, crayons there, and pencils everywhere. Before leaving the school, she decided to make a list of the activities she would do the next day.

"So am I disowned?" Kim said humbly as she stood in the classroom doorway.

Wendy looked up and for a moment was startled. She never expected Kim to show up at her job. It would have excited her to see Kim, except Wendy wasn't in the mood for a confrontation. "Me, disown you? Funny, I thought it was the other way around," she said, and continued what she had been doing.

Kim could sense the tension. "I never disowned you. I was just hurt and angry at the time."

"So what did you come here for? Sorry, but I don't need you letting off any more steam." Wendy was also hurt. Deep down she knew that Kim had every right to be upset with her. Yet Wendy couldn't get over how hateful Kim had been, especially the things she had said.

"That's not why I'm here." Kim stepped into the classroom and shut the door. Wendy looked up again. "I came to restore our relationship," Kim admitted.

"The last time I tried to do that you hung up on me, remember?"

Kim wanted to lash out and remind Wendy about the reason for the hang-up. She hadn't driven all the way across town to get rejected. She had half a mind to turn around and walk back out that door, but she couldn't. Marlene was right. Wendy was the only sister she had. She was determined to make things right with her. "Wendy."

Wendy ignored her younger sister. "*Wendy*," Kim repeated with a little more force this time, and walked directly in front of her desk.

"What?"

"I'm sorry."

There was silence in the room as both ladies waited to see who would make the next move.

"I truly am sorry," Kim broke the silence. "I had no right to speak to you the way I did."

"I'm sorry too," Wendy admitted, and stood up. "I never should have lied to you."

"I really can't blame you. I can't say that I would have been eager to have everyone find out about my doctor's visit. I probably would have made up something also."

"So you talked to Mama, did you?"

"Yes. She told me how you found out about Kevin."

"Kim . . ." Wendy's voice began to quiver and she paused for a minute. There she was, in her classroom, about to burst into tears. Most of the teachers were gone by now, but there were probably a few of them left in the building. Wendy no longer cared. She had put on a front for so long that now she just wanted to be real. "I'm scared."

Kim had never heard her sister admit to being scared of anything. She set her purse on the desk and slowly walked around it to Wendy.

"Nothing has gone the way I thought it would go. I'm separated from my husband, getting ready to be jobless and a mother all in a short amount of time. It frightens me. I admire your strength and the way you handled the situation with Darius. I just don't know if I have that same strength."

"Sure you do. We are two peas from the same pod. What's in me is in you."

"But I don't want to be alone with a child for the rest of my life. You were lucky to have Terrance by your side. I have no one. Look how long it took for me to find Kevin. He's about as successful as they come and look where that got me. Alone, pregnant, and with an STD that fortunately could be cured with a few antibiotics."

"Quit saying you're alone. You're not. You have your family. Wendy, you have me."

"Yeah, I know," Wendy said.

"You say that as though I'm not good enough," Kim kidded. "I can't do the things Kevin did for you and, honestly, I don't even want to think about everything he did." She winked and Wendy gave a slight grin. "However, I will do any and every thing I can to help you with this baby. Shoot—if you still feel that you need a man, if we can't find you one, we'll rent one for you every now and then," she said jokingly.

Wendy finally chuckled. "You're wrong for that."

"Hey, I'm just trying to help a sista out. Desperate times call for desperate measures."

"I think I'll hold off on the rent-a-man idea. Besides, I'll have this lil' man to keep me busy for a while," Wendy said, and patted her protruding belly.

Kim picked up on her reference to the sex of the child. "You know it's a boy?"

Wendy nodded.

"Why didn't you tell me? Wait, don't tell me you knew all along and decided to keep it from me," Kim said. She was joking, but in a way she was also serious. Wendy had kept so much from her that it really wouldn't surprise her.

"No. I didn't know all along. I found out last week when I went for my checkup."

"Why didn't you call and tell me?"

Wendy looked at her sister as if to say *Duh, you were mad at me, remember?* Kim changed her question. "What made you decide to find out?"

Wendy shrugged her shoulders. "I don't know. My appointment was on the day of my birthday. At that time, it seemed like everything around me was falling apart: my marriage, my relationship with you. With the uncertainty of my future, I guess I wanted one thing that I could be certain of, so I asked Dr. Korva to tell me the sex of the baby."

"We're having a boy!" Kim proclaimed excitedly. She didn't care whether it was a boy or a girl. All she cared about was being a part of this child's life. "Do we have a name yet?"

"No." Wendy knew Kevin wanted to name him Kevin

Jamal Phillips Jr., but she was not sold on that idea since they were separated.

"Speaking of birthdays," Kim announced, "I still owe you a present. How about I take you out to dinner tonight?"

"Sure, why not?" Although it was a school night, Wendy knew that if she went home she would do nothing but mope around and feel sorry for herself in her big, empty house.

"Oh, I'm sorry, Ms. Phillips. I didn't know anyone was still in here," said the maintenance person walking into the classroom. He was making his rounds, checking to see that the building was clear and that all the doors were locked.

"That's okay, Otis. We're getting ready to leave anyhow." She saw Otis eyeing Kim. "This is my sister, Kim." Wendy introduced the two.

Otis walked up to shake Kim's hand. "You're not a teacher here, are you?"

"No," Kim replied.

"I didn't think so. I couldn't live with myself if I had missed noticing someone as fine as you." He smiled.

Wendy rolled her eyes. Otis Edward Thornton never passed up an opportunity to flirt with women. He was probably in his late thirties and looked like he had been taken out of the eighties and placed in the twenty-first century. He was nearly six feet tall and very thin. What stood out most about his smile was the gold tooth he had implanted on the upper right side of his mouth. The tooth, of course, matched the color of frames for his glasses. His Jheri Curl was usually dry and uneven. For some reason he couldn't grow a full beard, but that didn't stop him from showing off the handful of hairs on his face.

Otis was so dark that he took being black to a whole new level. He thought he was fine, though, with his fake gold necklace and rings. To most ladies, he was hard on the eyes. He probably wouldn't have looked as bad if he would invest more time and money in his appearance.

"Back up off my sister, Otis, or I'll have to hurt you," Wendy teased. She knew Otis was harmless, but he could be quite annoying sometimes.

"Oh girl, I ain't worried about you. Besides, you'll hurt yourself trying to hurt me." He pointed to the child she was carrying inside of her.

"Well in that case, I'll just call my future brother-in-law and *he'll* hurt you."

"You gettin' married?" he asked Kim.

"Yes, next summer," Kim stated. She was ready to go.

"Well, congratulations. How long have y'all been together?"

"Over six years."

"Well looks like ol' Otis is about seven years too late, huh?"

"Seven years ago ol' Otis would have been looking at jailbait," Kim remarked. She would have been only seventeen at the time.

"Still, do you think I would have had a chance?" Once again Otis gave what he thought was a killer smile.

Kim had to laugh at his ridiculousness. "I really don't think you want me to answer that question."

"C'mon, now. You can tell the truth," he said, and adjusted his pants. "I'll tell ya, there ain't nuttin' like an Otis!"

"You are definitely right about that." Kim rubbed her nostrils after the aroma of his cologne attacked her.

Wendy picked up on Kim's behavior. Otis didn't know that if he continued pressing Kim, she would eventually tell him what she thought of him. Wendy knew this, and tried to save him from embarrassment. "Slow your roll, Otis. We have to get going and you need to finish locking up." Wendy looked at Kim. "You ready?"

"No better time than the present."

"Okay, then. I think we can all go." Wendy motioned toward the door. Otis walked out, then Kim, then Wendy. She was about to pull out her keys and lock the classroom door.

"Don't worry about that. I'll get it."

"Okay, thanks. You have a good evening."

"You too, Ms. Phillips." He flashed a smile at Kim. "Nice to meet you, young lady."

"Um-hmm." Kim turned around as she and Wendy proceeded to walk down the hall.

"Ooooh-weee. You sho' is a PYT—pretty young thang!" Otis checked Kim out as she walked away. "Let me know if those marriage plans don't work out. You just don't know, there ain't nuttin' like an Otis. You hear what I say, girl? There ain't nuttin' like an O-teese. No other man takes better care of his women than me."

Kim didn't even respond. Rather, she and Wendy continued walking to the parking lot. Once outside, they cracked up. "What was that?" Kim asked Wendy, laughing hysterically.

"Girl, I think Terrance may have a lil' competition.

You heard him, didn't you?" Wendy changed her voice to imitate the maintenance guy. "There ain't nuttin' like an Otis."

Wendy left her car at the school and rode with Kim. The two of them laughed all the way to the restaurant.

# Chapter Fourteen
## The Uninvited Guest

"THEY'RE HERE!" Marlene called after she looked out the window and saw Kim and Wendy pulling into the driveway. Everyone jumped out of their seats and scattered as though someone had yelled *fire*. They had all parked their cars down the street so that Wendy wouldn't suspect anything. Marlene continued peeking out the window until the girls got out of the car.

She giggled as she watched Wendy waddle up the driveway. Wendy was now in her seventh month of pregnancy, and Marlene could swear her daughter was having twins. Wendy had gained a lot of weight in the last couple of months, but she looked so adorable! Marlene and Kim often teased her about the weight she had gained, but they knew it was only temporary. Wendy vowed that once the baby was born, it would only be a matter of time before she regained her old shape.

Being hardheaded, Marlene and Kim had ignored Wendy's statements about not wanting a baby shower and planned one anyhow. Although she hadn't joined the church, Kim had begun going to Sunday services regularly again and had also attended that month's Soul Sistas meeting with Wendy, all of which had enabled her to spread the news about Wendy's surprise baby shower. Gwen had given Marlene the numbers of some of Wendy's friends, since they both knew many of the same people. Marlene was able to invite them to the shower. The result was a baby shower that consisted of about twenty women with whom Wendy associated.

All the guests stiffened up and quieted as they heard the front door opening. "Hello," Marlene said, and went over to hug Wendy and rub her belly.

It annoyed Wendy when people touched her stomach. Not only was she feeling the strains of having another individual grow inside of her, but she had also watched her stomach stretch out beyond recognition. Her hands, feet, and ankles were swollen; her back hurt, her head hurt, her legs cramped up, she had heartburn, and she couldn't sleep well because the baby decided that he only wanted to kick during the night. On top of all of that, everyone she encountered—family, friends, and even strangers—took it upon themselves to rub her belly whenever they saw her and she just had to grin and bear it. She figured that she was getting paid back for all of the times she had done that to other expectant mothers.

Wendy had come over to her parents' house with Kim because she thought she was going shopping for baby stuff with her mother and sister. Although Wendy had gone out and bought a fashionable maternity wardrobe thanks to Kevin's Platinum Visa, today she wore just a plain, white maternity tank top with blue stretch shorts to make sure that she would be comfortable.

"Are you ready?" Wendy asked her mother.

Marlene stood with a big grin on her face.

Wendy glanced into the living room and saw that the furniture had been replaced with folding chairs and a futon. Marlene had borrowed some chairs from the church, and the futon had come from the basement, where the furniture was temporarily being stored. Wendy also noticed that there were decorations all over the place. "What is—" Before she could finish her question, the guests jumped out of their hiding places and yelled "Surprise!"

"Oh my goodness!" Wendy said, and covered her mouth with her hands. She was speechless for a moment. "I cannot believe you guys did this," she said to her mother and sister with a smile.

"C'mon now, just because you said you didn't want a shower you didn't *really* think that we would give up that easy, did you?" Marlene stated.

Wendy shook her head in disbelief. "I should have known that y'all were up to something."

Kim, still standing behind Wendy when everyone emerged, held out her hands in case Wendy was so startled that she fell backwards. Truth was, if Wendy had fallen, Kim would have been in big trouble. Her small frame could not have handled all of the weight her sister had adopted.

Wendy finally caught her breath and walked into the living room to greet the guests. "They set me up," she said as she began hugging everyone. Marlene and Kim certainly had outdone themselves. There were pink and blue balloons all over the place. There were streamers, confetti, banners, and even a rocking chair in the middle of the room that had a sign on it: FOR PREGNANT WOMEN ONLY.

"I bet you had something to do with this too," Wendy accused Gwen as the two women embraced.

"You know I'll do just about anything for you, girl," Gwen said. Yesterday she had done Wendy's hair and put it up in a fancy french roll despite Wendy's protests.

"Guess who?" Someone sneaked up behind Wendy and covered her eyes, not caring that she'd interrupted a special moment between Wendy and Gwendolyn. Gwen gave the lady a dirty look.

"I don't know. Say something again," Wendy requested. She didn't recognize the voice.

"Don't tell me you forgot about me that quickly," the woman said jokingly before letting her hands go.

Wendy turned around, and her eyes got big. She was truly surprised to see one of her old friends, Natalie. "What are you doing here?" Wendy asked as she embraced her.

"Oh, so you don't want me here? Is that what you're saying?" Natalie teased.

"You know what I'm trying to say. I am so shocked to see you."

"In that case, I suppose I'll stay, then." She smiled. "I see that someone has something cooking in the oven." Like everyone else, Natalie took it upon herself to rub Wendy's abdomen.

"Yeah, I don't have too much longer to go."

"I can see," Natalie said, still touching Wendy's stomach.

Wendy politely grabbed Natalie's hand and squeezed it softly as people do when they are happy to see someone.

It was the only thing she could think of to get her friend's hand off her body. At that moment, Wendy swore to herself that she would never touch the belly of another pregnant woman as long as she lived. "I am still so shocked to see you. Are you still living in New York?"

"No, I moved back to town a couple of months ago because my mom is ill. I happened to run into your mother at Easton Mall. She told me that you were pregnant and that she and Kim were throwing a surprise baby shower for you. I gave her my telephone number and address and the rest, as they say, is history."

Wendy hadn't seen Natalie for over six years. She, Natalie, and Gwendolyn all had gone to high school together. Wendy managed to maintain her friendship with the two women despite the fact that they didn't like each other very much. Gwendolyn had never trusted Natalie, and she didn't like how Natalie always tried to be the center of attention. Wendy and Natalie had also attended Ohio State University together. After graduation, Natalie had moved to New York to pursue a modeling career.

The difference between Gwen and Natalie was that Natalie worked hard for the attention she got. For Gwen, attention came naturally; she didn't go chasing after it. Not only that, she handled it humbly, unlike Natalie, who was vain. Ever since Natalie had her first car, her personalized license plate had the letters Q T PIE. Natalie could have invented the slogan "All Eyes On Me." Natalie would never admit it, but she had always been jealous of the friendship Wendy and Gwen shared. That was why she didn't mind breaking up their tender moment; she wanted her own.

"You look great," Wendy said to her friend. Seeing

Natalie was nice, but Wendy felt like a whale standing next to her. Natalie had on a tight spaghetti-strap shirt with capri pants and one-inch-heel sandals. She was tall and slender, with honey-colored skin. Her thick lips and small, narrow eyes gave away her mixed ancestry. Her mother was white and her father was black, although there was some Indian ancestry on his side of the family. Natalie had dark hair that she used to wear long. Wendy was surprised to see that she had cut it. "I love your hair."

"Thanks. It's very low-maintenance." Natalie fluffed her fingers through her hair. "Your hair is cute too. Where'd you get it done?"

"Gwen did it for me. You know she owns her own shop."

"Oh, I guess I'll have to check it out sometime," Natalie said, unconvincingly.

"I'm sorry to hear about your mom. What's wrong with her?"

"She has cancer and has been having a tough time going through chemo. She's been getting treatments for about a year now, but she's getting progressively worse, so I had to make the move back this way, although I loved it in New York."

"How was modeling going for you?" Wendy was happy that she could use being pregnant as an excuse for her appearance right now. There was nothing worse than seeing someone whom she hadn't seen in a long time and they looked good while she looked like who-did-it-and-why.

"It was going okay. Not as well as I would've liked. I never made the front cover of any big magazines. Someone told me that I may be able to do some things locally, so I'm gonna look into it."

"You two will have to play catch-up another time," Marlene said. Everyone had been patiently waiting for Natalie and Wendy so that the party could start.

"Oh, sorry," Wendy said. She had been so wrapped up in the conversation that she had almost forgotten there was a shower being held in her honor.

Natalie sat down on the futon next to Gwen. Although it had been years since the two ladies had seen each other, there was no love lost between them. They greeted each other, but it was more of a "Since you're here I'll tolerate you" hug than an "I'm happy to see you" one.

"Thank you so much," Wendy said to her sister and mother as tears rolled from her eyes.

"Hey, don't you start that," Kim said jokingly.

"I'm not crying," Wendy said, and wiped her eyes. She very much appreciated her mother and sister. These days, it didn't take much to make Wendy cry. It had to be the hormones because Kim hadn't seen Wendy cry during her whole life as much as she had these last several months. Kim would not let her live down the day she went over to Wendy's house and found her crying because she couldn't get her hair to do what she wanted it to do. Kim had laughed so hard that Wendy had stopped crying and also laughed once she realized how ridiculous the situation was.

Kim kicked off the party by stating how excited she was about becoming an "auntie." Everyone then took turns giving Wendy a baby blessing. The first game they played was "Name That Baby Food." The guests were given a paper plate with eight samples of baby food. They were instructed to taste each one and write down what they thought it was. The person who could guess the most right was the winner. Wendy wasn't eligible to win any prizes, so she didn't participate. She wasn't sure if she would be able to stomach the taste of baby food, although many of the women didn't mind eating the fruits and desserts that they sampled. It was the vegetables, especially the peas, that distorted everyone's face and had Wendy cracking up.

For the next game, Kim brought out a big bowl that had been filled with safety pins and rice. The object of the game was to see how many safety pins one could dig out in sixty seconds while blindfolded. Each lady was confident that she would succeed, but they were wrong. Although she couldn't officially win, Kim made Wendy take part since she made a comment about it not looking that difficult. Everyone laughed hard as Wendy continued pulling out handfuls of rice from the bowl. When her time was up, she was sure that she had collected several safety pins. Contrary to her belief, there was not a single safety pin removed from the bowl.

Several other games were played and the ladies all had a ball. Wendy was having so much fun she didn't even notice that her grandmother wasn't there until Frances walked down the stairs.

"Hello, everyone," Frances said in a bitter tone of voice. She had been upstairs in her room the whole time.

"Hey, Gramma," Wendy said cheerfully. "Are you going to join us?"

"Oh, the shower was today?" Frances asked. "I had forgotten all about it. I'm sorry."

Marlene and Kim both knew Frances was lying. Marlene had mentioned the party to her earlier that week, and she claimed she wasn't going to come because they had kept her out of the loop when planning. She'd gone on and on about how she felt left out. She was still hurt because no one had told her about Terrance's plans to propose to Kim on Christmas and everyone knew what was going on with Wendy and Kevin except for her. Although Terrance's proposal to Kim had happened months ago, Frances couldn't let it go.

When Marlene told her about the shower, Frances had said that she would probably be busy doing other things. Marlene knew she didn't actually have any plans because she couldn't go anywhere unless Marlene drove her. Marlene wasn't in the mood for begging her mother's participation, so she told her that if she changed her mind, she was free to join them. If Frances had truly forgotten about the shower, she would have been wearing her blue robe that she normally wore around the house. Instead, she was dressed in regular clothing.

"Well, that's okay, Gramma. Have a seat," Wendy invited her.

"I don't know if I should. Your mama didn't tell me about the party until Wednesday. By then, I didn't have time to get you anything."

"Gramma, you know I'm not expecting anything from you," Wendy said honestly. She didn't want to harp on the fact that Frances didn't know about the party. If that was true, then she knew exactly why no one had told her. It was clear to see that Frances was getting ready to play the victim and try to have everyone feel sorry for her. Wendy was having a good time and didn't want her grandmother's attitude to ruin it, so she tried to ignore Frances's behavior and make her feel wanted. "I'm just glad that you came down. C'mon and hang out with us. I think they've played all of the games, but we're getting ready to eat in a few minutes."

"Well, all right," Frances said, and made her way to an empty chair.

During Frances's grand entrance, Kim went into the kitchen to bring out the food.

"Hello, Sister Frances." One of the ladies from church spoke.

Frances looked across the room and saw several church members there. She hadn't thought any of them would come, since she hadn't heard anybody at church mention a baby shower. She knew then that she needed to change her demeanor so they wouldn't see how she acted outside of the church walls. "Oh, Praise God. It's so good to see you all," she said cheerfully.

"Are you feeling any better? Marlene was telling me that you've been having some chest pains," another lady inquired.

"Yes, chile, I'm feelin' much better. I'm blessed and highly favored of the Lord." She waved her hand in the air like people did in church when they hollered *Amen*. Gwen, Wendy, and a few of Wendy's other friends snickered. Watching Frances in action was pretty comical.

Kim walked out with the food just in time to see her grandmother's performance. She looked at Wendy and shook her head. Wendy smirked at Kim as if to say *Let the show begin*.

"I take it you don't know if it's a boy or girl," Natalie stated, noticing that everything was pink and blue.

"Actually, I do. I'm having a boy."

"That's what the doctor said. But she's carrying that baby too high for it to be a boy. She's having a girl," Marlene interjected. She didn't care what the ultrasound showed. She predicted a baby's sex the old-fashioned way: Pay close attention to how the mother is carrying the child.

"My mother is in denial, as you can see," Wendy said.

"Do you want her to have a girl?" Natalie asked Marlene.

"No, it doesn't matter to me. I want her to have a healthy baby. I just know that doctors don't always know what they're talkin' about."

"Well, if it is a girl, Natalie would be a perfect name for her."

Both Kim and Gwen looked at each other when Natalie spoke.

"Well, that's not quite what I had in mind," Wendy confessed.

"Okay, fine. You don't have to name the baby after me since I'm already the godmother," said Natalie.

Wendy forced out a chuckle, but she really didn't think it was funny. She thought Natalie had some nerve expecting to be crowned godmother when the two hadn't spoken for years. Wendy knew that Natalie was just being Natalie. She could be so self-centered sometimes that it used to drive Wendy crazy. They would have to start building a whole new friendship again. So much had changed since they had graduated from high school and college. Wendy was hopeful that before long, she and Natalie could be as tight as they used to be. However, Natalie still wasn't in the running for godmother to her child.

"Sorry to tell you this, but Kim and I have already been selected as the godmothers," Gwen announced purposely to get under Natalie's skin.

"Oh," Natalie said quietly.

"Why don't you tell us what you plan on namin' the baby?" Frances asked.

"I don't really want to say yet. I haven't settled on a boy's name," Wendy said truthfully.

"Oh, I'm sure you and Kevin have picked out some possibilities," said Frances.

The mention of Kevin's name infuriated both Wendy and Kim. At that point, Wendy felt like she could strangle Frances for putting her in an awkward position. Besides her family, Gwen, and a few others, the rest of the guests did not know that she and Kevin were separated.

Marlene could see Kim's jaw tensing. She shook her head no to indicate that Kim needed to stay quiet and not make a scene. Wendy was now suddenly reminded of why she never wanted a baby shower in the first place. She didn't want to talk about Kevin. She was hoping to get through the shower without his name being mentioned. Leave it up to Frances to open that can of worms.

"Kevin—is that your husband?" Natalie asked.

"Yes. I guess it won't hurt to tell you the names that we're considering." Wendy wanted to cry, but she wasn't going to give Frances the satisfaction of embarrassing her that easily, nor was she going to risk her baby sister going to jail on her behalf. "The names we're considering are Kevin Jamal Phillips Jr. or Kevin Michael Phillips," Wendy said, trying to sound happy about it. She had been considering compromising and instead of having a junior, using her dad's name for the middle name.

"What if it is a girl? Then what?" Natalie spoke again.

"I don't think it's a girl, but if it is, then I guess Maya Nicole."

"That's pretty," Natalie confirmed.

Everyone else seemed to agree. The mention of Kevin's name brought on other questions about him from Natalie. She hadn't been around to know how long he and Wendy had been married, where he was from, or what he did for a living. Wendy knew Natalie was asking innocently, so she suffered through her questioning.

To break the cycle of questions about Kevin, Marlene announced that everyone should begin eating before the food got cold. The menu for that afternoon included a pasta salad, deli meats, cheese, crackers, pretzels, chips, and hot and mild chicken wings Marlene had made. Kim and Wendy had made a joke one time when Marlene had invited them over for dinner. Everyone knew that Marlene was an exceptional cook. Kim looked at Wendy and said that the food was so good, it made Kim want to slap the taste out of her mama's mouth. Wendy laughed and said, "Go ahead." It took a minute for Marlene to catch on to the joke but when she did, she laughed and told Kim that as long as she lived, she'd better not raise a hand to her. That was how good the wings were today. However, if Kim had the nerve to slap anyone, it would have been Frances for being ignorant.

As expected, several mini-conversations took place while everyone ate. When they were done, Kim moved Wendy's rocking chair to the table where all of the presents were. Wendy got a lot of things for the baby such as diapers, blankets, diaper bags, a high chair, a stroller, neutral outfits, a bottle warmer, and a baby monitor. Kim and

Marlene had bought her a deluxe baby crib that eventually turned into a toddler bed as the child grew older. Frances even reached down into her bosom and pulled out money to give to Wendy. She made sure Wendy and everyone knew that it was the *last* ten dollars she had from her Social Security check. Wendy tried to give it back, telling her grandmother that she didn't need the money, but Frances wouldn't hear of it.

Everyone helped Kim and Marlene clean up the paper from the presents. Gwen had written down what presents were from whom so Wendy could send out her thank-you cards. Wendy was surprised that she didn't get many duplicate gifts. Kim confessed that she had created a baby registry for Wendy at several stores to prevent that from happening. It seemed as though Kim and Marlene had thought of everything.

The doorbell rang just as the party was wrapping up. Neither Marlene nor Kim could imagine who would be at the door. It was not likely that any more guests would arrive three hours after the party had started. Marlene went to answer the door.

"Kevin? What are you doing here?" She was extremely stunned to see him. She hadn't seen or heard from him in months.

"I'm sorry. Did I come at the wrong time?" he asked.

Kim saw that Kevin was at the door and wanted to warn Wendy, but it was too late. Several other guests had taken notice of him.

"Cute man alert," Natalie announced.

Wendy turned around and saw Kevin standing there. Her heart raced. She and Kevin had minimal contact through e-mail and telephone calls, but they rarely saw each other. "Oh my goodness," Wendy said softly, and leaned back and began rocking in her chair. *What is he doing here?* she wondered.

"Whoever that is, he is fine!" Natalie whispered. Gwen finally told her that the man standing at the door was Wendy's husband. Everyone else recognized him from the church, or wedding pictures that Wendy showed of him. "You go, girl," Natalie said to Wendy.

"Wrong time for what?" Marlene asked Kevin. "We're just finishing up Wendy's baby shower."

Kevin looked clueless. "A baby shower? Oh God, are you serious? Ms. Gibson said that there was a family meeting today and asked me if I could come. She specifically said that everyone wanted me to be here."

"What!" She had been trying to keep her voice low, but her response quieted the room as everyone strained to hear their conversation. Marlene noticed that she and Kevin were the center of attention, so she asked Kevin if they could step outside and she closed the door.

Out of the four women in the Tibbs family, Frances was the only one who didn't look surprised to see Kevin. Kim had a few choice words to share with her grandmother, but she knew that she better get all of the guests out of the house first, especially the people from church. "Thank you all for coming. Y'all don't have to finish cleaning up. We can get everything from here. Those of you who want a ride back to your car, I can take a couple of groups at a time in my mother's van." The walk to their cars was only about a block, so no one took Kim up on the offer. She ignored comments from several guests who couldn't help but wonder why the party was being brought to such an abrupt end.

It wasn't difficult to tell that Wendy's mood had changed dramatically. She was embarrassed, angry, and hurt all at the same time. She desperately wanted to find out why Kevin was there, but she wanted everyone to go home first. She tried her best to force a smile and thank all of her guests for their presents despite the offended looks on many of their faces at their being rushed out of the house. Before she left, Natalie and Wendy exchanged telephone numbers. "Be sure to call me," Natalie stated.

As Gwen gave Wendy a final good-bye hug, she asked if Wendy needed her to stay. She knew that Wendy had not been expecting to see Kevin.

"No, I'm fine. But thanks anyhow."

On the way out, Gwen told Kim that if they needed anything to call her. "Thanks, we will. I just want to try and get everyone out of here so we can find out what the"— Kim paused to choose her words carefully—"*heck* is going on," she said, trying not to slip.

"Just stay calm. You know Wendy doesn't need to be upset any more than she already is."

"Yeah, I know."

"Call me later."

"Okay," Kim said, and Gwen walked out the door.

The guests started filtering out of the house and making their way down the street to their cars. Marlene and Kevin were still outside talking, so whenever the door opened and someone walked out, they quieted down.

Kim looked around and saw Frances sitting on the couch singing "What a Friend We Have in Jesus" to herself. She opened the door and told Kevin and Marlene they could come inside since everyone had left.

"So what's going on?" Kim asked Kevin with an attitude after he and Marlene were inside. "Why did you come over to my mother's house uninvited and unwelcome?"

"Kim, calm down. It's not his fault," Marlene said in Kevin's defense.

"Kim, I swear to you that I didn't know what was going on today. Ms. Gibson called the office yesterday and said that your family wanted to speak with me. When I saw your car in the driveway, I assumed she was telling the truth. I am *so* sorry. I swear to you that I didn't intentionally try to upset anyone."

"Mama, why would you invite Kevin over here today knowing that we were having Wendy's baby shower?" Marlene asked before Kim got a chance to respond to Kevin's explanation. Marlene's voice escalated with each word she spoke, showing how irritated she was with Frances.

"I told you that I had forgotten all about the shower bein' today." Frances tried to sound sincere. Her words didn't soften anyone's demeanor.

Marlene had her hands on her hips and Kim's arms were folded. Kevin kept his hands in his pants pockets while Wendy rocked slowly in the chair and looked out the window.

"Yeah, right!" Kim responded. "Then what did you want to talk about with him?"

"I know that he and Wendy are havin' some problems," said Frances. "No one will tell me what's goin' on, but that's beside the point. Anyhow, it's been a long time since we've had Kevin over and I thought that maybe if ev'ryone could come over and get together and have fun then it would make him and Wendy think twice about separating. I thought that I was doin' a good thing. I was tryin' to save my granddaughter's marriage," Frances defended herself.

"Oh *please*, that's a bunch of bull—"

"Kimberly Michele Tibbs, you know better!" Marlene said before Kim could finish her sentence. If looks could kill, Kim would have been struck down at that very moment. Kevin's, Wendy's, and Frances's eyes got big at Kim's daring attempt to say a curse word in front of Marlene.

"I'm sorry," Kim repented.

Marlene turned her attention back to her mother. She was heated. She could see right through Frances's defense. "Why didn't you tell us he was coming when you came down the stairs?"

"I don't know. I guess I forgot. You know I'm gettin' old. I can't remember a lot of things."

"When did you say she called you, Kevin?" Kim asked.

"She called me yesterday."

"What?" Wendy said. "Gramma, you couldn't have forgotten that quickly. You said that Mama told you about the party on Wednesday."

"I did?"

"Yes—you—did," Kim replied.

"Well, like I said, I'm gettin' old. Y'all know that I ain't been feelin' well." Frances rubbed her chest as though it was hurting. Kim thought that she deserved an Oscar for the forced look of sincerity she put on her face.

"Mama, I really don't understand why you treat your granddaughters the way you do."

"What did I do? I was tryin' to do a good thing."

"You forgot about the party being today, right?" Kim asked.

"Right," Frances replied.

"You invited Kevin over so that everyone could possibly spend time together and have fun. You hoped that it would cause Wendy and Kevin to think twice about their marriage, right?"

"*Yes*," Frances said. It was clear that she was getting tired of being interrogated.

"Well, tell me this: If you didn't know that the baby shower was going to be today"— Kim paused while everyone looked at her, waiting to see what she was going to say—"how did you know that Wendy and I would be here when we never got a phone call from you inviting us over for a family meeting?"

Kevin, Marlene, and Wendy turned to Frances for a reply.

"I . . . um . . . I . . ." Frances couldn't think of anything to say. At that moment she knew she was busted. "I don't have to explain myself to none of y'all. I'm the oldest one here and you sittin' up here questionin' me like a chile. I ain't gotta put up with this." Frances got up and stormed up the stairs.

Kevin apologized to everyone, especially Wendy. "I hope you know that I would have never tried to ruin this day for you."

"Yes, I do." Wendy looked at her husband. She really wanted to jump up and hold him, but a little voice in her head prevented her from doing so. *Remember what he did to you.* She looked away to hide the tears that were about to drop from her eyes. If they were together still, she and

Kevin would have celebrated their first wedding anniversary that month.

Kevin asked Wendy to e-mail him after her doctor's appointment next week.

"I will," she replied without looking up.

Marlene walked Kevin to the door while Kim stayed behind to talk with Wendy. She would finish cleaning up, and then take her sister home. She planned to call Terrance and tell him that she would be spending the night at Wendy's. With everything that had just happened, Kim wasn't going to leave her sister alone.

After Kevin left, Marlene marched upstairs to Frances. She was still bothered by her mother's actions and had a few things that she needed to get off her chest. Marlene opened Frances's bedroom door without knocking and screamed. There, Frances lay unconscious on the floor.

## Chapter Fifteen
# The Familiar Stranger

IT WAS WEDNESDAY AFTERNOON. Marlene had been at the hospital since Saturday, when the ambulance had brought in her mother. From the looks of things, they'd be there for a while. Frances had collapsed because her blood pressure had gotten dangerously high, which caused her to develop atrial fibrillation. The upper chambers of her heart were beating up to six times the normal rate due to the improper flow of blood. In order to regulate her heart rhythm, the doctors had installed a pacemaker. They warned Marlene that Frances would need to make efforts to maintain a healthy blood pressure or else she would face further complications later.

Marlene sat in the hospital room and looked at Frances's sedated body. *Lord, watch over her and give me the strength to deal with her.* She wondered if Frances would learn anything from this event.

Marlene hadn't forgotten the stunt her mother had pulled at Wendy's baby shower, but it seemed minuscule now, considering her condition. Frances could have very well lost her life if Marlene had not walked into the bedroom when she had. She had every intention of telling her mother that if she didn't start treating Kim and Wendy with respect, she would find herself back at the senior center. She knew Frances would be hurt, but she was tired of Frances hurting her daughters. Marlene vowed to care for the woman who gave birth to her; she also vowed to protect the women she had given birth to. Sometimes those roles in her life clashed with each other. If she had been forced to choose between the two last Saturday, out Frances would have gone. *I can't deal with her. Lord, if You don't speak to her heart and change her ways, I will lose my mind.*

Marlene got up from the chair she had been sleeping in uncomfortably for the last couple of days. She was reminded how much her body ached as she slowly walked out of the room, rubbing her back and rolling her neck to stretch it out. She headed toward the cafeteria to buy a much-needed cup of coffee.

"Harold Wallace, please report to the front desk in the lab. Harold Wallace, report to the lab," she heard announced over the PA system.

*Harold Wallace.* For some reason she recognized that name, but after searching her mind for clues as to why, nothing came of it. She shrugged it off as one of the many names she'd come across during her years of nursing. Still, curiosity got the best of her and she found herself going in the opposite direction from the cafeteria, to the lab.

Moments passed as Marlene sat in the waiting area,

looking at every person who walked up to the desk. She strained her ears to hear who would mention the name that sounded strangely familiar to her. The idea that she would know this person seemed ridiculous, yet she had nothing but time to waste since Frances wasn't going anywhere anytime soon. Looking for the infamous Harold Wallace broke up the monotony of the day.

"Ma'am, have you been helped?" the lady at the receptionist desk asked Marlene. The lab waiting room wasn't busy, and Marlene stood out like a sore thumb. Several pairs of eyes gazed at her when attention was brought her way.

"Uh, I'm fine, thank you. I'm waiting for someone," she responded and the woman continued about her work.

*See, God, I told you I was going to lose my mind.* Marlene wanted to laugh at how odd she must have looked staring at the face of every individual who walked by. She decided to go to the cafeteria as she had planned, originally, before anyone else said something to her. She would wait a few more minutes and then try to slip out quietly.

"There you are, Mr. Wallace." The same lady who had addressed Marlene spoke in a high-pitched voice and smiled at the elderly gentleman who had just entered the room. "I thought I was going to have to page you again." Marlene zeroed in on their conversation.

"So what's the verdict?" the man said. "Am I gone live a lil' longer?"

"Looks that way. As usual, your blood work came back fine."

"Well, thank you very much. I'll see you next month."

"Okay. You have a good day, Mr. Wallace."

"I most certainly will. You do the same, hear?"

"Yes sir."

From the way he and the woman talked to each other, Marlene could tell this was not the first time the two had spoken. It reminded her of how she would develop casual relationships with patients she saw on a regular basis. *Harold Wallace . . .* There was something about his name that continued pestering her. She wasn't able to get a good look at his face because she could see him only from the side.

Marlene studied his features as best she could. From what she could tell, he looked like he took very good care of himself. He was tall and slender, about five-nine or so. *No, it can't be.* Her eyes widened as she suddenly remembered why the name seemed so familiar. *It can't be.* She watched as the elderly man turned to walk out of the room and she saw the back of his bald head. *The scar! He has the same scar. Can that really be him?*

The moment he twirled his hat around his finger several times before placing it on his head Marlene knew for sure who he was. *Oh my God! It is him!* She covered her mouth as though she had spoken out loud. Twirling his hat before putting it on was something she had seen only *him* do. It *had* to be him. Who else could it be?

Without even thinking, Marlene got up and followed the elderly man. She had no idea what she was going to say, but she couldn't let the moment pass without saying anything. *Wait. What if he doesn't remember me—then what?* Wishing she had gotten a better look at his face,

Marlene hesitated for a moment. *C'mon, Marlene, do you really think he would look exactly the same after over forty years? What if it's not him? This man will think I'm crazy. But what about the scar and the hat . . . that's too much of a coincidence. I know it's him. It has to be.*

"Hello, sir. How are you doing?" She walked up beside the man and spoke.

Turning and smiling, he said to her, "I'm fine, young lady, and yourself?"

*Yep, it's him.* The smooth, dark chocolate skin Marlene remembered now had a few wrinkles, but he still looked great for his age. The voice was a little raspy and the facial hair was gray, but there was one thing time couldn't change: that smile. Harold Wallace, with his dimples and pointed chin, had the kind of smile that would light up a room. This man was Uncle Harry, all right. Marlene was sure of it. "I—um—I'm fine."

"Good, glad to hear that." Harold kept walking toward the exit door.

Marlene froze in her tracks. *Wow! It really is him. Okay, what do I say? Hi, Uncle Harry, remember me?* she considered. *Naw, that sounds corny.* Besides, he wasn't really her uncle. He was a friend of her parents and that was just what she had always called him. She hadn't seen him since before her daddy died. She thought it would be a little presumptuous to walk up to him after forty years and refer to him by the name she'd used as a child.

After a minute or so of contemplating what she would say next, Marlene decided to wing it. Whatever came out of her mouth, she would flow with it. She headed toward the door Harold had gone through. She reached the exit just in time to see him get into the passenger's side of a white, four-door Buick. *No!* She desperately wanted to speak with him, but it was too late. The car drove away and Marlene was left standing outside, wondering if she would ever see that smile again.

# Chapter Sixteen
## Name Change

*I* WANT IT NOW!" Wendy screamed at the nurse who refused to send the anesthetician into her room.

"Mrs. Phillips, I'm sorry. We just gave you some Demerol. You can't get the epidural until you have dilated five centimeters," the nurse spoke smoothly.

Wendy closed her eyes and groaned in agony as the labor pains shot through her body.

"C'mon, you can do it." Kim tried to comfort her sister. "Just continue taking deep breaths." She had brought Wendy to the hospital several hours ago. The two of them had just finished getting the baby's room together when Wendy's water broke. It was exciting, but unexpected, since the baby wasn't technically due for another two weeks.

"If you want, Mrs. Phillips, you can try and go for a short walk up and down the hall. Maybe that'll help you dilate a little faster. It works for some women."

Wendy wished she could get up and slap the nurse for saying something so stupid. Walking was the last thing she wanted to do right now. Instead of speaking, she gave the woman a look that indicated exactly how she felt about the suggestion.

"I'll try and find Dr. Korva and have her come back in to check your progress," said the nurse, picking up on Wendy's glare. "You were two centimeters an hour ago. Since you're in a lot of pain, you may be farther along than we think," she admitted before slipping out of the room.

Kim held Wendy's hand. Gwen, Marlene, and Kevin should all be on their way. Kim had called them once Wendy got settled into her room. Michael said to call him as soon as the baby was born. He and Marlene didn't want to leave Frances at home alone. It had been less than two months since she had gotten her pacemaker and they wanted to keep an eye on her. Evelyn had the kids and would keep them while Terrance went to work tomorrow.

*This is finally it*, Kim thought as she anxiously antici-pated the birth of her nephew. She was definitely excited about becoming an aunt. Wendy was the only means she had of achieving that status, because Terrance was an only child. Kim planned to spoil this child rotten then send him back home to his mother, like Wendy had done with her children.

"I hear you're in quite a bit of pain." Dr. Korva walked into Wendy's room.

"Um-hmm," was all Wendy could manage to say.

"Well, I'll get you checked out and we'll see what we can do for you."

"I'm gonna wait outside for Mama and Gwen," Kim

said, trying to find an excuse to leave the room. She remembered how uncomfortable it had been to have her dilating progress checked during labor when other people were in the room.

Wendy's nod indicated that she understood the real reason behind her sister's exit. Kim gave her sister's hand one last squeeze before leaving. As soon as she walked into the hall, Kim was met by Kevin.

"Hey, how's Wendy doin'?"

"She's in a lot of pain. The doctor is checking to see if she is ready for an epidural, so now is not a good time to go in there. That's why I came out."

"Oh. Well, I'll be right back. I need to go downstairs and use my cell phone. I'm gonna call and leave a message for my secretary so she knows I won't be in tomorrow."

"Okay," Kim said and walked away. *Is it really your secretary you're calling?* she wondered. She hadn't seen Kevin since he'd crashed Wendy's baby shower. She had mixed feelings about him. Yeah, Kevin would be her nephew's father, but it didn't mean she had to be his friend. She had called and told him about Wendy being in labor because it was the right thing to do, considering that it was his child. Plus, she didn't want to hear her mother complain. Kim could hear her now, saying "Two wrongs don't make a right."

"Kim!" a voice yelled from behind. She spun around and saw her mother and Gwen coming up the hall. Both were dressed in sweatpants and T-shirts with night scarves tied around their heads. "So what's happening with Wendy?" Gwen asked.

Kim repeated exactly what she had told Kevin.

"Did you call Kevin like I told you?" Marlene questioned.

"*Yes*, Mother. He's here. In fact, you just missed him. He *said* he was going to call the office and let his secretary know he wouldn't be there tomorrow."

Marlene rolled her eyes at Kim's implication that Kevin was up to something. "He very well may be calling the office. The man does run a business, you know."

Kim didn't respond. Deep down, she knew her mother was right. It was almost midnight and there was no telling how long Wendy would be in labor. Kevin probably had meetings set up for the next day, so it was likely that he would call and make alternate arrangements.

The ladies sat out in the waiting room for a little while and Kim filled them in on all of the details that had brought her and Wendy to the hospital that night. Dr. Korva walked by and recognized Kim sitting in there.

"Your sister has been given an epidural. It's okay to go back in there if you want. She's sleeping, though."

"Okay, thanks," Kim responded. Her mother and Gwen had been at the hospital for about thirty minutes and Kevin was nowhere in sight. *It doesn't take that long to leave a message*, she thought as they headed toward Wendy's room.

Marlene quietly opened the door so she wouldn't wake her daughter. Wendy was now resting very comfortably, thanks to modern medicine. Next to her bed, in the chair Kim had once sat in, was Kevin. He slept also. His body was in the chair but his head rested next to Wendy's stomach.

Kim felt guilty for thinking the worst about him. It looked as though the two were a happy couple awaiting the birth of their first child. However, the three ladies who entered the room knew that things between Wendy and Kevin weren't exactly how they appeared to be. Each of them located a spot on the furniture where they intended to rest until the baby arrived.

⁓

"I still can't believe this," Wendy said. After thirteen hours of labor, she looked at the baby with admiration while the child stared blankly at her face. Kevin, Gwen, Marlene, and Kim all hovered over her shoulders. "You lil' booger, you tricked me." Wendy tugged at the baby's fingers.

"You tricked us all," Gwen cooed at the baby.

"She tricked y'all, not me. I knew it wasn't a boy. I told you that," Marlene said smugly. Her prediction of the baby's sex had overridden that of the obstetrician, who had used high-tech medical equipment.

Wendy and Kim just shook their heads. They knew their mother would gloat about this for years to come. Wendy continued holding the baby even though she knew everyone wanted a turn, especially Kevin. She felt that she had the right to be a little selfish. The pain she had gone through hours ago didn't compare to the joy she felt now that her baby rested in her arms.

"What did you have as a girl's name again?" Gwen asked.

"Maya Nicole, but I'm thinking about something different, so we'll see."

Kevin didn't like the sound of that. He thought they'd committed to naming the baby Maya Nicole if it was a girl. To him, there was nothing left to think about, so why was Wendy having second thoughts? *Forget it. It's not worth arguing about,* he told himself. Although he would be hurt, the baby's name was the least of his problems. Looking at the child, Kevin was even more desperate than ever to put his family back together. He couldn't imagine missing one moment of his daughter's life. Getting Wendy to agree with him would be difficult, considering all that had happened between them.

The nurse who assisted Dr. Korva walked into the room. "What is her name, Mom?" she asked.

"We were just talking about that. I don't know yet."

"Well, can I steal your baby for just a little while? The doctors want to run some tests on her. It's common with all newborns just to make sure they are healthy. I promise it won't take more than a half an hour, if that. Dr. Korva will probably stop in and say good-bye before she leaves."

Wendy nodded her head and handed the baby over to the woman, even though she didn't want to let her go. The nurse placed the infant in the roll-a-way carrier and went out of the room. Kim playfully stuck her bottom lip out like she was pouting. "I want to hold her first when she comes back."

"Well, what about me? I'm the grandmother. I think my rights supercede yours," Marlene said jokingly. She glanced at Kevin, whose demeanor gave away how much he wanted to hold his child. He bit his lip as though he were fighting the urge to say that his rights as the father superceded everyone else's except for Wendy's. "Technically we *should* let Kevin hold her since he *is* the baby's daddy."

*Thank you,* Kevin internally whispered to Marlene.

She winked at him. Marlene had always tried to be a peacemaker. She didn't approve of Kevin having an affair, but that shouldn't mean that his rights as the baby's father should be null and void. Like it or not, he'd be around, so Wendy, Kim, and Gwen had better get used to it. Marlene and Michael had agreed not to discuss their daughter's marriage and not to railroad Kevin.

"Fine, I'll wait until you and Kevin hold her. Gwen can even go in front of me—that way we can save the best for last."

"You can skip me. I don't like holding newborns," Gwen said. She did not have an ounce of insecurity, except when it came to holding newborns. She was fearful of dropping a baby so small.

"Oh that's right—you're scared of babies," Kim recalled.

"I'm not scared of babies." Gwen got defensive. "I just would prefer to wait until she's older."

"That's cool. I'll take your turn." Kim looked at her mother mischievously. "I'll get to hold her twice as long as you 'cuz I have two turns to your one."

Marlene playfully hit Kim. "I'm gonna run and get some coffee while the baby's out. Does anyone want anything?"

Gwen spoke up. "I'll come with you. I want some water."

"The truth is, I wanted to get away by myself for a few moments," Marlene insisted. "I may try to hunt down some of my former colleagues and visit for a few minutes."

"Will you bring me back a bottle of water, then?" Gwen started reaching in her pocket for some money.

"I would like a Coke or a Pepsi." Kevin handed Marlene a twenty-dollar bill. "You can get your coffee, Gwen's water, and whatever Kim wants out of this."

"I don't want anything," Kim said, refusing to allow Kevin to buy his way back into her good graces. Marlene and Gwen both thanked Kevin for his generosity.

Wendy dozed off and Marlene didn't bother asking her if she wanted anything. It was probably too early after giving birth for her to eat or drink anyhow.

"I'll be back." Marlene walked toward the door.

"If you're not here when the baby comes back, you'll lose your turn," Kim teased.

Marlene stuck out her tongue before leaving the room. She felt a slight bit of guilt for leaving under false pretenses. She did intend to see some of her former co-workers, but she was also planning to make a pit stop at the lab to see if, by chance, Mr. Wallace would be there. He must come frequently since he and the nurse seemed to know each other fairly well. Marlene had even tried looking him up in the telephone book. She had found several Harold Wallaces. After calling each one, she discovered none was the Harold Wallace she'd been searching for. If she ever saw him again, she wouldn't hesitate to approach him.

When Marlene had come back from Tennessee after living with her grandmother, she had never expected to see Harold again. She asked her mother about him, but Frances had claimed she didn't know where he was or how to get ahold of him. Marlene was hurt by the fact that he hadn't come by to see her after her daddy died. After all, he was supposed to be one of her parents' closest friends and a surrogate father to her.

"Excuse me," Marlene said as she walked through the door of the lab, past someone who was coming out. She glanced around. No Harold Wallace. Disappointed, she immediately left.

"You're lucky—you came just in time." Kim smiled when Marlene walked back into the room. "Kevin was about to give her up and I was going to take your turn."

"Nuh-uh. Give me my granddaughter." Marlene gave her coffee, Gwen's water, and Kevin's pop and money to Kim while she took the baby from Kevin.

"Mama, make sure you hold her head." Wendy woke up in time to see her mother getting the baby from her husband.

Marlene gave Wendy a look as if to say *Don't start trippin'. I had two kids. I even raised you and you came out all right so apparently I know how to hold a baby.* She put on her cooing voice and talked to her newest grandbaby. "Hey, punkin. How is Gramma's suga-wuga?" Marlene forgot all about her coffee and sat down on the couch talking to the baby.

"So what's up with a name?" Kim asked. "Suga-wuga isn't gonna get it."

"Tell me about it." Wendy hesitated for a moment. "Kevin wanted to name her after his sister, but I came up with another idea," she confessed without looking at Kevin. "I think it'll only be fair if we name her after both of our sisters, not just one."

Kim's face lit up. Wendy couldn't be talking about anyone else but her.

"Her name is going to be Kimberly Maya-Nicole Phillips."

Gwen started laughing. "What ever happened to two middle names being ghetto?" she teased. Wendy once had accused Gwen of being very tacky and ghetto when she named her son Galvin Cortez Vincent Simmons. "It's not natural for children to have more than one middle name," she had said.

Wendy smiled. She had known that her best friend would give her a hard time, and she was prepared. "She only has *one* middle name. It's Maya-Nicole with a hyphen, *not* Maya Nicole."

"Um-hmm. You think you're slick, but either way you spell it, with or without a hyphen, it's still two middle names."

"Wow." Kim had been letting the announcement of her niece's name sink in. "I'm truly honored."

"No, I'm honored to have you as my sister. Thanks for sticking by me. I love you."

"I love you too." Kim gave Wendy a hug. She turned to Marlene, who was still talking gibberish with the baby. "Give her up, Mama. I think my rights supercede yours now that she's my namesake."

Kevin sat quietly in the corner. He was fine with the baby's name. He only wished Wendy had had the courtesy to talk to him about it before making a change. The fact that she hadn't indicated to him how little she valued him as the baby's father.

## Chapter Seventeen
# Whoop-De-Do

WHAT NOW? Wendy thought when the doorbell rang. It had been less than five minutes since her mother, Gwen, and Kim had walked out the door. She figured one of them had forgotten a purse or something. Wendy glanced around the living room to see if she spotted anything that wasn't hers, but she didn't. She hurried to the door to see what they could possibly want.

She loved those three ladies dearly, but they had driven her crazy with all their unwanted parenting advice. Kim and Gwen weren't that bad, although they did sneak in remarks every now and then. Her mother seemed to act like she had an honorary pediatrician's degree.

"It don't hurt them babies to lie on their stomachs. That's how you and your sister were raised and y'all never died of SIDS," Marlene had said earlier. Wendy had ignored her and laid Kimberly on her back as the doctors had recommended.

"That's what's wrong with kids today," her mother had continued. "Too many parents listen to what the so-called experts say and kids grow up out of control. Parents don't want to whup their kids anymore because *they* say it damages a child's self-esteem. When you chastise them while they're young, you won't have many problems when they get older. Common sense will tell you that."

"Mama, what does laying my baby on her back have to do with her growing up out of control?"

"Nothing. I'm just saying that sometimes them doctors don't always know what they are talking about."

"I'm sure they know something—that's why they are called doctors."

"Okay, smarty pants. If they know *so* much, why did you think you were having a boy instead of a girl? I told you it was a girl, but you chose to listen to the doctors. When they tell you not to whup your child, you gonna listen to that too?"

Wendy had rolled her eyes. She had been a mother for only six weeks, and already her mother was getting on her nerves. The correlation between whupings and laying the baby on her stomach didn't make sense. After the three women had walked out the door, Wendy vowed to spend what was left of her Saturday evening peacefully.

Wendy looked through the peephole. *Dang it!* It was Kevin. She opened the door, trying not to let her irritation with his coming by unannounced show.

"Is this a bad time?"

"No, I was just looking forward to relaxing a bit, since I just had company."

"I cannot exactly be considered company, seeing how my name is still on the mortgage," Kevin reminded her. "If you want, I can take the baby off your hands for a few hours."

"No thanks," Wendy snapped, and then realized she had answered him in a sharp manner. "I mean, the baby isn't a problem. I just don't have any breast milk pumped for you to take with you."

"Oh." Kevin sensed that Wendy wasn't ready to be separated from Kimberly. "Would you mind if I hung around here for a few hours so you can take a nap, relax, or do whatever you want to do?"

Wendy was silent.

"Are you going to let me in? It's a little windy out here, you know."

Wendy moved out of the way so Kevin could enter the house. She had nothing against him coming to see Kimberly, though it would have been courteous for him to call first, considering their circumstances.

"Is Kimberly up?"

"No, I just laid her down for a nap about twenty minutes ago. You're welcome to go in her room and see her if you want. Try not to wake her because Mama, Gwen, and Kim were here and they kept her up, so I think she's a little cranky."

Wendy walked with Kevin to the baby's room. Kimberly lay on her back in her bassinet. Kim had been kind enough to redo the room so it would be fit for a baby girl. Originally, the room had been decorated with a sports theme, but now the walls were light purple with a Winnie-the-Pooh border.

Kimberly's little eyes fluttered while she slept. Kevin looked down at his daughter with admiration and fought off the urge to pick her up. "How long do her naps usually last?"

"She'll be asleep for at least another hour or two. If she

doesn't wake up on her own I'll wake her, because I have to feed her anyhow."

"Do you mind if I stay until she wakes up? I would really love to spend time with her." On the other occasions when Kevin had come to visit, Wendy's family had been around. He would be so glad to have a chance to be alone with Kimberly.

"Sure, why not." *What in the world are we supposed to do until she wakes up?* Wendy wondered. Wendy and Kevin really hadn't spent much time together since he'd moved out over nine months ago.

"What were you planning to do before I came?"

"Just relax."

"Do you want to watch a movie or something?"

*No, I don't even want you to be here!* "Sure, why not." Wendy repeated her same dry response.

They walked to the living room. Wendy sat on the couch and stretched out her legs so Kevin couldn't sit directly next to her. As a result, he sat at the opposite end. She began watching something on Lifetime, trying to pretend Kevin wasn't there, but he refused to sit quietly.

"Have you contacted an attorney yet?" he asked, fishing for information.

"About what?" Wendy knew very well that he was referring to their getting a divorce, but she opted to play stupid. She wasn't in the mood for this.

"About us?"

"No. Have you?" she asked.

"No, I wasn't planning to. In fact, I really don't want to."

Wendy flipped through the TV channels. *Here we go. You think having a baby will change my mind. Once a cheater, always a cheater.*

Kevin forcefully moved his wife's feet out of his way so he could sit closer to her. "Wendy?"

"What?"

"I love you."

Before she could stop herself, she said, "I love you too." She hadn't meant to speak out loud. It was a Freudian slip. She did love Kevin, but she couldn't forgive him for what he had done to their relationship. How would she ever be able to trust him again?

Kevin smiled. "You don't know how good it is to hear you say that."

"What I meant is that although we're not together, I still care about you. I hope we can remain civil to one another for Kimberly's sake."

"So that's all you meant, right?"

Wendy was silent.

Kevin shook his head. "I don't know why you have to be so stubborn. So you're trying to say that after all we've been through together, you don't have feelings for me."

"If you would *listen*, that's not what I said. I said that I care for you."

"Do you still love me?"

"Can we not talk about this, please?"

"No, I want to know. Are you still in love with me?"

"All right then, since you have to bring it up." Wendy tried her best to lie: "No."

Kevin laid his head back on the couch. He was hurt and irritated at the same time. "I can't believe that even after reading that letter I gave you months ago, you would still push me away like this."

*Oh, yes, the infamous letter that would explain it all.* In all fairness, she had intended to read it the night he gave it to her, until she'd seen the lie about not cheating on her. She couldn't even remember what she had done with the stupid thing. "You promised that if I read the letter and didn't take you back then you would leave me alone about us getting back together. I read it and I'm not changing my mind."

"I know, but it's just so hard to believe that you would be like this. Did you not believe what I said about Joanne?"

"Who?"

"The lady I told you about in my letter."

"Oh, her." *Why does that name sound familiar?*

"Why didn't you call her and ask her what happened between us? I gave you the number in the letter."

"What do I look like calling the woman my husband had sex with? That's real stupid." Wendy turned off the television and got up from the couch. "I don't want to talk to you about this. All you are doing is getting on my nerves. I'm going to lie down. Why don't you go somewhere and I'll call you when my baby gets up and you can come back and see her." She got up and proceeded to walk down the hall.

"Did you hear what you said? You said *your* baby. Like it or not, she's *our* child. It's about time you start to realize that and quit making decisions concerning her by yourself."

Wendy stopped, turned around, and glared at him with her hand on her hip. Her voice rose. "What in the world are you talking about? I should have the right to make decisions about her. I'm the one raising her, aren't I?"

"But you're not doing it alone. If you think I am going to sit back and be a passive father, think again. I very much intend to have a say in her life. Don't think you're going to keep making all of the decisions."

"What decisions have I made?" Wendy yelled.

Kevin raised his voice. "Like her name, for one."

"What?"

"You heard me. When did we decide that her name would be Kimberly?"

"That's what this is about? Her name? Grow up. I don't have time for this." Wendy turned and continued walking. Kevin jumped up from the couch, ran in front of her, and grabbed her by the arms.

"Make time," he said angrily. Truthfully, he had gotten over the name incident. It was hearing Wendy say that she no longer loved him that had incited this set of emotions. He wanted his wife back.

"Get off of me!" Wendy struggled to get free from his grip.

"I'm sorry." Kevin loosened his hands after realizing what he had done. "I just . . . I have lost you. I don't want to lose her, too."

Wendy's temper flared. He had some nerve, grabbing hold of her like she was a child. "You should have thought about that before you cheated on me!"

"Oh, so now you want to use her as leverage to get back at me?" He continued blocking the hall so Wendy could not walk by.

"I'm not using anyone."

"Then what do you call all this?" he asked, pointing around the house. "I feel like nothing more than a pimp. You treat me more like your suga' daddy than your husband."

"Whatever, Kevin. Move out of my way." Wendy pushed him to the side and walked past him.

"It's true. I'm good enough to pay the mortgage, give you money to go toward the baby and yourself, but you can't have a conversation with me for more than a few minutes. Yet you seem like you get an attitude when I don't call before coming to see *my* daughter."

Wendy turned to respond. "You are the one who said you would do those things. I never made you."

"Yeah, but you took advantage of me. You knew that I wouldn't let you and the baby struggle for anything."

Kimberly started crying.

"Whoop-de-do. Do you expect to receive a Father of the Year award or something? Take your house, take your money, take whatever. But know one thing: Me and *my* baby will survive with or without your help."

Kevin stood there and watched Wendy walk into the nursery and slam the door. In frustration, he hit the wall with his fist before going back into the living room. He kicked the coffee table, and the two-thousand-dollar porcelain lamp shattered when it hit the floor. Kevin grabbed his keys and stormed out of the house.

# Chapter Eighteen
## Nothing to Lose

I'LL TAKE A HEINEKEN, PLEASE," a distraught Kevin said to the bartender at the club. Once he received his drink, Kevin laid a hundred-dollar bill on the table. "Keep the change," he said, and turned to face the dance floor.

He took a long gulp of his drink. It burned a little on the way down, but after a few more swigs he'd get used to it. This particular dance club wasn't one of his regular hangouts, but he had heard a lot about it. Wendy would never listen to him long enough to find out that he had stopped hanging around the people he used to, and he didn't drink, smoke, or party any longer. Tonight was the first night he was having a drink in several months. It also was the first drink he had ever paid a hundred dollars for. Money meant nothing to him tonight. He would happily lose all of his money if it meant that he could get his wife back.

*Face it, Kevin: you messed up. She's not going to take you back, so you need to get over her and move on with your life.*

With the exception of going to church, he had made all the changes Wendy had been nagging him to make. Now he felt a day late and a dollar short. If only the changes had been made before she'd confronted him about having chlamydia. *It doesn't matter now,* Kevin thought to himself. *My marriage is over.* He gulped down the beer before ordering another one.

"Hello, how are you?" a sultry, smooth voice said as she sat down on the empty bar stool next to him.

"Terrible." Kevin snickered.

"C'mon, things can't be that bad."

"Easy for you to say. Can I buy you a drink?"

"Sure. I'll have a piña colada."

Kevin motioned for the bartender. "Can you get the lady a piña colada, and a rum and Coke for me, please?"

"Comin' right up," the bartender said.

"Thank you."

"No problem."

"By the way, my name is Renée." She held out her hand and smiled.

"Oh, I'm sorry. I guess I should have introduced myself, huh? I'm Kevin."

They shook hands. "Very nice to meet you, Kevin."

"You too."

Kevin laid another hundred-dollar bill on the counter when the bartender returned with the drinks. "Keep the change." He downed the rest of his second beer before giving Renée her drink and taking his.

"Thank you." She took a sip of her cocktail. She had spotted him when he first walked into the club and was immediately attracted to him. She had doubted he would give her the time of day, but he had, and she was enjoying the attention. Her cheek-length hair was pulled back on the sides with barrettes. It used to be shorter, but she'd let it grow out over the summer. Her tight shirt and pants showed off every curve of her tall, slender frame. "So do you want to talk about whatever is bothering you?"

Kevin shook his head. "There's no point." He began drinking his rum and Coke.

"You know you can always dance your sorrows away rather than drink them away," she said, flirting.

"You know what? That might not be a bad idea," Kevin considered. Why shouldn't he dance with a pretty girl? He'd been accused by Wendy of doing much more.

Renée fluttered inside. She didn't know exactly what was bothering him, but she knew that at least for the moment, she would be the distraction he needed. They finished their drinks and then proceeded to the dance floor.

Just as they were starting to dance, the DJ announced that the next song would be an oldie-but-goodie. The song: "Computer Love" by Zapp and Roger. Renée pressed her body up against Kevin's, and the two danced like they were the only ones in the room. It had been a very long time since Kevin had been this close to any woman. He was definitely turned on by the beautiful Nubian princess he held in his arms.

They danced a couple more songs before going back to the bar. They spent the evening talking and laughing. Renée provided a great ending to Kevin's tumultuous day.

Before the night was over, she managed to convince Kevin that they should exchange telephone numbers, although he was reluctant to at first.

⌒

"Hello?" Kevin didn't recognize the strange number on the caller ID of his cell phone at three in the morning. It hadn't been long since he got back from the club. He'd had only enough time to take a quick shower, turn off the lights, and hop into bed before the phone rang.

"I'm sorry. I hoped you were still up," the woman said.

"Who is this?"

"Renée."

"Oh, hey, what's up? I wasn't sleeping."

"I'm sorry. I know it's probably tacky for a woman to call a man—especially this late."

"No, you're fine. You just caught me off guard, that's all. It doesn't bother me that you called."

"Good. I just wanted to say how much I enjoyed your company tonight. I hope to see you again."

"Uhh . . . there's something I think you should know."

"What's that?"

"I'm married."

"Oh." She sounded surprised.

"But my wife and I are separated. Looks like we're heading down the road of divorce, but no one has made the first move."

"So what are you saying?" she inquired. "Does this mean you don't want me to call you anymore?"

"No, I'm not saying that at all. I don't want to mislead you into thinking that there will be more to us than there can be. Truth is, I still love my wife. If I could, I would be with her now. Normally I'm not that outgoing with women at clubs, but tonight was a rough night for me. My wife shut me down and I guess I just needed to let out some frustration."

"Well, I hope you enjoyed yourself, at least."

"Of course I did."

"Maybe we can do it again sometime. I am really interested in you, but I understand where you are coming from. We can be friends, can't we?"

"No doubt."

"Well, friends it is." Renée really had her hopes set on something more, but she wouldn't press her luck. Besides, if he really was getting a divorce, it would only be a matter of time before their friendship went to another level.

They continued their phone conversation for a long time. When Kevin looked at the clock again, it was almost five. Now that he lived separate from Wendy, he didn't have to worry about her yelling at him to get up and go to church in the morning. He couldn't believe he and Renée had shared such an intense yet intriguing phone conversation. He had enjoyed it. They talked about everything from his marriage to her career goals. To his surprise, he had told her everything about what happened to split him and Wendy up.

*Maybe exchanging numbers with Renée wasn't a bad idea after all.* He pondered this after they had finally gotten off the phone. She seemed like a very nice person and even though he was married, Kevin could not deny the fact that she was gorgeous. Talking to her couldn't damage his marriage any further; he was already on the verge of losing it all. There was nothing more to lose.

# Chapter Nineteen
## Four-Letter Word

T EARS WELLED UP in Kim's eyes as she listened to the special news report on the television.

"A man walked into the Mid-Western Steel Plant and fired a semiautomatic, killing over twenty-eight people and wounding several others before turning the gun on himself. Columbus police are not certain as to what led forty-nine-year-old Victor Davis to this point. Investigators say that when they went to his home, they found his wife and three children shot to death in the basement. At this point, CPD is not sure whether it was Mr. Davis who shot his family. Sources reveal that Mr. Davis had gotten laid off at the plant several months ago. However, CPD has not yet confirmed these allegations. Ballistics will determine whether the bullets found in the victims at the plant match those found in the suspect's dead wife and children. We'll give more information on this story as details become available."

Kim sat there in despair thinking about the lives of all those individuals who, without warning, had been snatched away. She had never thought much about death before, but in a world where so many people were dying so needlessly, Kim couldn't help but wonder about the condition of their souls. Had they gone to heaven or hell? More importantly, would she go to heaven or hell if her life was suddenly taken away? It was a scary thought, yet it was a question that would inevitably be answered one day.

"Hello?" She wiped her eyes as she answered the phone.

"Hey, sorry I'm just now calling you back. I was out all day yesterday." It was Wendy.

"Why didn't you go to church?"

"I was going to, but your niece kept me up most of the night on Saturday, so I slept in."

"Oh." Yesterday wasn't the first time Wendy had missed church. There had been several occasions when she was a no-show, which was abnormal since she was usually zealous about going. Each time she had used now three-month-old Kimberly as an excuse. It was interesting how the baby never caused Wendy to miss a hair appointment or a meeting with her personal trainer. She'd even skipped out on last month's Soul Sistas meeting held at night because Kimberly had been fussy all day. Kim had gone to that one by herself.

"What did you want?" Wendy asked.

"Nothing, I just wanted to see why you didn't come to church, that's all. Mama asked about you."

"Dang. What, are y'all on pew patrol?" Wendy kidded. "Truthfully, I probably could have come, but then Nat called and wanted to know if the baby and I wanted to go shopping, so we did."

"What did you buy?"

"Girl, some of everything—jewelry, clothes, shoes, handbags. I went from one department to another in Nordstrom. I bought a few things for Kimberly, but nothing big. She still got clothes that she hasn't worn yet. I told Natalie that, but she insisted on buying an outfit for her anyway. It's cute. I can't wait to show it to you."

"Umph."

"Don't start."

"Start what?"

"I know that you and Gwen have your hang-ups about Natalie, but that's not going to stop me from talking to her."

"Nobody said you had to."

"Anyhow, the outfit Nat bought is really cute. I'm sure both godmothers would approve of her taste."

Kim didn't feel like talking about Natalie. "Did you see the news?"

"No, why?"

"This man walked into a plant and killed twenty-eight people and shot some more."

"Really?"

"Yeah, they also said that his wife and kids were found dead in the basement of his home. They don't know yet if he did it."

"See, that's why I don't watch the news too often. It's too depressing."

"But don't you think it's scary that your life can be over within minutes?"

"Yeah I guess, but when it's time to go, then it's time. There's pretty much nothing that can be done about it."

"Doesn't it make you wonder about—" Kim heard the sound of glass shattering through the telephone. What startled her was not the glass breaking, but Wendy's reaction. For the first time in her life, Kim heard Wendy utter a four-letter word. "Wendy!" Kim said in disbelief.

"What?" responded a voice of frustration.

"Are you okay? I've never heard you talk like that before." It was as if Wendy had spoken a foreign language. Kim had stopped swearing months ago, after Tori had conned her into going to church.

"Sorry. I was getting some water and accidentally knocked the glass off the counter."

"Okay, but is it really that serious?"

Kimberly started crying in the background.

"Great," Wendy belted. "Look, girl, I gotta clean up this mess. I'll talk to you later," she said before hanging up the phone, leaving Kim bewildered.

If it had been someone other than Wendy, Kim would not have been so taken aback. To Kim's knowledge, Wendy had never sworn before. In fact, whenever Kim would curse around her sister, Wendy would get offended and politely tell Kim that she needed to "watch her mouth." Now it seemed like the roles had been reversed, except Kim wasn't offended, she was shocked. So much so that she held the phone in her hand for a moment as she reflected on what had happened. To Kim, Wendy's swearing and then being nonchalant about it was an obvious sign that her relationship with God wasn't as strong as it used to be.

## Chapter Twenty

## *Just Friends?*

LOOKING FOR SOMEONE SPECIAL?" Renée whispered in Kevin's ear when she walked up behind him at the Bar and Grill Restaurant.

"There you are." Kevin beamed and put his arm around her shoulder. "I was starting to think you stood me up."

"You should know I wouldn't do that to you." She smiled. "My mother's doctor appointment ran later than I thought it would."

"Ma'am?" Kevin motioned to the hostess. "My guest is here. Can we have a table for two, nonsmoking, please?"

The restaurant was pretty busy that afternoon. Dozens of mini-conversations overshadowed the music playing in the background. Kevin helped Renée off with her suede coat after they were led to a booth.

"You look nice." He complimented her on her hip-hugger jeans and baby-blue cashmere sweater. Since they first met her hair had grown longer, and she was now able to pull it back into a ponytail.

"Thanks." She sat down. "I was surprised that you wanted to come here for lunch."

"Why?"

Renée shrugged her shoulders. "With you being at work, I guess I figured you would want to go somewhere more formal. I didn't think you would be dressed casually."

Kevin, dressed in a pair of khaki pants and plain polo shirt, looked down at his attire. "Are you implying that there is something wrong with the way I am dressed?" he kidded.

"No, not at all." Renée blushed.

"Actually, I am usually so busy that I normally don't have time to go out to lunch unless I'm going with a client and it's part of the business transaction."

"What happened to change the routine today?"

"You—and the fact that today was dress-down day. We sort have a tradition in my office of wearing jeans the Friday before a holiday week. Since next week is Thanksgiving, today is dress-down day."

The waitress walked up to the table. "Are you all ready to order or do you need more time?"

"Oops. We haven't even looked at the menu. I'm sorry— can we have a few more minutes?" Renée requested.

"Sure, no problem. Can I get you something to drink?"

"May I have a glass of water for now—with no lemon?" Renée asked.

"I'll take a Coke, please," Kevin stated.

The woman scribbled on her order pad and placed it back in her apron. "Okay, I'll be back shortly with your drinks," she said before walking away.

Both Kevin and Renée picked up their menus. After discussing several items that looked good, they decided to order separate entrées and share them. The waitress came back with their drinks, took their orders, and left again. Renée decided to pick up on their previous conversation.

"You were saying that you have dress-down Fridays before holiday weeks."

"Uh-huh."

"Sounds like you're a pretty nice boss."

"I try to be. Who knows what they say about me when I'm not around." He took a sip of his Coke. "What are your plans for Thanksgiving?"

"Since my mom is sick, I'll cook dinner. My mom's boyfriend will most likely come over and eat with us."

"My mother, brother, and his wife are supposed to fly in from Philly so they can see my daughter. She's four months old and my family has never seen her except through a few pictures my wife gave me."

"Do you have a picture of her with you?"

"Yeah, I do." Kevin reached in his back right pocket and pulled out his wallet.

Renée couldn't help but notice the wad of cash he had.

"This is my baby girl. Her name is Kimberly Maya-Nicole."

"Oh, she is so beautiful." Renée gazed at the picture of Kimberly in a red and black velvet dress.

"Thanks. *Supposedly* my wife is going to allow me to get her on Thanksgiving so my family can see her."

"Why do you say it like that?" She picked up on Kevin's uncertainty about the arrangements.

"I don't know. I guess I'm afraid she'll change her mind at the last minute because it's a major holiday. I'm thinking about going to Philadelphia for Christmas instead of hanging out here by myself. I know she won't let me take the baby there." He placed the wallet back in his pocket.

"You do have the right to see your daughter, you know. Especially since you're paying virtually all of the bills and she's not teaching anymore."

"How did you know she was a teacher?"

"You told me," Renée said quickly. "Duh? How else would I know?"

"Yeah, well she has savings from when we were together, mutual funds, and stuff like that. But you are right. I am paying for everything."

"It doesn't bother you that she's basically being kept?" Renée asked with a twinge of jealousy.

Kevin was silent at first. "Initially it did, but now I try to think of it as I'm doing it more for my daughter rather than her. Wendy's a good mother and as long as she continues to be, I'll be able to deal with the rest. Would you believe that tomorrow will be the first time since my daughter has been born that I will have her overnight?"

"You can't be serious."

Kevin nodded. "Yep. I am. Normally, I visit her at the house. Wendy has never let me keep her for more than a few hours at a time. But it's cool. I get her tomorrow and hopefully again on Thanksgiving, so I won't complain."

"What's so special about tomorrow?" Renée asked curiously.

"Honestly, I don't think she had any other choice. Her sister is getting married next year and they're going shopping for wedding dresses. I think her mother is going also."

Renée paused to consider her words carefully. "How are

things going between you and Wendy?"

"Cordial. We haven't had any arguments since the one we had the night I met you awhile back. I decided that I am going to leave her alone about getting back together. That's what she wants, so I have no other choice."

"Which one of you will make the first step?" She was referring to the divorce and Kevin knew it. She had been advising him that it was not healthy to hang on to a dead-end relationship. She didn't like it when Kevin mentioned still having feelings for his wife. It made her a little resentful toward Wendy.

"I don't know. I guess we'll just take it one day at a time."

At that moment their lunch was brought to the table and the two enjoyed a wonderful meal together without any further talk of Kevin's marriage.

⌒

"Thanks for lunch," Renée turned and said to Kevin after being escorted to her car. Standing so close to him caused her body temperature to rise despite the cold air.

"My pleasure. I enjoyed your company." The chilly wind formed a cloud around his words and the mist came so close to Renée's mouth that a bystander would not have known which one of them actually spoke.

"I expect to see you tonight," she stated, referring to the club that had been their weekly hangout since they met.

"Of course you will," he responded.

"You know I may get a little jealous watching you

dance with other women." Renée spoke softly and smoothly. Kevin kept his eyes on her luscious lips, which were very tempting for him to kiss. He fought the temptation by backing up from her a little, although he didn't think she would oppose if he had tried.

"How can I make you jealous if we're just friends?" he playfully challenged her.

They hugged and Kevin closed the door when Renée finally slipped inside.

He was trying hard to maintain a platonic relationship with her, at least until he knew for sure when his marriage with Wendy would be over. However, he could not deny the attraction between the two of them. Being a man of his word, he promised himself that he would wait until one relationship was over before getting into another one. That was how he got in the mess with Wendy in the first place. Kevin wasn't about to make the same mistake twice.

# Chapter Twenty-One
## Lady and the Tramp

GWEN IS IN THE BACK WAITING FOR YOU. She said to tell you as soon as you came in," one of the ladies who worked in the hair salon said to Kim the moment she walked through the door.

"Okay," Kim responded. Before going to the back, she checked the appointment book. *Whew.* She was relieved to see that she hadn't missed any scheduled appointments. Even when she was with a client, Gwen would excuse herself for a moment and request a meeting in the backroom whenever any of the stylists missed appointments. She did not believe in reprimanding her workers in front of each other or in front of clients. Since Kim had never been summoned to the back before, her first instinct was to think she had done something wrong when her co-worker relayed Gwen's message with such urgency.

"Hey, you wanted to see me?" Kim said to Gwen.

Gwen was putting towels up on the shelves, but when she saw Kim she stopped and turned with a serious look on her face. "Shut the door." The bright smile that usually greeted everyone she came in contact with had faded.

"O-kay," Kim said slowly. She took off her coat and hung it up on the coatrack. "What's going on?"

"You will never believe who I saw last night at Maxine's." Gwen referred to a popular dance club.

Kim scrunched up her face. "Since when did you start hanging out down there?" Nothing was wrong with Maxine's, but whenever Gwen and Kim used to go out together, Gwen never wanted to go there. She preferred another popular club on the north side, and that was where they always hung out.

Gwen rolled her eyes. "Girl, believe me, it wasn't my idea. That's Anthony's spot."

"Who's Anthony?"

"The guy I went on a date with last night."

"Uhhhh . . ." Kim said with a slur and sly smile. "I haven't heard you mention him before. When did you meet him?"

"Honestly, I just met him last night. It was sort of a blind date as a favor to my cousin, who is dating his brother. Don't worry. We didn't hit it off. You won't hear me mention him again."

Kim laughed. That was a typical Gwen statement. When she was through dealing with any man, she was through and never sailed backwards.

"Anyhow, I'll tell you about him later. That's not why I wanted to talk to you. I saw Kevin at the club last night."

Kim shrugged her shoulders. "What's so special about that?" It was no secret that one of the problems with

Kevin's and Wendy's marriage was the fact that he hung out a lot.

Gwen lowered her voice. "Would you believe he was dancing with Natalie?"

"*No!*" Kim's eyes grew bigger.

"*Yes!*" Gwen said angrily. "I wish you had seen the way she was hugged all up on him. It was almost as if she had to be peeled off."

"Nuh-uh."

"She was on him like white on rice." Gwen shook her head as though she were trying to erase the image from her mind.

"Did she see you?"

"No. I don't think she or Kevin saw me. I wish I had said something to her last night, though. I could just kick myself because I didn't. I couldn't do anything without Dumbo following me around."

"Who's that, Anthony?"

"Yeah. I went to the bathroom. When I came out, this fool was waiting for me outside the door. He was relentless." Gwen looked disgusted, as if she were reliving last night's event.

"Did it look like Natalie and Kevin came together?"

"No, I guess not, since they both danced with other people. Plus, I saw Kevin leave like an hour before she did, but they sure had a few side conversations off the dance floor."

"Are you going to tell Wendy?"

"I don't know. Do you think I should? She seems a little edgy lately. I don't want to upset her unnecessarily."

"I know what you mean. Did I ever tell you she cussed?"

"Quit lyin'." Gwen was shocked.

Kim raised her right hand in the air. "Honest to God, I'm tellin' the truth."

"What happened?"

Kim quickly recapped the day when she'd spoken with Wendy and Wendy had sworn after dropping a glass.

"I can't believe it." Gwen shook her head. Like Kim, she had never heard Wendy come close to swearing in the twenty-something years they had been friends. Gwen might swear occasionally, but not like she did in high school. Still, Wendy was always determined not to succumb to using foul language. "Naw, I don't think she needs to know about Natalie and Kevin, at least not yet."

Kim nodded in agreement. "I agree. If his only crime was dancing, then we're all guilty. When I used to go out, I danced with other people besides Terrance even if he was there."

"True. Me too. But I seriously doubt you danced with other men the way Natalie was dancing with Kevin last night. As a matter of fact, I *know* you wouldn't do that and neither would I. I may start popping up at Maxine's to see if they are ever like that again."

"You know if she sees you, she won't dance like that with him, especially knowing he's Wendy's husband."

"Yeah, you're right. I guess that won't really work. I do know someone needs to keep an eye on her, though. I know for a fact that she doesn't mind going behind her friends."

Gwen was referring to the incident that happened between Natalie and Charlene, a former friend of theirs from high school. Natalie had starting dating Charlene's ex-boyfriend three weeks after he and Charlene broke up.

Fortunately, Charlene could have cared less. She said that if Natalie liked garbage then she could pick up her trash. Although Natalie apologized to Charlene after the relationship with her ex didn't go anywhere, Gwen believed Natalie was sorrier that the relationship hit a dead end than she was about betraying her friend.

"Excuse me." The backroom's door opened and Denise, who had delivered Gwen's message to Kim earlier, poked her head through the door. "Kim, your nine-o'clock appointment is here."

"Okay, thanks. I'll be right up."

Denise shut the door.

"You had me thinkin' I messed up this morning the way she said that you wanted to see me. She jumped down my throat as soon as I came in."

Gwen laughed. "My fault. I probably did seem sort of hysterical. I was eager to tell you about last night."

"Thanks for telling me. Don't forget I'm leavin' early today. I just have this appointment and one more, then I'm gone."

"Oh, that's right. You're going to look for wedding dresses today, aren't you?"

"Um-hmm. My mom, Evelyn, and Wendy will all be there." Kim was silent. "I wish you were able to come with us."

"So do I, but I have to close up the shop today because no one else was available. There's a cost to being the boss." Gwen always planned her Saturday events around the schedule of her employees. If they couldn't close, she didn't have a choice. "Call me and let me know what you find. If you see a dress for me, let me know and I'll go and check it out."

"I will." Terrance and Kim had decided to have only one person stand up for them. His best man was going to be his cousin. However, Gwen would still participate in the wedding as the soloist. Among her other qualities, Gwen had the voice of an angel. Kim opened the door to go out. "If I don't call you tonight, I'll give you a call after church tomorrow."

"All right. Tell everyone I said hi. Tell Wendy to call me too." Gwen paused for a moment. "Truthfully, I don't know what your sister sees in Natalie. I never understood it. They make an odd pair of friends. I think of them as Lady and the Tramp. Wendy's the lady and that other thing is the tramp."

Both Gwen and Kim laughed. "You're silly," Kim said as she walked out of the room.

# Chapter Twenty-Two
## *Whooo?*

HEY, EVERYONE." A cheerful Natalie walked up to the ladies at the bridal store.

"Hello." Evelyn spoke to be courteous, but she had no idea who this woman was.

"Hi, Natalie. How are you?" Marlene asked.

"I'm fine, thanks."

"Natalie, you remember Evelyn, don't you? Kim's future mother-in-law."

Both Natalie and Evelyn exchanged weird looks. Neither of them recalled meeting before.

"Oh, that's right." Marlene corrected herself. "I was thinking that you two met at Wendy's baby shower, but, Evelyn, I forgot you were out of town that weekend. Natalie is one of Wendy's best friends."

"Hi, nice to meet you," Natalie said, and extended her hand.

"You too," Evelyn responded.

"Kim, you didn't tell me Natalie was coming," Marlene said to her daughter.

"That's because Kim didn't know." Kim intentionally referred to herself in the third person.

*Yikes.* Evelyn tried to keep a straight face after sensing the sarcasm in Kim's response.

"Has Wendy gotten here yet?" Natalie asked Marlene, searching for her comfort zone.

"No, she should be on her w—"

Wendy came rushing up to them. "Sorry I'm late, guys. I was waiting on Kimberly to get picked up."

"Did everything go okay?" Marlene asked.

"Yes. Her dad was just running a little behind, that's all."

"Hey, Nat."

"What's up?" Natalie was glad to see Wendy's smiling face.

"Hi, Evelyn. It's so good to see you!" Wendy hugged her.

"You too, sweetie. How is the baby?"

"She's doing really good. She's a chubby little thing."

"I know. Kim gave me the pictures you sent. Thank you."

"You're welcome. She's only four months and already weighs sixteen and a half pounds."

"Are you serious? She certainly is a doll baby. You need to bring her by sometime to see me."

"I will, I promise," Wendy assured her. "You're looking good, as always."

"Oh, bless your heart. Thank you," Evelyn said humbly. As usual, she wasn't dressed as casually as everyone else. Evelyn's idea of "dressing down" was a pair of slacks and a nice shirt, which most people would call business-casual attire. "You look great yourself. I can't even tell that you had a baby."

"I've been trying. I owe all the credit to my personal trainer and those kick-boxing classes he has me taking." Wendy turned to Kim. She could tell by the look on her sister's face that Kim was not happy. "Uh . . . Can you come with me for a minute, please?" Wendy grabbed Kim by the arm. "Excuse us for just a moment," she said to her mother, her friend, and Evelyn. She and Kim walked to another part of the store.

When Wendy let go, Kim stared at her sister with her arms folded. She didn't have to say a word; her demeanor said it all. "Before you get all bent out of shape, I didn't invite Natalie here," Wendy explained.

"So tell me how she knew where to come, then."

"Listen, she called me this morning and said that she wouldn't be able to come over tonight as we had planned. She asked if we could do something earlier today."

"Um-hmmm."

"I told her no because I was meeting you here today to look for stuff for your wedding. Next thing I knew, she said she would try and meet me here. I didn't know what to say, honestly."

Marlene, Natalie, and Evelyn observed the way Kim was standing. No one said anything, but everyone pretty much figured that Wendy was explaining Natalie's presence. "So, Natalie, how long have you and Wendy known each other?" Evelyn asked, trying to strike up a conversation so they were not just staring at the two sisters.

"I've known her since high school."

"Oh, so you must also know Gwen?"

Natalie didn't like the fact that Gwen's name was being mentioned, but she swallowed her pride and said yes.

"I have known Wendy and Kim since they were young girls," said Evelyn.

"What about us?" Kim heard their names mentioned as they were walking back to where everyone was. She sounded normal.

"Evelyn was just telling Natalie that she has known you and your sister for a while." Marlene looked at her watch. "I think you better tell the lady that we're ready now."

Kim went to find the woman with whom she had set the appointment. She wasn't thrilled about Natalie being there, especially after what Gwen had told her this morning. However, she wasn't going to let it ruin her day. They had a long day ahead of them, as Kim had made appointments at several other bridal shops as well.

"She wants us," Evelyn said to everyone after she noticed Kim motioning to them. They walked over to where she was standing. Beside her was a woman who favored the actress who played Janet from the television show *Three's Company*, with her dark hair and round face.

The bridal consultant introduced herself with a bright smile. "Hi, I'm Amy."

Everyone said hello.

"As I was telling Kim, I want to concentrate on finding her something first. You all are welcome to look around for dresses that interest you or you can help find something nice for her."

"I want to help her look," Wendy said.

"Me too," both Marlene and Evelyn agreed. Natalie was silent.

"I don't know, Mama," Kim kidded. "I've seen some of those dresses you pointed out in the catalogs—they weren't too attractive."

"Oh shut up. You keep messin' with me and I'll wear one of them myself."

Amy laughed with everyone else. She had no idea what

style of dresses Marlene had picked out, but she had worked with numerous brides-to-be and the majority of them had ideas that varied drastically from their mothers'. "Well, how about this? Before we get started, Kim can give everyone a rundown of the kind of dress she's most interested in, and that way we'll have a guideline and pick out stuff that she'll have a better chance of liking."

Kim thought the idea was perfect and gave a general overview of what she was looking for. The next two hours were spent with Kim trying on one dress after another. She intended to wear a white dress and wanted purple and silver as her wedding colors. Wendy found a purple dress that she considered buying at that particular store. Marlene and Evelyn, who would be wearing silver, also found dresses that interested them. However, everyone agreed that it would be better to look around at the other shops first in case they found something better.

While everyone looked for dresses, per Kim's suggestion, Natalie was stuck with baby-sitting the purses and coats. If Natalie had to be there, Kim was determined to find something useful to do with her and keep her out of the way.

⁓

"You're back!" Amy said in a high-pitched voice. She was happy to see Kim and her family return to the store. It had been several hours since they had left, but they had asked her to hold all the dresses they liked and said they would come back if they couldn't find anything else. They even had allowed her to take their measurements earlier. Their return ensured her commission.

"We came to narrow down our choices," Kim said. She was worn out, hungry, and ready to select her wedding gown.

"Follow me." Amy signaled for everyone to walk back to the dressing rooms. "I may have to go back and forth between you and another lady who has an appointment in a few minutes," she turned and said to Kim.

"That's fine. I understand."

The shop had gotten busier while they were gone. Fortunately there were enough rooms available for each lady to try things on at the same time. Marlene, Evelyn, and Wendy were at the opposite end of the hall from Kim, who was able to get a very large dressing room specifically for brides-to-be.

"Natalie, can you come help me zip up this dress?" Kim yelled out to the waiting room.

Natalie jumped at the opportunity. It was about the most excitement she had experienced all day. She knocked on Kim's door. "It's Nat."

Kim let her in. "Oooh, I like that," Natalie said after seeing the gown Kim had on.

"Really?"

"Yeah. I think you should get it."

Kim agreed. She had seen no other dress that could compare with this one. She turned and faced the mirror so Natalie could zip up the back. "So tell me about Kevin." She'd been waiting for the opportunity to confront her all day. Now she finally had her chance.

"Whooo?" Natalie was blindsided by the question.

"Whooo?" Kim raised her eyebrows and imitated Natalie. "You sound like an owl."

Natalie felt extremely uncomfortable and realized that Kim didn't necessarily want her help with the wedding dress; she wanted an interrogation. "I—I'm not sure what you're talking about," she responded cautiously.

"Yeah, I bet." Kim sneered and turned from the mirror to face Natalie, who was quite a few inches taller than she. "I'm talking about the guy you were plastered all over at Maxine's last night. Tall, dark, handsome real estate investor. You know Kevin, otherwise known as my sister's husband."

"Look, I don't know what you're talking about. I dance with a lot of guys when I go out. If I was dancing with Wendy's husband, I didn't know. I've never met him, so how would I know it was him?"

"But I know you have seen him. You were there when he came over to my mother's house the day of her baby shower. And if I'm not mistaken, you commented on how *fine* he was."

"Do you know how long ago that was?" Natalie said defensively. "I don't remember what he looked like."

Kim just looked at her. Maybe Natalie was telling the truth. Kim didn't know what to think, but she would sure make it clear that Natalie needed to stay away from him.

"I swear to you, I don't even remember meeting anyone last night whose name was Kevin." Natalie appeared to be hurt by the fact that she was being accused of betraying Wendy.

"Maybe, but I know that someone *did* see you with him. Be more selective about who you talk to. If you're spotted with him again, I will make sure my sister finds out."

"Hey, are you done yet?" Wendy knocked on the door. "We're all waiting to see which dress you decided on."

Kim gave Natalie one last look of warning before step-ping outside of the room.

The gown she had selected was a very fitted, long dress with wide straps. It was satin with an overlay of sheer lace. The lace was decorated with clear sequins in various places, even on the train. Marlene, Wendy, and Evelyn agreed that she looked gorgeous in it. It was the perfect dress to fit her slender, petite frame.

After the long, tiring day, they were all ready to eat. They decided to go to one of the nearby restaurants. How-ever, Natalie declined. Kim had offended her, and she didn't think she would be able to enjoy herself. Plus, she had other plans for the evening. She said good-bye to everyone and headed in the opposite direction.

⸺

Kevin answered his phone. "Hello?"

"So how are Daddy and baby doing?" It was Renée.

"Hey, we're doing pretty good. She's demanding all of my attention, but that's cool, though. What are you up to?"

"Nothing. I'm on my way back home. I was out with some friends earlier."

"Are you going to the club tonight?"

"Naw, I'm sort of getting tired of that place."

"What? That's surprising. I thought Maxine's was your spot."

"It was, but . . ." Renée was silent for a moment. "I guess it's just doing the same thing and seeing the same people week after week that's getting old to me."

"So are you gonna take up sewing or something like that?" Kevin kidded.

Renée laughed. "You're so silly. I don't know what I'm going to do. I would like to come and see your baby tonight, if you don't mind." Truthfully, she could care less about visiting the baby. Saying she wanted to see Kimberly was an excuse to spend time with Kevin.

"I don't know if that'll be a good idea," he admitted.

"Why not?"

"Because . . ."

"Because you think that I'm gonna try and seduce you or something?"

"I just don't want either one of us to do something we might regret, that's all."

"Kevin, I know you're married and that you still have feelings for your wife, but I would be lying if I said that I didn't find you attractive."

"Same here."

"If things were different, I would like to be more than just your friend, but right now, I'll take whatever I can get. If all you have to offer currently is friendship, then friendship it is."

"You're certainly being very candid tonight. Is everything okay? You sound a little frustrated."

"Everything's fine. I wish you would trust me and stop thinking that my goal is to try to get you in bed."

"Look, I didn't mean to offend you. I just want to make it clear that I do not intend to get involved with anyone until my wife and I have signed our divorce papers."

"I *know.*"

"Well, if you know, then quit trippin' and come on over."

"Really?" Renée was excited. "You'll have to tell me

how to get there. It'll be a minute, though, 'cuz I wanna go take a shower and change clothes first. I've been out all day."

"Okay, but wear some sweats and a big T-shirt. Don't come over in your lil' tight jeans and shirt or I won't let you in," he teased.

"Oh you'll let me in, 'cuz you know you want to see me," she responded seductively. It didn't matter what she wore, Kevin would still find her attractive, and she knew that.

Kevin gave Renée directions to his apartment. "I got another call comin' in so I'll see you when you get here," he said after hearing a beep.

"Okay."

Kevin clicked over and Wendy was on the other line. "Hi, how's the baby doing?"

"She's fine. How'd it go today?"

"Good. We all found our dresses."

"That's good."

"Are you sure you want her overnight?"

"Yes, I'm sure. She's fine, Wendy. I won't let anything happen to her."

"I know. Give her a kiss for me."

"I will."

# Chapter Twenty-Three
## Wishes Do Come True

"HI, IS THIS PAT?" Wendy asked the woman who answered Kevin's phone.

"Yes, it is."

"This is Wendy," she said to Kevin's mom.

"Hello, how are you doing?"

"I'm fine, thank you. How about yourself?"

"I'm doing pretty good. I'm enjoying spending time with Kimberly. She's as cute as she wants to be."

"Thank you."

"Kevin keeps telling me that I'm gonna have her too spoiled 'cuz the minute she looks like she gonna cry, I'm picking her up."

"Uh-oh. I bet she's lovin' that."

"Oh, I tell you, she is absolutely adorable. I wish I could take her back to Philadelphia with me. Did Kevin tell you that Kyle's wife is pregnant?"

"No, I didn't know that."

"Yeah, she's due in March."

"That's nice. Tell them that I said congratulations,"

Wendy said. She had never really gotten a chance to know her in-laws well. She'd talked to Pat on the phone while she and Kevin were still together, but the two women hadn't spoken since Wendy was supposed to go to Philly with Kevin last Christmas. Wendy had never called to explain why she hadn't come, so she knew that Pat must have been disappointed. "May I speak to Kevin, please?"

"Sure, hold on." It sounded like Pat put her hand over the phone, but Wendy could still hear what she said. "Renée, can you go tell Kevin that he has a phone call, please?" Pat removed her hand. "Just a second. He's in the back changing the baby."

"Okay," Wendy said quietly. She could have sworn that Kyle's wife's name was different, although she couldn't remember what it was.

"I got it, Ma," Kevin said after he picked up the phone.

"Okay. Nice talking to you, Wendy. You take care."

"Thanks, you too."

Pat hung up the phone.

"Hello?" Kevin said.

"Your mom told me Kyle's wife is having a baby."

"Yeah, she is."

"What's her name again?"

"Valerie. Why, what's up?"

*Valerie—yeah, that's it,* Wendy thought to herself. "Then who's Renée?"

"What are you talking about?"

"I heard Pat talking to someone named Renée. Who is she?" Wendy demanded as curiosity got the best of her.

"Oh, she's a friend of mine," Kevin admitted.

Wendy couldn't explain why, but she was upset. "What do you mean, she's a friend of yours? How come I never knew her?"

"Wendy, please. Now is not the time for this."

"Why is that? 'Cuz your lil' girlfriend is there?"

Kevin rolled his eyes and sighed. "I *told* you that she's a *friend* of mine. She's not my girlfriend."

"Did she eat dinner with y'all?"

"Yes."

"I don't have dinner on the holidays with my *friends*," Wendy said sarcastically. "I spend that time with my family."

"Wendy." Kevin tried not to raise his voice. "What do you want? Surely you didn't call here to talk about this."

"I want you to bring my baby home."

"There you go with this foolishness about Kimberly being *your* baby. I thought we agreed that she could spend Thanksgiving here because you wanted to be with her on her first Christmas."

"We did, but that was before I knew you would have your girlfriend there."

A frustrated Kevin gritted his teeth and spoke into the phone. "How many times do I have to tell you that she's *not* my girlfriend?"

"Yeah, whatever."

"You know what? I'm not going to talk to you about this. You're jealous because I'm not sweatin' you anymore and now you want to put Kimberly in the middle of it."

"You—" Wendy tried to speak, but Kevin cut her off.

"I'm not bringing her home right now. She will spend the day here as we had planned, and I will drop her off in the morning."

"*What?*" Wendy was irate. "How dare you tell me that you won't bring her home. I—" Before she knew it, Kevin had hung up the phone on her. She immediately called back.

"Don't answer that!" Kevin yelled from the bedroom. The phone continued ringing until it clicked over to voice mail. A few minutes later it rang again. By the third time Wendy called, Kevin had taken Kimberly to the other room with everyone else. He went back into the bedroom and answered the phone. "I wish you would quit acting childish."

"Me, acting childish?"

"Yes, you. Instead of acting like the jealous wife, you should just go back over to your mother's house and spend time with your family like I am trying to do."

"Oh, so Renée is part of your family now. I thought you said she was your *friend*," Wendy mocked.

"You know what I mean."

"How about I just come over there and get my child?"

"Whatever. You won't be able to get in." Kevin wasn't concerned about that at all. He knew Wendy couldn't get to his apartment unless he let her in. After realizing that his separation with Wendy was permanent, he'd bought a luxury condominium in a gated community. She couldn't get through the gate without a visitor's pass or her name being on the guest list with the security officer.

Wendy was fuming. "Well, I'll call the police then," she threatened.

"What can they do?" Kevin said calmly. "I am the father. I *do* have a right to file for visitation if we can't work it out ourselves."

"Don't threaten me, you jerk."

"Take it as a threat if you want, but I promise that if you call the police I'll take it to the courts."

"Ugh!" Wendy screamed.

Kevin heard a thump. Wendy had hit her fist on the table.

"I knew you were no good. That's probably the tramp you gave me the disease from," Wendy accused.

Kevin defended her. "First of all, she's not a tramp. Second of all, you are out of control. I am going to hang up, turn all of my phones off, and spend the rest of the evening with my family. I advise you to calm down. I will bring Kimberly home in the morning as we had planned."

"How can you do this to our marriage?" Wendy yelled.

"How can I do what to our marriage?" Kevin screamed back. "I tried to get back with you several times if you would recall. *You* are the one who told me over and over how you didn't want me. *You* are the one who said you didn't love me. *You* are the one who said you were moving on. So don't ask me how I can do this to our marriage. I *tried* to fight for our marriage, but you chose to let it go. You wanted me to leave you alone and I did. You ever heard the phrase 'Be careful what you wish for because wishes do come true'? Now you want to act like you care because I have a female friend over for Thanksgiving. You want to renege on our agreement and you want me to bring Kimberly home. Forget it, Wendy! I'm not giving in to you and your little tantrum. Call the police if you want, but be prepared because I will fight you on the issue." Kevin hung up the phone once again.

Wendy sat in her bedroom and cried. She hated the thought of Kevin having someone else over there spending Thanksgiving with her daughter. She had spent the early part of the day at her parents' house. Marlene had held her celebration earlier than normal because Kim and Terrance had to go over to his parents' house. They wrapped up about four, and Wendy had spent the rest of her evening at home. She'd really called Kevin just to see how the baby was doing, but somehow the whole thing got off track. She tried calling back again, but no one answered. He must have turned the phones off, like he said he would.

Wendy tortured herself the rest of the evening wondering about Kevin's *friend* Renée. *Is she pretty? How many times have they kissed?* Although she wasn't ready or willing to get back with him, it bothered her to know that he was taking an interest in someone else.

# Chapter Twenty-Four
## Two Can Play That Game

IT WAS THE DAY AFTER THANKSGIVING. Kimberly was playing in the nursery while Wendy and Natalie talked in the living room. Natalie had been keeping Wendy company most of the day. Wendy was still upset about Kevin having a female friend at his house. Neither Kevin nor Wendy had had much to say to one another when he'd brought the baby home that morning. He asked her when would be a good time to come back and get Kimberly, but Wendy's response was "We'll see," and then she shut the door.

"I'm telling you you should call him," Natalie urged Wendy as she came out of the kitchen carrying two strawberry daiquiris.

"You didn't put alcohol in mine, right?" Wendy looked at Natalie suspiciously to confirm that her drink wasn't spiked.

"*No.* I told you I wouldn't."

"Don't roll your eyes at me. I just wanted to double-check." Wendy took a sip of her daiquiri. It tasted fine.

"Anyhow, I'm not calling Jaylen, so you can forget about it. For all I know, he gave me the wrong number."

"You'll never know if it's the wrong number if you don't try it."

"Then I guess I'll never know." Jaylen was Wendy's ex-boyfriend. She had told Natalie about running into him a few weeks ago at the gym. Wendy had finished her workout and he was signing up for a new membership. They talked briefly and Jaylen asked for Wendy's telephone number. When she refused, he gave her his number instead.

"Why not?"

"Because technically I'm *still* a married woman."

"On paper only. Girl, you and Kevin have been separated for almost a year. It's time to move on."

"I know, but—"

"Oh, *please* don't tell me you're having second thoughts about him."

"No, not really. I guess I didn't realize how definite our situation was until yesterday when he had that woman over."

"What do you mean you didn't recognize how definite your situation was?" Natalie exclaimed. "He gave you a sexually transmitted disease, for God's sake. How much more definite does it need to get?"

Wendy took in her friend's advice. *She does have a point,* she thought.

"You know you want to call Jaylen," Natalie continued. "Why would you keep the number if you didn't?" She gave Wendy a smile that clearly said *Busted.*

"Oh shut up," Wendy said playfully. There was some

truth to what Natalie was saying, but Wendy wouldn't admit it. She had definitely been attracted to him when she ran into him that day. He seemed to look even better than he had when they were a couple. His arms were so defined that his muscles rippled under his light-colored skin. He also had a tiny gap between his front two teeth that proved to be sexy rather than unattractive. Wendy had always been attracted to tall men, and Jaylen was no exception.

"For your information, I only kept the number because I didn't want to be rude and throw it away in front of him. If I had really wanted to talk to him, I would have given him my telephone number—so there."

"*Sure*," an unconvinced Natalie slurred. "You could have thrown it away when you got home. You want to call him. You might as well get it over with and do it. Since I've been back in town, I've never heard you mention anything about him until you got his number. I didn't even know you had an ex-boyfriend named Jaylen."

"How could you? You went MIA after we graduated from college. Remember?"

Natalie stuck out her tongue at Wendy.

"Besides, I don't want to make any hasty decisions. I have Kimberly to think about. Maybe Kevin and I could possibly work things out."

"That's bull!" Natalie seemed slightly irritated. "You had Kimberly to think about all along and you didn't want to get back with him. You're just jealous because he's seeing someone else. You don't want him, but you also don't want anyone else to have him. Now you're using Kimberly as an excuse."

"I am not." Wendy defended herself, although she knew Natalie was telling the truth.

"If you really are concerned about Kimberly, consider this: She'll respect you more if you aren't willing to settle for less than you deserve and move on instead of staying with her father just for his money."

Wendy was offended by her friend's insinuation. Their conversation had started off light, but now both women were serious. "First of all, I was never with Kevin because of his money. When I met him I didn't know he even had money."

"Maybe that's true. But how can you explain this sudden change of heart that you're having about him?"

"I don't need to explain anything." Wendy set her drink on the table and looked Natalie straight in the eye. "But, for the record, I have always loved my husband for himself, *not* for his money. He hurt me by cheating on me. I never wanted to get back with him because I didn't think I could forgive him."

"So what has changed? Can you forgive him now?"

Wendy didn't answer and looked away.

"All I'm saying"—Natalie put her daiquiri down and leaned closer to Wendy, demanding eye contact—"is that you deserve more. Don't let this other woman pressure you into taking him back if you don't want to. Explore all of your options and see which one benefits you the most."

"Yeah, well I don't think Jaylen can exactly be considered an option. He broke my heart too, you know." Wendy recalled how Jaylen had dumped her when she wouldn't have sex with him.

"That's because he had the upper hand last time. This time, you do."

"And how is that?"

"What's the first thing he said when he saw you?"

"That he was sorry and that he regretted the way our relationship ended." Wendy put a slight smile on her face. "He even said that he missed me."

Natalie grinned also. "You see what I mean? If you give him a call and y'all do end up hooking back up, the relationship will be on your terms this time, not his. Girl, if Kevin wants to have another woman, then show him that two can play at that game."

Natalie and Wendy finished their drinks before getting second rounds. The rest of the evening, they laughed and joked about guys and how Wendy could have Jaylen eating out of the palm of her hand if she wanted him to. It was almost midnight when Natalie left. Before doing so, she advised Wendy not to delay calling Jaylen any longer. Wendy didn't want to call that late. However, Nat convinced her that if Jaylen was serious, he wouldn't mind her calling. Wendy took her friend's advice and dialed the number she had kept in her purse.

⸻

"Hi, Jaylen. This is Wendy. Did I wake you?" She was nervous. "I know it's late. I'm sorry."

"No, don't apologize. I was just lying in bed, but I wasn't asleep."

Wendy knew he was lying. She could tell from the hoarse sound of his voice that she had woken him up. Nevertheless, she was flattered by his anxiousness to talk with her. "I can always call you another time."

"No, please don't hang up. I'm glad you called."

"Are you *sure* I didn't wake you?"

"Okay, you got me. I *might* have dozed off, but I'm up now." It sounded as though Jaylen sat up in the bed. "What's up?"

"Nothing. I just called to say hi." Wendy felt like a schoolgirl holding the phone in one hand while twirling her hair with the other.

"I'm glad you did."

Wendy and Jaylen spent the next twenty minutes playing catch-up. She found out that after finishing graduate school, he'd started teaching at the community college. He admitted how insensitive he had been to Wendy's feelings when they were dating and apologized again for mistreating her. When asked what brought the change of heart, he said that none of the girls he dated after her were able to make him feel special the way she did. Wendy had been attentive and he missed that. He never realized how much he enjoyed spending time with her until he no longer had the opportunity to do so.

Wendy told him about Kimberly and that she and her husband were no longer together. She didn't use the word *divorced* because it would be a lie, and she didn't want to scare him off by saying she was separated. They ended their conversation by agreeing to talk the next day. Wendy felt a little guilty about calling her ex-boyfriend. Her guilt was eased by replaying Natalie's words in her mind: *If Kevin wants to have another woman, then show him that two can play that game.*

# Chapter Twenty-Five
## A Chance Encounter

ATTENTION, SHOPPERS!" the man on the PA system announced. "The store will be closing in fifteen minutes. Please make your final selections and go to the registers. We will reopen the day after Christmas at nine A.M. Thank you for shopping with us, and Happy Holidays."

"Here Comes Santa Claus" played in the background while Marlene stood in line double-checking her grocery list to make sure she had gotten everything she needed for Christmas dinner tomorrow. She had so much to do today that she had thought she would never make it to the store on time. She would have liked one of the girls to go for her, but neither one of them was available. Kim and her family were spending Christmas Eve at Terrance's parents' house, and Marlene had no idea where Wendy was.

"Five dollars and thirty-four cents is your change," the cashier said to her.

"Thank you. Merry Christmas," Marlene responded before walking away. She held her money in her hand. *I hope the representative from the Salvation Army is still out there collecting money.* She felt bad about how she had rushed past the gentleman on her way into the store. She'd been trying so hard to make it in and out of the store before it closed that she couldn't recall even speaking.

Marlene was pleased when she heard the ringing bell outside and hurried to drop her money in the red collection bin. "God bless you, darlin'," the man said.

"You too, Merry—" She looked up and her words got stuck in her throat.

"Ev'rything all right, ma'am?" he asked, still ringing his bell.

"Um, yes sir. I—I, um . . ." Marlene couldn't figure out what to say. Sitting in front of her was the same guy she had seen at the hospital back in June. It was Harold Wallace. He was bundled up in a hat, coat, gloves, and a scarf, but she hadn't forgotten his face. She had given up on the idea that she would ever see him again.

"You have a good Christmas, hear?" he said.

"Yes, thank you. You too." She proceeded to walk away slowly. *No, say something to him!* She convinced herself and turned around. "Excuse me, sir?"

"Yes ma'am?" He smiled, still ringing the bell. Several more shoppers were coming out of the store and donating money.

"Are you . . ." Marlene fumbled for words. She had run out of the house so quickly that she hadn't taken the time to dress properly. The cold air caused her to tremble a bit, but she was also nervous. "Is your name Harold Wallace?"

He chuckled. "I hope so. That's the name I been usin'

for the last seventy-six years. If it ain't, I'm sho' in a heap of trouble." He was exhibiting the same wit and sense of humor Marlene remembered. "How can I be of service to you, young lady?"

"Were you at Memorial Hospital in June getting some kind of lab work done?"

"Oh, honey, I'm there ev'ry month. You see, I got suga and so I goes to make sure ev'rything all right with my blood. I'm gettin' up there, but I wanna take care of myself. Why, do you work at the hospital?"

"No. Well I used to, but not anymore." Marlene took a deep breath. She was stalling. "You may not remember me. . . . My name is Marlene Tibbs. I mean Gibson. It was Marlene Gibson at the time."

The bell stopped ringing and Harold dropped the smile from his face. He looked as though he had seen a ghost. "You serious?"

"Yes sir. Do you remember me?"

He closed his eyes and nodded. "I've never forgotten you." He reopened his eyes and looked at her solemnly. "You know, I didn't recognize you. You were ten years old the last time I saw you."

A manager walked out of the store. "Excuse me, sir. The store is closed. We're doing some paperwork and then we're taking off. We can't leave you out here. I can let you come in and call for a ride if you need to."

"No, that's okay. My nephew is sittin' right over there." Harold pointed across the parking lot. Marlene turned and saw the same four-door Buick that had picked him up from the hospital the day she first saw him.

"Okay. Well there are no more customers inside, so we need you to wrap it up if you can, please."

"Yes sir. I'll be leavin' in a minute."

The manager turned around and walked back inside.

Marlene stood there while Harold started packing up his stuff. She wasn't sure whether approaching him had been a good idea. He seemed so withdrawn and didn't really say much. She explained their first chance encounter and how she recognized him. "Sorry to bother you, sir. I just wanted to say hello."

"When I said I never forgot you, I meant it." Harold reached in his back pocket and pulled out his wallet. He opened it and handed it to her.

Marlene was shocked to see a black-and-white picture of herself as a little girl. "Oh my God!" she exclaimed. "How old was I in this picture?"

"I think you were about seven or eight at the time."

Marlene couldn't believe how much the picture resembled Tori, but she was more shocked about the fact that Harold had kept it for such a long time.

She gave him back his wallet and noticed that the manager had peeked out of the window. "I think we better get out of here. They've turned several lights off inside and that guy just looked out the window."

"Yeah. Well, thanks for sayin' hello. You don't know how good it is to see you again."

"Mr. Wallace . . . I know this is awkward, but do you and your family have plans for Christmas dinner tomorrow?"

"It's just me and my nephew. I raised him after my sister died. We usually go to the church and eat there."

"Would you be interested in joining my family and me for dinner tomorrow instead? I'm sure my mother would love to see you."

"I'm not sure we'll be able to make it," he said without looking at her.

"Oh, *please*, Mr. Wallace. It would mean a lot to me—I promise."

"We'll see, darlin'. I'll have to check with my nephew."

Marlene got a pen and paper out of her purse. Her fingers were numb by this time. "Here's my number and address. *Please* try and come. If your nephew doesn't want to, then I'll even pick you up. It really would be nice to have you," she pleaded.

"I'll see what I can do. I won't make any promises, though." He took the information and placed it in his back pocket.

Without thinking, Marlene hugged him. It was sort of instinctive, as she used to give him hugs all the time as a child. "We're gathering together at four. I really hope you can make it."

Harold nodded. "I'll see what I can do," he repeated before going to meet his ride.

# Chapter Twenty-Six
## Guess Who's Comin' for Dinner?

I AIN'T STAYIN' IF THAT MAN IS COMIN' OVER HERE, and I mean it!" Frances said defiantly. She had been asleep when Marlene returned home and hadn't found out about Harold coming for dinner until this morning. Marlene thought Frances would share her excitement. Instead, her mother was livid. "How do you even know that was really him? 'Cuz of some scar? Do you know how many people have scars? Ain't no tellin' who you got comin' over here. That man could be some type of serial killer."

"It *was* him, Mama. He even had a picture of me in his wallet."

"I don't care what you say. If he's comin' then I'm leavin'."

"Suit yourself. I've invited him over and I won't take back the invitation." Marlene was stern. She left her mother sitting in the living room pouting and went into the kitchen to prepare Christmas dinner.

Michael was at the table drinking a cup of coffee. "I can't believe how irrational that woman is. I'm starting to believe I was adopted," Marlene said, then kissed her husband on the forehead. "Either that or I inherited all of my daddy's characteristics." She walked over to the sink and began running water.

"So she doesn't want this Harold person to come over, huh?"

"Yeah. I don't know what her problem is. You would think she'd be happy to see someone who was at one time a good friend of hers."

"Apparently they weren't as good friends as you thought."

"No, they were. My mother is just fickle." She turned off the water and placed the ham in the sink. "She went from one extreme to another about it not being him. She even accused him of being a serial killer."

"I will have to admit, honey," Michael said cautiously, "it does sound sort of weird for him to have a picture of you after all these years."

"So you agree with her that I shouldn't have invited him over?" She turned around, daring him to say yes.

"No, I'm not saying that. You must have meant a lot to him, like he did to you. All I'm saying is that you have to think about how it sounds. If you hadn't told me about seeing him that day at the hospital, I would probably be a little leery also. Maybe you should have told your mother about that."

"Yeah, maybe. At the time I figured she would be more concerned about her health than anything else."

"Michael." Frances burst into the kitchen. "Can you give me a ride to Sis' Binford's house? I'm spendin' Christmas with her and her daughter since my daughter prefers to spend the day with strangers."

Marlene didn't even turn to look at her.

"Sure, let me finish my coffee first," said Michael. He would gladly get rid of his mother-in-law for a day. Frances turned around and walked back out.

"Don't forget to take your medicine with you," Marlene yelled. "Especially your blood-pressure medicine, since you're so angry. I don't want you going over there gettin' sick."

Frances never responded.

Michael gulped down the last of his coffee and took his cup to the sink. He whispered in Marlene's ear, imitating Arnold Schwarzenegger as the Terminator: "I'll be back."

"If you don't feel like taking her, then don't. She's acting silly."

"I'd rather take her than listen to her gripe for the rest of the day. Who knows? This may be our best Christmas yet." He gave Marlene a devious smile.

Marlene knew he was saying that because Frances was leaving, so she playfully hit him. "Stop it. Just go—and be careful."

"I will." He kissed her on the cheek. "Merry Christmas, honey."

"Merry Christmas to you too."

⌒

"Are you serious?" Kim asked Marlene while laughing.

"Yes! Ask your dad. She was furious with me for inviting him over." Marlene had just explained to her girls and Gwen why Frances wouldn't be celebrating Christmas with them today.

"That is too funny," Gwen said. Her son, Galvin, was

spending Christmas with his father's side of the family. Beside Galvin and a cousin, Gwen had no other relatives in Columbus. If she didn't travel to see her family during the holidays, she usually spent that time alone or with the Tibbs family.

"That's your mama," Kim said to her mother.

"Not by choice, honey—believe that," Marlene responded. "Did y'all have a good time at Evelyn's yesterday?" she asked Kim.

"Yeah, it was great. Wendy, she said to remind you that you still haven't brought Kimberly over to see her."

"I know. I'll get to it, I promise."

"Where were you yesterday?" Kim asked Wendy. "I tried calling to see if you wanted to come over there."

Wendy was caught off guard by the question. "I was out runnin' around."

"I tried to call you too," Marlene admitted. "You must not have had your cell phone with you."

Wendy had spent the day at Jaylen's place. The two of them had talked, watched movies, and even made plans for New Year's Eve. She hadn't told Gwen or Kim about the possibility of their getting back together yet, and she wasn't going to do it now with her mother sitting there. "Excuse me for not being available when y'all wanted me," she kidded.

Gwen gave Kim a look that Kim clearly read as *Something's going on*.

"Well, both of y'all missed the Christmas Eve service yesterday. Pastor Jones knows he can preach," said Marlene.

"He sho' can," Gwen agreed, although she hadn't gone

yesterday. She didn't belong to Marlene's church—or to any church, for that matter. However, she had heard Pastor Jones on several occasions and enjoyed each of his sermons.

Marlene looked at her watch and was a bit anxious. "It's almost four now. I better start setting the table."

"I'll help," Kim volunteered.

"Me too," Gwen said.

"While you guys are doing that, I'm going to change Kimberly." Wendy got up from her chair. "Mama, do you want me to tell Daddy and Terrance to wrap it up?"

"Yes." Michael and Terrance had been involved in a very intense chess game downstairs while Tyler and Tori were also down there playing with their new toys. Marlene mistakenly spoke her thought out loud: "I hope Mr. Wallace decides to join us." She had neglected to get his information, so she couldn't follow up with him.

Kim tried to comfort her. "If he doesn't, don't feel bad. You did the best you could do."

"Yeah, I know," Marlene said before going into the kitchen.

Gwen and Kim followed behind her.

After changing the baby, Wendy went down to the basement. "It's time to eat, guys," she said to the children.

"Aw, man!" Tyler moaned.

"Aw man nothing. These toys will be here when you get done, so go," she said sternly, and pointed up the stairs.

"Aunt Wendy, can Kimberly sit by me?" Tori asked.

"I'm sure that can be arranged."

"Goody," Tori said, running up the stairs.

Wendy overheard Tori teasing Tyler about not being

able to sit next to the baby. She shook her head and laughed. *Kids*, she thought, and walked to the back room where Terrance and her father had settled.

"Checkmate!" Wendy heard Terrance yell.

"Wait a minute," Michael protested.

"Give it up. You have nowhere to go," Terrance gloated. "I gotcha!"

"I want a rematch."

"Cool. It doesn't bother me if you wanna get whipped again." Terrance taunted his future father-in-law and began setting up the chessboard.

"Y'all don't have time for that now," Wendy interrupted. "Mama said it's time to eat."

Michael looked at Terrance. Both of them knew that if they started another game now, it would not be over before Marlene summoned them again. "After dinner, be prepared to take a beating, boy!" Michael declared.

"You may want to brush up on your game a lil' bit and read instructions on how to play."

"Just come on," Wendy said on her way back up the stairs. She did not feel like hearing the two of them talk trash.

Kim stood at the bottom of the stairwell that faced the front door. "Tori and Tyler, get down here *now!*" she yelled up to her children, who were playing in the bathroom. The water was turned off and their little feet scurried down the stairs. "I don't know why y'all didn't wash your hands when you were in the basement," she commented because it didn't seem rational for them to go all the way upstairs when there was a half-bath down there.

"My fault," Wendy confessed. "I wasn't thinking. I told them to go upstairs."

Kim looked out the living room window. "Someone just pulled up in the driveway."

"I'll get the door if you go tell Mama that her guest is here," Wendy said.

"Wait and make sure it's him first. I don't want to get her hopes up."

Kimberly lay on her back, kicking her legs and making baby noises. Kim went over, scooped her up, and kissed her.

"You can take her in the dining room," Wendy said, walking toward the door. "Oh, and put her high chair between Tori and me. Tori wants to sit by her."

"Any more orders you want to give while you're at it?" Kim asked her sister half jokingly and half seriously.

Wendy laughed. "Sorry. I guess I should have said please." She looked out the peephole and saw two people walking toward the door. "*Oh no!*" she said out loud.

"What's wrong?"

Wendy looked at Kim with a strange grin. "Guess who's comin' for dinner?" She opened the door just as the person was about to ring the doorbell.

"Ms. Phillips?" He looked perplexed. "What are you doing here?"

"My mother lives here."

"Hot diggety dog!" he proclaimed and snapped his fingers. "If I had known that we were spending Christmas with your family, we would have been here much earlier."

Wendy laughed. "We're glad to have you, Otis." She stepped away from the door so that he and his uncle could come in.

Kim overheard the name and remembered the maintenance man from the school where Wendy used to work. She hurried to tell Marlene that her guests had arrived.

"Hello, sir. I'm Wendy. You must be Mr. Wallace. Otis and I used to work together." Wendy held out her hand to shake his.

"It's a small world. Well, nice to meet you, Wendy."

Marlene walked up with her apron on. "I'm so glad you could make it." She hugged him.

"This is my nephew, Otis. This is Marlene."

"Woo, I see why your daughters are so fine. They get it from their mama."

Marlene chuckled. "Thank you. I haven't gotten a reaction like that from anyone in a long time."

"Mama, I already know him. He and I used to work together at the school."

"Wow, that's great." Marlene was excited. "Let me take your coats and then I'll introduce you to the rest of my family."

Harold and Otis dusted the snow off their boots and politely took them off, since they noticed that no one else was wearing shoes. Marlene took the coats but passed them to Wendy, who hung them in the closet. By this time, Terrance and Michael had come from the basement into the living room. Gwen, Kim, and the kids were called by Marlene from the dining room.

"This is my daughter Kim," Marlene said after introducing her husband.

Harold politely said, "Nice to meet you," while Otis gave his charming smile. "Did you get married yet?" Otis asked.

His looks hadn't changed since the day he and Kim had first met. He had on different clothes but the hair, tooth, fake jewelry, and curl were still there. "No, not yet, but soon," she said.

"Well, remember what I told you. . . ."

"What was that?" Terrance came and put his arm around Kim.

"Uh . . ."

"This is my future son-in-law, Terrance." Marlene continued with her introductions. "These are their two children, Tori and Tyler. The baby Kim is holding is actually Wendy's, my oldest daughter's, child."

"That's right! You look so good that I almost forgot you had a baby," Otis turned and said to Wendy. "You need to bring her up to the school sometime."

"I know." Wendy had sent pictures, but she hadn't taken Kimberly to see any of her former co-workers. Otis didn't ask about Kevin, which indicated to Wendy that somehow he had heard about their separation. Several of her co-workers had been getting suspicious when he no longer attended school functions. Wendy hadn't confirmed or denied their suspicions. She'd kept quiet because she didn't want them in her business.

"And this is Gwen, a very good friend of the family. She's like a daughter to me," said Marlene.

Otis eyed Gwen from head to toe. She was dressed in black and red leather. Her hair was in a ponytail with spiral curls. She looked good, and Otis wasn't oblivious to that. "You know, I like a woman with a lil' meat on her bones," he said after kissing her hand.

Harold rolled his eyes. "Excuse him. This is my sista's child. He inherited his personality from his daddy's side of the family."

Everyone laughed. Gwen wasn't offended, nor was she flattered. Otis had a long way to go before he could compare to the guys that she was used to going out with.

"Where's your mother?" Harold asked.

"She decided to spend the holiday with one of her friends."

"Is it because she knew I was coming?"

"No . . . she . . ." Marlene was having trouble lying. "Yes."

"Dang, Unc, what you do to run the woman off?"

"Probably nothing," Marlene said to Otis. "You have to know my mother. She'll get mad over simple stuff and not speak to you for weeks."

Harold put his head down. "I'm sorry to cause so much trouble."

"Don't be," everyone said in unison, except the kids, who weren't paying attention. Both Otis and Harold were shocked by how quickly they responded.

"Mr. Wallace, you have no idea how peaceful it's been today. Thank you for coming," Michael said, and they all went into the dining room, where dinner was waiting.

## Chapter Twenty-Seven
# Baby-Mama Drama

*Dear Kevin,*

*Welcome home! I just wanted you to know that I missed you and thought about you A LOT. Call me. Maybe we can bring in the New Year together.*

*Love, Your Friend,*
*Renée*

KEVIN WAS TOUCHED by the handwritten Christmas card Renée had mailed to him while he was away. Inside were three red rose petals. He immediately picked up the phone to call her.

"Hi, it's me. Leave a message," the recording on her cell phone answered.

"Hey, it's Kevin. I wanted to let you know that I made it back. Thank you for the card. It was really sweet of you. It means a lot to know that you care—and, uh . . . in case you're wondering, I missed you too."

Kevin laid the card on the coffee table and walked to

the bedroom so he could unpack his suitcase. He'd missed Kimberly while he was gone much more than he missed Renée. Flying to Philly to be with his family helped him overcome the loneliness he would have otherwise felt that day. His mother wanted him to stay through the New Year, but Kevin was eager to get back before then. As cute as Renée was, there was only one female Kevin would like to be with tomorrow for New Year's Eve. After unpacking, he decided to call Wendy and make arrangements to spend time with his daughter.

"Hello?"

"Hi, Wendy. This is Kevin."

"Um-hmm."

He could feel the tension. "Listen, I was thinking that if you didn't have any plans tomorrow night—"

"I do," Wendy said quickly.

"O-kay. Is Kimberly involved in your plans? 'Cuz I was kind of hoping that—"

"Kim is picking up the baby tomorrow night at eight. Kimberly is staying overnight with her."

"What are you doing during the day? Can I—"

"I plan on visiting Terrance's mother. She's been asking to see the baby."

"Wendy, would you stop it?" Kevin was getting upset.

"Stop what?"

"Stop using Kimberly to get back at me!" He raised his voice. "I'm sure Kim wouldn't mind if you called and told her that Kimberly is coming with me. I—"

"I'm sure that Tyler and Tori will be looking forward to her staying with them."

Kevin felt like throwing the phone against the wall. Wendy was irritating him with all of her excuses. "The kids were able to spend Christmas with her. I *would* like to see my daughter. Will you stop acting so childish and let her spend the night with me?"

"Don't you mean you and your girlfriend?"

Kevin spoke firmly. "I *don't* have a girlfriend."

"Yeah, whatever. I don't care anymore. I've made plans with one of my *friends* also." She intentionally emphasized the word *friends*.

"You are trying your best to pick an argument and I'm not in the mood to get into it with you. Just call me when Kimberly comes back from your sister's house."

"Fine."

Kevin hung up the phone without saying good-bye. It upset him that Wendy was using Kimberly to get even with him for having Renée over during Thanksgiving. Since that day Kimberly had not been to his place, and he had seen her at the house only for an hour or two on several occasions. During the visits, Wendy would disappear into another area of the house so she wouldn't have to be in the same room with him. Whenever he suggested getting Kimberly overnight or for a day, Wendy always made up an excuse like she had just now. If her behavior continued, he planned to take legal action in order to obtain regular and permanent visitation rights.

The phone rang. "Hello?" Kevin barked, his tone clearly indicating that he wasn't in a good mood.

"Ugh. Did you go to Philly and come back with an attitude?" It was Renée.

"No, I'm sorry. I'm just a little frustrated right now."

"What's wrong?"

Kevin sighed. "I don't even feel like getting into it."

"More baby-mama drama?"

"What else is new?" he said sarcastically.

"Is she still actin' funny about you seeing Kimberly?" Renée asked, ignoring Kevin's statement that he didn't want to talk about it.

"Yeah, I asked to get her tomorrow. I figured that since I've been out of town, she would let me spend a little time with her. I didn't get to see my baby for Christmas, I got stuff for her, my family sent stuff for her, and Wendy tells me that Kimberly is staying the night with her sister tomorrow. Then, on top of all of that, she tried to make me jealous."

"How'd she do that?"

"She mentioned having plans with one of her friends. She said it like she wanted me to think that it was a guy, but I didn't pay her no mind."

"Would you be jealous if it was a guy?"

"I don't know. I guess I would be more hurt than anything. I mean I know you and I spend time together, but there's nothing going on with us."

*Not yet*, Renée refrained from saying out loud. "Why would you be hurt, though, if you all are not going to get back together? She's the one who never gave you a second chance."

"I know. It doesn't make sense. I know my marriage is over. . . . I guess I'm just in denial, which is why I haven't made any moves. If Wendy starts dating someone else, I guess I will have no choice but to come to grips with reality."

There was a strange silence as both Kevin and Renée reflected on his words.

"But there's really no need to talk about her seeing anyone else, because she's not like that. She probably doesn't have plans tomorrow. If she does, she's going to church. She's just trying to get under my skin, that's all."

"Well, she seems to be doing a good job at it."

"It just bugs me that she puts our baby in the middle of our problems."

"You shouldn't have to ask for permission to see your child, you know?"

"Yeah, I know."

"Just go by the house and get your daughter. She can't stop you from seeing her."

"She'll be sure to catch an attitude if I drop by unannounced."

"So what?" Renée was harsh. "You have every right to stop by when you want. You're paying for the house. You need to stop letting her control when you can and cannot see *your* daughter."

"I know. . . . I guess I'm hoping that things will work themselves out on their own."

"They won't. You need to take the initiative, like contacting an attorney, for example."

Although it wasn't meant to be funny, Kevin laughed. "You're just saying that 'cuz you are anxious for me to be a free man," he teased her.

"Oh, be quiet. I want to get it through your thick head that you need to be proactive on a few things. If you want to see your daughter tomorrow, then go get her. Don't let your wife dictate your actions."

"Right now the only thing that's going through my *thick head*, as you put it, is that I don't feel like talking about this anymore. Why don't we change the subject? For instance, I appreciate the card. It was very nice of you to send that to me. Thank you."

"You're welcome," she said. Kevin had hit the nail on the head when he said Renée was anxious for him to be free. She desperately wanted him for herself and was getting impatient with his marital situation. "So if you don't have Kimberly tomorrow, what are you going to do for New Year's Eve?"

"I'm not quite sure yet. Why? What are you doing?"

"I don't have any definite plans. I wouldn't mind spending time with you."

"Don't take this the wrong way, but if I feel tomorrow like I do right now, I might be better off hanging out with myself." Kevin was pretty bummed about not seeing Kimberly, and Renée was no substitute for that.

"Oh."

He could tell she felt slightly rejected. "It's not that I don't want to see you. I just need some time to myself to think things through."

"Okay."

"How about I call you tomorrow if I'm up to doing something?"

"You expect me to sit around all day waiting for the phone to ring?"

"No, I don't *expect* you to do anything. If you want to do something, then go ahead. Either I'll catch up with you later or I'll miss out." This phone call was not going well. Kevin figured it was his fault for being in a foul mood when she telephoned. "I'm sorry if it sounds like I don't want to spend time with you. I do. I'm just afraid of getting into a new relationship before I'm completely out of one. I think you're a great girl. I really do. I know you're attracted to me, and I feel the same way about you. But I gotta get my head together or I won't be any good to you or myself."

"So what are you saying?"

"I'm saying that I don't want you to wait on me for anything. I can't make you any promises about our future."

"I never asked you to."

He detected bitterness in Renée's voice. "Look, how about we both get a good night's sleep and possibly talk to one another tomorrow?"

"Fine," was the last thing she said before their conversation ended.

Kevin wondered if he was making the right decision concerning her. *Are you crazy? It's obvious that she likes you. She's a wonderful person. Why are you afraid to explore what could be with her?* He knew the answer to his last question: Renée was sexy and sweet, but she was not Wendy. Kevin still loved his wife despite how she felt about him. He didn't want to get into a rebound situation that would only spell disaster in the long run. If he and Renée were meant to be more than friends, time would tell. Right now his focus was not embarking on a new relationship; his only focus was trying to work things out amicably with Wendy so he could be a vital part of Kimberly's life.

# Chapter Twenty-Eight
## Diging a Grave

ARE YOU GOING TO BE ABLE TO KEEP Kimberly for me tonight, or what?" Wendy asked her younger sister. Yesterday she had neglected to tell Kevin that she hadn't yet spoken with Kim about baby-sitting.

"Well . . . I . . ." Under different circumstances, Kim would have gladly said yes. However, she wasn't comfortable with the idea of baby-sitting so Wendy could spend time with one of her ex-boyfriends. Wendy had filled Kim in on her plans for the night. "I *did* tell Mama that I was going to Watch Night service with her," Kim admitted. "I would ask Terrance to baby-sit, but he won't even have our children. He is going out with his cousin. The kids are staying with his dad because Evelyn is going with Mama and me. You're still taking Kimberly to see Evelyn, aren't you?"

"Yeah. So your answer is no, right?" Wendy was a little frustrated. She was counting on Kim. Unlike when she and Jaylen had spent Christmas Eve together, Wendy wanted them to have the evening to themselves.

Kim spoke candidly: "I don't think you need to get involved with Jaylen again."

"Why not? All we're doing is seeing if we're compatible. I haven't committed to being in a relationship with him," Wendy explained.

"I don't see how you are checking your compatibility with someone else other than your husband. You do remember that you're still married, don't you?"

"So what are you saying? That I need to get back with Kevin?"

"No. But honestly, it seems like y'all want to get back together. Neither of you has filed for divorce."

"I'm leaving that up to him."

"Why? Especially since you're *checking your compatibility* with other people."

"So is he. I told you about that woman being at his house."

"If it upset you that he is with someone else, then you need to divorce him, not try to get even." Kim was amazed by how much her sister had changed. She never thought in a million years that she would be advising Wendy not to go out with someone outside of her marriage.

"If I file for a divorce, then Kevin may think that I am trying to go after his money."

"Are you?"

"No," Wendy said defiantly. "I just don't want to make the first move, that's all."

"I hope you feel that way tonight with Jaylen. I hope both of y'all feel that way and nobody makes the first move."

"Relax. I'm not gonna do anything crazy."

"It sounds like you already have."

"I know what I am doing. Trust me."

"I don't see why y'all have to be cooped up in the house for New Year's Eve. Go out somewhere where there are other people around to ensure that you don't do anything you'll regret."

"Remember what happened last year when I went out for New Year's? I let my persistent little sister talk me into celebrating downtown and I got busted for not being out of town. I didn't want to go, but *somebody* pressed the issue. If I'm seen out with Jaylen, I can only imagine the trouble that will cause."

"As I recall, it was your deceitfulness that got you busted, not the mere fact that you were downtown. If you and Jaylen aren't doing anything wrong, then you shouldn't be afraid of being seen in public with him."

"I'm not afraid."

"Okay, then why won't you tell Mama that you and Jaylen are testing your compatibility?"

"She'll never understand and you know it."

"Um-hmm." Kim didn't understand either. It was ironic that she was planning a wedding and the woman who would stand by her side was on the verge of becoming an adulteress. "Why don't you see if Natalie or Gwen has plans for tonight?"

"I haven't told Gwen about Jaylen, and I'm not sure I want to if she'll respond like you." Wendy sighed. "I can't see Nat sitting at home on New Year's Eve baby-sitting. I'm sure she wants to go out."

"So Natalie already knows about Jaylen?"

"Yes."

"I can't believe you would tell her before Gwen and me!"

"That's because she doesn't trip on me the way y'all do."

"I'm sure she wouldn't," Kim snickered.

"What do you mean by that?"

"Nothing." Kim was slightly jealous that Wendy felt more secure talking to Natalie than to her. Wendy had never been told about Natalie and Kevin dancing together at the club a while ago. Gwen hadn't seen them together again since that time. Both she and Kim figured that it was a chance meeting and that Natalie really didn't have any idea she had run into Wendy's husband. Of course, Gwen still didn't trust Natalie. Kim, on the other hand, was willing to give her the benefit of the doubt. "If it seems like I'm trippin' it's because I don't want you to get hurt. Does Jaylen know you are married?"

"Not . . . exactly."

"Wendy!"

"I sort of gave him the impression that I'm divorced even though I didn't tell him so directly."

"How could he get that impression, then?"

"Because I often refer to my marriage in the past tense as though I am divorced, even though I don't come out and say so. If it looks like our relationship is going to go somewhere, then I'll tell him everything. I promise."

"Oh my goodness, girl." Even if Kim wasn't going to church she would refuse to baby-sit now for sure. If her not baby-sitting meant that Wendy had to cancel her plans with Jaylen, Kim preferred to see that happen. "You are digging a grave for yourself."

"Relax—Oh crap!" Wendy blurted out loud.

"What's wrong?"

"I just remembered that I need to call ADT and have them come out to look at this system."

"Why, what happened?"

"The alarm isn't working. I couldn't get it to come on last night before going to bed. It doesn't even chime like it's supposed to when the doors open."

"At least you don't have to worry about break-ins where you live."

"Yeah, but I still feel more secure with the alarm on at night than I do with it off, since the house is so big."

"Maybe God's trying to tell you something."

"Like what, call ADT?" Wendy replied cynically.

"Like *maybe* you should be spending the time with Him tonight instead of with an ex-boyfriend."

"Whatever. I'm gonna get off the phone and call this alarm company. I don't know if they'll come out today, but it's worth a try. I don't feel comfortable staying another night alone in this house with a broken alarm."

"You won't be alone. Kimberly will be with you, won't she?"

"That's only if I don't find a baby-sitter. Besides, if something happened, she couldn't do anything."

"I hope you're not planning on asking Jaylen to stay the night."

"Naw!" Wendy was offended by Kim's implication. "If I can't get it fixed, then I can't get it fixed. Nothing else to it. Jaylen and I are bringing in the New Year together then his butt is going home—for real."

"I'm just double-checking . . ."

"Well, let me go so I can get everything I need done."

"Okay. I'll talk to you later. Wendy . . ."

"Yeah?"

"Please be careful tonight."

"Would you calm down? I know what I'm doing."

"I hope so," Kim said in despair before hanging up the phone.

# Chapter Twenty-Nine
## *All About You*

IT WAS 9:30 P.M. Kevin sat alone in a booth at Horizons, a popular restaurant near the Ohio State University campus. He'd been there for at least an hour. The place was packed with dozens of loud people eating and drinking while waiting until the clock struck twelve. Kevin had so much going through his mind that he was able to block out the noise and quietly sip on his Coke.

It was the most depressing New Year's Eve he had ever experienced. Even when he'd gone to Philly last year without Wendy it wasn't as bad. He had come back to Columbus with the hope that the two of them would be able to reconcile. They hadn't, and it was not likely that they ever would. Tonight Kevin was trying to come to grips with that fact.

He never did call Renée to make plans for the night, nor did she call him. He figured she was still upset with him because of their conversation yesterday. Renée was always a fun person to be around. They went to the movies, out to dinner, or just lounged around one of their places. It had been a while since they had gone out to a club. Kevin didn't mind. He really didn't want to get back in the habit of partying every weekend. If it wasn't for his argument with Wendy the night he met Renée, he wouldn't have been at Maxine's then.

*She's right*, Kevin thought to himself, remembering Renée's advice that he needed to be proactive in filing for divorce. *There's no point in holding on to a dead marriage. She doesn't love me. And if she does, she doesn't want me. New Year's Resolution Number One: Move on with my life.* He looked down at the table solemnly. Moving on meant taking the necessary steps to end his marriage.

"Hey, Kevin. What's going on, man?" Kevin looked up from the table and saw Terrance standing next to the booth.

"What's up?" said Kevin, standing to greet Terrance with a handshake and a one-armed hug. "How ya been doin'?" he asked. The two of them hadn't seen each other since he and Wendy separated.

"Good. How about yourself?" asked Terrance.

"I'm hangin'," was the only answer Kevin could think to give. "What's been goin' on with you?"

"A lot. Kim and I are getting married next summer."

"Yeah, I heard. Congratulations, man. You ready?"

"As ready as I'm gonna be. I think it'll be great. She's a good person."

"I hope y'all make it, man, I really do. Marriage is a wonderful thing if you have a good one," Kevin said, and sat back down in his seat without looking at Terrance.

"You here by yourself?" Terrance asked.

"Yeah . . . go ahead and sit down." Kevin pointed to the other side of the booth.

"Naw, that's all right. I got my cousin over there waiting for me." Terrance pointed in the direction of his cousin. There was a crowd of people standing around so Kevin couldn't discern who he was referring to. "I just wanted to stop by and holla at you."

"I'm glad you did. Y'all plan on staying here the rest of the night?"

"Yeah. How about you?"

"I'm not sure yet."

"Well, you're welcome to hang with us if you want."

"Thanks. I might end up going home before midnight hits. I really wanted to spend tonight with my baby girl, but I hear your wife-to-be got first dibs."

"Huh?" Terrance was confused, and frowned slightly.

"I'm talking about Kimberly staying the night at your house tonight," said Kevin.

"Oh . . . okay." Terrance had no idea what Kevin was talking about, but he would play it off like he did.

"She is there, isn't she?"

"Uh . . . yeah, sure."

Kevin picked up on Terrance's hesitancy and looked up at him. "Terrance, please don't lie to me, man. I thought we were better than that. Is my baby at your house?"

Terrance sighed. "I really don't know," he admitted, and shrugged his shoulders.

Kevin laid his head back on the booth. He couldn't explain it, but all day he had had a funny feeling about his conversation with Wendy yesterday. "Can you call Kim for me and find out?"

"Look, man, I don't know what's going on, I swear. I can call Kim, but I doubt that I will get ahold of her. Last I knew, she was going to church with our mothers. It *is* possible that she has Kimberly with her."

"Did your kids go to church also?"

Terrance hadn't anticipated stumbling into a web of deceit by coming to speak to Kevin. He hated being in the middle of any kind of conflict. He knew about all the drama that had caused the separation between Wendy and Kevin. Kim had also told him about many of the things Wendy had done, like considering an abortion, swearing, and even trying to find a baby-sitter so she could be alone with her date tonight. Terrance wouldn't dare tell Kevin any of that. Originally, Kim had said that she wasn't going to baby-sit, but it was possible she had changed her mind. "No . . . they're with my dad, but—"

Kevin wasn't sticking around to hear any buts. He left his Coke and Terrance at the booth and fought his way through the crowd to his car.

⸺

"Sorry I took so long." Carrying a bowl of popcorn, Wendy walked back in the living room, where Jaylen was sitting. "I wanted to check on the baby."

"Is she still sleeping?"

"Soundly. I don't think she'll be waking up anytime soon, but I still want to stay up here." Wendy sat down on the couch. While she was getting their snack, Jaylen was supposed to be looking through the movies and deciding which one he wanted to watch. However, Wendy returned to the living room and heard the sultry sounds of Luther Vandross playing on the stereo, and the lights were dimmed.

"That's fine with me," Jaylen said. Wendy had originally planned for them to sit downstairs in the recreation room, but since she was unable to get the security company out to fix the alarm, she was more comfortable staying upstairs. In the basement she had a seventy-five-inch theater-like television screen with surround sound. The basement was fully furnished with a wet bar, a full bath, a pool table, and a lot of other luxuries Kevin wanted. That was where Kevin would entertain his guests. Wendy showed Jaylen around the place and carefully manipulated her words, telling him that she got the house as part of the "agreement" between her and Kimberly's father.

"I still can't get over how fabulous you look," Jaylen commented on Wendy's figure.

"Thanks." She was flattered.

"I'm serious. Most women *blow up* after they have kids. But you look great!"

"My sister's not fat. Remember, she has two kids."

"Yeah, Kim is an exception too. But why turn the focus on her when you're sittin' right next to me lookin' very good?" Jaylen gave a charming smile.

Wendy laughed flirtatiously. She had made every effort to look good that night. She was dressed casually in a Nike jumpsuit she'd recently bought. She'd specifically chosen to wear it tonight because it showed off the after-pregnancy figure she had worked very hard to achieve. Her hair was pulled up in a clip with a few curls hanging down in the back. Her eyebrows were newly waxed, and she had given herself a facial before Jaylen arrived to make sure that her skin would look radiant. "You're not too shabby yourself, mister." She playfully poked him in the chest, displaying her professionally manicured nails.

He scooted closer to Wendy and put his left arm around her shoulder. The two had been talking on the phone since the night after Thanksgiving, but this was only the second time they had seen each other outside of the gym. The closest contact between them on Christmas Eve had been a hug, although Jaylen wished he had decorated his place with mistletoe so he could have used the excuse to kiss her. Tonight he planned to make it clear that he was serious about taking things to the next level.

With his arm around Wendy, Jaylen reached over in her lap and picked up one popcorn kernel with his right hand. Instead of eating it himself, he put it in Wendy's mouth. He spoke in a soft and seductive voice, "I am really glad you called me—you know that, don't you?"

"Why are you so glad?" Wendy could have cared less if they watched a movie or not. Her ego preferred that she listen to Jaylen's flattering remarks.

"I feel like I've been given a second chance. This time I'm gonna do things right," he said.

"Um-hmm, you're just saying that," she teased.

"No, for real. You have no idea how much I've thought about you."

"And just what would you think about?"

"Everything: the sound of your voice . . . your smile . . . the way you made me laugh . . . your morals and values. You are perfect. I didn't appreciate your discipline with remaining celibate until the women I dated after you seemed so eager to give it up. I guess it was then that I realized that intimacy meant more than just sex. We didn't have a sexual relationship, but we certainly had an intimate one. I have never stopped thinking about you."

"Look at you, trying to run game. You probably did think about me, but I'm sure it was more like 'Man, I wish I had hit that' instead of appreciating my discipline." Wendy wouldn't admit it to Jaylen, but she was not one hundred percent sure she wouldn't give it up this time around. She'd tried being the good girl and it hadn't gotten her anywhere. She threw a popcorn kernel at his face and it landed in his lap. He picked it up and put it in her mouth.

"What you said isn't true. I wasn't thinking or wishing we had done anything. At first I was, but then I was getting it regularly—"

Wendy held her right hand up. "Please spare me the details."

"Is someone getting jealous?" Jaylen chuckled. "Ahhh . . . I see you're the one who wishes we had done more."

"Oh, don't flatter yourself, buddy."

"Would you believe that I've been abstaining from sex for almost a year?"

Wendy laughed. "Yeah, right!"

"I swear I have."

"Whatever—game recognizes game. You are not gonna get me with that one."

"How about I get you with this?" Before Wendy could respond, Jaylen held her chin and kissed her passionately on the lips. His lips were so soft and full. Each second he pressed them against hers, Wendy loosened her grip on the popcorn bowl a little more. Kissing him felt very good, and her hormones were raging. After about fifteen long seconds, the kiss was over and she was left stunned.

She took a deep breath. "Um . . ." She couldn't formulate any words to say. She had wanted and even expected Jaylen to kiss her, but she was startled by the intensity of the kiss. She was startled even more by the combination of frantic doorbell ringing and banging at the front door.

"Open the door!" Kevin shouted from the other side. He had parked his Hummer next to the black Camry sitting in the driveway. He had no idea whose car it was, but the churning in his stomach had signified that he wouldn't like what he was about to discover.

Meanwhile, Wendy was frozen and Jaylen stared at her, wondering who was at the door and why she wouldn't get up to answer it. Even though Luther Vandross was still belting out sounds on the stereo and the lights were still dimmed, the mood for the evening had taken a turn away from being romantic.

Betting that she had never gotten around to changing the locks, Kevin used his old house key and within moments he stood over Wendy and her beau on the couch. "Happy freakin' New Year!" Kevin said sarcastically and threw his arms up in the air.

Jaylen stood up. He didn't know who Kevin was. However, he had enough sense to know that the man was not happy about him being there. If something were to go down, he was better prepared on his feet than on the couch.

Wendy looked petrified and accidentally dropped the popcorn on the floor.

"Naw, man—have a seat," Kevin said to Jaylen. "Continue doing whatever it was you were doing with my wife before I came."

"Your *wife?*" Jaylen turned to Wendy for an explanation.

"Yeah, that's right—my wife. Did you forget to tell the man we're married, Wendy?"

Wendy put her head down and covered her eyes with her hand. Whatever emotions she'd felt from Jaylen's kiss were now replaced by fear. *Oh God, please . . . this can't be happening. It can't be!*

"I'm not sure what's going on, but I'm gonna leave and let y'all figure this out. Look, dawg, I didn't mean to disrespect you or anything like that," Jaylen explained. "I—"

"Slow your roll, partnah. I ain't got a beef with you. Handle your business. I'm getting my baby girl and I'm out." Kevin turned and walked away.

"No!" Wendy got up from the couch and ran after him. Jaylen took the opportunity to get his coat and leave.

"Get off of me!" Kevin pushed her away so hard that she fell and broke one of the nails she had gotten done earlier. By the time Wendy got up, Kevin had made his way to Kimberly's nursery. He shut and locked the door.

"No! Kevin, please don't do this," she cried. "Kevin, please. Please don't take Kimberly. I'll listen to anything you have to say now, I promise. Just don't take my baby . . . please!"

Kevin was angry. Not only had Wendy lied to him, but she also had the audacity to have another man in *his* house. He was hurt. Kevin snatched one of Kimberly's baby bags off the dresser and stuffed it with as many things as he could find. Kimberly had slept through all of the ruckus so far. She whined a little when Kevin picked her up and placed her in the carrier. Wendy continued pleading with him on the other side of the door.

"Kevin . . . baby, please don't do this."

Kevin opened the door. With Kimberly's baby bag on his shoulder and her carrier in his hand, he walked right past Wendy without saying a word.

She held on to his arm with tears streaming down her face. "Wait . . ."

"Leave me alone, Wendy."

"I'm sorry—I swear. Let's talk. Let's try and work things out," a desperate Wendy begged, holding on tight to Kevin as he went into the kitchen in search of milk and bottles. He didn't respond to Wendy's plea. "Kevin . . . c'mon, baby. Please don't do this—please . . . let's just talk."

"About what, Wendy? I hate to think about what would have happened between you and dude if I wasn't here," he shouted. Kimberly started crying.

"Nothing, I swear . . ."

"The least you could have done was let me have Kimberly for the night. But you couldn't even do that. You shoved her in the nursery so you could whore around." Kevin became angrier by the minute. By now the carrier and Wendy on his arm were heavy and it was difficult for him to gather Kimberly's bottles. Kevin cautiously set Kimberly down on the floor and used his free arm to hold Wendy at arm's length so that he remained closer to the baby. Kimberly began crying louder.

"Me! What about you and Renée?" Wendy retorted.

"Oh, so you're trying to get back at me? You wanna know about Renée? I'll tell you about her. She's mad at me because I didn't want to go out with her tonight. For months she has made no secret about being interested in me. But I haven't done anything with her—*nothing*—because of you!" Kevin squinted his eyes and pointed at Wendy. "It's been all about *you* the entire time. I've been about you—you've been about you. Everything has been centered around you!"

"That's not true!"

"Oh, it's not? How many mortgage payments have you paid since I moved out? How is it that you're still driving a BMW but you don't have a job? You have used Kimberly as an excuse in order to use me," he said as he got a few bottles of breast milk out of the refrigerator. Five-month-old Kimberly was squirming and wailing in her carrier now. "I didn't realize it until tonight. But no more. Things are about to change." Kevin picked Kimberly back up.

Wendy grabbed the cordless phone off the wall.

Kevin gave her a disgusted look. "I hope you're not calling the police."

She stood silent.

"Go ahead. I dare you to call. They won't take me to jail. Kimberly *is* my baby. The worst thing they'll do in a domestic dispute is order one of us to leave. Remember, this house is in my name. If anyone has to go, it'll be you. And I will make sure that Kimberly stays with me because the car, that's in my name too. It's a long walk from here to your parents' house. I'm sure the cops would agree."

"I hate you!" Wendy yelled.

"You know, tonight has totally changed everything I thought about you. You're pathetic. If I had any hope of us getting back together I don't now. If it wasn't for you being the mother of my child . . ." Kevin was so frustrated that he couldn't finish his sentence.

Wendy stood speechless with eyes full of tears as Kevin stormed away. She threw the phone across the room after she heard the door close and fell to the kitchen floor. She sobbed and said out loud, "God, how can You allow him to do this to me?" She felt an urge to pray, but she really wasn't making a sincere appeal to God for answers. Doing so would have required her to examine her behavior that night. However, Wendy was so wrapped up in what Kevin had done to hurt her that she failed to acknowledge her own faults.

# Chapter Thirty
# Can You Hear Me Now?

W ENDY!" Her mother and sister both called out after rushing into her house. "Mama, she's in the kitchen," Kim yelled to Marlene as she saw Wendy lying on the floor. Marlene had gone to check another part of the house, but ran into the kitchen once she heard Kim.

"Wendy, get up," Marlene said to her daughter. She and Kim bent down in their church clothes and high heels, trying to lift Wendy, who was still crying frantically.

"He took my baby," Wendy sobbed.

"Who, Kevin?" Marlene asked.

Wendy nodded her head.

"Get off the floor and tell me what happened. You can't lie here all night."

Wendy was not cognizant of the time. It was a quarter to two in the morning and she had been in the same position since Kevin had left, a little after ten. After service, Kim had dropped Evelyn off and was on her way to take Marlene home when she noticed a voice message waiting on her cell phone. It was Terrance calling to tell Kim about seeing Kevin at Horizons. Kim then told Marlene how Wendy had lied to Kevin about her baby-sitting earlier. Marlene asked why Wendy hadn't wanted to go with them to church, and Kim simply said that she had other plans. Until she heard Terrance's message, Kim had no idea that Kevin wanted to keep Kimberly.

Kim and Marlene managed to help Wendy into one of her kitchen chairs. Wendy sat in the chair, crying and looking at the floor. Kim left to get a washcloth from the bathroom so she could wipe Wendy's face. On the way down the hall, she stopped in the living room to turn off the stereo that was still playing. She looked at the popcorn scattered about the floor and used her imagination to piece together that night's events. In the kitchen, Marlene knelt down in front of Wendy and said, "Tell me what happened."

"Mama . . . he took my baby. . . . Kevin took my baby," she cried. The breaks between her words were the pauses she took whenever she had to catch her breath.

"Okay, calm down, sweetie. Why did he take her?"

"'Cuz . . . he was . . . mad at me."

"What did you do? Why was he mad at you?"

"Because . . . Jay—Jaylen was here." Wendy's tears fell in her lap.

"What!" Marlene was stunned. She didn't bother asking any more questions. Like Kim, she could put the pieces together from there. "Oh Wendy." Marlene rose, leaned forward, and laid Wendy's head on her shoulder. "What in the world has gotten into you, baby?"

Kim came back with the wet washcloth and handed it to Marlene, who wiped Wendy's face. Kim didn't know what to say. She felt horrible watching Wendy cry. She wished she had been able to talk some sense into her earlier. Either that, or she wished she hadn't given Wendy such a hard time about baby-sitting. Kim sat down quietly at the table and let Marlene do all of the talking.

"Honey, why did you tell Kevin Kimberly was with your sister?"

"I—I don't know. . . . He just came and took her, though."

"Shhh, stop crying like that. You're gonna make yourself sick."

"He . . . I want to call . . . the police."

"I don't think you should get the police involved."

"But what if he doesn't bring the baby back?" Kim spoke up.

Marlene didn't respond at first. Instead, she stopped consoling Wendy with hugs and pats and sat down in a chair at the table. "Kimberly is Kevin's daughter also." Marlene was concerned about had what happened tonight, but she had more wisdom than her daughters and did not want to respond emotionally. "Even though he has taken her, he will not hurt her. I'm sure of that."

"But Mama—"

"But Mama nothing," Marlene replied to Kim's protest. "Listen to me. Kevin is hurt and angry—honestly, I can't say that I blame him."

"But . . . he cheated on me . . . first," Wendy rationalized.

"I know that you know better than to use that as an excuse with me about your behavior tonight. I raised you better than that." Marlene was stern. "Two wrongs do not make a right. You've made your bed, now you have to lie in it. Kevin loves that baby just as much as we do. He would never let anything happen to her. He needs this

time with her, so let him have it. Look at me, Wendy."
Marlene demanded her daughter's undivided attention.
She pointed at Wendy as she talked. "If you get the police
involved, that's going to make Kevin even angrier, and
then you don't know what he'll do."

"But what if he . . . takes her out of town or . . . something?" Wendy said. She still had tears streaming down
her face, but she wasn't crying hysterically like she had
been when her mother and sister first arrived.

Marlene stopped pointing. "You watch too much television. The man has a business to run. He's not going to
take her anywhere."

Kim decided to ask another question. "How do you
know for sure?"

"I don't know for sure. I'm praying that I'm right. Give
him a day or so. If he doesn't bring Kimberly back or call,
then we'll see what we have to do."

Wendy didn't want to hear that. She wanted her baby
right that minute. However, deep down she knew her
mother was right.

"In the meantime, you need to try and get the best
night's sleep you can, considering the circumstances. Kim,
take your sister and make sure she gets ready for bed."

Kim got up from the table and held her hand out to
Wendy. "C'mon." Kim looked at Marlene and gave her
the car keys. "I'm gonna stay the night with her. You can
take the car."

"No, I'll stay also. I need to call your daddy and let him
know what's going on." Marlene looked for the kitchen
phone and saw it shattered on the floor. She went into the
living room to call her husband as Kim and Wendy
headed toward the bedroom.

*Father,* Marlene began to pray silently, trying to step over the spilled popcorn on the living room floor on her way to the phone. Marlene wiped the tears that fell from her eyes. Her heart ached for Wendy. *I'm turning her over to You. She's Your child. Help her to get back on the right path and straighten out this mess she has made.*

Marlene filled in a half-asleep Michael on everything that had taken place. He had driven separately to church and had done Marlene a favor by picking up Mr. Wallace, who also attended service. For some reason, Frances didn't want to come. She was still offended about how things had gone down on Christmas. Her version of the story was quite different from the way things had actually happened that day. After speaking with her husband, Marlene swept the popcorn off the floor and lay on the couch, where she fell asleep.

⌒

On January third, Wendy received a phone call from her mother. "Wendy?"

"Yes?"

"Kimberly's here!" Marlene sounded relieved and cheerful.

"What?" Wendy needed Marlene to repeat herself to confirm that she'd heard right.

"Kimberly's here. Kevin just dropped her off."

"How is she? Is she all right?"

"She's just fine. Do you want me to bring her or are you going to come and get her?"

"Just stay there. I'll be right over." Wendy hung up. She was anxious to see her baby and didn't want to wait for

Marlene and her slow driving. Since Kimberly had been gone, Wendy had barricaded herself in the bedroom, coming out only when absolutely necessary. Gwen and Kim had visited several times, trying to get her out of the house, but Wendy had refused to budge. She didn't want to go anywhere until her baby was home.

Natalie left a few messages wanting to know how her evening with Jaylen had gone. Wendy hadn't returned any of the phone calls. She didn't feel like rehashing that horrible night. She also regretted letting Natalie convince her to call Jaylen. At first Wendy was mad at Natalie, but then she realized that she had no reason to be. Natalie hadn't forced her to do anything she didn't want to do. Jaylen hadn't called. Odds were he never would again. At this point in her life, Wendy didn't care.

She was a little disturbed by the fact that Kevin had taken Kimberly to her mother's instead of bringing her home. Maybe he thought that he could avoid an argument that way. Wendy tried to call him several times, but he never answered the phone. Luckily, he had brought Kimberly back. She had planned to give him another day, and if she didn't have her baby or at least hear from him, she was going to call the police no matter what her mother said.

Wendy hurriedly grabbed her car keys and went through the house to the garage. *What in the world?*

She looked and saw that her BMW sedan was no longer parked inside. In its place was a used two-door Geo Metro. She walked slowly toward the car and looked through the window. There was an envelope on the seat. She opened the door and picked it up. Inside were keys and a letter.

Wendy:

As you can see, I took the car and bought you another one. The car has been thoroughly checked out and is in great condition. Don't worry about insurance for it—I already have that covered. I know that it is essential for you to have transportation, especially where Kimberly is concerned.

From now on, I will no longer give you money to pay the mortgage, utilities, or anything else. I am having all household bills mailed to me and I will pay them directly. Whatever Kimberly needs, tell me and I'll buy it.

As far as money for yourself, you're on your own. I hope you have not drained your savings. You might want to look into getting your old teaching position back for next year. Of course, I'll cover all of Kimberly's child-care expenses.

Apparently you didn't listen to one thing that I tried to tell you in my first letter. You can disregard that letter as I'm sure you already have. Be sure to read this very carefully because I want to make sure that you can hear me now! Just in case you think you have it made, you don't. Nothing I'm doing is for you, it's for my daughter. Don't get too comfortable—these arrangements are only temporary.

—Kevin

*You jerk!* Wendy threw the letter down on the garage floor and got inside the car. Except for the AM/FM radio and heating/cooling system, it was empty. There was no CD player, sunroof, automatic windows and locks, map navigator, or any of the other luxuries Wendy had gotten used to.

*The BMW was paid off; there's no reason why he had to take it. He's being spiteful. He's probably going to give it to his new girlfriend.* Wendy's mind was about to run wild with thoughts of Kevin and Renée until she remembered how sincere he'd looked when he said they hadn't done anything. *So what if he didn't do anything with her—he did do something with somebody at one point in time,* Wendy reminded herself as she backed out of the driveway and headed toward her mother's house.

# Chapter Thirty-One
## Ditch of Lies

KIM PULLED INTO HER PARENTS' DRIVEWAY and sat in the car for a few minutes. She knew that Marlene and Michael had gone to their weekly deaconate board meeting at the church. Kim hadn't come to see them. She purposely came to speak with her grandmother while they were out.

January had been a hectic month, and Kim was really glad it was almost over. On top of worrying about her sister, she and Terrance had shifted their wedding plans into high gear. Last week they had met with Shelly, the wedding coordinator, to discuss some ideas for their upcoming event. Shelly was highly recommended to Kim by one of her clients at the salon. Kim was immediately impressed with how professional and well organized she was. She was also full of ideas. One of her suggestions was for Terrance and Kim to acknowledge their grandparents during the ceremony.

Unfortunately, both sets of Terrance's grandparents were dead and Frances was the only living grandparent

Kim had left. Shelly thought it would be great to include Frances in the ceremony, but Kim wasn't so sure about the idea. Shelly didn't know what a pain Frances was to deal with. Kim and Terrance talked about the suggestion later, and eventually concluded that it wouldn't hurt to ask Frances to be a part of their wedding.

*The worst she can say is no,* Kim said to herself before getting out of the car. She didn't even care if her grandmother attended the wedding, let alone participated in it, but she was trying hard to be the bigger person. Even though it was likely that Frances would decline to participate, at least she wouldn't be able to say they'd excluded her.

The air was cold on Kim's face as she ran to the front door with the house key in hand. Although both girls had lived on their own for years, they still kept keys to their parents' house. It was the house the two of them had grown up in and would always be a place they called home.

Kim walked inside, dusted the snow off of her boots, and placed them near the front door. *Maybe I should have called first.* She wondered if Frances was sleeping, though she heard the television playing from her room. That wasn't unusual. Frances would often leave the TV on all day, even if she was doing something else. Before taking off her coat, Kim decided to go upstairs and see if her grandmother was awake. If she was taking one of her afternoon naps, Kim would come back later. A fully awake Frances was cranky enough to deal with, yet was ten times better than a Frances who had been woken unexpectedly.

As Kim reached the top of the stairs, she heard Frances

talking on the phone. *Great. With her on the phone I'll never get out of here,* she thought. Whenever Frances was engaged in a phone conversation with one of her buddies, it was guaranteed to last for a while. Kim was on her way back downstairs when something about Frances's voice caught her attention. It was bizarre. Frances didn't appear to be having a casual conversation. Kim didn't hear the loud laughter that usually accompanied Frances's gossip sessions. Rather, she sounded distraught, almost afraid. Kim crept closer to her grandmother's bedroom door and peeked through the crack. She observed Frances sitting on the edge of her bed with the phone up to her ear. Frances's face was covered with her other hand.

"Why are you tryin' to cause trouble with my family?" Frances said to the caller. "Your mere presence causes trouble. Marlene is happy. If you really care about her happiness and her family, go away and leave them alone!"

Kim's curiosity got the best of her. She tiptoed into her parents' bedroom to eavesdrop on Frances's conversation. As always, Marlene and Michael's king-sized bed was neatly made with the comforter folded back just enough for the pillows to show. Kim could hear herself breathing as she unplugged the telephone cord from the wall and picked up the receiver. She pressed the mute button before reinserting the cord into the phone jack.

"I'm really not tryin' to cause trouble, Frances. I do not intend on tellin' Marlene anything. I just want a chance to get to know her—you stole that from me," a man responded.

"Please don't do this, Harold," Frances pleaded. It was definitely fear that Kim heard in her grandmother's voice.

"It's too late to change what happened in the past. If you continue to come around, Marlene is bound to find out the truth. Your nephew already knows."

Kim was even more confused than ever. *She's talking to Mr. Wallace. What truth are they talking about?*

"I had to tell Otis so he could quit flirtin' with them girls," said the man.

*What does Otis have to do with this?* Kim wondered.

"I wish you had never come over for Christmas. You're gonna want to tell her, I know. We've been through this before. That's what caused my husband's death."

"Don't you dare blame Frank's death on me! He died because you lied to him." Harold Wallace spoke angrily. "You lied to us all—that's why we're in this mess. I said I wasn't gonna say anything and I'm not. I didn't think I would ever be able to get over how you handled things, but I did. And now I refuse to be forced out of Marlene's life a second time."

"You leave us be. Do you hear me? Leave my daughter and her family alone. Don't ever call here again!" Frances yelled and slammed down the phone.

Kim held the receiver in her hand, stunned by what she had heard. *What is going on?* She waited a few minutes, left her parents' room, and knocked on Frances's door.

There was no response at first. Through the crack in the door Kim observed Frances wiping her face. *Is she crying? No, she can't be!* Frances could be so mean that it was hard to believe she even produced tears. Kim knocked again.

"Who is it?" asked Frances.

She pushed open the door. "It's me, Gramma."

"Your mama and daddy ain't here. They went to some kind of church meeting."

"Yeah, I know." Kim stood awkwardly in the doorway. Frances wouldn't look up at her. She pretended to be searching for something on her dresser. Even if Frances wasn't pretending, it would be hard to find whatever she was looking for, considering how unorganized her room was. Her dresser was cluttered with books, papers, clothes, and any other thing she could store there. Frances's room was by far the messiest room in the entire house. "I-I came to talk to you."

"About what?" Frances said dryly. Kim figured that now was not a good time to talk about the wedding.

"Never mind. It can wait until later. Is everything okay? I thought I heard you yelling on the phone."

"Yes . . . um, somebody kept calling here with the wrong number."

*Why is she lying to me?* Every instinct in Kim's body told her that Frances was hiding something big. "Since you're busy, I'll come back at a later time or I'll give you a call."

"Do you want me to tell Marlene you stopped by?"

"No, that's okay." She shut Frances's door and went down the stairs. She thought about calling Mr. Wallace. *No, he probably won't tell me the truth either. . . . Otis!* Kim was determined to find out what Frances was hiding. She remembered Harold saying that Otis knew what was going on. She couldn't guarantee that Otis would tell her anything, but it was worth a try. Kim checked her watch. It was one o'clock. She knew exactly where she could find him. He still worked at the school where Wendy used to teach. Kim put her boots back on, fastened her coat, and headed out the door.

~

Hearing a knock, Wendy opened her front door slightly to keep the wind from gushing in. "Yes?"

"I have a certified letter for Wendy Phillips," the mail carrier at the front door announced.

"That's me."

"I need you to sign here, please." He directed her attention to a dotted line.

"Okay." Wendy was forced to open the door completely. "It is really chilly out here, isn't it?"

"Yes ma'am, it is."

It never crossed Wendy's mind to let the gentleman in the door, so she signed the necessary papers standing in the doorway while the cold air forced its way inside the house.

"We're all set." He handed her the mail. "You have a nice day, ma'am."

"Thanks. You too," Wendy said, and shut the door. She looked at the return address. It was from a law office. Her heart pounded so heavily against her chest that she forgot about the goose bumps she had gotten from the wind. Kevin had to be behind this letter. The two of them had not said much to each other since the horrible ordeal on New Year's Eve. He had picked Kimberly up on occasion with no problem from Wendy. During those times, there were barely three sentences exchanged between them.

Wendy checked on Kimberly, who was having a good

time in her baby swing. Next, she went into the living room and sat on the couch as she nervously began to open the letter. She had a feeling that she already knew its contents.

⌐

Kim had no idea where the maintenance office was located. She didn't want to wander around the halls for fear of looking suspicious. Instead she went to the front office to ask for help.

"I'll be with you in just a minute," a lady said to her.

Kim noticed the nameplate on the lady's desk. *Donna Burchett!* Wendy had told her several stories about this nosy woman.

"I'm sorry to keep you waiting. How can I help you?"

"I need to speak with Otis, please." Kim couldn't remember his last name. She didn't think it was Wallace because Otis was Harold's nephew by his sister.

"Otis Thornton, the maintenance man?"

"Yes, that's him."

"One moment. Let me call and see if he's available. May I tell him your name?"

"Kim, Kimberly Tibbs."

"Tibbs. By any chance are you related to Wendy Phillips? Her last name was Tibbs before she got married."

"Yes. Wendy is my sister."

A huge smile crossed Ms. Burchett's face. "Oh, she is! I thought you resembled her, but I wasn't sure. How's the baby?"

"She's doing fine. Growing like a weed."

"I bet. How old is she now?"

"Six months."

"It's funny how fast these kids grow up. How's Wendy's husband?"

"He's fine."

"We didn't see him much during the last school year. I don't recall him being here on Mrs. Phillips's last day, either." Ms. Burchett scrunched her face and looked toward the ceiling as though she were thinking. "As a matter of fact, I know he wasn't here because a few of our men helped load some of her heavy things into the car."

*Oh no, she ain't trying to get information from me.* "Wendy's fine, Kevin's fine, and the baby is fine. Everyone is doing just fine," Kim said bluntly. "Now can you see if Otis is available, please?" she asked impatiently.

Ms. Burchett looked indifferent as the smile faded from her face. She dialed some numbers on her telephone. "Hi, Otis. This is Donna Burchett in the front office. There's a Kimberly Tibbs here to see you—Mrs. Phillips's sister." There was a pause. "All right, I'll send her down." She hung up the phone. "Do you know how to get to his office?"

"No."

"Okay, go back out of this door. Make a right, then go left down the first hallway. You'll pass several classrooms. Once you go past the rest rooms, make another right. Go straight down that hall. His office will be the last one on the left."

"Thanks," Kim said, and proceeded to follow directions. It didn't take long to get to Otis's office from the front office. She gently knocked on the door.

"Come in."

Kim opened the door slowly and let herself in. "Do you want me to shut it?" she asked.

"Sure." Otis leaned back in his chair and put his hands behind his head. It was as if he knew this day would occur. "So what's going on?"

"I'm not sure. You tell me." Kim sat in the empty chair in front of his desk. She was convinced that Otis knew something. She had seen him only on two occasions previously, and this time it was different. He was different. He didn't have his usual sense of humor or the corny pickup lines. The smile he loved to show off had vanished. He looked serious.

"What am I supposed to tell you?" He removed his hands from his head.

If Kim had been in a different frame of mind, she would have laughed at how he wiped the Jheri Curl oil from his hands on a paper towel sitting on his desk. *At least it's not dry this time* was the first thought that crossed her mind. "I don't have time to play guessing games. I know that you know something about what's going on between my grandmother and your uncle."

"I'm not sure I know what you're talking about," Otis said. He looked away and pretended to write something on a notepad. Kim could tell he was nervous.

"I'm gonna just give it to you straight before you dig yourself into a ditch of lies. I overheard a telephone conversation between the two of them, and your name was specifically mentioned as knowing the truth, whatever that may be." Kim lifted her hands and simulated quotation marks around the word *truth* as she said it.

Otis laid down his pen and looked directly at her. He had had nothing to do with what had happened, but he carried the burden of knowing too much. "I am not the one you should be talking to about this. If you want to know what's going on, your grandmother would be the best person to speak with."

"She's not going to tell me anything. That's why I came to you."

Otis shook his head. "I don't want to get in the middle."

"Dang it, Otis!" Kim responded. "Something serious is happening and I think I deserve to know, especially since *my* mother is involved somehow and so is *my* grandfather, whom I never got to meet because he killed himself. According to the phone conversation I overhead, my grandmother thinks that your uncle was responsible."

"That's not true!" Otis snapped. "That's not true at all."

"Then tell me what is true."

"I can't. . . . I don't want to cause trouble."

"Funny, that's the same thing your uncle said." Kim got up from the chair. "Too late. The trouble has already been started. I'm gonna tell my mother the little bit that I do know. She'll get to the bottom of this. I guarantee that if Mr. Wallace is responsible for my grandfather's death . . ." Kim was so angry that she didn't know how to finish her sentence. What could her family do if Harold had killed Marlene's father? It was over forty years ago and the death was ruled a suicide.

"You're way off base."

"Whatever. I'm out. Just tell your uncle to prepare himself to face murder charges."

"Kim, sit down," Otis requested.

She ignored him and walked toward the door.

"Sit down!" Otis said with more authority in his voice.

Kim turned around and looked at him. *Who does he think he is raising his voice at?* She didn't speak her thoughts out loud, though. Instead, she slowly took a seat in the chair.

# Chapter Thirty-Two
## When Darkness Comes to Light

KIM HAD A PLETHORA OF EMOTIONS running through her mind. She left Otis's office in a rage and couldn't wait to get back to her parents' house. Like Otis, she was now burdened with the truth. *There's no way I can tell Mama. I can't even tell Daddy.* Telling Michael would be like telling Marlene. The two of them shared everything. He wouldn't be able to hold his peace, especially with Frances living in their home. *Wendy is too emotionally unstable right now to handle this.* Kim started to call Terrance but stopped herself. *Never mind; I'll wait.* She had a feeling that he would try to talk her out of going to see Frances. She wasn't in the mood to hear that. Even if she had to carry this information to her grave, she wouldn't do so without telling her grandmother exactly how she felt.

She pulled into the driveway so fast that she almost ran the car into her parents' garage. The seat belt hugged her chest and prevented her from bouncing forward as the car came to an abrupt stop. She jumped out of the car and burst through the front door. Frances was sitting in the living room watching TV.

"Your ma—" Frances was starting to say, but Kim interrupted her.

"Well, well, well . . . if it ain't Miss Lie About My Baby's Daddy." Kim leaned her right shoulder against the wall with her arms folded, glaring at Frances, who looked uneasy. "Yeah that's right—I know. I know *everything*."

"Kim . . ." Frances began to say.

"Don't *Kim* me!" she yelled. This was it. She was at her breaking point. Like an atomic bomb, Kim was about to explode. "You are *the* most hypocritical person I have ever known in my entire life. Unfortunately for me, you happen to be my grandmother."

The remote control tumbled out of Frances's hands and onto the floor. The television show she had been watching was drowned out by the piercing sound of Kim's voice.

"A grandmother who made me feel like crap both times I got pregnant." Tears formed in Kim's eyes as those hurt feelings resurfaced. A year ago, she would have used a more vivid word to describe her feelings. Now she tried hard to keep her language clean despite the fact that profane words ran through her head. Somehow, she managed to filter them before they came out of her mouth. "When Terrance and I moved in together, you made it your business to *continuously* remind me that we weren't married." Kim wiped the tears from her eyes. "All the while you were no better than me. In fact, you're a lot worse."

Frances stared blankly at her without saying a word. Goose bumps spread over her flesh, and she knew there would be no way to stop her granddaughter from speaking, although she desperately wanted to.

"*You* are responsible for my grandfather's death! Oh, that's right—Frank Gibson wasn't really my grandfather, was he?" Kim asked sarcastically. "Harold Wallace is."

Frances's heart sank.

"You remember him, don't you? The handsome young soldier you met and didn't tell that you were married. The same man you became pregnant by. The same man who didn't know that you were his army buddy's wife until the day he saw you and Granddad together." According to the story Otis had been told and had repeated to Kim, Frances was a few months pregnant by the time Harold saw her with Frank. He later questioned her about the child. However, Frances swore that the baby was her husband's. Even though he still speculated about being the child's father, Harold kept quiet about the affair because of his friendship with Frank, and unselfishly put his suspicions aside. "*For years* Mr. Wallace watched *his* daughter call another man daddy because *you* lied to everyone about who Mama's father was." Kim's voice grew louder with each sentence.

Frances closed her eyes, as she too was crying.

"Please spare me the tears," Kim barked after noticing Frances's emotions. "I'm sure you played the grieving widow at my granddaddy's funeral when technically you might as well have pulled the trigger." She wiped her face again. "Mama never knew why her daddy went into a depression, but you did. He found out. Somehow he found out that he couldn't have children."

Frances held up her hand as an indication that she had

heard enough. However, Kim continued speaking. "My grandfather confided in Mr. Wallace, who, by that time, was one of his best friends and Mama's godfather. From what I understand, Mr. Wallace came to you and said that he wanted to tell Granddad about the affair, but you refused to hear of it. Sadly, you even threatened to tell Granddad that Mr. Wallace raped you. Neither of you knew that my grandfather overheard your conversation until the next day when he killed himself."

Frances closed her eyes even tighter as she visualized the night she'd seen her husband's dead body spread out on the wooden bedroom floor. Luckily Marlene had stayed over at a friend's house that night. It had been raining when Frances got home from work. In those days she worked as a maid cleaning houses for wealthy Columbus families. It wasn't a job Frances enjoyed, but her bosses paid her a fairly decent salary so she tolerated it. Plus Frank hadn't been able to keep a steady job for a while due to his drinking habit.

134 Oak Street was where the Gibsons lived. Frances had walked into the small brick eight-hundred-square-foot home expecting to find the usual: her husband sprawled out on the couch after having one too many beers. When she pulled up to the house, it was pitch black like no one was home, even though Frank's rusty blue pickup sat in the driveway. She got out of the car and ran to the front door because she had forgotten her umbrella. "Frank?" she had called out once inside, but there was no answer. *Someone must have come to pick him up. Ain't no tellin' when he'll be home.* Frances had flipped on the light, taken off her coat, and gone upstairs to get out of her wet clothes.

She had opened the bedroom door and seen Frank Gibson lying in a pool of blood. Frances screamed as she knelt down beside her husband's lifeless body. Next to it was a suicide note.

*Frances:*

> *I have known for a while that I couldn't have children. Yet, there was a precious little girl living under my roof that called me daddy whom I loved with all of my heart. I wanted to confront you, but I didn't have the emotional strength to do it. All I knew was that my world had been turned upside down. I was angry and I hated you. Even though she didn't carry my blood, I still loved Marlene. I STILL LOVE MARLENE.*
>
> *How ironic . . . of all the people in the world, it had to be Harold. He should have told me about y'all . . . you should have told me about y'all . . . somebody should have told me! How many other affairs have there been, Frances? I guess I'll never know the answer to that one. I do know that you had at least one affair. . . . Marlene is proof of that.*

Embarrassed by the contents of the letter, a distraught Frances had confiscated it before authorities arrived. She had blamed Frank's death on Harold and sent Marlene away to Tennessee. Consequently, Harold never saw Marlene again.

Kim continued snapping at her grandmother, "I used to feel bad for not liking you. But now I realize that I have every reason to hate you. You're lucky that I love my mother *more* than I hate you. Because of that, I will never tell her about Mr. Wallace. But also know that I will never forgive you. It's too bad Granddaddy didn't take you with him." Kim spun around so fast that her purse knocked over one of Marlene's knickknacks and it fell to the floor and broke. It was a ceramic sculpture of a young African boy playing the drums. Frances opened her eyes to see what had happened. Kim didn't want to stay in the presence of that woman any longer than need be, so she wasn't going to take the time to pick it up. "I'm sure you'll think of something to tell Mama about that," she said, referring to the broken item. "You're good at lying," she snorted before storming out of the door.

As soon as Kim was gone, Marlene appeared in the kitchen doorway. Frances sat paralyzed as their gazes met.

"Mama, please tell me none of that is true," Marlene pleaded as a flood of tears poured down her face. "Tell me you didn't let me live a lie for *fifty-two years!*" she yelled. Kim hadn't been aware that her parents' meeting had let out early that day. Michael had brought his wife home, then gone out again. Marlene had been there the entire time and had heard every word that was said.

Frances couldn't bear looking at Marlene's horrified expression. Though she wished she could, Frances Eileen Gibson could not deny the accusations against her. She was speechless. She remembered how her mother used to say "Be mindful of what you do. Everything that's done in darkness will eventually come to light."

# Chapter Thirty-Three
## *Romans 8:28*

"MAMA, I AM SO SORRY!" Kim apologized to Marlene for the hundredth time. It was Saturday afternoon and Kim was helping her mother pack some things in Frances's room.

"Would you stop it? I told you I'm not mad at you." Marlene held up her hand to simulate a stop sign. All of Kim's apologizing was starting to get on her nerves.

"I know, I just feel so bad," Kim admitted. The day after she had found out about Harold being her grandfather, Michael had come by her place to tell her that he had moved Frances back into the senior center. Kim's first thought was *Good*, until Michael informed her that Marlene had heard the things she'd said to Frances. That had been several weeks ago now, and Kim had been apologizing ever since.

"What's done is done. No one can undo the past. We have to pick up the pieces and move on."

"Okay, but I'm still sorry."

*"Kim!"* Marlene stopped what she was doing and widened her eyes as she looked at her daughter.

"I won't say it anymore."

"Thank you." Marlene returned to boxing Frances's books. Michael was going to take the rest of her belongings to the senior center that evening when he got home. The day Frances had left she'd shoved whatever would fit into her duffel bag. Everything else was left in her room until this week, when Marlene had finally had the emotional strength to pack it up. Although she hadn't made her way to the center yet, Marlene had had a few brief conversations with her mother.

"Mama, I have to admit you're taking all of this much better than I thought you would. When Daddy told me that you were here that day, I was so worried about you."

"Yeah. I've had some rough days, but I thank the Lord that each day is easier than the day before. I try not to focus on the pain. I'm asking God what He wants me to learn from all of this." Marlene looked down and shook her head. "There's no need to worry, baby. Everything you see me handling is a result of the God in me. It's not me. The pain is still very raw, but Pastor Jones has been helping me work through it."

"We did it, Mama."

"Did what?"

"Terrance and I explained to Tori that he's not her biological father." Kim had some notebooks in her hands that belonged to Frances. "Is there room in that box for these?"

"Yeah, hand them here." Marlene grabbed the items. "So how did she take it?"

"Good, I guess. She had no idea what the word *biological* meant. We explained it in terms of her not having

Terrance's blood, but having someone named Darius's blood."

"Did she ask who Darius was?"

"Yes. We said that Darius was a friend of mine a long time ago. I told her that I didn't know where he was because he moved away. Terrance made sure to tell her that he *is* still her father no matter whose blood she carries. She asked him how. She had heard the word *stepfather* before and asked if that's what Terrance is."

"What did y'all say?"

"That technically, Terrance is her stepfather, but he's really so much more. Terrance stressed how much he loved her and he wanted to be with her. It was hard. I'm glad she didn't start crying or anything like that 'cuz I'm not sure if I would have been able to handle it. After we talked, she got up and played like nothing had ever happened."

"Good. That signifies that she was okay. Kids are like that. It's better that you told her now instead of lying to her all of her life and she finds out later." Marlene was speaking from her own experience. "You never know, Darius might try to come back into her life."

"I wouldn't put it past him after she's grown and he doesn't have to assume any responsibility for her. I wish I had never gotten involved with Darius and that Terrance was actually her biological father."

"You can't really say that, honey."

"Why not?"

"Had it not been for Terrance stepping in when Tori was a baby, you and he may have never become involved."

"Not necessarily."

"Even if you had, you two might have had a child, but

it wouldn't have been Tori. It's easy to wish things away, but if things were exactly how we wanted them, then they wouldn't be how God ordained them to be. Tori is supposed to be here, even if she wasn't born under ideal circumstances."

"So what about you? Are you saying that Gramma was right to have an affair?"

"Heavens no! What I do believe is that I was meant to be here. God wouldn't have allowed her to get pregnant otherwise." Marlene closed up one box and started folding shirts to put into another one. "Pastor Jones is a prime example of how God ordains lives even if a child is born from an adulterous affair."

"What does he have to do with this?"

"He can relate to what I'm saying. He was born out of adultery too."

"Nuh-uh."

"Yes, he was. His mother actually had an affair with a married man."

"You can't be telling the truth."

"I know you're not calling me a liar." Marlene put one hand on her hip and teased her daughter. "I *am* telling the truth." She returned to folding.

"I never knew that." Kim paused as though she were letting everything sink in.

"I don't think many people do. It's not something he goes around town bragging about. But look at how many lives he's impacted. Look at how he's helped me deal with this mess. God had a purpose for his life, and he's living it out as a pastor. Talking with him has helped me understand my situation. Everything happens for a reason, you know."

"I believe what you're saying about Pastor Jones, but I'm not sure if I buy into that everything-happens-for-a-reason philosophy."

"Why not?"

"Take Wendy's life, for example. Look at what has happened to her marriage in less than two years. It's scary. Kevin started out being a prince; now we find out he's really a frog. I'm still trippin' over him taking her car. That was just wrong." On the same day Kim went off on Frances, she had also found out that Kevin had filed for divorce. Wendy called her that night in tears. Until the actual divorce hearing took place, Kevin requested regularly scheduled visitation rights. In addition, he filed for joint custody and petitioned to have her move out of the house. Wendy had been given six months to find a job, a new place to live, and a baby-sitter for Kimberly. She had the right to file for full custody, child and spousal support. However, if she didn't comply with the other stipulations, Kevin could get temporary custody of Kimberly until the divorce hearing.

The news of Wendy's divorce hadn't come as a shock to Marlene, considering what had happened on New Year's Eve. "Now, now. Kevin is not the only one at fault here. Wendy had no business having Jaylen in that man's house."

"True, but—"

"But nothing. You want to take her side because she's your sister. That's fine, *but* right is right and wrong is wrong. A year ago when she found out that Kevin cheated on her, she should have left him then, if that's what she wanted to do."

"Where would she have gone?"

"Your daddy and I have made it no secret that our house will always be your house. She could have come back home. She didn't *have* to stop teaching."

"She wanted to be there with the baby."

"Key word: she *wanted*. I understand that. There are many women who want the same thing. However, the reality is they do what they *need* to do in order to take care of the child. I'm not working. I would have kept Kimberly for that girl. She ought to know that she wouldn't have had to pay me 'cuz I keep your kids for free whenever you need me to."

*True*, Kim thought to herself as she continued listening to her mother.

"Wendy wanted her cake and she wanted to eat it too. There's no doubt in my mind that she was hurt by Kevin. She may have wanted to leave him, but she didn't want to leave the lifestyle he provided for her. Kevin and the lifestyle come as a package deal. She thought she could have one without the other. That's why she finds herself in the predicament she's in. It's not Kevin's fault. He's like any other human being with sense. He's only going to allow himself to be used for a certain amount of time."

"I see your point, but that also proves my point."

"Which was?"

"There's nothing good that came out of this. Everyone loses: Kevin, Wendy, and, most of all, Kimberly. She can't even walk or talk yet and already comes from a broken home."

Marlene chuckled.

"What? Why are you laughing?" Kim frowned.

"I'm sorry—it wasn't funny. I laughed because someone who doesn't know the Bible might agree with you. You sound so convincing. However, my mind keeps coming back to Romans 8:28. It doesn't matter what the situation looks like, honey—it's the end result that counts."

"Okay, Mama. You gotta help me out now. I'm slowly learning this whole Bible thing, but you know that I can't quote scriptures. What does that passage say?"

Marlene rolled her eyes. "Girl, if I didn't know any better, I would think that you never cracked open a Bible before in your life. I know that's a lie because I used to take you and your sister to church with me all of the time." As an adult, Kim hadn't retained much of what she'd learned in church as a child. She knew a few basics like Psalm 23 or verses about sparing the rod and spoiling the child. However, in general she wasn't good at con-necting scriptures with their specific books in the Bible. "Do you even know whether or not the book of Romans is in the Old or New Testament?" Marlene playfully asked.

"Yes—I—do, thank you very much! It's in the New Testament, immediately before First Corinthians—so there." Kim sounded like Tori did when she made a point with Tyler. Except Tori was serious and said it with a lot of attitude. Kim was kidding.

Marlene lifted her hands in the air. "Thank You, Jesus. Something soaked into that child's head."

"I know where the book is at. I don't know that scrip-ture, though."

"Well, Romans 8:28 says that 'all things work together for good to them that love God, to them who are called according to His purpose.' You see, honey, when you really get serious about seeking a relationship with God, you don't have to worry about trials and tribulations that arise in your life. We all have them. As Christians, we may not know all the roads we have to take, but that's okay. Just go along for the ride because if we truly love God, then we know how things will end—all things *will* work out for our good. Your situation with Darius, my situation with Harold, and even your sister's situation with Kevin. Sure, it seems ugly right now. But God *can* make something good come out of it. We don't know what He has in store. That's why we just have to trust Him."

"That's just like a mama—when you think you got a point, she starts throwing scriptures up in the air to refute it."

Marlene laughed. "You know they say 'Mama knows best.' "

"Last time I checked it was 'Father knows best,' " Kim said wittily.

"You're right. It is 'Father,' but our Heavenly Father, see, He knows what's best for us. He knew that I probably wouldn't have been able to handle the news about Harold until now."

"Well, I'm still sor—" Kim was about to apologize again.

Marlene quickly stepped in. "Shh! I don't want to hear it. If you want to apologize for something, apologize for breaking my figurine and give me the two hundred dollars to replace it," she kidded.

"Two hundred dollars!" Kim was stunned. "It *really* cost that much? I can't believe y'all would pay that much for something so small."

"It was handmade. I know it sounds expensive, but it was well worth it, especially when you consider how much time and effort the person put into making it." Marlene really wasn't concerned about Kim replacing the figurine that had accidentally been knocked over. She had intentionally broken a few things herself after she found out about Harold. When Michael returned home that day, dinner was burning on the stove, Frances was a frozen fixture on the couch, and Marlene was an emotional basket case. Frances never said a word to Marlene that day. She humbly had told Michael that she believed she had worn out her welcome and requested to be taken back to the senior center. Of course, Marlene had no argument with that.

A few days later, Marlene called Harold. Her phone call was no surprise to him. Otis had already told him about Kim's visit and how angry she was. Harold was glad Marlene had made the call. He'd wanted to, but didn't know how she would react. Initially, Marlene was upset and asked why he hadn't told her the truth. Harold apologized numerous times. He said that he loved Marlene and was more concerned with not hurting her than he was with setting the record straight. So much time had passed since Frank's death. Instead of causing turmoil in her life, he just wanted to have some type of relationship with her, even if she never knew he was her father.

After their conversation, Marlene understood how difficult the situation was for him also. Frances had betrayed everyone: Marlene, Harold, and her husband, Frank Gibson. Pastor Jones became very instrumental in helping Harold and Marlene work through the pain of her discovery. As Pastor Jones suggested, they began counseling together.

"Will it be okay if I pay you back on the thirtieth of this month?" Kim said, referring to the item she had broken.

"You really don't have to. I was just playing, but I sho' won't stop you if you want to." Marlene laughed.

"Sure, no problem." Kim kissed her on the cheek. "Anything for my dear mother."

"Aren't you sweet."

"Yep!" Kim checked her watch. "Mama, I gotta go. Terrance and I have a meeting with Shelly."

"Who's that?"

"Remember, the wedding coordinator?"

"Oh, that's right. Are the kids staying with Evelyn again tonight?"

"Yes, but I'm going to pick them up in the morning and take them to church. Tomorrow is Evelyn's fiftieth birthday."

"Are you serious? That woman doesn't look a day over thirty-five."

"I know," Kim agreed.

"I'm surprised that you and Terrance aren't celebrating with her."

"Doug is taking her to some fancy restaurant downtown. I believe he has an evening for two in mind 'cuz Terrance and I were told about it, but we weren't invited." Kim winked.

"*Oh*, I see."

"Anyhow, we bought her a gift certificate to Charles Penzone."

"She'll love that."

"Yeah, she will. She's mentioned before that she would like to go there." Evelyn faithfully got weekly facials, massages, and other beauty maintenance treatments. She'd just never been to that particular day spa before, though.

"I'll give her a call in the morning to wish her happy birthday. Maybe I'll run out today and try to find her something."

"Okay. Well, I better get going."

"All right, honey. Thanks for coming by. I'll see you at church tomorrow."

"Okay." Kim headed downstairs, giggling to herself as she put on her coat and boots.

"Wait a minute!" Marlene yelled. She walked out of the bedroom to the top of the stairs. "There aren't thirty days in this month—it's February!"

Kim looked up and grinned. "I know."

"You brat. I should make you give me my money for real."

Kim looked very seriously at Marlene. "Mama, you do love God, don't you?"

Marlene frowned. "Yeah. What kind of question is that?"

"Then you should know that the figurine being broken will work out for your good. That's what Romans 8:28 says, right? If you believe that, then it doesn't need to be replaced because somehow my breaking it will benefit you in the end." Kim laughed hysterically at herself.

Marlene laughed and threw a shirt down the stairs. Kim ducked to the side as it flew past her. "Get out my house," she teased her daughter, and walked back into the room.

"Bye, Mama! I love you." Kim picked up the shirt and laid it on the railing.

"Love you too!" Marlene replied.

# Chapter Thirty-Four
# *One of Those Faces*

KEVIN AND RENÉE WERE ENJOYING A QUIET DINNER at Skyler's, one of Columbus's classiest downtown restaurants that overlooked the Scioto River. The soothing sounds of classical music played in the background, creating a very elegant atmosphere. Skyler's was known for its tableside menu. Dressed in black slacks, a white shirt, and a tie, the server would carry out the food on a cart and then describe, in detail, all of the choices. Meals ranged from fifty-one to seventy-five dollars per person. Skyler's was the type of place where guests didn't know how much a meal had cost until the bill came.

Renée was dressed in a snug-fitting brown satin pantsuit. Because she hadn't seen Kevin for quite some time, she wanted to make sure he got a good look at everything he'd almost let go. Since their spat on New Year's Eve, the two of them hadn't spoken until this past week, when Kevin called to invite her to dinner. At first she refused. She had left several messages for him in the last few weeks, and he had waited until February was nearly over before calling her back. Renée did not appreciate his actions. Kevin apologized for not getting back to her sooner. He told her what had happened with Wendy and explained that he needed time to sort things out by himself.

At first Renée wasn't willing to give him the time of day. She had never been rejected by any man and was used to getting what and whom she wanted. It wasn't until he uttered the word *divorce* followed by the sentence "Give me a chance to make things up to you" that Renée was certain of Kevin's interest in her. Then, for the greater good, she was willing to overlook his not calling—the greater good being that in due time, she would reap the benefits of dating a wealthy man.

The money, that was what Renée's pursuit of Kevin had been all about. He was just too blind to see past her facade. He thought she liked him for qualities such as his personality, chivalrousness, sense of humor, and attractiveness. All of that was true, but what Renée liked most about him was his success.

"Do you know how much longer the divorce is going to take?" Renée asked.

Kevin wiped his mouth with his napkin. He had just taken the last bite of his sautéed shrimp entrée. "Honestly, I'm not sure. It depends on how big a fight Wendy puts up. My attorney hasn't heard from hers yet. She has six months to adhere to all of the terms I set out, and then we go from there."

"Oh," Renée mumbled and put her fork down.

"Don't 'Oh' me. I know what you're thinking."

"And what is that, Mr. Mind Reader?"

Kevin laughed. "You're going to continue giving me a hard time, aren't you?" He pushed his plate aside, folded his hands on the table, and looked her straight in the eye. "I don't think either one of us got all dressed up to sit here and talk about my divorce."

"Sounds like an interesting topic to me." Renée took a sip of her wine.

"I have a better topic, if you're interested," Kevin said.

"Like what?"

"Let's talk about us. If you're still willing to be friends, I want to try again. This time, with the understanding that we are definitely more than *just* friends."

Renée gave a sly grin.

"I still want to take things very slow, though," Kevin admitted. This divorce was not easy for him. He still had a few unresolved feelings about Wendy. However, she had apparently moved on, and so would he. Kevin thought that Renée was a great girl and didn't want to miss the opportunity for a wonderful relationship with her.

"And how slow is slow?" Renée inquired. "We've been through slow before."

"Let's just say that it would be at least a few years before I think I would be ready to remarry, *but*"—Kevin emphasized the word *but* after Renée rolled her eyes—"I think we've graduated from the hug to the kiss stage," he teased.

"Oh, really?"

"Really," Kevin stated with an affirmative nod.

Roberto, the Italian, dark-haired waiter, walked up with his food cart. "Excuse me, would either one of you be interested in having dessert?"

"I think we're having dessert at his place tonight,"

Renée responded to the waiter, but kept her eyes on Kevin.

Kevin chuckled and adjusted his tie. Renée's forwardness in front of the waiter was unexpected, but flattering. "No sir—we're fine. I'll take the check now."

"Yes sir. I'll be back in a few moments," he responded.

Kevin looked at Renée. "I can't believe you're that anxious for a little peck on the cheek. You do know that is what I was referring to, right?"

"Yeah, whatever."

He poured the remaining wine into their glasses. "Let's make a toast"—he held his wineglass up to Renée's—"to us . . . to the start of something new."

"To us," she repeated. They both took a drink. "Will you excuse me for a moment while I go to the ladies' room?" she asked.

"Sure."

Renée got up and Kevin continued sipping his wine. Instead of taking her to his place, he would drive her back home. He had every intention of kissing her good night, but that was all. He wouldn't take it any further. Wendy had already accused him of adultery, and he wanted to make certain that the accusation remained false.

"Evelyn?" Kevin said to the person walking by his table.

Evelyn turned. She smiled when she saw Kevin and took a few steps backward. "I didn't even see you sitting there."

"How are you doing?" Kevin stood up and gave her a hug.

"I'm fine. I haven't seen you in a month of Sundays."

"I know. It's good to see you. What brings you out here?"

"My husband brought me here to celebrate my birthday."

"Is that right? I guess you only turn twenty-five once."

"Oh boy, stop it," Evelyn said in a flattered tone.

"Where is Doug? Are you coming or going?" Kevin noticed that she had her coat on.

"We're just getting here. Doug is sitting over there." Evelyn pointed to her left. Kevin looked across a few tables and waved. Doug waved back. "I was just on my way to the rest room."

"Here you are, sir." Roberto handed the check to Kevin, who was still standing with Evelyn. "I'll take that whenever you're ready."

"I'm sorry. I don't mean to inconvenience you, but can you add the cost of a private room to this bill?" He looked at Evelyn. "It's my birthday present to you."

"No, you don't have to do that." Evelyn looked at the waiter. "I'm fine, really."

"No, I insist." Kevin turned and gave the waiter his debit card. "Please see if you have a private room. Thank you."

Roberto left.

"You didn't have to do that."

"No problem at all. It's good to see you. Man, it's been what, over a year now since I last saw you?"

"Yeah since you—" Evelyn cut her sentence short and there was an awkward moment of silence. Neither one of them wanted to mention Wendy or the divorce. Evelyn knew about Wendy's and Kevin's separation in general, but she didn't know many of the details. "You have a beautiful baby," she stated.

"Thank you. She's pretty special."

"Here you are, sir. I have revised the bill." Roberto gave Kevin the payment slip and turned to Evelyn. "Ma'am, we'll get you seated in a few minutes."

"Thank you very much," Kevin said, signing the receipt and giving Roberto a large tip. "I appreciate your service."

"You're welcome, sir. Thank you, and have a nice evening."

"You too," Kevin responded.

Renée walked up to the table. "Sorry I took so long. I—" She stopped speaking when she saw Evelyn.

"Evelyn, this is my friend Renée; Renée, this is Evelyn." Kevin introduced the two. "Evelyn is the future mother-in-law of my soon-to-be ex-sister-in-law." He smirked. "That sounds crazy, doesn't it?"

"Haven't we met before?" Evelyn asked her with a hint of uncertainty in her voice.

"No, I don't think we have," she responded with a straight face and held out her hand. "Nice to meet you."

Evelyn gripped Renée's hand. "You look very familiar to me. I'm sure I know you from somewhere," she now said with conviction.

"I guess I just have one of those faces." Renée felt uncomfortable as she pried her hand from Evelyn's grip. She turned to Kevin. "Are you ready?"

"Sure." He hugged Evelyn one more time. "It's good to see you, it really is. Happy Birthday!"

"Thank you. You take care."

"I will."

Instead of going to the rest room as she had originally planned, Evelyn walked over to where her husband was sitting.

Kevin assisted Renée with her coat. The two of them walked out of Skyler's hand-in-hand as Evelyn stared after them.

# Chapter Thirty-Five
## *Something Like That*

KIM BURST THROUGH THE FRONT DOOR of Kevin's office building like a bull that had spotted red. Late last night, Evelyn had called her with concerns about possibly seeing Kevin out with one of Wendy's friends. She couldn't remember her name, but the woman last night introduced herself as Renée. Evelyn talked about the eerie resemblance Renée had to the lady who had accompanied them the day Kim picked out her wedding dress. Instantly, Kim knew it was Natalie. Once she heard how upset Kim was, Evelyn tried suggesting that maybe it could have been a cousin or a sister of Natalie's, but Kim knew better. Natalie didn't have any siblings. Plus, Kim had never known Natalie to have any relatives in Columbus, besides her mother. She told Evelyn about the time Gwen had seen Natalie and Kevin together. Kim could kick herself for believing that it had been just a coincidence. She now had a gut feeling that it had been much more. It was a premeditated attempt by the two of them to carry on a relationship behind Wendy's back.

It was after midnight when she and Evelyn got off the phone, and Kim didn't want to call Wendy that late with such disturbing news. She planned to go over to her house today. First, she wanted to let loose on Kevin the words that had tumbled through her mind the entire night. The next time she saw Natalie, she would have a few choice words for her, also.

Kim was so angry that it was impossible for her to get any sleep. She got a glimpse of how horrible she looked from her reflection in the building's glass doors. Most of her hair was pulled into a ponytail with the exception of a few strands that had gone astray. She wore a pair of faded black sweatpants with a gray Ohio State sweatshirt of Terrance's that was too big. Kim was so fired up that she had mistakenly left home without a coat. For a person who did not like being cold, that morning she had been unaffected by the weather. Her body temperature had been rising steadily since Evelyn's phone call.

Kevin's office building was a large three-story brick building that housed his real estate company, an insurance company, and a law office. Kevin owned the building and ran his company from the third floor while leasing the remaining office space. "Hi, can I help you?" A woman in her mid-thirties with short, reddish brown hair smiled at Kim.

"I need to see Kevin Phillips, please," Kim stated without smiling back.

"Do you have an appointment?"

"No."

"I'm afraid Mr. Phillips is not available right now. He's on a conference call. You're free to make an appointment or wait until he gets off the phone and I'll see if he can fit you in."

"I'll wait."

"Okay. Have a seat and I'll let you know if and when he can see you. May I tell him your name, please?"

"Ki—can you tell him that his good friend Natalie is waiting to see him?" Kim ignored the woman's request to sit down and leaned on the desk instead. Gwen closed the salon on Sundays and Mondays so Kim didn't have to work that day. It was a quarter to ten now. The kids didn't have to be picked up from school until three-thirty. She would wait all day if she had to.

The lady who had greeted Kim answered the phone. "Thank you for calling Phillips Realty. Leanne speaking—how can I direct your call? Mr. Phillips is on another line right now. Would you like to be connected to his voice mail? One moment; I'll transfer you."

Kim stared at the nameplate hanging on the door behind Leanne's desk. KEVIN PHILLIPS, CEO. If he didn't get off the phone soon, she didn't know how long she could continue to resist the urge to march right into his office and terminate the call.

"I believe he's off the phone now," Leanne confirmed.

*Thank You!* Kim silently prayed.

Leanne picked up her phone receiver and dialed Kevin's extension. "Mr. Phillips, I just transferred a call to your voice mail and there's a woman named Natalie here to see you. She said she's a friend of yours." She used her hand to cover the mouthpiece of the phone and spoke to Kim. "Ma'am, would you mind stating the nature of your visit? Mr. Phillips apologizes, but he can't recall knowing anyone by that name."

"Oh, he knows me, all right." Kim strutted past Leanne.

"You can't go in there. . . ."

It was too late. Kim entered Kevin's office and slammed the door behind her. The door shut so hard that the framed college degree that hung on Kevin's wall rattled.

Kevin looked up with a surprised expression. "Kim?" Leanne must have said something to him through the phone. "No, there's no need to call Security. It's my sister-in-law," he responded, and hung up. "What is this business of you saying your name was Natalie?"

"You dirty dawg!" Kim walked up and yelled across his desk.

"Wait a minute. If you're here to badger me about the divorce, I'm not talking to you about it. It's between Wendy and me, so I suggest you stay out of it."

Kim gave him a fierce look. "Don't you dare try and play stupid. You *know* why I'm here. How could you go out with Natalie behind Wendy's back? It's not enough that you're taking everything away from her, is it? You have to rub salt in her wounds by having an affair with her friend?"

Kevin stood up. "First of all, you need to calm down—"

"Don't tell me what to do!"

"I believe that I have the right to, since this is my office," Kevin said smugly, as he owned all four hundred square feet of that room and then some.

"Whatever."

"Either you lower your voice and tell me what's on your mind or I *will* have Security escort you out."

"Oh, excuse me. I forgot. You're Mr. Big Shot. Mr. Moneymaker. Mr. Not-only-did-I-cheat-on-my-wife-and-give-her-chlamydia-but-now-I'll-continue-trampling-on-her-feelings-by-sleeping-with-one-of-her-best-friends," Kim said sarcastically.

"What are you talking about? Cut to the chase and tell me what has gotten your feathers all ruffled or get out."

"Why, Kevin? Out of all the women in Columbus, why did you have to pick Natalie?" Kim asked in a hurt tone.

Kevin looked puzzled. "*Who* is Natalie?"

"The lady you were seen with at Skyler's yesterday."

Kevin sat back in his chair and leaned backward. "So that's what all of this is about? Evelyn told you about seeing me with another woman yesterday. Tell your mother-in-law that she needs to remember names correctly if she's going to report them. Her name is not Natalie, it's Renée. Furthermore, I really don't have to explain anything to you because Wendy and I are getting a divorce, remember?"

"I know all about how you introduced Natalie as Renée. Did the two of you really think you could get away with this without anyone finding out?"

"Finding out what? You're not making any sense. I don't care who sees me with Renée. I'm not going to hide my relationship with her because you, Evelyn, Wendy, or anyone else feels uncomfortable. Get over it!"

Kim looked disturbed and spoke her thoughts aloud. "Renée?"

"Yes, her name is Renée." The phone rang, but Kevin didn't answer it.

"Oh my goodness," Kim exclaimed as this new revelation sank in. "It's Renée!"

"Look, I would love to sit here and keep saying her name with you, but I have a business to run." Kevin reached for his telephone.

"By any chance is her last name Coleman?"

"Yeah. How did you know?" Kevin stopped short of picking up his phone and looked at Kim strangely.

"Oh my God . . ." Kim plopped down in the chair behind her and smacked her forehead with the palm of her hand. "Why didn't I figure this out before?"

"Figure out what?" Kevin looked confused.

"You seriously know her as Renée, don't you? Is she the same person you had over for Thanksgiving?"

"Yes."

"Oh my God."

"What?" Kevin was stressed. "Quit saying that and tell me what's going on."

"She knew. . . . Gwen was right about Natalie the first time."

"Right about what? Who in the heck is Natalie?" Kevin assertively inquired.

"Natalie is Renée."

"What? That's ridiculous."

"Natalie Renée Coleman. That's her name."

"Whose name? Renée's?"

"Yes. Her full name is Natalie Renée Coleman. She and Wendy have been friends since high school."

"No, that can't be true. There has to be a misunderstanding. Renée would never deceive me like that. Even if she does know Wendy, I'm sure there's some kind of rational explanation here. Wendy never mentioned anyone by the name of Natalie or Renée to me before."

"That's because Natalie has lived in New York for a number of years. She just moved back in town within the last year."

"*New York?*" Kevin thought it was a strange coincidence, but he still tried to make sense of the situation. "That still doesn't prove that Renée did anything wrong. *If*, in fact, she is Natalie. We had never met before."

"When you did meet her, she knew exactly who you were. I can guarantee it."

"But how?"

Kim told Kevin about Natalie being at the house the day he showed up during Wendy's baby shower. He was having a hard time believing it all, but there were too many similarities between his Renée and Natalie. Kim and Kevin talked for at least an hour, during which time Leanne forwarded numerous unanswered calls to him.

Kevin told Kim about the argument with Wendy that drove him to the club the night he met Renée. When asked why he cheated on Wendy in the first place, Kevin also told his sister-in-law about the letter he had written Wendy explaining how she'd ended up with chlamydia. Kim was astonished. She admitted to Kevin that there was a good chance Wendy had never read his letter.

"What do you mean she never read it?"

"I truly don't think Wendy has any idea what really happened between you and this other woman. If she does, she sure didn't tell me. Until this very moment, I always believed that you committed adultery."

Kevin turned his leather swivel chair around and looked out the window. He was more confused than ever. He had been under the impression that Wendy had read the letter and just didn't care.

Kim had come into to the office ready to kill Kevin; now she was ready to console him. "Are you going to be all right?"

She watched the back of Kevin's head as he nodded and softly said, "Yes."

"I'm sorry, Kevin."

"For what? None of this is your fault. If you don't mind, can you leave? I need time to process all of this."

"I understand. I just . . ." Kim slowly got out of her chair. She wasn't sure what else to say. She walked toward the door and left with every intention of visiting Wendy.

"Mr. Phillips?" A frustrated Leanne came into his office after Kim walked out.

Kevin turned around. "Yes?"

"Jacob Bailey had a ten-o'clock appointment with you. He waited for a while then left without saying anything."

"Oh, man." Kevin rested his left hand on his forehead. "I completely forgot." Mr. Bailey was one of Kevin's potential clients who had been interested in purchasing a large amount of land owned by Kevin's company. Jacob Bailey was not one who liked to be kept waiting and Kevin had some serious damage control to do. "See if you can get him on the phone and try to reschedule. Tell him I'm really sorry, but an emergency came up."

Leanne puckered her lips as if to say *That lady who was here didn't look like an emergency to me*. "There's a Renée Coleman holding for you on line one. She called here four times already," Leanne stated in a bothered tone of voice before walking out.

Kevin stared at the blinking hold light on his telephone. He took a deep breath before answering, "This is Kevin."

"It's about time I got ahold of you. I don't like that secretary of yours. She's got an attitude."

"Hi, Renée." His voice quivered.

"Hi, Renée? That's the best I get the day after we shared our first kiss?" she teased.

Kevin didn't respond.

"Hello?"

"Yeah, I'm still here."

"Ugh . . . did someone get up on the wrong side of the bed this morning?"

"No, I've just been having an interesting day today, that's all. What's up?"

"Are we still on for tonight?"

Kevin had forgotten about the dinner plans he had made with Renée for that evening. "Um . . ."

"Don't tell me you have to cancel." She sounded disappointed.

"Well I-I—no, I don't have to cancel. I forgot to make reservations."

"That's okay, I can do it. Where do you want to go?"

"Let's do Skyler's again."

"Skyler's? Two nights in a row?"

"It's one of the best formal dining places around. Why not?"

"I didn't know we were going for formal tonight, but I can deal with it. What time should I make the reservations for?"

"Seven."

Leanne crept back into Kevin's office. "I have Mr. Bailey on the phone for you," she whispered.

"Listen, I have an important call I have to take."

"What time are you going to pick me up?"

"Things are so hectic today that I may not get out of here in time to come and get you. Can you meet me there?"

"Sure."

"Also, see if Skyler's has any private rooms available."

"Want to be alone, do you?"

"Yeah, something like that. I'll see you tonight."

"Okay, you know I can't wait."

"Yeah, me too," Kevin said before ending the call.

## Chapter Thirty-Six
## Stuck with the Bill

KEVIN AND RENÉE ATE THEIR DINNER in a secluded room at Skyler's. It was a pretty big meal. Because of Kim's visit and rescheduling with Jacob Bailey, Kevin had skipped lunch. He had managed to smooth things over with Mr. Bailey and close the deal despite the earlier mishap. Renée was wearing a form-fitting black dress. Like the pantsuit she'd had on last night, it showed off every curve on her body. Her hair was pinned up, and she wore a fancy pearl necklace and earring set. She looked like a million bucks even though she wasn't worth it.

Kevin remained quiet during dinner. He'd been contemplating the right time to ask Renée about her relationship with Wendy. Renée talked nonstop about a photo shoot she'd had that afternoon. In light of his conversation with Kim, it was becoming painfully obvious to Kevin how self-centered Renée was. *Why didn't I see this before?* He questioned himself as she continued babbling. *Probably because I never wanted to. I wanted to believe she was a fabulous person, but she doesn't even know me. The only thing she knows about me is about my relationship with Wendy. That's all she's ever been concerned about. She doesn't know my favorite color, when my birthday is, or what types of movies I like. It's been all about her. Her favorite color is red. Her birthday is May tenth. Her favorite types of movies are drama movies—go figure.* "I'm sorry, what did you say?" Kevin unconsciously had drowned Renée out to the extent that he hadn't realized she'd asked a question until she said his name.

"I *said*, are you okay? You seem a little different."

"How so?"

"I don't know. You came in and sat down. You didn't give me a hug, a kiss, or nothing."

"Sorry, I told you that I had a hectic day."

"Well, you sure worked up an appetite. At least you thought you did. It looks like your eyes were bigger than your stomach." Renée commented on all of Kevin's uneaten food. He couldn't decide among the lobster, steak, or chicken entrées so he'd ordered all three. Kevin had also ordered a very expensive bottle of Italian wine.

"I guess I'll have a lot of leftovers this week, huh?"

Renée spoke flirtatiously. "At least you won't have to eat them alone. I'll help you out."

"I'm sure you would," Kevin murmured under his breath.

"Have you spoken with your wife today?" Renée inquired before she parted her lips to drink.

"No, I haven't. Have you?"

Renée began coughing as the shock of Kevin's question sent the liquid down the wrong pipe. He stared blankly, waiting for a response. "Boy, you're so crazy," she joked after calming herself and wiping her mouth. "I hope I never have to see that woman after all she's put you through. She's a trip."

"Why don't you tell her that yourself, Natalie?"

"Huh?"

Kevin spoke more slowly. "Why don't you tell my wife how you feel about the situation?"

"What did you call me?"

"Natalie. That is your name, isn't it? You know Evelyn, the lady who was here yesterday—she recognized you."

Renée was silent.

Kevin shrugged. "You might as well admit it. I already know that you introduced yourself to me using your middle name."

"So," Natalie said dryly. She really thought she had fooled Evelyn by remaining calm and pretending not to be bothered by her presence. "That's not uncommon. A lot of people use their middle names."

"Oh, I agree with you. What is uncommon is for you to go months without telling me that you are friends with my wife."

"I didn't know she was your wife when we first met. You told me you were married. You didn't say to whom." Natalie had been practicing that line since she and Kevin had met. She knew this moment would come one day. However, she'd thought it would be after the divorce. That would have given her more time to sink her claws into Kevin.

Kevin laughed to himself sarcastically. "I had a feeling you would go that route. Before you travel any further, let me just say that the day we met is different from the day you first saw me. I know you were at my wife's baby shower."

"I might have glanced at you that day, but I certainly didn't put two and two together until recently."

"Do you think I'm gullible enough to believe that?"

"It's the truth."

"How can you justify keeping your relationship with my wife a secret from me all these months?"

"I don't have to," Natalie snapped.

"What?" Kevin was astonished by her response. "You don't have to? What kind of heartless woman are you?"

"The same woman that comforted your butt when Wendy hurt your feelings. Now all of a sudden I'm heartless? You didn't seem to think so when you were spending so much time with me. You especially didn't think so last night when you wrapped your lips around mine."

"Yeah, well, I see I made a big mistake by trusting you. You had the perfect opportunity to tell me the truth after we saw Evelyn, but you didn't."

"I *said* I didn't know the woman. I meet tons of people in my line of work. People tell me that they have seen me before all the time. Do you actually think I remember every face I see?"

"You really expect me to believe that?"

"Believe whatever you want. I told you I didn't know what's-her-name last night, and I don't."

"Okay, then what about Kimberly? You've spent time with my daughter and me. You've also spent time with Wendy and Kimberly. You can't tell me you didn't know it was the same baby."

Natalie sighed and spoke unremorsefully, "I'm sorry I didn't come clean with you. Can we just finish dinner? I'm sure after you calm down you'll see things from my per-

spective. We can get past this, you know?" she said to
Kevin, and took a bite of her food.

Kevin shook his head. "Unbelievable! You really have
no shame, do you?"

Natalie ignored him and continued eating.

"I . . . I gotta go to the bathroom." Kevin got up, threw
his napkin down on the table, and walked out of the
room.

Natalie put down her fork and took another drink of
her wine. Now that everything was out in the open, she
expected to hear from Wendy soon. *I'll tell her that I would
have never had the opportunity to take Kevin from her if she
wasn't already giving him away.* She sat at the table smiling
deviously. *He'll want to be with me rather than her, especially
after what happened with Jaylen. Kevin and I have had too
much fun together to separate now. He'll get over this. He just
needs a little time. Wendy doesn't have a chance in this world
of getting him back. Besides, I have way more to offer than she
does,* she thought to herself.

"Excuse me, ma'am—will this be with cash or credit?"
a short, bald Caucasian waiter named Paul asked. He was
certainly the least attractive of all the servers at Skyler's.

Natalie looked at the waiter. "I don't know," she said
with an attitude. "You'll have to ask my boyfriend. He'll
be back—he went to the rest room."

"Are you referring to the gentleman who was just in
here with you?"

"Yes." *Dumb question. Who else would I be referring to?*

Paul frowned. "Ma'am, he left. On the way out, he said
you were ready for the bill. Again, will this be cash or
credit?"

"What! You have got to be kidding me!" She stood up and snatched the bill out of his hands. "Oh my God!" She grabbed the table to keep her tall, slender frame from falling when she saw the total printed in bold, black ink at the bottom. The cost of the dinner came to $567.98, including tax, tip, and the service charge for using a private room. "I-I-I can't afford this," she stammered.

"You are Renée Coleman, correct?"

"Yes."

"Ma'am, I'm sorry but the reservation was made under your name. You *are* responsible for tonight's meal."

"Wait a minute. There has to be a misunderstanding here. I'll just call Kevin and clarify this whole thing. I'm sure he probably meant to give you his credit card or pay for it before he left." Natalie nervously got her cell phone out of her purse and dialed Kevin's number. She had less than twenty dollars in her purse, and all of her credit cards were maxed out.

"Yeah?" Kevin answered the phone very calmly.

"Where are you?" Natalie demanded.

"I'm in my car driving on the freeway."

"How dare you leave without telling me. You forgot to pay the bill."

"No I didn't."

She turned away from the waiter and whispered into the phone, "Kevin, I know you're upset, but this is not the time for games. I don't have any money."

"Aw, I'm sorry to hear that. I hope you can come up with it somehow. Skyler's does prosecute people who leave without paying. It's called theft of service."

"Theft of service!" Natalie looked behind her. Paul

impatiently tapped his foot on the floor, waiting for payment. Natalie turned back around and pleaded with Kevin. "Look, Kevin, please come back and pay this bill. Hate me if you want to, but don't leave me in this position. You're the one who ordered *three* entrées, not me."

"Sorry, Natalie, Renée, or whatever your name is, but I'm afraid I can't help you out."

"You idiot!" she screamed. "How can you justify doing this to me?"

"Let's see. . . . What was that you said to me when I asked you how you could justify your deceptiveness these last few months? Oh, that's right, you said, 'I don't have to,'" Kevin retorted sarcastically and hung up, leaving her stuck with the bill.

## Chapter Thirty-Seven
# In the Master's Hands

WENDY SAT AT THE DESK IN THE STUDY trying to figure out what to do next. She had thought she could trust Natalie but now knew she couldn't. She should have trusted Kevin and hadn't. *How did my life get so out of control?* she wondered. Wendy was dumbfounded after what Kim had told her earlier. "No, not Natalie," she'd kept repeating. "She wouldn't do this to me. She's my friend." Wendy desperately wanted to believe in her friendship with Natalie, but the writing was on the wall. It couldn't be any clearer. Natalie encouraged Wendy to call Jaylen and forget about Kevin. All the while, she'd known the truth. Natalie knew that Kevin had never cheated on Wendy and didn't tell her. *How could I be so stupid?* she asked herself.

It burned Wendy up inside to know that it was Natalie who had been at Kevin's place on Thanksgiving. Wendy's first instinct was to go and beat the life out of her. She had never been in a fistfight, but she had been ready to try out her fighting skills on Natalie that day. Surprisingly, it was Kim who talked her out of having any verbal or physical confrontation with her backstabbing friend. Kim admitted that she initially wanted to tell Natalie a few things, also. However, after her conversation with Kevin, she realized that Wendy bore the burden for the way things had played out, not Natalie. "You should have read his letter," Kim had declared. As much as Wendy still wanted to strangle Natalie, she knew Kim was right. If Wendy was to blame anyone, she first had to point the finger at herself.

The guilt of not believing Kevin when he professed his innocence was magnified when she read the letter. It took some searching, but she managed to find it. It was right inside the desk where she had put it more than a year earlier. Wendy recalled being angry and stubborn the night Kevin came to visit her after he'd returned from Philly. She didn't think there was any other explanation besides him cheating on her. In her mind, he was guilty and there was nothing he could say to get out of it. She now held the emancipation letter that declared her husband's innocence.

*Dear Wendy,*

*If you're reading this letter then it must be the last chance I have of making things right with you. I'm sorry for everything that happened. I swear to you that I didn't cheat on you. Well, how did I get chlamydia, then? you're wondering. It's a long story, but I will explain it as quickly and as well as I can.*

*Remember I told you about a friend of mine named Joanne? I said that we grew up together. Back in the* day, she was one of my best friends. When I first moved here for college, I didn't know anyone in Columbus. I was homesick. I missed my family, my boys, and even Joanne. Out of all my so-called friends, she was the only one who would come and visit me periodically. I felt special. You know, like she really cared about me. At first her visits were platonic, but eventually they turned into something more. We tried dating for a while, but the distance was hard on us both, especially since we were both college students with very little money to continue flying back and forth. We mutually agreed to just be friends. Every blue moon she would come and visit, but not as often as before.

Whenever I went back to Philly, I would see her. Although we called our relationship a "friendship," we still remained sexually active. I'm not proud of this, but Joanne and I had an understanding that this was the nature of our "friendship." Even when we were involved in other relationships, we still hooked up. This went on for a number of years and we were both okay with it.

Do you recall the trip I took to Philadelphia a few weeks after you and I had met? There's no easy way to say this, so I'll just spit it out. Joanne and I got together then. But this time it was different. I felt guilty. I had always been able to rationalize my actions when I was dating other females. Either I suspected they weren't faithful or I knew they were not marriage material for one reason or another, so it didn't matter to me that what I was doing was wrong. But you, Wendy, you were not like any of the other women I had dated, including Joanne. You were smart, funny, beautiful, caring, gentle, etc. You had goals. Life wasn't all about partying and seeing which guys you could run game on. You were a lady with class, and I fell in love with you way before I uttered the words.

You don't know how much it meant to me that you didn't go to work and unexpectedly met me at the airport when I returned to Columbus after that visit. You said that it was all because you missed me. Seeing you at the airport confirmed what I had already concluded in Philadelphia: I needed to let Joanne go. That night I called her and told her it was over. She thought we could revert back to being strictly platonic friends, but I believed we had gone too far over the platonic line to go back. I didn't want anything or anyone to stand in the way of my relationship with you. I should have told you, but I feared I would lose you if I did. I had no idea that I would one day be in the position that I am in now.

Over the holidays, I contacted Joanne. She was surprised to hear from me. Believe it or not, she was afraid that you and I had broken up and that I was calling her to see if we could hook back up. She intended to tell me no because, like me, she had found true love. It was weird, but I asked her if she ever had chlamydia. She told me yes. I explained to her the situation I was in with you. She apologized for never calling and informing me that she had it. She said I had made it very clear that I was ceasing all contact with her and, initially, she was bitter about the way I abruptly ended things. Neither one of us can say who gave it to the other because we both had practiced unsafe sex with more than one partner. Just so you know, I have been treated and no longer have the dis-

*ease. Anyhow, Joanne is willing to verify my story. If you don't believe me, call her yourself. Her number is 267–555–3273.*

At the beginning of the letter, I said that I never cheated on you. I guess in the larger scheme of things, technically I did. I'm hoping that you will forgive me for the one indiscretion that I committed back when we first met. Since that time, I have never touched another woman and I don't ever want to.

Wendy, I am so sorry. I am willing to do anything to make our marriage work out. I don't want to lose you. I know you complain that I go out too much and you get mad because I don't go to church with you regularly, but please give me some time. I didn't grow up in a Christian home like you did. This is all new to me. I apologize for not being more sympathetic during the times you've tried to talk to me about these issues. I guess I can understand now why you would think that I committed adultery. Baby, finding out you're pregnant should be a joyous occasion for us. We're starting a family. I want many more children with you. One of my New Year's resolutions is to be a better husband so that I can be a good father. I want to prove to you how much you mean to me. I will stop smoking—it's unhealthy for me anyhow and it certainly wouldn't be good for any of my clients to find out. I'm also giving up my party life. To be honest, I was getting pretty bored with it anyhow. Part of me was being rebellious because I didn't want to give you the power of telling me what to do. So the more you pressured me about not going out, the more I went out. I'm sorry. I'm willing to make improvements in every area of my life where I have let you down. And *yes, I'll even TRY to go to church with you more often. All I need is for you to give me another chance. I love you.*

*Kevin*

That was it. That was the letter that explained the side of the story Wendy never knew. It made perfect sense. Kevin had already been infected with chlamydia when he and Wendy married. Dr. Korva said that it wasn't uncommon for infected persons not to have symptoms or for the symptoms to go unnoticed. Had she not gone to the gynecologist due to her pregnancy, there's no telling how long she and Kevin would have carried the disease. It wasn't like she was faithful in scheduling her annual exams. Unless she was having problems, she procrastinated doing so. In her opinion, most single women went to the gynecologist for fear of being pregnant or to make sure they didn't have any diseases. Neither reason applied to her, so she often delayed her annual checkups.

Wendy didn't believe it would be necessary to call Joanne. "Hello, I was just wondering if you had casual sex with my husband and in the process gave him chlamydia." That would be a strange conversation. For hours, she had been wanting to call Kevin, but she didn't know what to say. *He probably hates me by now after all I've put him through*, she thought.

Wendy could hear that Kimberly was still awake through the baby monitor. Tears dropped from her eyes as she thought about how Kimberly's life would be affected by this whole ordeal. *You just wouldn't listen to him, would you?* she badgered herself. *He tried numerous times to get you to listen, but you foolishly pushed him away every time, how could you be so stupid?*

The doorbell rang. She looked at the clock. It was after nine. *Who's coming to visit this time of night? Probably Kim and Gwen coming to throw a pity party.* On the way to the door, Wendy tied her robe, and wiped the tears from her cheeks. Once there, she looked out of the peephole and gasped. Standing on the other side wasn't her sister or her best friend; it was her soon-to-be-ex-husband.

He rang the doorbell again.

"Hey," she said solemnly once she opened the door.

Kevin noticed the traces of dried tears on her face. "Is this a bad time?"

"No, come in." She moved out of the way so he could enter the foyer. "Do you want me to take your coat?" she asked after shutting the door.

"No, I'm not going to stay long. Um . . . has Kim been by today?"

"Yes . . ."

"I just wanted to come by and apologize."

"You don't owe me an apology. I'm the one at fault. I also blame Natalie because she betrayed me, but I really can't say the same thing about you."

"Wendy, I swear I didn't know who she was. I promise," Kevin pledged as they stood near the door.

"I believe you and I really appreciate you coming all the way over here just to say that."

"No problem." He gripped the doorknob. "Well, I better go. I have a long day at work tomorrow."

"Wait!" Wendy placed her hand on the door to prevent

him from opening it. She wasn't ready for him to leave. "Do you want to see Kimberly?"

"Is she still up?"

"Yeah—at least she was a minute ago."

"Of course I want to see her."

"She's in the nursery."

Kevin walked behind Wendy to Kimberly's room. Kimberly's head lifted up when the door opened and she started fussing. Kevin took off his coat and spread it over the back of the rocking chair. When he walked over to the crib, he smiled as Kimberly reached her arms out to him. "How's Daddy's baby doing?" He spoke in a soft child-like manner and kissed his daughter on the cheek. "What are you still doing up, young lady? I think it's past your bedtime."

"Maybe she sensed that you were coming."

"Is that it, pretty girl? Did you know your daddy was coming over?"

Kimberly made a baby noise that sounded like she answered yes. Her parents laughed. Wendy wiped the baby's slobbering mouth while Kevin held her.

"I'm sorry," Wendy blurted, and started crying.

Kevin looked at his wife.

"I'm *really* sorry for not believing you. I read the letter. I know it's too late to change the past, but I'm sorry."

Kimberly yawned and laid her head on Kevin's shoulder. He patted her back.

"I don't think we should talk about this right now."

"I know. I hate the fact that I have been so stubborn."

"Me too," Kevin sighed.

"Do you—do you think we could try again? I mean, I

know you already started the divorce and all, but I'm willing to make it work this time."

Kevin stared at the Winnie-the-Pooh decorations on Kimberly's wall. "Why? Why do you want to make it work now? I'm honestly not sure what the right thing to do is. There were a lot of things said and done that I just don't know if we'll be able to get past."

"We can try counseling or something."

"What happened to the woman who didn't love me anymore?"

"I've always loved you." Wendy owned up to her feelings. "I was hurt"—Kevin looked like he was going to speak, but Wendy stepped in. "I know, I know . . . had I read your letter, this would have all been cleared up. But I didn't. I can't change what has happened. I wish I could. God, I wish I could," she belted. "I don't want my marriage to end."

Tears hadn't fallen out of Kevin's eyes yet, but he couldn't hide the quivering sound of his voice. "You know, Wendy, if I hadn't caught you here with that guy, I might believe that you want to try. I thought you were just mad at me and so you were trying to make me jealous that night you said you had plans. Renée wanted to go out with me and I turned her down. Seeing you here with another man devastated me. It became painfully apparent to me that you had moved on." Kimberly had fallen asleep on Kevin's shoulder, and he placed her in the crib.

"No, I didn't. I was trying to because of what happened on Thanksgiving. At that time, I didn't want to be with you because I thought you had betrayed me, but I hated the thought of you being happy with someone else."

"But *why?*"

"I don't know, Kevin—because I still loved you. I just didn't like what I thought you had done."

"Do you really love me, Wendy? Or do you love everything that I provide? Do you not want to get a divorce because you don't want to give up the house, you want your car back, you don't want to have to work—what is it? Is it me or is it all of the luxuries that come with me? That's what I'm confused about. I'm trying to convince myself that you really loved me, but it's hard. It's very hard after everything that has happened." He took his coat off the chair. "I need to go. I have a lot of work to catch up on tomorrow that I didn't get to finish today."

Wendy was crying so hard that the tears blurred her vision. "It's you that I love. . . ."

Kevin grabbed her and she cried in his arms. "I'm so sorry," she sobbed.

He kissed the top of her head. "Me too, baby . . . me too." He let her go. "Take care," he said before walking out of the room. He didn't want to talk about the divorce right now. He needed to leave before Wendy saw his tears fall.

Wendy slumped into the rocking chair in Kimberly's room and continued crying. *God, I want him back. I want my husband back. Not his money, not his cars, but him. I am so sorry for everything. Please forgive me for what I did to him, but, more importantly, forgive me for what I did to our relationship . . . my relationship with You.* She thought about all the ungodly decisions she had made since her separation with Kevin. *I want back into Your throne of grace,* she silently prayed.

She got up, made sure the door was locked, and turned on the alarm before going in her room. *Though He slay me, yet will I trust Him*. Wendy inadvertently recalled the words of Job when it seemed like God had turned against him. It was a strange recollection for her, considering it had been months since she'd even cracked open her Bible. She pulled it out from the nightstand and unzipped it. At least a dozen slips of paper fell out of it. Wendy laughed. She used to be embarrassed for others to use her Bible with all of the stuff she kept in it. Notes, Sunday programs, and even a few slips of paper with church members' numbers could be found stashed inside. She bent over and picked up the items that had fallen. She noticed one Sunday program with the sermon title "When God Allows All Hell to Break Loose."

The title caught her attention because she noticed the date. Pastor Jones preached this sermon on the day of her father's fifty-fifth birthday. It was also the day before she went to the gynecologist and was diagnosed with chlamydia. She looked at the notes that were scribbled on the program. *3 Reasons Why God Allows Pain in Our Lives: 1.) Pain teaches us how to handle blessings humbly. 2.) It teaches us how to submit to God's will. 3.) Pain and problems teach us to rely on God.*

Wendy didn't remember paying much attention that day, let alone taking notes. Her mind had been preoccupied with the phone call she had received from Dr. Korva's office. A closer look at the program revealed that the notes were not taken by her; unbelievably, it was Kevin's writing.

Wendy hadn't gotten Pastor Jones's message then, but she certainly understood it now. She had been frustrated with Kevin for months before that day. The main reason was because he wasn't who she wanted him to be. She wanted him to be the perfect Christian husband. She desired for him to go to church every Sunday, go to Bible study, pray, fast, and participate in various ministries. He didn't do any of it, and it angered her. Could God have possibly allowed things to go haywire in her life to show her that she wasn't as perfect as she had thought? In one year alone, she had told numerous lies, almost had an abortion, and even knocked on the door of adultery.

After all of that, she had no choice but to be humble, submit to God's will, and rely on Him for strength and direction. If her marriage with Kevin was ever going to work out, Wendy realized that she had to let go of the steering wheel and let God take control. Every problem, every challenge, and every hurt feeling had to be left in the Master's Hands.

# Chapter Thirty-Eight
## Only God Knows

ONLY A COUPLE OF WEEKS BEFORE EASTER, and Marlene had let another afternoon pass without getting what she needed to make Easter baskets for her grandchildren. *I'll get the stuff this weekend,* she promised herself on the way home. Unlike the other days when she neglected to go shopping, Marlene felt that her time today had been well spent. She had been at the senior center with her mother the entire afternoon. It was the best visit the two of them had together since Frances moved out. It had been only within the last couple of weeks that Marlene had worked up the strength to see her mother. Prior to visiting, she would speak with Frances on the telephone, but even that was hard at first because Marlene felt so betrayed. However, she prayed her way through the pain, and consequently the bitterness of the betrayal didn't take root in her heart.

Frances had become a different person. She was cheerful and so full of energy. She had also gotten involved in several activities at the center. Today, Marlene had accompanied Frances to her sewing class, Bible study, and then they ate lunch together. Marlene really enjoyed herself. She couldn't recall the last time she and her mother had shared so many laughs. Today was symbolic of Frances's desire to be forgiven and Marlene's willingness to forgive. Before she left, Marlene made sure to tell Frances that she loved her. Frances gave a huge smile and said, "I love you too, baby."

The phone was ringing when Marlene entered the house. She dropped her purse on the floor and ran to answer it before the voice mail kicked in. She figured it was Michael calling to see what she was preparing for dinner. She had planned to cook steaks, but had forgotten to take the meat out of the freezer before she left the house earlier.

Marlene hurriedly answered the phone. "Hello?"

"Hi, this is Barbara from the Lovelace Senior Center. May I speak with Marlene, please?"

"This is she. Is everything all right?" Marlene asked nervously. She had just left there thirty minutes ago.

"Well . . ."

"What's wrong?"

"A staff member found your mother on the bathroom floor. We don't know if she slipped and fell somehow or if she passed out, but she's being taken to Grant Mercy Hospital as we speak."

"Oh no!" Marlene panicked. "I'm on my way." She hung up the phone and raced out of the house.

⌒

"Are you all right?" Terrance asked Kim as they walked down the hall of the intensive care unit.

"Yeah, I'm straight," she said quietly.

Frances had been hospitalized due to her passing out at the senior center yesterday. Her prognosis wasn't good. Even with the pacemaker that had been installed last summer, her heartbeat was less than thirty percent of the normal rate. The doctors weren't sure what to do this time. They discussed installing a different type of pacemaker, but feared that her heart muscle was too weak right now for the surgery. It was a no-win situation, because either way Frances risked dying.

When Kim first received the phone call that her grandmother was in the hospital and that Frances had asked to see her, she was nervous. It wasn't that she didn't want to see Frances; she was just apprehensive and wasn't sure what to say. The two of them hadn't spoken since the day Kim went off on her.

*Frances E. Gibson*, read the handwritten tag on the outside of her room. Terrance gently squeezed Kim's hand, and she took a deep breath as he opened the door and the two of them went inside.

The sound of beeping monitors cut through the stillness in the air. Kim's stomach churned when she saw her grandmother's sedated body. Her eyes were closed, and several tubes ran through her arms and nose. Kim was not used to seeing Frances look so vulnerable, and it scared her. She almost preferred to see the strong-willed, obstinate woman rather than the sick individual who lay before her.

"There you are." Marlene rose to greet her daughter and future son-in-law with a hug. "You've just missed your sister and daddy. They left about ten minutes ago to get some food. I told them to pick up something for y'all just in case you hadn't eaten."

"Thanks, but I'm not hungry," Terrance said.

"Me neither," Kim responded.

Marlene turned her attention to Pastor Jones. "Have you ever formally met Terrance?"

Pastor Jones stood up and shook his hand. "No, not really, but I've seen him at the church a few times. How are you doing, young man?"

"I'm fine, sir, thank you."

"Kim, it's always good to see you, sweetheart," Pastor Jones said and gave her a hug.

"You too." Kim turned her attention to Marlene. "How is she?" she asked out of concern for Frances's well-being.

"She's doing a little better than she was when they first brought her in," she answered. "They had her on oxygen until a few hours ago. If you ask me, she still needs to be on it, but she claims she's all right."

"Why did they take the oxygen off of her?" Kim further inquired.

"Her vitals were looking pretty good and they told her that if she felt fine without the mask, they could leave it off for a while. She has an emergency button on her bed to press if she needs to. I'm concerned because she seems short of breath when she talks. I can't discern whether she's gasping for air or just taking really deep breaths."

"I'm . . . fine," Frances said, opening her eyes. She had woken up in time to hear the last part of Marlene's statement.

"Okay, Mama. If you say so."

"Hi, Ms. Gibson."

Frances turned her head and smiled when she saw Terrance standing next to Kim. "How . . . long have . . . y'all been here?"

"We just got here a few minutes ago," Terrance answered.

"Hello, Kim . . ."

"Hi, Gramma," she whispered.

"I'm going to leave now. I have a few errands that I need to finish," Pastor Jones announced. "You take care, Sister Frances." He patted her arm. "I'll stop by and check on you later."

"Okay, thanks for coming."

"No problem. God bless you, darling." Pastor Jones turned to Terrance. "I'm sure I'll be seein' you around."

"Yes sir," Terrance said as the two of them shook hands again.

"Terrance, why don't you and I walk out with Pastor Jones?" Marlene suggested, hinting to Terrance that they should let Frances and Kim be alone.

"Oh . . . okay," Terrance said, feeling he didn't have much of a choice. He'd picked up on what was going on as well as Kim.

Kim's knees began to get weak. She was not prepared to visit her grandmother alone. She would have been at the hospital sooner, but she had waited until Terrance came home. He had been out with his cousin looking at tuxedos for the wedding. When he returned, Kim told him about the phone call she'd received from her mother. They dropped the kids off at his parents' house and then came to the hospital.

"Have a . . . seat," Frances said to Kim after everyone else had left the room.

She clutched her purse and obediently sat down in the chair next to Frances's bed. It was hard for Kim to look directly at her, so she tried to look past her and still appear to be attentive.

"Kim . . ."

"Yes ma'am," she answered.

"I know you're probably still mad at me. . . ."

"I—"

Frances held up her hand. "It's okay. . . . You have ev'ry right to be." That comment surprised Kim, and she looked at Frances. "I just wanna say that I'm sorry."

*She's sorry? She has never apologized to me for anything before.* Kim was bewildered and continued listening.

"For years . . . I hated myself because of . . . what happened to my husband. I became a prisoner of my past. Instead of comin' clean, I allowed my life to be driven . . . by guilt. . . . I turned my self-hatred outward. I took my frustrations with myself out on others. Especially those who made mistakes. I took a lot out on you."

Kim spoke softly, "Why?"

"Honey, I can't say for sure. There's . . . no rational . . . explanation for how I have treated you. . . . I know I can't take back any . . . anything . . . that I have said but I . . . at least want you to know that I am sorry . . . and I want to thank you."

"For what?"

"For givin' me the chance to be set free . . . free from the burden of guilt that I . . . carried since your mother was a baby. . . . It was hard at first, but I feel that I have . . . enjoyed my life more these last few months . . . than for the last fifty-two years. You know . . . for years I professed to be saved, but because of bitterness that I harbored in my heart, I wasn't *really* livin' a Christian life."

*She has been given way too much medication*, Kim thought. The grandmother she knew would never have made such a confession.

"You see, I was in church, but Christ wasn't really in me." Frances tried to give a short chuckle, but ended up coughing instead.

Kim jumped up out of concern. "Do you need me to push the emergency button?"

Frances shook her head no. She tried to reach for her water, but couldn't quite get it. Kim picked it up and held it while she sipped from the straw.

"Thank you," Frances was able to say.

"You're welcome," Kim said before putting the water down and sitting back in the chair.

"As I was tryin' to say . . . I know now that I wasn't an exemplary Christian. . . . I tricked myself into believin' that I was 'cuz I knew the Bible." Frances gave a sly smile and looked at the ceiling. "I knew the Bible so well that I could pour out scriptures like I was pourin' a glass of water."

Kim laughed.

"I knew that book from Genesis to Revelation. . . . I spoke the words, but I did not bear the fruit of the Spirit referred to in Galatians 5: 22. . . . I didn't have love, joy, and I definitely didn't have peace, not to mention the others." Frances looked directly at Kim. "Your mama tells me that you are becomin' more and more involved in the church."

"Yeah, I guess you could say that."

"Have you . . . accepted Jesus Christ as your Lord and Savior?"

"No, not really. I'm trying, though."

"Honey, it's not hard, trust me. . . . You don't need to try, just do it."

"But I was going to wait until after the wedding. Terrance and I aren't married yet, and I know it won't look right with us living together."

"Are y'all havin' relations?"

*Relations? Now that's definitely something an older person would say.* Kim wanted to laugh but couldn't because Frances was serious. "We're sleeping together, like in the same bed, but we're not *sleeping* together as far as intimacy is concerned." *Did you just hear what you said? You're telling her about your and Terrance's sexual intimacy!* Kim couldn't believe what was happening. She and Frances had never engaged in this kind of conversation before.

"How much longer do you have before the wedding?"

"It's the first weekend in August. Not too long after Kimberly's first birthday."

"Listen to me. . . . Don't wait to ask Jesus into your life. You and Terrance can make alternate livin' arrangements until August if that's what it's gonna take. But don't wait. . . . Tomorrow is not promised. Don't do like I did and take chances with your soul."

Kim nodded.

"I'm serious, baby. . . . I'm just glad God has given me another chance. He really didn't have to. . . . He could have snatched me from the face of this earth a long time ago. But He showed undeservin' mercy on me. He has given me a chance to make it right before He takes me home."

"Don't talk like that." Kim started to get teary-eyed. "You're gonna be okay."

"I know that's what we all want to believe. But the truth is, I'm not concerned about what these doctors can or can't do. It really doesn't matter. I have the blessed assurance that all is well with my soul and that gives me a peace that passes all understanding."

Frances reached out her hand for Kim to hold. Tears fell onto Kim's cheeks as she saw her grandmother crying. "I wanna tell you exactly how I feel." She squeezed Kim's hand. "I am so proud of you. You have grown up to be a beautiful and smart young lady." Frances paused for a moment. "I know you might not believe me. I really can't blame you, considerin' the way I've treated you all these years. I'm glad . . . you came. I asked the Lord to keep me alive long enough so that I could tell you that I'm sorry and that . . . I love you."

"I . . . love you too," Kim managed to say despite the tightness in her throat. She couldn't stop the waterfall from her eyes.

A nurse entered the room. "Ms. Gibson, I need to check your tubes. We're getting some strange numbers on our screens out there."

Kim got up so she could move out of the nurse's way. "Gramma, I'll be back. I'm gonna get Mama."

"Okay, baby. . . . Bye . . ." Frances said before Kim walked out of the door. "Thanks for coming."

"I'll be right back in a few minutes, I promise." Kim wiped her face before going out into the waiting room. This time with her grandmother was something that she definitely had needed. It gave her a new outlook on their relationship. Kim was looking forward to the day when

Frances got out of the hospital. She was eager to talk to her about Shelly's idea about acknowledging her during the wedding ceremony. Shelly's suggestion had been completely rejected after Kim found out about Harold. Now it was at the forefront, but this time Kim would ask Frances because she wanted to and not because Shelly suggested it to her.

"Are you okay?" Marlene asked her daughter when she walked into the waiting room. She noticed that Kim had been crying.

"Yeah, I'm fine." She gave a reassuring nod.

Michael and Wendy were back with the food that they had bought. Terrance, who had claimed earlier that he wasn't hungry, was wiping his face and hands with a napkin.

"Kim, there's more chicken if you want some," Wendy said. "Daddy figured that y'all would be here by the time we got back."

"No, I'm fine." Kim sat down in the chair next to Terrance and laid her head on his shoulder.

"How was she doing?" Michael asked.

"The nurse is checking on her right now. Mama, I told her that I was coming out here to get you."

"Okay, I'll give the nurse a few minutes to do what she needs to and then I'll go back in there," Marlene stated in between bites of her chicken.

Kim had picked up a magazine and begun flipping through it when an alarming cry went out over the ICU airways.

"Code Blue . . . 4736 . . . Code Blue!"

Kim felt a knot in her stomach as her gut told her what was going on. 4736 was Frances's room number. She dropped the magazine and instantly ran through the ICU doors, followed by her family. When everyone arrived in Frances's room, doctors swarmed around her with machines trying to save her life. But there was nothing that anyone could do for Frances. Her monitors had flatlined. A solemn atmosphere arose as the doctors pronounced the time of death.

"No!" Kim cried, and thrust herself into Terrance's arms. "No!" she repeated. "Why . . . Why now? She said that she loved me. Why did she go now?"

Terrance held Kim tight as she sobbed. "I wish I had an answer for you, baby, I really do. Only God knows," he sighed.

Michael put his arms around his wife and Wendy. Neither of them was as emotional as Kim. Both ladies had prepared themselves for this. Even still, the reality of death was very unsettling.

# Chapter Thirty-Nine
## *Not Guilty*

THOSE WHO WEREN'T ALREADY CRYING were soon brought to tears while listening to Gwen's rendition of "Precious Lord." Frances lay in her bronze-colored casket looking so peaceful dressed in a navy blue and white suit. If she could, Frances would probably have chosen to wear the blue house robe she loved so much. However, Marlene allowed Kim and Wendy to pick her mother's burial outfit. Instead of choosing among the clothes Frances already had, the girls decided to buy her something new. Marlene was pleased with their selection and appreciated how her daughters were so eager to assist with all of the funeral arrangements.

The church was packed with many members who came to pay their last respects and offer words of encouragement to the family. Frances was well known at Mount Calvary Missionary Church even if she wasn't well liked. She'd had a reputation of being nosy and a gossip, and, unfortunately, very few members had gotten a chance to see how much she had changed in the last couple of months.

Because it was more convenient for her to do so, Frances had been attending services at the senior center. Those who had spoken with her before she passed away and seen how different she had become were especially saddened by her untimely death, including Harold.

Unbeknownst to anyone, Harold had taken a bus to visit Frances at the senior center a couple of weeks before she died. She was surprised, but glad to see him even though she hadn't known he was coming. Besides the day he'd called for Marlene, when Kim eavesdropped on their conversation, it had been over forty years since the two of them had spoken. It was a tear-jerking moment. Unlike Marlene, who had noticed his scar, Frances took one look at him and instantly knew who he was.

"Harold," she said the moment he walked into her room.

"Um . . . I know you didn't expect me—but—I . . ." he stuttered. The two of them stared at each other for a few seconds. Both were uncertain about what to say. Harold wasn't exactly sure why he had come in the first place. Part of him just wanted to see Frances and make peace with her after all these years.

"I'm sorry"—Frances finally broke the silence and tears burst from her eyes—"I'm so sorry for keepin' Marlene away from you."

Harold began to cry also. He hadn't been sure she would welcome his visit, let alone apologize. Frances invited him to sit down, and the two of them spent an hour or so making amends with one another. "Take care of our baby," were the very last words she spoke to him. Harold held her hand and promised that he would. He left the center that day and never saw Frances again until today, when she lay in her casket.

Unfortunately, Otis didn't attend the service. He hadn't been to a funeral service since his mother died when he was eleven years old. He hoped to attend only two more during his lifetime: his uncle's and his own, although he wasn't looking forward to either of them. Plus Otis had never met Frances, so he didn't feel that his presence was needed. However, he did send his condolences, along with a beautiful floral arrangement.

After Gwen's solo, Pastor Jones took his place in the pulpit as he prepared to share the things that were on his heart. "Today, we are gathered together because five days ago, one of our members departed from this earth and entered into the other side of life called eternity. I must warn you"—he paused—"I am not going to deliver a typical eulogy. As a matter of fact, I'm not sure that this should be called a eulogy at all. Usually when someone dies, we have a whole list of good things to say about that person's life. That's not the case here, is it? It's no secret that Sister Frances wasn't the most exemplary member of our church. In fact if y'all are honest, most of you who *really* knew her did not like her," Pastor Jones said without biting his tongue.

Several people in the congregation gasped, as no one had expected such an unusual introduction.

"Sister Frances lived seventy-five years, and I believe that it was in the last few months of her life that she truly lived. You wonder what I mean by that, don't you?" He smirked, knowing he had grabbed everyone's attention. "I saw Sister Frances on several occasions before she passed away. I visited with her a few times when she was at the senior center, and I also saw her at the hospital the day she died. During all of my encounters with her, there was something different about her—something that brightened her smile, something that gave her peace, something that I'm not sure many of you have yet." Pastor Jones took a sip of his water from the glass that sat on the podium.

"At the age of seventy-five, Frances Eileen Gibson had developed a relationship with the Lord. That's why the family has called this a 'Home-Going Service.' When Frances died, several days ago, she did so with peace because she knew that she was going home to be with the Lord. How many of you can honestly say the same thing? If, in the next hour, you took your last breath, would you spend eternity in heaven or hell?"

The church was so silent that it was possible to hear a pin drop. Kim recalled wondering the same thing the day she heard on the news that a former employee of the Mid-Western Steel Plant had walked in and killed several of his co-workers. Without warning, their lives were rushed into eternity, but to which place?

"What is the one thing that determines our destiny after we leave this earth?" Pastor Jones asked, although he was prepared to answer his own question. "I'll tell you what: The only sure way to guarantee that you don't spend eternity in hell is to have a relationship with Jesus Christ. In the last few months of her life, Frances got a revelation of what it really meant to accept Jesus as her savior and *instantly* she got a new start. *Everything* she had done wrong in her life became covered under the blood of Jesus when He died on the cross. Thus, Frances was free from the guilt of her past sins. We all have to stand before God one day. We will all be accountable to Him for the things that we've done in this life. But will we all be rendered a verdict of Not Guilty like Sister Frances was?"

Pastor Jones searched the crowd for unbelieving faces. "Just in case you doubt what I have said, let me back it up with scripture. Turn to Second Corinthians 5:17." He opened his Bible and waited while those who volunteered with the media ministry projected the scripture onto the overhead screen. "Two Corinthians 5:17 states 'If any man be in Christ, he [or she] is a new creature: old things are passed away; behold, all things are become new.'"

"Perhaps many of you have become burdened by the sins of your past. Maybe you had children out of wedlock, were addicted to drugs, or you were promiscuous, you lied to people, you've stolen from people, or maybe you've basically been a good person all of your life and haven't done any of these things. It's funny that we put weights on sin. In our scheme of thinking, telling a small, white lie is not as serious as committing adultery. But in God's eyes, it doesn't matter how serious or minor our actions are—sin is sin, and the *only* way to be cleansed from sin is by accepting Jesus as your Lord and Savior. It's very simple to do." Pastor Jones took another drink of his water.

"Turn to First John, first chapter and ninth verse. 1 John 1:9 says, 'If we confess our sins, He is faithful and just to forgive us our sins, and to cleanse us from all unrighteousness.'" He shut the Bible. "Frances did just that. She confessed her sins and she was forgiven of them. The Bible says that God is no respector of persons, meaning that what He did for Sister Frances, He'll do for you if you're willing to live your life for Him. He did it for me, as well as several others who are present in the church today.

Just because I'm a pastor it doesn't mean that I was born saved. There was an anointing on my life to preach, but I had to confess my sins and accept Jesus into my life just like everyone else."

The musicians and choir took their cues from Pastor Jones and began to play a hymn softly. "Perhaps you want to give your life to Christ but you are afraid of what others will say. Those who know the things you've done wrong wouldn't likely accept you or believe you if you were to tell them you got saved. Fortunately, salvation frees us from being bound by other people's opinions or perceptions of us. God doesn't care what people think about us, especially when we first get saved. One of the tricks that satan uses to deter us from salvation is whispering in our ear that no one will believe us. But guess what? Actions speak louder than words. Over time, those people who initially doubt your salvation will be able to see the difference in your behavior. The change that takes place on the inside of you once you accept Jesus Christ as your Savior will display itself on the outside. It's inevitable. *The* most important thing you can do is give your life to Christ. No matter how much money you make, what kind of titles you hold, how many committees you serve on, God is not impressed. To Him, it's the condition of every soul that matters. *Your* soul matters! I know this is a burial service, but I feel led by the Holy Spirit to open the altar for anyone who is ready to accept Jesus. Won't you come today and make the decision that will give you the assurance of knowing that, if you never see another day on earth, you will spend the rest of your days of eternity in heaven?"

The musicians were still playing softly as Kim considered Pastor Jones's plea. *Is this my time?* she thought. *Can I really commit to Christ?*

A little voice inside her head cried out, "Yes!"

*But how? My sister backslid, and her entire life she has been more faithful to God than I have been.*

"*You're not accountable for the actions of others, only your own.*"

*But what about all of the things I have done wrong? I'm no angel, you know.*

"*Yes, I know. All you have to do is accept and acknowledge Me as your Savior and I will take care of the rest.*"

*But what about—*

"*What about Me? I am everything you need. You have sinned, but I have come that you may have life and have it more abundantly!*"

There was nothing left to ponder. Kim hearkened unto the voice and was among the first to walk up front. Surprisingly, she was not alone. Terrance felt led to walk up with her, as he too desired to be saved.

"Maybe you have already given your life to Christ before, but for one reason or another you have strayed away from Him," Pastor Jones said. "Sometimes situations happen in our life and instead of turning to God, we turn away from Him. But what I love about God so much is that even though we may give up on Him, He never gives up on us. In Jeremiah 3:14, God says that He is married to the backslider. He wants to restore the relationship you once had. In fact, He wants to make it better."

Wendy wept as she realized she had made a mess of her marriage this past year. Mainly because she hadn't sought God's help in solving her problems; she had always tried to do everything on her own. It had been six weeks since she had discovered that Kevin really hadn't committed adultery. Although the two of them had spoken since then, neither had brought up their marriage or pending divorce. Wendy still wanted to give her marriage another try, but she wasn't going to force the issue with Kevin. Before she could restore her marriage, she knew that she needed to restore her relationship with God.

"I'm so sorry!" she said to God and fell to her knees and cried. She hadn't even noticed that Kim and Terrance had walked to the altar, although they were all sitting in the same row. Wendy momentarily had tunnel vision. The only thing she could see was the need in her life for God. Without Him, nothing else mattered.

Wendy continued sobbing and asking for forgiveness until she felt someone tap her shoulder. It was Kevin. She got up and hugged him. She thought he'd come up merely to offer moral support, but Kevin had other plans in mind. As he listened to Pastor Jones, he recognized the need in his life for Jesus and wanted a relationship with Him.

"Together we'll live out our Christian walk as husband and wife," he whispered to Wendy, and gave her a warm smile.

Wendy's mouth fell open and Kevin embraced her. "Thank You," she whispered to God, closing her eyes.

The musicians began to play even more softly as Pastor Jones got ready to pray with those who had come forth. Kim, who hadn't wanted to interrupt Wendy earlier while she was praying, took the opportunity to hold Wendy's hand after she and Kevin finished their embrace.

Pastor Jones looked at the number of people who had come forth. He smiled when he saw Wendy's husband standing next to her. He had been praying for them since the day he'd run into Wendy at the diner. "Praise God," he said aloud. "I want all of you to repeat this prayer after me." Line by line, Kim, Wendy, Terrance, Kevin, and all the others who wanted to give their lives to Christ repeated the following words:

*Dear Heavenly Father,*

*I confess that I am a sinner. I come to You in the name of Jesus asking for forgiveness of my sins. I believe in my heart that Jesus died on the cross for my sins, was raised from the dead, and is the only Lord and Savior of the world. Right now, I ask Jesus to come into my heart and cleanse me from all unrighteousness. I believe that I am saved. I believe that my past is forgiven. I believe that I am a new creation in Christ Jesus. Thank You, Lord, for saving me. Amen.*

Marlene was filled with joy. After Frances had died, she'd spent her private time with God asking Him to help her understand what good could come out of her mother's death. She loved Romans 8:28, but she couldn't comprehend why Frances had died just as they were rebuilding their relationship. Today, God answered that prayer by using Frances's death to bring her family closer to Him. No matter what Terrance, Kim, Wendy, Kevin, or anyone else had done, if they met God tonight, all would be rendered a verdict of Not Guilty.

# Chapter Forty
## Unconditional Love

THE CROWD BROKE OUT IN·CHEERS when Gwen caught Kim's bridal bouquet. She had mesmerized the wedding guests during the ceremony when she sang "Unconditional Love," a song she'd written specifically for Kim and Terrance. Now she stood next to the gentleman who'd caught the garter belt as they posed for a picture with the bride and groom.

Terrance and Kim made a good-looking couple. He was dressed in a black tuxedo with a purple vest and a silverish purple tie. Kim was absolutely stunning in her wedding dress. She had found white satin shoes with clear heels to match the sequins on her dress.

"Baby, I'll be back. I see one of my relatives I want to say hi to," Terrance said to his wife.

"Okay," Kim said, and gave her husband a peck.

"Oh, *please*," Gwen teased. "Y'all can do better than that!"

"Oh, be quiet. We'll see how you do on your wedding day," Kim responded.

Gwen gave her a smirk as if to say *Don't even get started.*
She knew that Kim was going to pick on her about her
new beau since she'd caught the bouquet and he'd caught
the garter belt.

"This just may be a sign—the two of you seem to be
getting pretty cozy," Kim said, unable to resist the temptation.

Gwen and her friend laughed.

"I will have to admit the two of you look very good
together." She pointed at the gentleman. "I just can't get
over how much you've changed. You're not all scrawny
like you used to be."

"Why, thank you, lil' 'cuz," Otis said, and flexed his
muscles. "I guess drinking milk did my body good after
all," he joked. Otis had indeed stepped up a few notches
and had changed himself from a pseudo-pimp into a nice-
looking man. He had stopped wearing his fake gold jewelry, invested in some contacts, and started working out
that year. The locks of his Jheri Curl were now in the trash
as he sported a nice, clean cut. He had sort of a Wesley
Snipes appeal going on. There was, however, one thing
Otis wasn't willing to change about his appearance. No
matter what, he wasn't ready to get rid of his gold tooth.
It had been his trademark for many years.

In her wildest dreams, Kim would never have imagined
that Gwen and Otis would be compatible. The two of
them had become interested in each other about a month
ago at a barbecue Marlene had held at her house. Otis had
debuted his new look then. In fact, Gwen barely recognized him from the time she had met him at Christmas.
Otis kept Gwen laughing the entire day. When the bar-

becue was over, the two of them exchanged telephone numbers and had been getting to know each other ever since.

Kim never saw anyone put a sparkle in Gwen's eye the way Otis had done during the last few weeks. "When you two stop professing to be just friends, let me know and I'll help with the wedding arrangements." Kim winked.

"Girl, you know there ain't nuttin' like an Otis." Gwen repeated Otis's signature line, sending Kim away giggling.

She walked past the table where her parents, Terrance's parents, and Harold sat. Kim blew a kiss to her father, who pretended to catch it and place it over his heart. She smiled and looked around for Terrance but didn't see him. It was getting pretty muggy inside, so she stepped onto the balcony for some fresh air.

Once outside, Kim placed her hands on the rail and looked at the stars. *We did it,* she thought. Today she and Terrance had pledged their love for one another in front of their family and friends and had become one in the sight of God. The wedding ceremony itself hadn't lasted too long, but the memory of the event would last a lifetime.

Tori and Tyler enjoyed the attention they got as the ring bearer and flower girl. Tori looked so cute in her white, frilly dress laced with purple trim. Gwen had done her hair in Shirley Temple curls that lay perfectly around the tiara she wore. Tyler's tuxedo was similar to his dad's, which made his resemblance to Terrance stand out even more. The kids were excited about Kim and Terrance getting married. Although they didn't understand what it meant spiritually, naturally they understood that the four of them had truly become a family.

*Family*—that word meant a lot to Kim. Each and every member of her family was important to her, including the new additions, Harold and Otis. To make sure that they knew how much she valued having them as members of her family, she had included them in the wedding cere-mony. Otis was asked to be an usher and Harold was acknowledged as being her grandfather. It was the first time Kim had called him by that title. Even though her children now referred to him as Grandpa Harry, Kim had continued to call him Mr. Wallace, although she felt that doing so seemed very impersonal. She had made the mental transition from thinking of him as Mr. Wallace to Grandpa, but she had not yet been able to make the verbal transition. That is, until today. Harold heard Kim call him "Grandpa" for the first time and he, along with Marlene, had been brought to tears.

Harold's presence brought life back into the Tibbs family despite Frances's death. Harold's mere existence was enough to put a smile on anyone's face because he was such a pleasure to be around. Marlene never went back to work after her mother died, so she was able to spend a lot of time with Harold. They laughed together, cried together, prayed together, and, most importantly, enjoyed their time together.

"I know you're not having second thoughts already." Terrance walked up behind Kim on the balcony and put his arms around her. He kissed her on the cheek.

Kim turned around, leaned her back against the railing, and put her arms around his neck. "Not a chance."

"Good, 'cuz I plan on keeping you for a very long time."

"Even after I gain about sixty pounds, my teeth fall out, and I go bald?"

"I'll put you on a diet, get you some dentures, and buy you a wig," he kidded. "But most importantly, I will never . . . ever stop loving you," Terrance said before kissing her.

Like typical newlyweds, the two of them got lost in their love for one another. There was a long silence while nothing else around them mattered. If it hadn't been for the sound of someone clearing their throat, it might have been a few more moments before their kiss ended.

"Perhaps y'all should get a room," Wendy teased. She looked gorgeous in her deep purple satin dress. It came off her shoulders slightly, giving her a sexy yet very elegant appearance.

"We already got one." Kim grinned and stuck out her tongue.

She and Terrance let go of each other. "I'm gonna go back in and let y'all talk," he announced, and looked at his watch. "Wendy, don't keep my wife out here longer than five minutes or I might have to put a choke hold on you," he jestfully threatened his sister-in-law.

She pushed him playfully. "Boy, shut up! The ink's not even dry on your marriage license and you're already acting crazy!" Terrance laughed and left.

Wendy walked over to where Kim stood and the two of them leaned against the rail. "I am so happy for you," she said sincerely.

"I . . . I can't begin to describe how excited I am about today. It's amazing. I look forward to spending the rest of my life with Terrance. . . . I really do."

"I pray that the two of you have a wonderful, healthy marriage."

"Thank you. Today was one of the most memorable days of my life. I'm so glad you were a part of it."

"Thank you for allowing me to stand up for you. Lord knows I had enough drama going on that I really didn't act like a matron of honor should have."

"All that is behind us now. You're my sister and there's no one more deserving to be my matron of honor than you. I just wish . . ." Kim became silent.

"You wish what?"

"Nothing."

"C'mon, what were you going to say?"

"Never mind. Girl, you'll probably think I'm crazy."

"I already know you're crazy." Wendy gave Kim a humorous look. "Nothing you say will surprise me."

"Believe it or not, I wish that Gramma was here." Kim shrugged. "It's weird. I spent so many years hating her. She was always around when I didn't want her to be. Now she's not here and I would give my right arm to see her again."

Wendy looked up at the sky. "You know, I would bet that she's looking down, smiling at you this very moment."

Kim looked up also. "Yeah, she's probably saying 'Now Kim, you're showing too much cleavage in that dress.'"

Both women laughed. "Then she'd say, 'But that's all right—I love you anyhow,'" Kim added seriously.

Wendy put her arm around Kim's shoulder. "It's been a rough year, but we made it through. Yep, I think we're all going to be all right."

"How are things with you and Kevin?"

"Things are great. I'm learning day by day that I can fight for my marriage most effectively through prayer." Since the day Wendy had rededicated her life to Christ and Kevin had gotten saved, their marriage had been much better than before. The two of them were able to discuss all the things that had transpired throughout the course of their marriage. They had also attended several marriage-counseling sessions at the church. They had encountered some challenges, but they both were committed to making their marriage work, and neither was willing to give up. Eventually, Kevin stopped the divorce proceedings and moved back into the house.

To celebrate their second wedding anniversary, Kevin and Wendy took a much-needed vacation to Florida, where they rented a secluded beach house for a week and cut themselves off from the outside world. Marlene was the only one who had a telephone number to reach them, and that was only to be used in case of an emergency because she had kept Kimberly while they were away. A couple of weeks after their return from Florida, Kevin, Wendy, and Kimberly flew to Philadelphia to visit his family. They got to see Kevin's niece for the first time, as his sister-in-law had given birth this past spring, around the time of Frances's death. Wendy had not only reunited with her husband, but she had bonded with her in-laws, too. Although her family would be disappointed, she was looking forward to spending this coming Christmas in Philadelphia with them.

"So things are going good, huh?" Kim asked Wendy.

"Yes!"

"Well, I am so glad to hear that."

"We're trying. With the help of the Lord, we are definitely trying. Prayer most definitely changes things." Wendy turned to face Kim. "Guess what?"

"What?"

"I'm going to have a baby."

"No way!"

"Yes way. You're going to be an auntie again."

Kim's face lit up. "Wow. Does Mama know yet?"

"No, we just found out yesterday morning. I wanted you to be the first person I told."

"Wow! It sure sounds like you and Kevin have been doing a lot more than *trying* to work things out. I'm so excited for you." Kim hugged Wendy.

"Thank you. Do you think you and Terrance will have any more children?"

"Girl, please. Tyler is now six and Tori is eight. It'll be like starting over. I don't know if I'm ready to go through all the baby stages again."

"*Accidents* do happen, you know?"

Kim laughed. "Yeah, but if I get pregnant again, it will be much more than an accident, it'll be divine intervention."

Just then, Kevin stepped outside. Kim looked at him with a girlish smile.

"I can tell by the look on your face that she told you."

"Yes, I'm so excited!" She ran and hugged him. "Congratulations."

"Thank you," he said, struggling to keep his balance since Kim's affection had caught him by surprise.

Kim walked toward the balcony door.

"Hey, where are you going?" Wendy asked.

"Inside so you and your *husband* can be alone. Besides, I think your five minutes is up. I have to keep Terrance from coming after you now that you're with child." She smiled and walked away.

"Uh-oh, what is going on with you and Terrance?" Kevin inquired as he walked up and put his arms around his wife.

"Long story."

"Well, tell me later, because right now I have something I want to tell you," he said seductively.

"Oh, really? And what might that be?"

"Not a day goes by that I don't thank God for blessing me with you. You're a great wife and mother." He smiled. "The baby told me to tell you that."

"Which one?"

"Both of them: Kimberly and the little one growing inside you. They said that they couldn't ask for a better mother."

"Um-hmm. That's funny, considering that neither one of them can speak."

"No, you just can't hear them. It's a special communication daddies have that mommies don't."

"Well, did the baby happen to tell you whether or not it was a boy or girl?"

"He's supposed to get back to me on that." Kevin smirked.

"Oh, so you think it's a boy, do you?"

"I think it may be." He looked at his wife. "But it really doesn't matter either way as long as I have you." Kevin pulled her closer to him. "I love you!"

"I love you too," Wendy said just before Kevin kissed her.

# Reading Group Guide

Note: Numbers correspond to chapter numbers.

1. Have you ever been pregnant? What are/were your expectations of the experience? How did the reality measure up to expectations?

2. Pastor's sermon talked about three reasons why God allows pain. What were they? How have you experienced those "benefits" in your own life?

3. Wendy reflects that all she ever wanted in life was marriage and children. Now she has both, but neither is proving to satisfy her. What do *you* want in life? Will those things satisfy? Why or why not?

4. Both of Kim's children were conceived and born outside of marriage, each by a different father. How would your family respond to such a situation? How would your church respond? How would *you* respond if Kim were your daughter? How would your faith influence your response?

5. Terrance proposed to Kim with both of their families standing by as witnesses. What is your ideal proposal setting? What would be the most romantic proposal you can imagine?

6. Abortion is a tough subject in America, even among Christians. How would you counsel a woman like Wendy? What would you choose in her situation? How would your faith influence your decision or counsel?

7. Why do women get married? What expectations and motivations do we have? What illusions are mixed in with those reasons? What reasons does scripture offer for marriage?

8. Wendy has a perfectionist streak. How has it set her up for failure? Is her desire for privacy (which makes her keep secrets from family, co-workers, etc.) legiti-mate—or just a justification for pride and deceit? Why?

9. Marlene asks Wendy, "Why is it that Pastor Jones knows more about you than we do?" When do *you* prefer to keep your business away from your family? Why?

10. Kim remembers the verse in PROVERBS 22:6 about "training up a child," but this chapter actually illus-trates ISAIAH 11:6, which says, "A little child shall lead them." When has a child led you into the right path? What have you learned from a child?

11. Why is Kim so interested in Pastor's series about "Living the Christian Life"? How is her interest a cau-tion to those of us who *do* embrace Christianity? (See MATTHEW 5:16.)

12. Love—and betrayal. How are they connected? Is it true that "if you really loved me, you wouldn't have betrayed me"? Why or why not? How have you handled betrayal in your life? How did Jesus handle betrayal in His? (See MATTHEW 26; MARK 14; JOHN 12–13.)

13. Kim wonders how she could possibly hope to do things God's way when her sister, "who had basically been a good girl all of her life," was having such trouble. How would you answer a friend who asked Kim's question?

14. How do you handle a family member like Frances? Do you strive to balance respect for elders with refusal to be abused and manipulated? Why—and how?

15. What biblical principles might help you in making difficult decisions concerning the care of aging relatives, particularly ones with physical challenges or difficult personal habits? What options have you considered—for yourself and for your loved ones?

16. Shakespeare asked, "What's in a name?" Scripture says, "A good name is valued above rubies." How was your name chosen? How did (or will) you choose a name for your child(ren)?

17. With whom do you tend to empathize more: Kevin or Wendy? Why? How do you (or would you) navigate such relational challenges? How might scripture guide you?

18. True or false: Does Kevin really have "nothing to lose"? Why or why not? When have *you* felt that kind

of desperation or resignation in life? How did you combat it, if at all?

19. Kim observes Wendy's changing behavior as signs that her relationship with God is suffering. What are the signs in *your* life that your walk with God has gotten detoured? How can you as a group hold one another accountable and get back on track?

20. Is it possible for a man and woman to have a platonic friendship, without sex getting in the way? Why or why not? How dangerous is it for a married person to have a close friendship with a member of the opposite sex?

21. What kind of "rules" do you have with your girl-friends about the men in your lives? Have you ever had a friend betray you or break those rules, as Natalie seems in the habit of doing? How did you respond?

22. Kim doesn't hesitate to confront Natalie about that dance with Kevin. Was Kim right or wrong in doing so—either in what she did or how she did it? How do you handle confrontation? What advice does scrip-ture have for dealing with conflict between friends or family?

23. Why do you think Wendy was so upset with Kevin for having a female guest for the holiday? Was her reac-tion fair or reasonable? Why or why not? What do you think is keeping her from dealing with her broken marriage in a healthier way?

24. What is your estimation of Natalie? Why does Wendy seem committed to the friendship—despite all the evidence that Natalie is *not* a good friend? When

have you been entangled in such a relationship? Why did you stay in—or get out?

25. When have you had a chance encounter that later proved to be a divine appointment (such as Marlene's with Harold Wallace)? How did you respond? How did you see God's hand at work in the encounter?

26. How do you spend Christmas—and with whom? Consider LUKE 2:14 in contrast with LUKE 12:51. How does your Christmas reflect one or the other of these possible influences that Jesus can have on the world? How do you reconcile the two in your own life?

27. Renée jokes about "baby-mama drama." What experience do you have with such relational dramas, particularly relating to a baby-daddy, or -mama? How have you handled it—for the good of the child? How would you advise someone else in Kevin's or Wendy's position? What is different about such dramas when God is an integral part of one or the other parent's life?

28. Think back to Chapter Two and the description of Pastor's sermon about the reasons God allows pain. How is Wendy's current situation a result of her less-than-ideal response to pain? How might she redeem the experience by turning to God—instead of away from Him?

29. Finally, Wendy has the urge to pray, but she really doesn't want to hear the answers, so the urge doesn't bear fruit. What keeps you from praying?

30. Marlene's prayer for Wendy is a classic "mother's prayer." When have you prayed such a prayer—or

been the subject of someone else's prayer? What results have you seen from that powerful prayer?

31. The consequences of deceit are a common theme in this story. It isn't hard to guess what secret Frances has been hiding. How do you think the truth might work to set the Tibbs family free (JOHN 8:32)?

32. Why do parents lie to their children? Is there ever a *good* reason for such a lie? Why or why not? What do scriptures such as 1 CORINTHIANS 4:5 seem to suggest about this question?

33. How have you experienced the truth of ROMANS 8:28 in your life? Where are you still waiting to see the good come from the ugly?

34. Renée wants Kevin for his financial success; his actual character is "gravy" as far as she's concerned. What qualities do you look for in a marriage partner? What compromises are you willing to make? What qualities does scripture recommend?

35. More than once we have witnessed Kim's temper flare. Mostly, it seems to be an example of how God makes good out of "ugly." Or is she exemplifying the righteous anger of Jesus in the temple courts (see MATTHEW 21)? Do the ends of such temper justify the means? Is that an appropriate interpretation of ROMANS 8:28? Why or why not?

36. "Why didn't I see this before?" Kevin wonders about Renée/Natalie. What blinded him to her true character? What has blinded you in similar relationships, whether with a girlfriend or a brother with whom you were involved?

37. In what ways do you struggle with a prideful and judgmental spirit, as Wendy recognizes she has done? How have painful experiences humbled you and taught you to rely on God's grace—both for you yourself and for others? What does MATTHEW 7:3–5 teach about such attitudes?

38. Frances turned her bitterness and guilt outward. Many people (especially women) turn it inward—where it manifests itself as depression, suicide attempts, eating disorders, substance abuse, promiscuity, and other self-destructive behaviors. How can acceptance of God's forgiveness (and the forgiveness of others) redeem us from such a burden of guilt and bitterness about the past? (See GALATIANS 5.)

39. Pastor's home-going sermon observes that we like to put weights on sin—to weigh one kind of sin as heavier than another. When is this appropriate? When is it not? Do you think God really sees all sin equally? Why or why not?

40. Considering the various trials that all the characters have experienced in this story, how would you, in the end, define "unconditional love"? How is it exemplified in each character's life? (Don't hesitate to refer to 1 CORINTHIANS 13—but put it in your own words, out of your own experience, too!)

Reading Groups for African American
Christian Women Who Love God and Like to Read.

# BE A PART OF
# GLORY GIRLS READING GROUPS!

## THESE EXCITING BI-MONTHLY READING GROUPS ARE FOR THOSE SEEKING FELLOWSHIP WITH OTHER WOMEN WHO ALSO LOVE GOD AND ENJOY READING.

For more information about GLORY GIRLS, to connect with an established group in your area, or to become a group facilitator, go to our Web site at **www.glorygirlsread.net** or click on the Praising Sisters logo at **www.walkworthypress.net.**

### WHO WE ARE

GLORY GIRLS is a national organization made up of primarily African American Christian women, yet it welcomes the participation of anyone who loves the God of the Bible and likes to read.

### OUR PURPOSE IS SIMPLE

- To honor the Lord with <u>what we read</u>—and have a good time doing it!

- To provide an atmosphere where readers can seek fellowship with other book lovers while encouraging them in the choices they make in Godly reading materials.

- To offer readers fresh, contemporary, and entertaining yet scripturally sound fiction and nonfiction by talented Christian authors.

- To assist believers and nonbelievers in discovering the relevancy of the Bible in our contemporary, everyday lives.